the christmas holiday

About the author

Sophie Claire writes emotional stories set in England and in sunny Provence, where she spent her summers as a child. She has a French mother and a Scottish father, but was born in Africa and grew up in Manchester, England, where she still lives with her husband and two sons.

Previously, she worked in marketing and proofreading academic papers, but writing is what she always considered her 'real job' and now she's delighted to spend her days dreaming up heartwarming contemporary romance stories set in beautiful places.

You can find out more at www.sophieclaire.co.uk and on Twitter @sclairewriter.

sophie claire

the christmas holiday

First published in Great Britain in 2019 by Hodder & Stoughton
An Hachette UK company

5

A CIP catalogue record for this title is available from the British Library

Paperback ISBN 978 1 529 39279 1
eBook ISBN 978 1 529 39280 7

Typeset in Plantin Light 11.25/14.75 pt by
Palimpsest Book Production Limited, Falkirk, Stirlingshire

Printed and bound in Great Britain by Clays Ltd, Elcograf S.p.A.

Hodder & Stoughton policy is to use papers that are natural, renewable and recyclable products and made from wood grown in sustainable forests. The logging and manufacturing processes are expected to conform to the environmental regulations of the country of origin.

Hodder & Stoughton Ltd
Carmelite House
50 Victoria Embankment
London EC4Y 0DZ

www.hodder.co.uk

To Bowdon Quilters: Jay Cawley, Elizabeth Craig,
Betty Croke, Val Imm, Marian Keall, Charlotte Logan,
Maureen Scapens and Glenys White.

Chapter One

Evie had a bad feeling about the place. Or perhaps it was simply the chill in the air as she hurried from her car to the Old Hall, carrying her heavy load. The forecast tonight was snow. She prayed it would wait until she'd finished what she was there to do and had driven back down the hill to the village. It should take her an hour, tops, and once she was home in her little cottage, it could snow as much as it liked: she'd be tucked up in bed with a warm quilt and a hot-water bottle. Tomorrow she'd email her invoice. The sooner she collected payment, the happier her bank manager would be. Maybe he'd even stop breathing down her neck.

She unlocked the door of the big house and flicked on the lights, accidentally knocking the coat stand. She caught it before it toppled, then scurried on towards the dining room. Two chandeliers lit it, and she saw her reflection in the tall, naked windows – her red coat was a beacon glowing brightly in the doorway. Carefully, Evie laid the curtain she'd made on the grand dining table. She flicked her long plait over her shoulder, then went back to her car. Floor-length, in a burgundy and gold damask that caught the light, the curtains would look perfect in that room, but they were so heavy she had to carry them in one at a time, all four of them.

As she scuttled back from her car for the last time, the first snowflakes began to fall. She smiled as they tickled her cheeks, but quickened her pace and closed the solid oak door, shutting out the icy air. Not that it was much warmer inside the huge empty house: her breath left a thin cloud in the air as she marched along the corridor. Perhaps the place would come to life once the new owner moved in.

Her foot caught something hard and she stumbled. A metal doorstop lay on its side. With her toe, she pushed it under the dining-room door to prop it open. She put her heavy parcel down with the others, stopped and listened.

Funny. She'd thought she'd heard barking.

But, of course, that couldn't be. Hers was the only car on the drive, and when she'd arrived the house had been in darkness. The owner wasn't due to move in for another week.

Evie brushed aside the thought and carried her step-ladder to the window. It squeaked loudly as she unfolded it. She unwrapped the first curtain from its plastic cover, lifted it expertly over her shoulder, and climbed up to the highest step. These windows were tall, and it was a balancing act as she supported the weight of the fabric with one hand and hooked the curtain with the other. She had finished one and was starting on the second when she heard barking again – louder this time. Perched on the stepladder, she stilled. It wasn't the tinny yap of a small dog, but a deep, loud bark.

Her heart thumped. What if a guard dog was patrolling? Surely not. She'd been given a key by the owner's PA, and tradespeople had been coming and going for weeks now.

Still, the owner might assume she would only seek access during the day. She looked at her watch. It was nine thirty now.

She heard footsteps approaching and the deep tones of a male voice. The dog's bark made her jump this time, and she heard the scrabble of paws as an animal – several, perhaps? – raced down the corridor. Frozen, she watched the open door, not daring to let go of the curtain, which was attached by only three hooks. Her eyes widened as a large Dalmatian bounded in and leaped up at her. She screamed and clung to the stepladder, which wobbled violently. The curtain was wrenched from her hands, she heard a creak – and looked up to see that the curtain pole was now hanging at a crooked angle.

'Smoke! Down!' the man shouted.

The dog ignored him, barked and jumped, knocking the ladder again. Evie gasped as it wobbled, then tumbled in a clatter of metal, fabric and barking.

She blinked. She and the curtains were in a heap on the floor. Instinctively, she lifted her arm to protect her face as the dog went for her, but instead of teeth, she felt only a warm wet tongue licking her hand.

'What the . . .' Shocked, she put her arm down and stared at the dog. It tilted its head to peer at her in turn, then whined affectionately. Evie laughed. 'After all that, you want your ears scratching? You silly dog!' She rubbed the Dalmatian behind the ears, and it made happy noises in return.

But her smile faded as she spotted the holes in the plaster where the curtain pole had been ripped from the wall. 'Oh, but look what you've done . . .' She tried to extricate herself from the curtains but she was well and truly tangled in them, and the combined weight of the ladder and the dog pinned her to the floor.

'Look what *he*'s done?'

She and the dog turned their heads at the sound of the disapproving male voice.

Now Evie got a proper look at the tall, unshaven man standing a few feet away. She guessed he was somewhere in his mid-thirties, though she couldn't be sure. He stepped closer to inspect the heap of ladder, metal pole and curtain in which Evie was trapped, and she caught a strong whiff of alcohol. The stubble on his chin gave him an air of menace, his hair was dishevelled, and when he turned his sharp gaze back on her she saw his eyes were bloodshot.

'He was simply protecting my property. The question is, what were *you* doing here?'

Not an outstretched hand to help her up, she noticed. No 'Are you hurt?' Just an accusing look, as if he'd caught her trespassing.

Her heart beat double-time. No one knew she was here – alone with this angry stranger and his dog. Suddenly she felt vulnerable.

'What does it look like I was doing? Breaking and entering?' He continued to glare down at her. She sighed and spelled it out for him: 'I was fitting these curtains, of course.'

'Of course,' he said drily. 'Because that's a perfectly normal thing to be doing at –' he looked at his watch, which glinted in the light of the chandeliers '– almost ten in the evening.'

Indignation bubbled up inside her. 'I have a key!' She wrestled to free herself from the fabric, but with no success. The Dalmatian stepped forward and nuzzled her hand. It was difficult to stay angry with the horrible man when his dog was so adorable.

'Really.'

His sarcasm was cutting. A picture of her ex flashed into her mind, but she pushed it aside to concentrate on the here and now. 'Yes!' She felt about for her pocket, but the tangle of curtains made it impossible. 'Heidi gave it to me.'

The flicker of recognition in his eyes reassured her that Heidi's name meant something to him. 'And did Heidi invite you to come here in the middle of the night?'

'It was the only time I could make it,' she said, through gritted teeth, as she finally managed to pull herself free and clambered to her feet. Pain shot up from her left ankle, making her gasp and lose her balance. She grabbed the nearest object – a chair.

'What's wrong?' he asked, sounding exasperated rather than concerned.

'Nothing.' She rooted in her coat pocket. 'Here's your damned key. Satisfied?'

He shot the medieval-looking piece of metal a cursory

glance, then turned his gaze back on the pitiful heap of curtains.

'Satisfied is hardly the right word. Have you seen the damage you've done?'

She followed his eyes to the holes in the wall where the curtain pole had been attached. Her jaw tightened as she bit back several possible retorts. She was aware that if he was the owner he was also her client, but she'd just been doing her job. She didn't deserve this treatment and he was by far the rudest customer she'd ever dealt with.

Although he wasn't the first man to make her feel small and wanting. Her ex, Tim, and this man were definitely cut from the same cloth. But if she'd learned anything from Tim, it was not to let another man walk all over her.

The dog ran excited circles around her, by turns sniffing at the curtains and rubbing his head against her leg. Evie gripped the chair and tried her best to keep her balance while not putting any weight on her left ankle. 'So, rather than apologise for your dog's behaviour, you're turning this back on me? I might ask who you are and why you're here.'

'This is my house. I don't have to justify my presence to you.'

Ah. So he *was* the client. And these curtains had cost a fortune in fabric alone. She couldn't afford for him to refuse to pay or she'd be in even bigger trouble with the bank.

'But – but Heidi told me you weren't moving in until next week!' If she'd known he'd be here she'd have called first.

And how she wished she had.

'When I move in is my affair,' he said brusquely. A strange expression flashed through his eyes before he looked away.

'Well, this is unfortunate. But I was just doing my job.' She lifted her chin. 'Perhaps if you'd kept your dog under control, there'd be less damage and I wouldn't have had the fright of my life.'

And she wouldn't have been hurt. She reached down to touch her ankle and the dog licked her hand.

'Smoke!' the man said sharply. 'Come here!'

The dog looked up at the sound of his name but ignored the command. The man glared at the animal as if it were a traitor, then sighed and set about righting the mess. He picked up the stepladder and propped it against the wall. The smell of alcohol grew stronger as he approached, and Evie watched him warily. He was angry and inebriated, and no one knew she was there.

She reached for the curtains, brushed off a small piece of plaster, and inspected them for damage. 'They seem to be fine, thank goodness. It took me hours to make them.'

She draped them carefully over the table so they wouldn't crease.

The man was picking up chunks of plaster. 'Tell me again why you're delivering curtains in the dark.'

Her fists curled in her pockets. Tim used to take the same disparaging tone with her when they were out with his colleagues and she spoke too much or said the wrong thing.

'I run a shop in the day,' she said, 'so I always deliver

my curtains in the evening.' Most clients appreciated this service, knowing that other suppliers expected customers to collect and hang their own curtains.

'You couldn't wait until tomorrow, given the weather?'

'No, I couldn't. Tomorrow is my friend's birthday and . . .' This red-eyed man wouldn't understand her cash-flow problems. He owned a hall, for goodness' sake. Not a house, but a hall!

'And?' he prompted.

She decided to admit the truth. 'And I needed to get them finished and delivered so I could invoice for them.'

Instantly, his eyes narrowed, as she had known they would. 'So, this is about money?'

'No! Well . . . yes.'

His bloodshot eyes became two red slits.

She added quickly, 'I've done nothing but work on them for the last week, and the cost of the material was in the hundreds – which creates cash-flow problems. I'm just a small business. I need to collect payment for them as soon as possible or my bank account will go into the red.'

'You couldn't send the invoice, then deliver them? You knew the place was empty.'

She looked at him in horror. 'I never invoice a customer until I've delivered the curtains and I'm satisfied they're the perfect fit.'

'Surely if you've measured correctly they'll fit.'

Spoken like someone who had never hung a pair of curtains in his life. 'It's not that simple – which is why I like to put them up myself and make sure they hang right.'

He raised a brow. 'Make sure they hang right?'

'Yes.' She was infuriated by his condescending attitude.

'What did you think – that the laws of gravity might not apply here in this house?'

If it had been anyone else, she'd have thought that was a joke. But he was just plain mocking. 'Clearly you know nothing about curtains.'

'You're right. Please enlighten me, because I've yet to see curtains that don't hang but float horizontally instead.'

She ground her teeth. 'Curtains can be the perfect measurements but if they aren't hung correctly with the pleats in the right places, they'll look stiff and – and awkward.'

'Awkward?' The corners of his mouth twitched with derision, which only raised her blood pressure even more.

'Yes! Which is why I like to dress them personally, so they look their best.' In her sewing bag she had extra weights she could slip into the lining if necessary, but usually it was simply a case of rearranging the pleats and fabric, and that was something experience had taught her how to do.

Somehow his silence was more damning than his caustic words.

'You can leave now,' he said eventually, with a nod towards the door. 'You've done enough damage. Your services are no longer required.'

Evie stared at him, a rush of jumbled thoughts filling her head. He was throwing her out after his dog had attacked her? And no longer required? Did that mean he wasn't going to pay her? Her heart raced as she thought of the grim warning the bank had issued. There would be no mercy if her account went into the red again.

'Now look here! You can't not pay for those curtains – especially when your dog was responsible for the damage, not me!'

'I'm not talking about the damn payment. Is everything about money with you?'

'No! But you said—'

'I asked you to leave. The door's this way.'

She glared at him, then snatched up her sewing bag and reached for her ladder.

'I'll take those,' he said, lifting them out of her hands.

She didn't have the fight to refuse. She hobbled after him, but every time she put weight on her left ankle pain ripped through it. She blinked hard. What a horrible, horrible man. The Dalmatian trotted happily beside her, occasionally nuzzling her hand as if to comfort her, bless him.

'What about the rest of the curtains?' she asked, glancing back at the pair still in their protective covers.

'I'll have to get someone in to repair the damage first,' he said, without so much as a glance in her direction.

'When they've been, I'll come back to finish the job.'

'That won't be necessary. I'll let you know if there's a problem – with gravity or otherwise.'

Evie shrugged. 'Suit yourself.'

A rush of cold air gusted in as he opened the front door, and Evie's eyes widened. Her car was sitting under a sparkling duvet, and snow spiralled down in a shimmering dance that lit up the night. It was coming thick and fast. At any other time it would have been beautiful – even magical – but tonight her heart sank. 'Oh, no . . .'

'Didn't you hear the forecast? They said it would snow.'

'I know. But it's the first of December. I didn't think there'd be so much of it!'

Snowflakes continued to float down like feathers and the air was eerily silent – although that was probably always the case up there on top of the hill. Evie was used to living in the village, with friends and neighbours close by.

'Where do you want that?' he asked, indicating the stepladder.

'In the back, please,' she said, and stepped outside to open her car. The snow crunched beneath her feet, and she was relieved that it hadn't got too deep yet. 'It fits in the footwell.'

He slid it inside, then regarded the car gravely. 'I'll help you clear the snow.'

His expensive-looking brogues were half submerged in it. Thank goodness she'd worn knee-high boots, Evie thought. 'There's no need,' she said quickly. 'I can manage.' She just wanted to get away from him. She'd be home soon, she reassured herself, as she scraped snow off the windscreen.

'Right. I'll be off, then. My name's Evie, by the way,' she said, and held out her hand. 'Evie Miller.' It was a bit late for niceties, but it felt wrong to drive away without introducing herself, particularly as tomorrow her invoice would be winging its way to him.

He looked at her hand, then shook it. 'Jake Hartwood.'

His hand was as cold as her own, but his grip was firm and strong. Close up, though, the stench of alcohol made her recoil. How sad that such a good-looking young man had turned out so embittered and unpleasant. He might have been attractive – if he'd had a different personality.

Still, at least she'd stood up to him. In fact, she'd surprised herself. Why couldn't she do the same with Tim? And her parents, for that matter?

'Drive slowly and stay in a low gear,' he warned, as she got into the car.

'I'll be fine. It's not deep.' She shut the door and looked at the long drive that snaked away into the snow-speckled darkness. In the doorway of the Old Hall the man and his dog watched as she started the car.

'Low gear indeed,' she muttered to herself, and pressed the accelerator. She couldn't get away fast enough. Goodbye and good riddance to him and his sour-faced advice.

The car moved quickly, and Evie smiled to herself. Thank goodness the snow wasn't too deep . . . but as the car gathered momentum, her smile slipped. She was turning the wheel to no avail. And the car was heading not down the drive but to the right. It was difficult to see, but she thought she remembered a steep slope down into the gardens. She pressed her foot hard on the brake. The car simply lurched forward. She turned the wheel as the drive wound to the left, but nothing happened. She touched the brake again. Her pulse revved up in panic. She braked harder, but the car only skidded, and the steering wheel felt loose in her hand.

'No!' she murmured, gripping the wheel harder. The car was picking up speed as it moved downhill. Muttering a prayer and a curse, she tried again and willed it to cooperate. 'Stop!' she cried, stamping on the brake pedal, and lifting the handbrake in desperation.

The car rolled faster. She yanked the wheel, pressed all the pedals, took it out of gear, put it back in – but still it gathered speed and slid uncontrollably. Her heart thumped crazily. Should she jump out and abandon it? No – she couldn't afford to pay for the repairs if it crashed. Then again, she wasn't in any position to prevent it crashing. She glanced back. Was Jake still watching? She couldn't see – and, anyway, at that moment the car left the drive and plunged down the slope.

Evie gasped as it stopped. She blinked.

The car was wedged at an angle, but she was unhurt, thank goodness. She tried to reverse, but nothing happened. She tried to go forward – it was optimistic, but if she could just turn the car, perhaps it could climb the hill back to the drive. She wound the window down, looked out, then tried the accelerator again. The wheels spun and the car sank deeper into the snow. She closed her eyes in despair. She had to face it: she was well and truly stuck.

Chapter Two

Jake Hartwood's face materialised through the snow. 'Are you hurt?' he asked.

'I'm fine,' she ground out.

He stepped back to survey the crooked angle of the car. 'Doesn't look good.'

'I don't know what happened – the car just wouldn't steer!'

'You mean you weren't aiming for the ditch?' There wasn't a trace of humour in his expression.

'Ha-ha, Mr Funny.'

She got out. He looked like the Grim Reaper, watching her through shadowed eyes.

This just wasn't her lucky night. First, she'd been knocked off her stepladder, and now she'd driven into a ditch. She'd always been accident-prone, but this took the biscuit.

'It's all right,' she told him brightly. 'I'll walk home and come back in the morning to collect my car.'

It was difficult to see, but she could use her phone as a torch. Hobbling, she set off, trying to shuffle through the snow, though it was deeper than it looked and her ankle made her unsteady on her feet.

'You're going to walk home?' he called after her disbelievingly.

'No, I'm going to build a snowman,' she joked, and faced him. 'Yes, I'll walk. It's not far.'

At least, it hadn't seemed far when she was driving to the Old Hall.

'You live in the village?'

She nodded and tried to move again. She couldn't decide which was less painful: putting all her weight on her injured ankle or keeping the foot flat on the ground and trying to shuffle forward through the snow, which was like wading through wet concrete. Perhaps if she found a large branch she could use it as a walking stick . . .

She took another step forward, but the ankle gave way and she collapsed into the snow.

Oh, great. Dazed, she lay there, watching as snowflakes fired down at her, stinging her face and settling on her eyelashes. Now she'd really made a fool of herself.

A pair of strong hands reached down and lifted her.

'Thanks,' she muttered, and brushed the snow off her coat. Her cheeks burned so hot she must be lighting up the place like a glow worm.

'You can't walk home,' he said quietly. 'The village is two miles away, it's dark, and it's still snowing.' He glanced behind him. 'I'd offer to drive you but I'm over the limit.'

She followed his gaze in the direction of the garage. So that explained why she hadn't seen another car when she'd arrived.

He sighed. 'You'd better come back inside.'

It wasn't the warmest of welcomes. She glanced at the house, then back at the drive. 'Are you sure? I don't want to be any trouble.'

'We don't really have any choice,' he muttered. 'This isn't how I planned to spend my evening.'

'Me neither!' she snapped. And cursed him: if she hadn't hurt her ankle she'd be halfway down that drive by now, marching off towards a hot bath and her own cosy bed.

'No use standing about here in the cold.' He scooped her up into his arms.

She yelped. 'What are you doing? Put me down!'

'Why? So you can bury yourself in the snow again? In case you hadn't noticed, the heating in the house isn't working yet. I really don't recommend getting yourself any wetter or colder than you already are.'

She blinked hard. Her pride was really taking a bashing tonight, along with her ankle. If anyone else had offered to carry her, she would have appreciated the gesture as a chivalrous act. But she was certain that Jake Hartwood didn't have a chivalrous bone in his body. He ploughed back up the hill through the snow – though, granted, he made a good job of pretending she wasn't heavy. She kept her eyes focused on the hall's front door because this was far too intimate and all types of awkward.

Smoke barked as they approached. Once they were inside, Jake kicked the front door shut behind them and it closed with a loud clunk.

'You can put me down now,' said Evie.

He shot her a stony look and continued down the hall.

He strode past the dining room, and Smoke trotted beside them, still barking with excitement.

'Put me down. I'm really heavy.'

He raised an eyebrow.

'Where are you going?' she asked, feeling the prickle of nerves as he passed door after door, turning left, right, then left again. This house was a maze. It felt as if he kept going for miles, his shoes clicking on the parquet floor.

'To the study,' he said curtly. 'The only room with a fire.'

Finally, he stopped in front of a door, which had been left ajar. He shouldered it open and carried her over to one of two armchairs that faced the fireplace. While he dragged a footstool in front of her, Evie looked around. This room was notably warmer than the rest of the house, and the charred remains of a thin log in the hearth explained it. She could see why she had mistakenly believed that she was alone here: the room was tucked away at the back of the house. In daylight it probably had a beautiful view of the gardens and perhaps down the valley to Willowbrook village below. Clearly, it hadn't been redecorated yet – the dark velvet curtains were worn and faded, and the panelled walls could have done with a lick of varnish – but it was cosy, and she understood why he'd chosen to hunker down in here rather than in one of the large reception rooms.

Her panic subsided, but she'd do well to keep her guard up: she knew next to nothing about him.

'Here.' He pointed to the footstool. 'Put your foot up.'

'Thanks,' she said, and removed her wet boots.

He closed the door, then knelt in front of the fireplace and added more logs. The flames climbed eagerly, making Evie feel better. She held up her hands to warm them and watched out of the corner of her eye as he took off his wet shoes and socks, placing them near the fire. He opened a small overnight bag and pulled out a pair of dry socks. Evie surreptitiously eyed the bag. He obviously wasn't planning to stay more than one night, and she wondered why he had come here. The fitted bookshelves and the desk behind her were empty: the place wasn't ready to move into yet. Had he dropped in to check on the decorating?

'Are you here on your own?' she asked warily.

He threw her a narrow-eyed look. 'Yes.'

He sat down in the other armchair. Beside him, on a small side table, were a bottle of whisky, half empty, and a glass. A couple of tiny melted ice cubes floated in the amber liquid. He refilled the glass and offered her some but she shook her head.

This isn't how I planned to spend my evening! he'd said. She wondered what kind of man locked himself away in a cold, empty house to drink alone.

'I know – I'll call a taxi!' she said suddenly, brightened by the idea.

He threw her a sceptical look but said nothing and sipped his drink while she fished in her pocket for her phone.

The taxi company's number was engaged. She tried again and again, until eventually the receptionist answered. 'I need a taxi,' Evie explained, 'to collect me from the Old Hall and drive me to Willowbrook village.' It wasn't far, so she'd make sure she tipped the driver generously to make it worth his while.

'I'm sorry. The gritters haven't been out and the main road is impassable.'

'Oh.' Evie's spirits plummeted again.

'No luck?' asked Jake, when she hung up.

She shook her head. 'The snow's stopped everything.'

Smoke moved restlessly between them, then finally settled beside her. She tickled his ears and noticed Jake shoot the dog another hard look. Silence crowded the room, making Evie uncomfortable. She wished she had her patchwork with her so at least her hands would be kept busy, but her sewing bag was in the car. If she was stuck here for the night, they couldn't very well sit in hostile silence all evening.

'So this is where you were when you heard me?' she said, reaching for the end of her long plait and absently winding it round her fingers.

'Smoke heard you,' he corrected.

At the sound of his name, the dog lifted his head and gave a small bark.

'Shush, Smoke. It's okay,' Evie soothed.

'I would happily have ignored an intruder, but Smoke wanted to investigate.'

The implication that she'd interrupted his evening was loud and clear. She'd never met anyone so unashamedly antisocial.

'You're a good guard dog, then, aren't you?' she told the Dalmatian, and he tilted his head for her to scratch behind the other ear.

She shifted in her seat, then winced at a shaft of pain from her ankle.

'The strange thing is that as soon as he saw you he switched from guard-dog mode to wanting to play. I'm afraid he hasn't yet learned that jumping on humans isn't well received.'

The corners of her mouth twitched at his words. 'But you don't know any better, do you?' she told Smoke. Then, to Jake, she said pointedly, 'he was just being friendly.'

Unlike his owner Mr Arctic.

Evie glanced around the room again, trying hard to look on the bright side. 'This house is so beautiful, isn't it?'

He didn't respond, but she didn't let that deter her.

'I heard it has incredible views, and it's so steeped in history. You must feel privileged to live here.'

His mouth pinched. 'I should have bought somewhere new, which didn't need so much work. It would have made moving in a lot simpler and quicker.'

'Oh, but this way you have the chance to decorate and adapt it to your taste. When it's finished, it will be exactly as you want it.'

She dreamed of having the chance to stamp her style on a place like the Old Hall. Somewhere as big as this offered so much scope. You could try a different colour scheme in every room, and different looks. State-of-the-art modern in the bedrooms, for example, and maybe a Shaker-style kitchen. But this room begged for a traditional look, picking up on all the original features, such as the wood panelling and the stone fireplace.

'In the meantime, however, I have no heating, no hot water, and the bother of workmen and people like you coming in and out.'

He was glowering into his whisky glass, and she wondered when – if ever – he'd last smiled.

'Well, at least the fire's going again and it's toasty in here,' she said cheerfully.

He choked on his whisky and looked at her in disbelief.

'What?' she asked.

'So to recap. I was counting on a quiet evening by myself, but instead you're here, having wreaked havoc in my newly decorated dining room, and we're snowed in. But it's all right because the fire's burning and it's "toasty in here".'

Her fists clenched. He sounded just like Tim: unkind and superior. 'I was trying to look on the bright side. Things could be worse.'

'Oh, great,' he muttered into his glass. 'And, to top it all, I'm stuck here with Pollyanna herself.'

'What did you call me?'

'Pollyanna.'

Her patience snapped. He might be her client, but she'd be damned if she was going to let another man make her feel silly and small again. 'You'd rather I was miserable and rude like you?'

'I'd rather you weren't here at all.'

Her nails dug into the arms of her armchair, and she didn't care if they left indents in the brown leather. 'So would I. But my power to influence the weather seems to have momentarily failed me. And, believe me, if I hadn't hurt my ankle I'd be halfway home by now. I'd rather have frostbite than spend the evening with you!'

The dog whimpered, upset by their arguing, and as she reached down to give him a reassuring pat, she realised she was beginning to sound like her reluctant host: sarcastic, crabby and not nice at all. Being trapped here with him was stressful: it was making her behave out of character. She resolved to keep herself in check. She was a cheerful person normally. He might have intended 'Pollyanna' as an insult, but she was a firm believer that if you looked for the good in this world you were likely to find it.

Although, right now, she was struggling to find anything good in him.

Jake slanted her a sidelong look. 'How bad is it?'

'What?'

'Your ankle.'

He sounded genuinely concerned. 'I'm fine.'

It was throbbing badly, but she couldn't bring herself to admit this – not to him.

'Let me see.' He got up and knelt beside her foot.

Her eyes narrowed with suspicion. 'Why?' Was he going to finish the job with a hammer, like the woman in that Stephen King film? No, of course not. He didn't want her to stay here a moment longer than necessary.

'Why do you think?'

She blinked and frowned. 'Well, it's not because you care, so I really have no idea.'

'I was trying to help.' His lips pressed flat, before he reluctantly added, 'I used to be a doctor.'

'Used to?' He motioned for her to roll up the leg of

her jeans. For some reason – perhaps because it really hurt – she complied with his silent instruction. 'Don't tell me – your bedside manner wasn't up to the job?'

He didn't respond. Instead he bent his head to concentrate on her ankle. His hands were disarmingly gentle, his fingers warm against her skin, and although she expected him to twist it or prod where it hurt, he didn't.

'Were you struck off?' she asked, tensing at the thought.

'No.'

She relaxed a little, but now her curiosity was piqued. 'Then why aren't you a doctor any more?'

'It's a long story.'

'I'm not going anywhere,' she said, smiling grimly at the prospect of being stuck with him for . . . Who knew how long? But since they were together they might as well fill the time. And she was genuinely curious, too. It took years to qualify as a doctor. Why would someone turn their back on such a hard-earned profession?

He sighed. 'Can you please stop talking and let me concentrate?'

She shrugged and watched him more closely. His stubble gave him a roguish air, but his dark hair fell in endearing waves and he had a strong jawline. She was almost disappointed when he released her ankle and rolled the leg of her jeans down.

'It looks like a simple sprain,' he said.

His eyes were blue, but one was darker than the other. Perhaps the dancing light of the fire was playing tricks.

'Ice will take down the swelling. I'll get some.' He got up and walked steadily towards the door.

The dog followed him.

'You coming?' Jake asked.

The dog looked back at Evie, hesitated, then made his choice and trotted back to her side.

'Suit yourself,' said Jake, and closed the door behind him.

Evie frowned at the half-empty bottle of whisky. Clearly the man could hold his drink. Or maybe she'd sobered him up with her unexpected intrusion into his evening.

'A doctor, eh, Smoke?' she said quietly. 'Who knew?'

She looked around the room. Next to his chair, in the corner, were a dog's bed, a lead, and a ball, which had been well chewed.

He returned a little later with a shop-bought bag of ice cubes, which he'd twisted shut and wrapped in a scarf. 'Hold this against the swelling for as long as you can bear it,' he told her.

He hadn't moved in yet and there was no central heating in this place, yet he'd come with ice cubes, whisky, and a bed for his dog. Curious.

'Thanks,' she said, placing the icy plastic against her ankle. 'So, if you're not a doctor any more, what do you do now?'

'I run a wine-importing business,' he said dismissively.

He didn't sound excited by it, and Evie would have thought being a doctor was much more rewarding, but they obviously didn't share the same values. Despite his gentle touch, she couldn't imagine that helping people and caring for the sick would come naturally to him.

She shifted a little in her chair, uncomfortable with the

silence. They couldn't sit here all evening without speaking. She looked around the room and thought of all the newly refurbished rooms in this grand house.

'Did you inherit this place?' she asked.

'Inherit? Why do you think that?'

'Because it's a big house and . . . you're young.'

'Not that young. And, no, I didn't inherit.' He picked up his drink and took a sip, but he didn't seem to enjoy it. He grimaced as he swallowed and put it down again.

'Do you drink this much every night?'

'No!' he said fiercely, but his anger was instantly transformed into an expression so wretchedly sad it almost made her feel sorry for him – until she reminded herself of how rude he had been. Her sympathy drained away.

'Listen, it's been lovely speaking to you, but do you mind if I curl up somewhere for the night?' She nodded towards the door. Even an unheated bedroom would be preferable to staying here with him. 'Only I've got a lot to do tomorrow. If I can just catch a few hours' sleep, I'll get up early and, hopefully, be out of your hair all the sooner.'

With any luck the snow would have melted by morning.

He frowned. 'I'm afraid the beds aren't due for delivery until next week.'

'A bare mattress will do.'

'You don't understand. There's nothing upstairs but empty rooms.'

'There are no beds in the house at all?'

'Not a single one.' He took another swig.

'So why are you here? Where were you planning to sleep?'

'I wasn't.'

She waited for him to go on. He swirled the last of the whisky in his glass, and his forehead became knotted as if some battle was raging inside him.

'I came here to . . . escape,' he muttered.

'And drink?'

He looked up. 'You really disapprove of the whisky, don't you?'

'I disapprove of people who drink so much they become unpleasant company.' Although for all she knew he might be unpleasant sober, too. She absently stroked the dog as she spoke. 'If you carry on at this rate, you'll still be drunk in the morning. Either that or dead of alcohol poisoning.'

He laughed bitterly. 'Roll on the morning.'

She hugged herself, disturbed by the look in his eye and the prospect of sharing the study with him all night, no possible escape from his sharp tongue and red-eyed sarcasm. She was finding it difficult to look on the bright side now. What if he carried on drinking? He clearly found her irritating. What if his patience snapped and he throttled her for saying something too upbeat? Her spine stiffened. No one even knew she was here.

'You're right, I should stop drinking.' He sighed, interrupting her chain of alarming thoughts. She watched in surprise as he tossed the rest of the whisky on the fire, making the flames flare, then subside. 'It wasn't helping anyway.'

Evie frowned. 'Helping what?'

He ignored her question and raked a hand through his

hair. 'How about I make us both a coffee? Or hot chocolate. I seem to remember I saw some in the kitchen. Heidi takes it with her everywhere she goes.'

She couldn't fathom his sudden change in attitude, but she was still a little cold and a warm drink was tempting. 'A hot chocolate would be nice, thanks.'

He threw a couple more logs on the fire. 'I'll be back in a minute.' He looked at the dog and patted his thigh. 'Come on, Smoke.'

The dog opened one eye to look at him but didn't move from Evie's side.

Jake glared at the Dalmatian.'Suit yourself.'

When he'd gone, closing the door behind him, Evie reached down and scratched between Smoke's ears. 'Sensible choice,' she told him. 'Why go out into the cold with him when you can stay here with me?'

The dog got to his feet and trotted to his bed. Evie pulled out her phone and typed a message to her friend Natasha: *Got snowed in delivering curtains to the Old Hall. Stuck here with a very rude man who claims to be Jake Hartwood. Letting you know just in case my corpse is found in the morning. He's not friendly at all.*

He could be wanted by the police, for all she knew, though when he returned with a tray of hot drinks and biscuits, it was difficult to keep hold of that thought. He placed a mug of hot chocolate on the small table beside her chair and took a black coffee for himself.

He glanced at Smoke and did a double-take. 'Did you move that?' He pointed to Smoke's bed, which had been dragged from the corner of the room to her side.

'No.' She giggled. 'He must have done it while I was texting.'

He threw a sharp look at his dog, but Smoke ignored him and closed his eyes.

'Maybe he wanted to be near the fire,' Evie suggested.

'Maybe,' he said flatly, and handed her half a packet of biscuits.

'Ooh, Hobnobs!' she said. 'My favourite.'

His brows lifted. 'They might be stale – the decorators left them. They also left milk, but that's definitely gone off.'

'And you didn't seize the opportunity to poison me with it?'

He didn't deign to answer that, but she thought he almost smiled. She offered the biscuits back to him, but he shook his head. Evie shrugged and helped herself to another.

'You seem hungry,' he said.

She stopped chewing. *Should you be eating that?* had been Tim's favourite question. Whenever he caught her tucking into anything tasty, he used to give her a look that made her want to shrivel up. She knew she was carrying a few extra pounds, but how gloomy would life be if all you ate was salad? Yet Jake's look wasn't so much disapproving as faintly curious. As if he were watching the monkeys at the zoo.

Her chin went up all the same. 'I'm starving. I worked late into the evening to finish your curtains.' Not that he'd appreciate that. And, to be fair, why should he? He probably couldn't give two hoots when his curtains arrived. 'I was going to eat when I got home – leftover lasagne,' she added wistfully, salivating at the thought.

'I'm afraid I have no food to offer you.'

'Not a problem. These are fine,' she said, holding up a biscuit before she bit into it. *You might even lose a little weight from missing a meal.* She quashed the memory of Tim's cutting words.

'So, you make curtains for a living?' he asked, after a long pause.

'I have a patchwork and quilting shop. The curtains are a sideline to pay the bills while my shop gets off the ground.'

'Patchwork and quilting?'

'I sell quilts, fabric, thread – everything you need for quilt-making.'

'What kind of quilts?' He looked bemused.

'The kind you might have on a bed – if you had any – or use as a throw. Patchwork.'

Understanding made his eyes brighten and it occurred to her that he might be good-looking if he didn't frown so much.

'We could do with one or two of those to keep warm right now,' he muttered.

She thought it was perfectly warm with the fire burning, but she didn't say so. Instead she said, 'Perhaps when your beds arrive I could interest you in buying some.' It was cheeky, but what was there to lose?

'Speak to Heidi. She's dealing with the refurb.'

Evie frowned. 'You mean you didn't choose any of it?'

He shook his head.

'Not even the colours?'

He curled his long fingers around his mug of coffee. 'That kind of detail doesn't interest me in the slightest.'

Evie stared at him, unable to hide her shock. Her shop was an Aladdin's cave of colours and patterns. Each time she began a new quilt she delighted in perusing the shelves, running her fingers over the different fabrics, choosing which colour combinations and designs to use. A warm autumnal palette, or fresh citrusy shades, a dainty flowery effect for a more romantic feel, or white with modern colour blocks . . . The possibilities were endless. She couldn't imagine moving into a house of this size and leaving someone else to choose the décor.

'What if she chooses a pattern you hate?'

'I wouldn't have a strong opinion about something so trivial. It's only curtains and wallpaper, after all.'

Trivial? Only curtains and wallpaper? This was his *home*. She ran her gaze over his black pullover and jeans. A long navy overcoat hung on the back of the door. He clearly wasn't into bright colours. Her curiosity was piqued. What must the world look like to somebody like him? Where she saw beautiful colours and patterns, what did he see? Nothing? Shades of grey?

'What's it called?' he asked.

Evie blinked.

'Your shop – what's its name?'

'Oh. The Button Hole.'

She thought he might smirk, but he simply nodded. She didn't tell him she had big wooden door handles in the shape of giant buttons, and fabric-covered buttons suspended from the ceiling inside in a colourful display. She regarded them as fun and quirky, but she felt certain he would look down his nose at them.

'And you live in the village?'

Evie smiled. 'Yes. Round the corner from the shop on Love Lane.'

'Seriously? Love Lane?'

She nodded. 'It's the cutest little place you've ever seen. The lane is too narrow for cars to drive along so it's really quiet, and the houses are pretty little terraced cottages built from sandstone with slate roofs.'

'You live cheek by jowl with your neighbours?' He looked horrified.

'I have the friendliest neighbours – old Dorothy on one side, and a retired fireman, George, on the other.'

He looked at her as if she was speaking a language he didn't understand. But, then, he'd chosen to live by himself up here on a hill in this cavernous place.

Then again, she thought suddenly, she didn't know that he lived alone. Perhaps he had a partner – or even a family – and he'd just come here to check on the refurbishment before they all moved in.

'So why did you move here?' she asked.

A shutter dropped over his eyes and she had the feeling she'd said something wrong.

'I'm making a new start,' he said, without any of the excitement or anticipation that a new start usually prompted.

Evie was willing to bet her shop that he was getting divorced. If so, her sympathies were definitely with his ex. No one could live with him. He was draining the oxygen from the room with his dour outlook. 'It's a big place.' She'd fitted curtains in four reception rooms so far, and she reckoned there must be at least six bedrooms upstairs. 'Is it just you moving in, or do you have a family?'

'Just me.' He glanced at the dog, now asleep beside her. 'And Smoke.'

She jumped as her phone trilled in her lap and a message popped up on the screen. It was Natasha: *The Old Hall? Jake is a friend of Luc's! Hope he's looking after you. Stay warm. x*

Evie's shoulders dropped with relief. He might be sour as a lemon, but he was unlikely to be wanted by the police if he was a friend of Luc's. 'You know Luc Duval?' she asked, looking up at Jake.

'Yes. Why?'

'His wife Natasha is a good friend of mine.'

He looked annoyed rather than pleased to learn of this connection. 'I chose this place because it's quiet, and I hoped I'd be left alone to mind my own business,' he muttered.

'Ha! That's never going to happen. Everybody knows everybody in Willowbrook, and we all look out for each other. It's a lovely village with a really close-knit community.'

'Oh, great.' He closed his eyes as if the news pained him. 'Luc forgot to mention that.'

His curt, disdainful attitude was exactly like Tim's. Yet she liked Luc and trusted his judgement. Maybe there was more to Jake Hartwood, if you knew him.

She drained the last of her hot chocolate and adjusted the ice pack, which was beginning to melt. The pain in her ankle had eased, and she was thankful because she couldn't afford to pay someone to mind the shop while she was laid up at home. 'Can I take this off now? It's so cold.'

'Yes.'

'How do you know Luc?' she asked, and rolled her sock back on. It felt warm and soft, and she wiggled her toes.

'We met years ago through a mutual friend. When I first set up my business Luc was very generous with his time and advice.'

She yawned. Maybe it was the heat of the fire, or the fact that she'd stayed up late last night making his curtains and then worked a long day today. 'Remind me what you do again,' she asked sleepily.

He shot her a sharp look. 'I told you – I import wine.'

'Oh, yes.' She stifled a yawn. 'It sounds very dull, but I suppose if you like drinking that must help,' she said, glancing at the whisky bottle.

He pressed his lips flat. 'You don't have to keep this up all night, you know.'

'Keep what up?'

'The pointless chatter. It's late and you talk too much.'

Pointless chatter? She talked too much? The cheek of him! 'And you're rude!' she fired back, stung by his words. How did he manage to make her feel so small? She'd only been making conversation – surely that was better than sitting here, two strangers, in silence.

'True.'

His acknowledgement was so unexpected, she blinked, then smiled. 'Yes.'

The corners of his lips lifted. 'Well, at least we agree

on something.' His tone softened a fraction. 'Why don't you try to get some sleep? You look tired.'

'Thanks a lot. You really know how to flatter a girl, don't you?' Her eyelids did feel heavy, though.

'I tell it like it is. That's all.'

She yawned. 'Didn't your mother teach you that sometimes it's kinder not to say anything at all?'

'Go to sleep. I'll keep the fire burning.'

'You're not going to sleep too?'

He shrugged as if he couldn't care less either way.

She sank back into the armchair and yawned again. Well, fine, he could have it his way. She'd quite like to close her eyes and pretend she wasn't here. 'This chair is so comfortable. Did Heidi choose these too?'

'The furniture that you see came with the house. The previous owners were downsizing so they left a few bits and pieces they couldn't take with them.'

'But no beds. Shame.'

He got up and placed a few more logs on the fire, then picked up the poker and prodded the base. The flames danced and twisted hypnotically. Evie closed her eyes. Tomorrow was Suzie's birthday, she thought drowsily. In a few hours she'd be in the pub with her and Natasha, and the prospect of seeing her friends was comforting . . .

A sudden thought made her open one eye. 'I left my car keys in the ignition.'

He was still stoking the fire but glanced over his shoulder at her. 'Don't worry about that now, Pollyanna. Your car isn't going anywhere tonight.'

'Stop calling me that. Anyway, I'm not worried; just saying . . .'

Her eyes drifted shut again. Smoke was snoring quietly beside her, and the sound was very soothing. 'Goodnight, Mr Arctic,' she murmured.

'What did you call me?' Jake turned to look at her, but she was fast asleep, her breathing deep and regular.

Mr Arctic. He chuckled softly to himself. She wasn't far wrong.

Satisfied that the fire was burning steadily, he returned to his seat. Evie's plait was draped over one shoulder. Her hair was thick, a warm chestnut colour woven through with streaks of honey. In that scarlet coat, she was a splash of brightness in the dark room. Shapely, too, and, despite her protests, she'd been light to carry. He supposed some men might call her pretty. But she smiled too much, and her inane, cheerful chatter riled him.

In contrast, he lovingly pictured Maria as he'd seen her so many times, seated by the window playing the violin. Tall and slim, she'd had a natural grace that he'd found mesmerising. He remembered sweeping her long dark hair away from her face. He could still feel the porcelain smoothness of her skin and see the love in her eyes. It made his chest pinch.

He'd come here to be alone with his grief. He was fed up with sympathy, with concerned family and friends turning up on his doorstep and inviting themselves in – for what? To keep him company? To distract him from the significance of the date? To cheer him up? He winced. They didn't understand that the pain was inescapable and that their prattling didn't distract him, just grated on his frayed nerves.

So he'd driven here on an impulse. He wasn't officially moving in until next week so he'd expected to have the place to himself. He'd settled the dog, then cracked open the whisky, drinking each glass quickly, hoping this would be the one that would send him into oblivion, wiping from his mind the memories and the deep cleft in his chest where his heart had once beaten – before grief had shrivelled it to a dried husk.

The liquid had burned his throat, as fiery as the logs that crackled in the stone fireplace, but he'd ignored the searing sensation and stubbornly kept on taking swig after swig, trying to douse the memories.

Until Pollyanna had arrived.

Smoke had heard her first. Jake would quite happily have ignored an intruder, but the dog wouldn't let it lie so he'd been forced to leave the study and investigate.

The Dalmatian gave a loud snore and shifted in his sleep before settling down again. Curious how the dog had run to Evie as if she were an old friend. Jake couldn't understand it. Smoke was normally wary of strangers, yet she had won him over almost on sight.

And now he was stuck here with her. The most irritating house guest possible. He tipped his head back and sighed. Every intake of breath was an effort.

He had hoped that coming here would help him turn the page and make a new start. Away from the house he and Maria had shared, the furniture sold, her clothes and other belongings gone, he'd hoped that the pain might ease a little, that living and breathing might become a fraction easier.

He had hoped – but he should have known not to hope. Because he knew exactly how punishing life could be. It seemed he was destined always to be anchored to this dark, leaden grief. Two years had gone by, but this day was still hard. Time hadn't lessened the unbearable ache or the anger he felt, nor closed the vast hole she had left in his life. Why her? Why so soon? Why, when she had been so talented and so necessary to him, hadn't she had her fair share of time on this earth? Why had she lost her life yet others, less deserving, were spared? The injustice of it ate away at him. He'd tried to accept it and move on, but he was stuck in this dark place of questions that no one could answer. And it was corrosive, he knew. It made him cynical. Antisocial. *Mr Arctic.* It prevented him from living.

He rubbed a hand over his eyes. They felt scratchy and sore, but he knew sleep wouldn't come tonight. He had to grit his teeth and bear it – he glanced at the whisky – without the anaesthetic of alcohol, because he wanted to be sober enough in the morning to drive Pollyanna home and out of his life.

Chapter Three

Evie opened one eye. It took her a moment to work out where she was.

Then she remembered. The snow, the red-eyed Jake Hartwood and his adorable but over-friendly dog.

Here in the study the curtains were drawn, but daylight had squeezed in around the edges – enough to give the room a haunted grey air. Jake was asleep in his chair, and Smoke was curled up exactly as he had been last night, his breath leaving tiny clouds in the air.

Evie sat up slowly. Her shoulders and neck were sore from having slept in the armchair, and her fingers were icy. She noticed the fire had gone out, which explained the chill in the air. She tried moving her ankle. It was stiff, but it didn't hurt as much today. Good. The dog stirred as she got up and she silently held a finger to her lips, smiling at him and hoping he'd stay quiet and not wake his owner. In sleep Jake's breathing was slow and deep, and his deep frown had been smoothed away. His long lashes rested peacefully on his cheeks. He looked far less intimidating like this, without a hint of disapproval. In fact, the tired lines around his eyes made him look almost . . . vulnerable.

She recalled his sarcasm last night and dismissed this last thought as her imagination running wild. Vulnerable? Him? Never.

Evie tiptoed away, carrying her boots in one hand and letting Smoke out, before closing the door as quietly as she could to leave any residual heat in the study.

Out in the corridor, Smoke seemed confident he knew the way and she hoped he would lead her either to the kitchen or the bathroom. In fact, they reached the kitchen where Smoke went straight to a side door.

'What's in here?' asked Evie, as she pushed it open.

A boot room, by the look of it, complete with umbrella stand and coat hooks. To one side was a small toilet, and Smoke made straight for the outside door, where he whined to be let out.

'Ah, I see,' said Evie, turning the key and opening it. 'You need the bathroom too.'

When they were both back in the kitchen, she remembered that Jake had said he had no food at all, but there was a bag of dry dog food for Smoke so she poured some out, then made herself a cup of black coffee while she worked out what to do next. She peered out of the window. The snow hadn't melted at all – in fact, it must have snowed more during the night because the marks in the drive where her car had skidded were barely visible now. She could try calling a friend, but if their car got stuck in a ditch, like hers, she'd feel bad. Or she could try walking home. Her ankle was less sore now, and she'd spotted a couple of old walking sticks in the boot room. She reckoned she might manage. Might.

'What should I do, Smoke?' she asked the dog, who had eaten hungrily and was now lapping water. 'Walk home? Call a friend? Try the taxi firm again? One thing's for sure. I can't stay here. Your owner is far too bad-tempered. Besides, I have lots to do today.'

'Morning,' said a gruff, deep voice.

She whirled round. 'Jake!'

She expected a sarcastic come-back, but he didn't say anything. From the way he was leaning against the door-frame, blinking and shielding his eyes against the daylight, she suspected he was paying the price for his drinking last night. Smoke bounded over to him, barking happily. Jake shushed him, but also gave him a friendly rub and she could see that, in his own stiff and restrained way, he was just as pleased to see his dog.

'Are you all right?' she asked, peering closer. His face looked gaunt beneath the stubble, and his skin was positively ashen.

'Headache.'

'I'm not surprised. You drank the best part of a bottle of whisky!'

He pulled out a bar stool, sat down heavily, and glanced at the bowls of water and dog food. 'Thanks for looking after Smoke.'

'No problem. He's delightful.' Unlike his owner. Although she couldn't help feeling a bit sorry for Jake seeing him suffer like this. She fetched a glass of water and set it down in front of him.

'Thanks.' He sipped it gingerly, then nodded at the window. 'The snow hasn't melted, has it?'

'No. If anything it's deeper. Did you say you have a car in the garage?'

'It won't be any use in this weather.'

'Oh.' She couldn't hide her disappointment.

'How's your ankle?' he asked.

'Much better, thanks. The swelling's gone right down.'

'You're still limping, though.'

'I'll be okay.'

He shook his head.

'What?' she asked.

'Pollyanna. "The swelling's gone right down."' He mimicked her in a high voice. 'But you can't put any weight on it.'

She pursed her lips. There was nothing like his sour-faced presence to focus the mind, and she made a swift decision because she couldn't wait to get away from here. 'Time for me to go.' She headed for the boot room to pick up a walking stick. 'Now it's light there's no risk of getting lost.'

'Wait!' said Jake, then winced and held his head.

She paused by the door.

He got up. 'There's a quad bike somewhere, I think.'

'You think? You don't know?'

'I seem to remember the estate agent pointed it out. The previous owners left it.' He opened a couple of kitchen drawers before finding the right one, then held up a set of keys triumphantly. 'Give me a few minutes, then meet me here at the back door.'

Minutes later, Evie heard the rough growl of an engine and he trundled past the kitchen window. Smoke barked excitedly. 'Sorry, Smoke,' Evie told him, 'but you're going to have to wait here.'

She opened the back door and cold air washed over her, making her shiver. Jake looked incongruous in his smart wool overcoat and brogues on a quad bike with enormous chunky tyres. Snow had covered everything in sight, reflecting the sun, so the whole landscape shimmered and sparkled, like a bride's wedding gown. 'Wow! It's so beautiful up here!'

'Jump on,' commanded Jake, and patted the seat behind him.

She hesitated a moment, then did as he suggested. 'Have you driven one of these before?' she asked.

'Once.'

'That doesn't fill me with confidence.'

'I can put it away, if you like. The vibrations are not helping my head, I can tell you. Here, put this helmet on.'

'What about you?'

'There was only one.'

'What if we crash? You'll get hurt.'

He shrugged as if his life was of no importance.

She frowned. 'Are you sure you're safe to drive? You had a lot to drink last night.'

'Not as much as I was planning to have,' he said. 'And I'm not over the limit – but whether I'm safe to drive this thing is a different matter. Hold on!' he told her.

Reluctantly, she put her arms around his waist. It felt far too intimate, but there was nothing else to hold on to. She tried to forget that he was her client and that they'd clashed horribly last night. She also tried to ignore how solid he felt as she gripped him tightly, lean and broad-shouldered.

He accelerated suddenly and she gulped in cold air as they began to weave down the drive towards the main road, passing her car along the way. The quad bike made light work of getting through the snow, and Evie's pulse quickened with excitement. The main road was just as thick with snow as the drive – clearly snow-ploughs would be needed to clear it – but the quad bike forged on.

By the time they reached the village, Evie was grinning. 'That was fun!' she said, as he slowed right down on the high street. He didn't reply, but she didn't let his scowl dampen her spirits and her exhilarated smile remained fixed to her lips.

The village was deserted and eerily quiet, apart from the low rumble of the bike. The shops were all in darkness. Some had signs on the doors saying *Sorry – closed due to weather*. A handful of dog-walkers were out, wearing sturdy boots and woolly hats. Evie waved as they passed Lynn, the postwoman.

'Where do you want me to drop you?' he asked.

She directed him to her cottage on Love Lane. Outside her front door, he cut the engine. Evie climbed off the bike and unfastened her helmet.

'You don't want a lift to your shop?' he asked.

She handed him the helmet. 'All the other shops are closed, so I think I'll do the same. I can't imagine many people will be shopping for fabric in this weather, and I have paperwork I can be getting on with at home.'

It would be good to rest her ankle today in the hope it might heal quicker because she couldn't afford any time off work right now.

'My invoice, you mean?' Jake said drily.

'No! I wasn't going to send that until the damage has been repaired and you're sure you're happy with the curtains.'

There was a moment's pause before he answered. 'I don't hold you responsible for the damage last night.' His blue eyes ducked away sheepishly, and was that an edge of remorse she heard in his voice? 'Besides, you've delivered the curtains, so go ahead and bill me.'

She blinked with surprise. 'Okay, I will,' she said, relieved as she thought of her bank balance. 'Thanks for the lift.' She limped towards her front door.

'You should see a doctor about your ankle!' he called after her.

She turned and grinned. 'Your hangover is more debilitating.'

His mouth twitched. 'Nothing that a few hours' sleep won't cure.'

She hesitated, then added quietly, 'Take care of yourself.'

He gave her a curt nod, then revved the engine and sped away.

She stared after him, wondering if his mood would improve when his hangover receded. He looked so grey and ill that it was easy to forget how rude he'd been and how unwelcome he'd made her feel last night.

Still. He *had* taken responsibility for the stepladder accident. That was something.

Jake strode along the woodland path, almost keeping up with Smoke, who scurried left, then right, sniffing and following trails, investigating tree roots, checking every now and then that Jake was still close by.

Jake was glad for the dog's silent, undemanding company. His head still ached at the thought of Evie Miller's relentlessly upbeat chatter. After leaving her at her cottage, he'd driven home and tried to rest, but sleep had evaded him, and Smoke had been keen to go out, so they'd set off to explore the grounds.

In this part of the woods pine trees prevailed so the ground was bare, sheltered from the snow by the canopy above. The fresh air washed over him, like cold water, and the only sounds were the crunch of his boots on twigs and the odd snatch of birdsong. What would Maria have thought of moving here? She had loved London. She always said she was a city girl. Living out here in the country she would have missed the university where she taught, the libraries, her books. She would have missed concerts, as well as the orchestras and groups she performed with. She would have appreciated the beauty of these rolling hills and historic stone cottages, but she would have found it too calm, too quiet.

Yet quiet was exactly what Jake sought. He was tired, he felt decades older than his thirty-five years. Now what he wished for most was peace. To live undisturbed. Because only when he was alone could he focus on getting through each day and easing the pain of living.

His head was just beginning to clear when the muffled ringing of his phone cut through the peace. He sighed and reached into the pocket of his coat.

'Jake, are you okay?' It was his sister, Louisa. 'You didn't answer your phone last night, you weren't in when I called by and the house was in darkness. I was so worried!'

He rolled his eyes as the banging in his temples started up again. 'I'm fine, Louisa.'

'Why didn't you answer the door or take my calls?'

'Because my phone was switched off and I wasn't home – at least, not in London.'

'Where were you, then?'

'I'm in the Cotswolds – at the new place.'

'I thought you weren't due to move for another week.'

'That's right. But I decided to escape for the night. I wanted to be alone.'

He hadn't planned it. The pressure had been gradually building as the day had crept closer, and in the end, it had got too much so he'd run.

'Oh, Jake. Is that wise?'

He chose not to answer. 'I brought Smoke with me. I thought it might be helpful for him to see the house and get used to it. Then, hopefully, it won't be as much of a shock for him when we move.'

'I wish you'd told me in advance. I didn't know where you were or if you were all right!'

'I'm fine. I'm a grown-up, Louisa. You don't need to mother me like I'm one of your brood.'

She said gently, 'It's only because I care about you, little brother.'

He sighed. Louisa meant well, but he simply wasn't ready to accept the kind of support she wanted to give. Since Maria's death, both his sisters had tried to draw him in with invitations to spend weekends, anniversaries and holidays with their young families. But being with others only made the difficult days more painful. The children's energy and joy were so at odds with how he felt, the effort required to feign good spirits with the adults so exhausting. Last year it had come to a head during Christmas dinner when Jake, unable to keep up the pretence a moment longer, had suddenly pushed his chair back and left. He simply couldn't carry on.

Louisa had been distraught, Scarlett angry. There'd been tears and questions. *What did we do? Was it something I said?* And Jake, overloaded with tension and suffocating grief, hadn't handled it well.

Which was why this year he intended to spend the holidays alone.

'Has it snowed where you are?' Louisa asked.

'Yes. There's loads of the damn stuff.'

'Same here. The boys were so excited this morning that they built a snowman before school and had a snowball fight, which involved shoving snow down each other's necks. They were wet through when they came in.'

His lip curled. 'That's boys for you.'

There was a moment's pause before she asked, 'So what did you do last night?'

'Oh, you know. Had a quiet night.' With a bottle of whisky. He didn't tell her that part.

Nor did he tell her about the woman who'd turned up unexpectedly and been snowed in with him. If he was honest, he didn't want to dwell on that. An uneasy feeling was beginning to take root and shame was licking at his heels. He hadn't been at his best last night. Had the tension of the date and the potency of the alcohol got to him? It wouldn't be the first time.

But last year's Christmas disaster was precisely why, yesterday, he'd tried to isolate himself. It wasn't his fault an unwelcome visitor had intruded on his evening.

'You mean you got horribly drunk and now you have a crippling hangover?'

'How did you know?'

'You sound rough.'

'Thanks, sis. You're full of compliments.'

'When are you going to stop punishing yourself like this? Alcohol isn't the answer.'

He stiffened. She made it sound so straightforward. She didn't understand what it was like or how it felt. How he was unable to let go of his love for Maria or dilute it in any way. How, alone, he hoarded the memories of their brief marriage, silently mulling over them, savouring them, yet at the same time flinching at the excruciating pain they provoked.

Smoke stopped suddenly and began to bark at a bird. 'Shush,' said Jake, catching up with him and giving him a reassuring pat on the back. 'Come on, boy. This way.'

'So when can we visit the new place?' Louisa went on.

'I'll let you know.'

'I still can't understand why you chose to move out to the sticks.'

'It's peaceful.'

'Lonely, more like.'

'I like being alone.'

He heard her sigh. 'It's not healthy, Jake. What will you do every day?'

'Same as I did in London: work, eat, sleep.'

'I mean when you're not working. Are you getting out? Meeting people? Or are you going to turn into even more of a recluse?'

'I do enough socialising with work.'

'Oh, Jakey, I'm worried about you.'

'Don't be.'

'Did you get in touch with that counsellor I recommended?'

'No.'

'Why not?'

'You know why not.'

'It might help you to open up and talk to someone.'

He sighed. How would that help? It would be like making an incision in an old wound. 'Opening up isn't my style.' His words were clipped.

Her tone softened and she said carefully, 'It's been two years now. Don't you think it's time you moved on?'

He inhaled sharply. 'Yes. You're right, big sister,' he

snapped. 'I'll just press the switch, shall I? The one to erase all memories and reset my emotional state of mind to "single and open to offers".'

'Jake! You know I didn't—'

He ended the call with an angry jab of his finger and switched off his phone. Then he closed his eyes, feeling bad. Louisa was only trying to help.

He realised Smoke had come to a standstill and was waiting for him because the path ahead had petered out, overgrown with what looked like brambles. Jake picked up a sturdy branch and ploughed through the thorny tangle, making sure Smoke had room to follow.

The trouble was, no one understood how he felt. He was sick of being told he should move on. What he felt for Maria wasn't fleeting; it wasn't superficial. He would always love her, always miss her.

The path emerged into the light, and he took a moment to get his bearings. Blinking against the reflection of sunlight on snow, he spotted the Old Hall up the slope to his left and headed towards it.

He simply wanted to be left to work through his grief in his own time, and in his own way. He needed to numb the pain using whatever means worked. And being alone was the best way to do this.

Ice had etched a delicate pattern around the edges of the cottage windows and framed the enchanting scene beyond. Evie sat in the window seat, her sprained ankle resting on a cushion, a cup of tea beside her, fingers moving quickly as she sewed. 'Somewhere Over The Rainbow' was playing, and she sang along as she made tree decorations to sell at the Christmas fair in just over a week's time. She had cut out red felt hearts and stars, which she was embroidering with white thread and the signature button to represent her shop, the Button Hole. But as she sewed, she was distracted by the snowflakes outside, which twisted and glided to the ground.

Snow was so magical and woke in her a childlike sense of awe and excitement. Was that because it happened so rarely? Or was it because it transformed a landscape so radically? Willowbrook always had a fairy-tale air about it – the narrow streets of tiny stone cottages with their slate roofs harked back to bygone centuries – but today especially so. The steep roofs were coated with white, the trees' branches traced filigree patterns against the pillowy clouds, and the only movement came from thin curls of smoke threading from the chimneys. It was as if an artist had taken a brush and painted out all the dark, dreary colours and hard edges, leaving only this enthralling picture. It was much easier to enjoy the weather, though, from the comfort of her well-heated cottage. She chewed her lip, wondering if Jake Hartwood would go elsewhere for the rest of his curtains after last—

The ring of her mobile phone pierced the air. Evie jumped, knocking over her tea. She was so busy trying to mop up the spillage with one hand, while fumbling for the phone with the other, that she didn't register the caller's name until it was too late.

'Evelyn.'

She frowned at Tim's voice, and her pulse hammered. The puddle of spilled tea would have to wait until she'd dealt with this. 'What do you want?'

'Have you reconsidered my proposal?'

'I told you – I have my own life now. I'm not coming back.'

'You don't mean that.'

'I really do!'

'Evelyn, you need to face facts. Opening that shop was an act of folly. You did it on the spur of the moment – I know you were angry, but now you must see sense. Come back to the city and give us another chance. I'll help you find a proper job. I have contacts I can—'

'I'm not coming back, Tim,' she cut in. Just picturing his sterile apartment made her stomach clench with tension. She used to hide her sewing because he'd disapproved of her hobby. She had constantly striven to meet his expectations – and constantly failed. When they were together, she'd felt she couldn't be herself because she was never good enough.

'You say that, but—'

'No buts. It's true, and nothing will change my mind. The sooner you accept that, Tim, the better.'

'Darling, don't be like this.' His tone softened to a deep purr. 'You know I never meant to hurt you . . .'

Tears sprang to her eyes and she shook her head. He hadn't meant her to find out, was closer to the truth.

But she had. Her heart thumped. She wound her long hair around her finger. It had been five months now – how did he have the power to upset her so much? After what he'd done, she should be immune to him. But each time his name appeared on her phone the memory stirred of him – the man she'd been engaged to – in bed with another woman. Along with the sickening realisation that if Evie hadn't chanced upon them, he would have gone ahead with their wedding.

'Tim, I want you to stop calling me.'

'Come on, darling, you don't mean—'

'I do mean it! I want no more contact with you, understand? No more calls or texts or anything else.'

He sighed. 'You're just being—'

'Goodbye, Tim.'

With a shaky finger, she did what she should have done months ago and blocked his number, deleted it from her contact list and put the phone down. Her breathing was ragged, her heart banging against her ribs. She looked through the window at the snowy scene outside, but the peace she'd felt earlier had been shattered. She ground her teeth, resentful that he'd intruded on her new life here in Willowbrook.

Well, she wouldn't let him, she vowed. She'd moved on, and hopefully now he would do the same.

Chapter Four

'Happy birthday, Suzie!' Evie, Natasha and Suzie chinked their glasses of prosecco.

The Dog and Partridge was quieter than usual due to the snow, but Suzie had insisted on meeting despite the weather, so the three of them had walked there. Their wellies were neatly lined up in the pub's entrance and they'd all brought a pair of shoes to change into.

She'd been living in Willowbrook less than six months, but already Natasha and Suzie felt like family. Closer than family, thought Evie with a nip of guilt.

'How did you hurt your ankle?' asked Suzie, with a nod to the walking stick Evie had borrowed from her neighbour, Dorothy.

Evie quickly recapped the previous night's drama.

'So you got snowed into the Old Hall with Jake Hartwood.' Natasha grinned and sipped her drink. She was a dab hand at nail art and today her nails were painted blue with glittery snowflakes.

'It was awful,' said Evie, with a shake of her head.

'Why?' asked Natasha. 'I've only met him a few times but I seem to remember that Jake is pretty hot.'

Evie thought of his bloodshot eyes and stubble. She

also remembered how solid he'd felt when she'd wrapped her arms around him on the ride home. She banished the thought. 'Good looks aren't enough to compensate for the fact that he has the personality of a grizzly bear. Plus it was freezing and he hasn't moved in yet so there were no beds and we had to spend the night together in his study.' She rubbed her neck. It was still a bit stiff, though at least her ankle was aching less.

'A grizzly bear?' Natasha repeated. 'Are we talking about the same person?'

'What did he do?' asked Suzie.

'He behaved as if it was my own fault that I'd got hurt, and made it very clear he didn't want me there.'

'Strange,' said Natasha. 'He's quiet, that's true, but he's always been impeccably polite when I've met him.'

'Politeness isn't in his vocabulary,' said Evie. 'Sarcasm, yes. Insults and cynicism, too. I'll be glad if I never meet him again.'

Which would be impossible, given that her car was stuck at his place, plus his curtain commissions were the only thing keeping her business afloat. Her cheeks heated at the thought of returning to the Old Hall. If he did order more curtains from her, she'd just have to do her damnedest to avoid him.

Suzie and Natasha exchanged a look.

'Perhaps something else was going on,' Suzie teased.

'What do you mean?' Evie frowned.

'Maybe there was some . . . chemistry between you.'

Natasha smiled and her white-blonde hair gleamed in the warm lighting as she nodded.

Evie laughed. Suzie couldn't have been further from the truth. 'What we had was the opposite of chemistry. It was . . .' she searched for the word, but it was difficult to describe how angry he'd made her, how he'd provoked so much indignation in her '. . . mutual dislike.'

And yet she hadn't been cowed by him. In fact, she was secretly pleased that she'd stood up to him.

Suzie smiled. 'So why are you blushing?'

'Because – because he was infuriating and – and so unreasonable!'

Suzie and Natasha exchanged another look. Evie sighed. If they'd heard the way he'd talked to her, they'd understand. 'If there was any chemistry at all, it was between me and his dog, Smoke – who was so cute you wouldn't believe!'

'The dog that knocked you off the stepladder?'

'Oh, he didn't mean to. He was just being friendly. He was probably delighted to meet a human being who isn't rude and drunk.'

'Drunk? Jake?' Natasha looked incredulous.

Evie nodded. 'Although he did sober up enough to drive me home this morning and I was grateful to him for that. I'd never been on a quad bike before. That was fun.' She couldn't help smiling at the memory.

'Jake has a quad bike? I thought he drove a classic car. He always struck me as being rather traditional.'

'It came with the house.'

'That makes sense,' said Suzie. 'That property includes the fields all around, and doesn't he own part of the woodlands too?'

Natasha nodded. 'That's what he liked about the place. It's secluded and private. Luc said he's become a recluse since his wife died.'

Evie had been about to take a sip of her drink but she stopped, the glass midway to her lips. 'His wife died?'

Natasha nodded.

'When?'

'I'm not sure. A year ago, maybe, or two. She was only twenty-nine. It was tragic.'

'I didn't know . . .' Evie murmured, distracted by the memory of the shocking phone call she'd received when her sister, Zara, had been killed in a road accident five years ago. She was only twenty-six. Far too young.

She thought of Jake's red-eyed bitterness, and it was difficult not to feel a stir of sympathy for him. She knew what it was like to lose a loved one. To have to rebuild your life, shell-shocked and broken, without them. Maybe what she'd interpreted as hostility had been a more complicated cocktail of pain and loss.

'Perhaps he came across as a little abrasive but he's a nice man underneath,' said Natasha. 'I really think you should give him another chance, Evie. You might find you have more in common than you think,' she finished, with a wink.

Her friends had totally got the wrong end of the stick, Evie thought. She had a quick sip of prosecco. 'Since the break-up with Tim, I've well and truly sworn off men.'

'Is he still bothering you?' asked Natasha.

Evie nodded. 'The woman he cheated with broke up

with him and he's been calling me ever since. He thought I'd come running back to him.'

'After what he did? He must have one hell of an ego.'

'They don't get bigger.'

Natasha touched her arm and smiled sympathetically. 'But you shouldn't let one bad experience put you off. Not all men are like him.'

'I know. But at the moment I need to focus all my energy on the shop.' Her forehead creased as she thought of her financial difficulties.

'Things are quiet?' asked Suzie.

She nodded. 'And now the bank's given me an ultimatum.'

'Oh, no!'

'I have until February to turn things around,' she said, trying to quell the panic. She'd been struggling to pay her bills and the rent, so she'd had to default on a couple of loan repayments. The maths was simple: she didn't have enough money coming in to cover the costs going out.

'And if you can't?'

'I'll lose the shop.'

Natasha's eyes widened. 'Oh, Evie. Let me lend you some money.'

'Absolutely not.' She held up one hand. 'It's very kind of you to offer, but I can't borrow from a friend when I already have a loan from the bank. No, I need to start making a profit or face up to the fact that my business has failed and it was a silly, childish dream to believe I could do this.'

'It's not silly or childish to do what you love,' said Natasha. 'Setting up my own flower shop is the best thing I ever did. It's been hard work, but I love it and wouldn't want to do anything else.'

'But the Button Hole isn't making any money. I'm just not getting enough customers.'

She could picture it now – having to hand over the keys to her little shop and admit that she'd failed yet again. She could see her parents' faces. Her dad would roll his eyes, her mother would give her that disappointed look, and then would follow what she'd heard so many times before: how her sister Zara had never let them down like this: Zara would have done the sensible thing and would never have spent all her savings indulging a whim. Zara had had a good job and an equally successful fiancé. She'd had her whole future ahead of her . . .

Evie dipped her head and tried to ignore the sliding sensation inside. To lose her shop would be like nailing shut her most precious dreams and laying them to rest. She had really hoped that just this once she might make a success of something. 'Still,' she said with a brave smile, 'Christmas is coming. Perhaps things will pick up.'

'Yes,' said Suzie. 'They're bound to. Everyone will be shopping for presents.'

'I hope so.' Evie tried to push aside her fears and stay positive. 'Plus these curtains for the Old Hall are keeping me busy. Hopefully the income from that will tide me over until the new year . . .' She didn't enjoy making curtains but it was her only source of income just now

'. . . though I'll have to make sure I deliver them when Jake Hartwood isn't around.'

By the next day the snowploughs had been and the roads were gritted, so people were out and about again, but Evie was pleased that snow still covered all the gardens, the roofs and the hills that encircled the village. Her ankle felt much better, and Saturday was her busiest day, so she reopened her shop. As soon as she had a minute, she would call the garage about recovering her car. If necessary, she could close the shop early to go to the Old Hall. The prospect of meeting Jake Hartwood again made her a little nervous, but she was fairly certain he'd be back in London by now.

The trill of the shop bell made her look up. A muscular-looking man stood in the doorway. He looked conspicuous in her shop, with his dirty hands and oil-stained overalls. Evie hoped he wouldn't touch anything. 'Can I help you?' she asked cheerfully.

'Evie Miller?' he asked, as he approached. 'I've just towed your car. Mr Hartwood asked me to deliver it to you. It's parked out there at the front.'

He held up a set of car keys and she recognised her heart-shaped keyring with her trademark button stitched in the middle.

'Mr Hartwood?' Her brows lifted in surprise. 'Thank you. How much do I owe you?'

The man shook his head. 'All paid for. I repaired the front light and checked for any more damage to the vehicle. I couldn't find any, but if you have any problems when you come to use it, let me know.'

'Right. Yes. Thanks.'

She was astounded. Jake Hartwood had had her car towed *and* paid for the damage?

The man looked around, taking in the quilts displayed on the walls and peering more closely at the basket of fat quarters beside the till. 'My missus loves this kind of thing,' he said, pointing to the quilt behind her. It was for a baby's cot, made up of squares of Liberty fabrics. 'She's always said she'd like to learn how to sew – do you run classes?'

'Yes. There's one for beginners on a Monday afternoon and Tuesday evening. She's welcome to come along to either. The first lesson is free, so she can try it before she pays.' Evie handed him a card with the shop's name and number.

'Thanks.' He was whistling as he left.

She ought to call Jake to thank him, Evie thought, as the door jingled shut, but she didn't have his number. She'd leave a note next time she delivered his curtains. His PA had ordered curtains for another three rooms, and he'd paid Evie's invoice immediately, just as he'd said he would. She was relieved. Her bank account would live to fight another day.

She didn't have time to dwell on the subject because the doorbell tinkled again and Natasha came in. She held a wreath in each hand. 'I made these this morning and thought you might like a couple for your shop and cottage.'

Evie's eyes widened. 'Oh, Nat, they're gorgeous!' The frosted pine cones and greenery sparkled and shimmered, and they smelt divine. She pointed to the white berries. 'Is that mistletoe?'

'It is,' grinned Natasha.

'I love the idea of my customers kissing under the mistletoe. How much do I owe you?' She reached under the counter for her purse.

'Nothing. They're a gift,' said Natasha. 'Like I said, I made a batch, and it's good advertising for my shop if people see them around the village.'

'Well, I'll be sure to tell—' The phone began to ring. Evie excused herself and picked it up. 'The Button Hole. How can I help you?'

'It's me.'

The sound of his voice made her still. 'Tim!' Her eyes narrowed. 'How did you get this number?'

Her skin prickled with goose-bumps. She hated him knowing where she was. This was her new life and her shop. It represented the fresh start she'd made when she'd left him.

'That doesn't matter. What matters is you and me. Can we meet?'

'No.'

'Please. Give me the chance to—'

'No!'

In an instant he switched from cajoling to belligerent. 'When are you going to see sense?'

Her teeth clenched. He was still making out that she was the silly girl who'd made yet another mistake.

Well, she hadn't. The only mistake she'd made had been to trust him. To believe him when he'd said he loved her and wanted to marry her. 'Tim, our relationship is over. You need to face up to that and stop calling me.'

'I know about your shop, Evelyn.'

'What do you mean?'

'I know you're up to your eyeballs in debt, and you haven't made a penny in profit.'

The back of her neck prickled. He didn't give her time to respond.

'It's only a matter of time until it goes down the drain and then you'll rethink. That shop is just another of your hare-brained fantasies. You can't run a business. You're hopeless – you break everything you touch. This will end in disaster, and you know it.'

Her hand shook. She didn't know what to say, so she slammed the receiver down instead.

Natasha was watching with concern. 'Are you okay?'

Evie's face was burning, anger and hurt simmering. After all he'd said and done, how could Tim still have the cheek to suggest she would come back to him? As if! It was only now that she'd spent a few months away from him that she realised how much he'd chipped away at her self-esteem. Constantly critical of small things – her hair, her clothes, her hobbies – he'd made her doubt everything about herself. She'd lived as if she were treading on eggshells, worried that she'd drop something and break it, or say the wrong thing and earn his disapproval.

But his words echoed in her head. *It's only a matter of time until it goes down the drain . . . You're hopeless . . .*

'Was that your ex?' asked Natasha.

'He just won't take no for an answer.'

'Surely he's got the message now. You were very clear.'

Evie shook her head and twisted the end of her pony-tail around her fingers as she tried to ignore the feeling of dread that crawled up her spine. 'Tim isn't a good loser.'

She was worried that that wasn't the last she'd hear from him.

Evie had the key in her pocket but rang the doorbell anyway. If she'd learned anything from her previous visit, it was that Jake Hartwood didn't like unexpected visitors.

Smoke's barking grew louder, and the wide oak door swung open. The dog pushed forward, wagging his tail excitedly, and rubbed his head against her knee. Evie bent to pet him.

'Oh. It's you.'

She thought she detected a hint of irony in Jake Hartwood's tone, but his dark eyes were as unreadable as ever. She straightened up. 'Yes, me,' she said. 'Like pizza delivery – only curtains.'

Jake didn't respond. Not even a smile. Okay, it had been a feeble joke, but couldn't he have pretended to find it funny out of politeness? No. After spending the evening with him, she knew he didn't do politeness or social nice-ties. Her pulse was rapid-firing, though she couldn't think why. It must be nerves. He made an imposing figure, filling the doorway and dressed in black jeans with a navy sweater. His chin was still dark with stubble, but his eyes weren't bloodshot, and he was almost good-looking –

although he scowled too much, and she couldn't forget how rude he'd been last time they met.

Smoke was turning circles around her, periodically pausing for her to stroke him. She chuckled at the dog's uninhibited friendliness. 'I thought you'd be at work – that's why I came in the day. I didn't want to disturb you.'

'I'm working from home.' His words were clipped.

'Ah.' It was evident he wasn't happy at the intrusion, but she pulled her shoulders back and did her best not be intimidated by his brusque manner. 'I must admit, I was a bit worried about coming back here, but I see you've had the drive cleared – that makes life a lot easier.'

The sterner he looked, the faster the words came spilling out of her mouth in a nervous stream of chatter. 'Oh, and thanks for having my car towed last week, by the way. The chap delivered it right to my door, and he said you'd paid for the repairs, too. It was really very kind of you.'

Too late she remembered what he'd said to her that night: *You talk too much.*

He shrugged. 'It was nothing.'

He was probably glad to be rid of her car and didn't want to risk another visit from her – but here she was on his doorstep again. Unfortunately, her visits couldn't be avoided: after all, he needed curtains and she needed his business.

Smoke finally stopped and sat beside her. Evie shifted from one foot to the other. When she realised Jake wasn't going to invite her in, she cut to the chase: 'I have a couple more pairs of curtains to hang downstairs, and I need to measure up in the bedrooms. Is this a good time?'

'You've made two pairs in less than a week?'

Was he disapproving or admiring? She wasn't sure. 'I thought you'd probably want all the decorating done before Christmas – in case you have family coming to stay.'

'Did you? Or am I your only customer?' he asked.

Her cheeks fired with heat, but there was no point in denying the truth, humiliating as it was. 'There is that, too,' she conceded quietly. 'Thanks for paying the invoice so soon, by the way.'

He gave a terse nod but still didn't move. Conscious that she was paying someone to look after her shop, Evie said, 'Right, well, I'll just get on with hanging the curtains, shall I? It won't take long – providing I don't get knocked off my stepladder, that is.'

She was sure his lip almost curled in the faintest suggestion of a smile. 'I was going out anyway.' He patted his leg for Smoke to come to him. 'Time for your walk, Smoke.'

Was that true, or was he just keen to avoid her? The Dalmatian didn't move but looked up questioningly at Evie. Jake reached behind the door and produced a lead, but his dog chose to follow her as she scurried to her car to fetch the curtains. She carefully lifted out thc soft modern tweed, pale grey shot through with dusky pink and blue.

'So you've moved in, then?' she said, when she returned.

'I have.'

She accidentally knocked the coat stand as she went past. It wobbled violently. Fortunately, Jake caught it in time and steadied it. 'Thanks,' she said, bracing herself for an angry reproach telling her to be more careful – she'd become so used to them with Tim – but it never came.

Instead he held up the dog's lead. 'Come on, Smoke.'

But the dog pointedly ignored him and trotted after Evie as she headed for the library. Jake hesitated, then followed too.

'Here, let me,' he said, with a nod to the curtains in her arms.

She caught the scent of his aftershave as he moved closer and it made her senses tingle. 'It's okay, I've got it.'

'Your ankle's better, then?' he asked, as she hurried on.

'Much better, thanks. Oh – you've had the plaster repaired!' She stopped outside the dining room.

The curtain rail had been put back up, her curtains too, and the room was filled with furniture. Yet, despite the expensive sideboard, the glittering mirrors and paintings, it still didn't feel homely – far from it. It looked like the home of a wealthy but lonely man, she thought, with a strange little tug at her heart.

'Yes,' said Jake, and stopped beside her. Smoke trotted around them both in figures of eight.

'Are you happy with the curtains?'

'They're satisfactory.'

Her head whipped round to look at him. 'Just satisfactory?' She felt a lurch of disappointment when she'd taken so much care over them and, quite frankly, was proud of the results.

'I mean they hang vertically and close when I draw them in the evening.' His mouth remained flat, but his eyes glinted with humour.

Evie felt a rush of relief and laughed. She told herself to ignore the sparking sensation in her blood. She wasn't sure what had caused it.

'And the move all went smoothly, I heard,' she said, continuing down the hall towards the library.

His brow pulled into a sharp frown. 'You heard? How? There was no one here but me and the removal people.'

He pushed the door open for her and motioned for her to go ahead. Evie glanced around her. The tall shelves had been filled with books, and the room was dotted with armchairs covered with the same tweed fabric as the curtains in her arms. It looked beautiful – if a little bare. A couple of rugs was what it needed, and a little lived-in clutter.

'Oh, everyone in the village has been talking about you.' She grinned, as she laid the curtains over one of the armchairs. 'Mostly they want to know if you're going to keep up the tradition of hosting a Christmas ball.'

She suspected she knew the answer. Hospitality was definitely not among Jake Hartwood's strengths.

'What tradition?'

'Every year the Old Hall's owners hold a ball for the village. There's been a ball here every Christmas for the last two hundred years, so I'm told.'

'Has there really?' he said flatly.

She turned and faced him. 'So will you?'

'Will I what?'

'Be hosting the ball?'

He made a rough sound, which might have been laughter. 'Definitely not.'

She bit her lip to stop herself smiling. The more horrified he looked, the more mischievous she felt. 'Oh, that's a shame. Everyone will be so disappointed.'

'I'm not opening my house for a village full of strangers to come and get drunk.'

Well, put like that, he had a point. 'I'm sure they'd all be well behaved.'

'It's out of the question. You may as well make it known that I don't do balls, parties or socialising.'

'What about community spirit, then?' It sounded like an innocent question, but she held his gaze.

His eyes narrowed. 'I don't do that either. I bought this house for the privacy it affords me.'

Natasha had said he'd been a recluse since his wife had died, and something inside her softened in sympathy. She knew how hard it was to lose a loved one. Still, it didn't have to make you prickly and antisocial. 'No one can live like that,' she said quietly, 'in complete isolation.'

Instantly his features hardened. 'I can.'

'We all have duties and responsibilities. We all need other people in one way or another.' She thought of her neighbours: old Dorothy, who was frail and couldn't get out easily, and George, who was physically strong but lonely living on his own.

'I don't.'

A muscle pulsed in his jaw and she knew she should keep quiet. It was none of her business how he lived his life. But the urge to help was too strong. It was in her nature to reach out to others.

'You must do! You have Smoke, for starters.'

'Okay, I have Smoke. I don't mind his company. He doesn't ask questions.' His blue-eyed gaze bored into her. 'It's the human, talkative type I avoid.'

Like her. She got the message.

He bent to stroke Smoke and clipped his lead on. 'Come on, boy. Let's get some fresh air and leave Pollyanna here to get on with her work.'

He threw her a sharp look and strode off, letting the front door slam behind him.

Evie stayed in the library and watched his tall figure stride across the lawn into the woods. If only she would hold her tongue around him and remember he was her client. *You're hopeless, you break everything you touch* . . .

Despite what Natasha said, Jake Hartwood was difficult to warm to. Not just cool but positively icy, and he revealed nothing. Except now and again when he showed flashes of dry humour – or was it sarcasm? – which broke through like unexpected beams of sunlight on a cloudy day.

Upstairs, she hung the curtains and measured up for the last few bedrooms, humming as she worked, double-checking all her measurements and calculations. Whenever she did this, she remembered her former maths teacher, Mrs Fox, who had handed out exam results saying, 'Evie Miller, bottom of the class.' With curtains of this size and quality fabric she couldn't afford to make any mistakes. Plus, she had the feeling that Jake wouldn't tolerate any more slip-ups on her part.

Satisfied that she had all the measurements she needed, she dropped her notebook into her sewing bag, picked up the stepladder, and made her way towards the staircase.

As she passed the master bedroom, she paused at the door and looked in, curious to see what the room revealed about its owner now he'd officially moved in. She glanced at her watch. How long had he been gone now? She didn't want to be here when he returned. Then again, his PA had ordered a couple of quilts for the two main bedrooms. It was unlikely Evie would have time to make them before Christmas, but if she took the measurements and jotted down notes on colour schemes, perhaps she could get started on them over the holidays when the shop was quiet and everyone else was spending time with their families.

Leaving her stepladder in the hall, she went in and measured the bed. It was enormous, bigger than king-size, with a biscuit-coloured headboard. The room's colour scheme was chestnut brown and cream, with the odd burst of berry red in a picture or cushion. The overall effect was masculine yet warm. It gave her lots of leeway for choosing colours to use in a quilt. It was also very tidy, she noticed, nothing like her own bedroom at home, which had piles of clothes, hairbrushes and -clips strewn around. Jake Hartwood clearly liked his life very ordered. Beside his bed there were only two objects: an alarm clock and a framed photograph. Evie tiptoed across to take a closer look. A woman with dark hair in a neat, super-elegant chignon smiled at the camera. Her skin was tanned and smooth, and her stylish navy silk dress and pearl earrings screamed sophistication. She was beautiful – and so, so young.

Just like Zara. Evie inhaled deeply as she fought off her own jagged memories of grief.

A dog's bark made her jump and through the window she saw Smoke bounding up the hill, Jake following. She checked her watch. She'd better scarper before he found her in here and she met with another of his disapproving glares. She snatched up her tape measure and sewing bag and hurried out of the room.

Jake rounded the corner of the house and just glimpsed Evie pushing her stepladder into the back of her car, then rushing to get in and driving away. She had left in a hurry. Coincidence? Or had she seen him coming?

Frowning, he stamped the snow off his boots and went inside. He didn't have the patience for niceties any more: he was short-tempered, intolerant and blunt. Normally he didn't care. So why did he find himself hounded by guilt, yet again, over the wounded look his words had provoked earlier in Evie Miller? After their first meeting he'd made sure she retrieved her car, that she was kept in pocket with work for his house, and thereby had assuaged his conscience. How was he going to put things right this time?

Avoid her. It was the simplest solution. Avoid all human contact.

He wasn't fit to be around people. They only irritated him. Alone he could indulge in the memories, replaying them, conjuring Maria's face in his mind, hearing her laugh, resurrecting their brief but acute happiness. Alone, he could sometimes trick himself into believing she wasn't gone, and when he turned around, she'd be there. Of course, the illusion lasted only a nanosecond, but the relief and the joy it brought were worth it.

Christ, I miss you so much, Maria. Forgive me.

He stopped at the bottom of the stairs and Smoke looked up at him with questioning eyes. Jake concentrated on breathing while he waited for the pain in his chest to ease so he could carry on. *Come on, Hartwood. One foot in front of the other.*

This time of year was the hardest. The anniversary was only the start: during the run-up to Christmas everything became more intense, and he could feel the tension already accumulating in his neck and shoulders. Just as it had done last year – before it had all come to a head on Christmas Day.

Upstairs, he was wearily exchanging his snow-dampened trousers for a dry pair when he noticed a notebook lying on his bed. He picked it up. Inside there were pages of measurements and sketches of what he guessed were patchwork designs. The last entry was headed with his name and read, *Bedroom no.1 Quilt. Colours: cream, chestnut brown, warm red.*

He frowned. She must have left it behind. He could let her know he had it and leave it by the front door for her to collect next time she was here. On second thoughts, he suspected it was probably something she used a lot. He'd be passing through the village tomorrow morning. He could drop by her shop then and return it to its forgetful owner.

Chapter Five

Jake pushed open the shop door, rolling his eyes at the oversized wooden handles shaped like giant buttons. He stood aside to let a young girl pass. 'And thanks for the ribbon, Evie!' she called on her way out. The shop door swung shut behind her.

Inside, he glimpsed Evie standing behind a table talking to a couple. Jake had her notebook in his hand, but she was clearly busy serving customers, so he filled time by wandering along the narrow aisles. Giant buttons wrapped in bright fabrics, and supersized cotton reels wound with chunky glittering wool hung from the ceiling. They spun gently, and he had to duck his head to avoid one. He ran his gaze over the shelves, with their neat lines of fabric. The price label of one caught his eye and he raised a brow. Expensive stock. No wonder she was worried about her finances: the initial outlay on a place like this must have been enormous.

'When are you going to stop dreaming and be sensible?'

The raised voice made Jake stop. He noted the plummy accent.

'You had a perfectly good job in London and a man who was willing to marry you. Who still wants to marry you – if only you'd see sense!'

Concealed by the shelves of fabric, he listened more carefully to the conversation he'd accidentally intruded on.

'Dad, if you've come here to try to persuade me to go back to Tim, you're wasting your time . . .'

Jake frowned. Not customers, then, but her parents.

'. . . It wasn't working between us. I'm happier without him.'

'Nonsense! The two of you have been friends since you were knee high.'

'No.' She sighed. '*You*'ve been friends with his parents, so we were obliged to spend time together – that's not the same thing.'

She was speaking quietly and patiently, but her father's voice was only getting louder and more irate.

'Tim's a decent chap with an excellent position and even better prospects. Only a fool would walk away!'

Jake peered around a corner and saw that the vivid colour in the man's cheeks contrasted sharply with the green of his tweed jacket. Beside him, a slim woman with silver hair was biting her lip.

'Dad – please keep your voice down! What if a customer comes in?'

Evie reached for the end of her long plait and wound it around her fingers. Jake recognised the nervous habit from when they'd been snowed in together.

'Customers?' the man sneered. 'You're hardly rushed off your feet. The place is deserted. And when you do get someone coming in to buy, you give away your stock for free!'

'I gave her a piece of ribbon, that's all. She had already bought a piece of fabric!'

'It's no wonder you're not making any money.'

'Which is why we're here, Evie,' said the woman. 'Darling, you know we worry about you. Please reconsider – before it's too late and Tim finds somebody else.'

'Has he put you up to this?'

'No of course—' her mother began.

'Well, he—' her father said simultaneously.

There was a pause. Then her father said, 'His parents came to see us. Asked us to talk some sense into you. He's distraught. Says you got hold of the wrong end of the stick and overreacted.'

Evie sighed. 'I knew it.'

'He won't wait for ever,' her father continued.

'Good. Maybe he'll stop harassing me. He doesn't seem to understand the word no.'

'He's waiting for you to finally see reason.'

'Dad, I don't want anything more to do with Tim. I'm sorry if that's difficult for you to—'

'Difficult is an understatement, my girl. Do you have any idea how strained this has made our relations with his family?'

'I'm genuinely sorry for that. But I've made up my mind. I'm not going to marry someone because it's convenient for you or his parents.'

'Evie, please—' the woman began, but was immediately interrupted.

'You're living in La-la Land!' said the man. 'Leaving Tim to come here and set up shop in the middle of nowhere, selling things no one wants to buy. You played games of make-believe when you were a child, but you're twenty-eight now, Evelyn – it's time to grow up!'

Jake frowned. He stepped forward to make his presence known, but none of them noticed. Evie was blinking hard. She seemed deflated. Defeated. And it was so unexpected that Jake felt a stirring of concern. Where was the fight in her? The woman he'd met at the Old Hall had been fiery and defiant. Now she looked like a little girl lost. She wore a bright green dress with striped sleeves that appeared to have been cut off a jumper and sewn on, but the colourful outfit only emphasised how pale her cheeks were. Her hazel eyes shimmered in the shop lighting.

'You've spent enough time – and money – on this place. Enough is enough!' Her father picked up a square of folded fabric and slapped it down on the table. 'Do you think I don't know how much you borrowed from the bank? This shop of yours has failed. It's time you faced up to reality and recognised that!'

Jake cleared his throat and stepped forward. All three whipped round and stared at him, clearly startled to see him there.

'Jake!' whispered Evie, and her horrified tone matched the look in her eyes.

'Evie,' he responded, with a nod, then asked mildly, 'How long has your shop been open?'

'September, so – er – three months.' Her cheeks flushed a pretty shade of raspberry.

He turned and addressed her father. 'It takes more than three months for a business of this kind to get off the ground. Your criticism is unreasonably harsh and premature.'

Silence ricocheted around the shop. One of the giant buttons spun slowly to the right, then back again. Jake got the feeling that this couple, with their tailored tweed and heirloom wristwatches, were not used to meeting with opposition. Tough luck.

Jake had always been a sucker for siding with the underdog.

'Who are you?' the man demanded to know.

'M–Mr Hartwood is a client,' said Evie.

Her father lifted his chin and swept an assessing gaze over Jake. 'Of course, we expected things to be slow at first, but this place is quiet as a morgue. She'll be bankrupt by spring.' He looked at Evie. 'You're not even covering your costs. No one wants to buy those – those things!' He gestured to the quilt hanging behind her. Below it was a neat price label displaying a three-figure sum. 'Especially at that price!'

'It's a handmade quilt!' Evie said indignantly. 'And the price reflects that.'

'It's overpriced. People won't pay that!'

Evie looked stricken. She tried to keep her chin up, but Jake could see the sheen in her eyes. Where was her fire, her gusto?

'But everyone needs curtains,' Jake said smoothly.

This seemed to catch her father on the back foot. A sharp frown cut through his brow.

'You sell curtains?' he asked his daughter.

'I make and sell them.'

'She made mine,' said Jake. 'I can vouch that they're excellent quality. Far superior to anything off the shelf and, of course, tailor-made to my specifications.'

The man's eyes widened. His mouth worked, but he seemed momentarily lost for words.

Evie stared at Jake, astonished.

'Well, one pair of curtains isn't enough to clear your debts,' her father continued. 'It's time you put an end to this dreaming and got yourself a real job.'

'Dad,' she said, and moved towards the shop door, 'this is my job now, and I have customers to see to. It's very kind of you both to visit, but this isn't a convenient time for me. I – I'll call you.' The bell on the door jingled as she opened it and waited.

Jake silently commended her for quietly asserting herself and recovering control of the situation.

The couple grumbled, but moved to leave, and Jake could see the relief on Evie's face when they finally stepped outside and she was able to shut the door behind them. The bell jingled one last time, and she let out a long breath. 'Thank you,' she said quietly.

Jake shrugged. 'What for?'

'Vouching for my curtain-making service and . . .' her eyes still gleamed, but then she blinked and the vulnerable shine in them disappeared '. . . and standing up for me.'

'I only spoke the truth.'

She stared through the glass door at the street outside. 'Oh, God, that was just awful! I'm so embarrassed you heard that conversation!' Colour bloomed in her cheeks.

'They're your parents, I take it?'

She nodded. 'Dad can be . . . a little overbearing sometimes.'

He raised an eyebrow. 'A little?'

She laughed nervously. 'They have very clear ideas about how I should lead my life, and I – I only disappoint them. Repeatedly.' She looked down at the floor but not before he'd glimpsed the sorrow in her eyes.

'Do you? Or do they make unreasonable demands of you?' Her head lifted and she blinked at him in surprise. 'I mean, it's a bit archaic to choose your daughter's husband for her, don't you think?'

She laughed. 'I suppose. But they also disapproved of my decision to leave my old job and open this shop.' She sighed. 'And they're right about the money side of things. I'm up to my eyeballs in debt, and the way things are going, I'm not sure I'll ever be able to repay it.'

'The curtains and quilts you're making for my place, won't they be enough to tide you over?'

'Yes! They will – they are. And I'm very grateful for the work.' She straightened a bolt of fabric. 'But when I've finished working for you, I need to know that I'll still be able to pay the rent. The curtain-making was supposed to be a temporary thing while the shop got up and running. I really need this place to start turning a profit.'

Jake looked around him. She'd decorated the shop with eye-catching displays, but he could see it was a specialist shop. After all, who sewed, these days?

'To be honest, I'm not sure I'm cut out for this. Dad's right – I can't afford to be giving out freebies to customers like I did earlier.'

'How much did that freebie cost?'

'A piece of ribbon? About two pounds.'

'I'd say that was two pounds well spent. The customer will remember, and she'll want to come back to this shop next time she needs fabric. She'll also tell her friends what a friendly shopkeeper you are, helpful and generous.'

Her cheeks flushed the colour of a fruity rosé. 'Well I never!' she said.

'What?'

She grinned. 'Mr Arctic paying me a compliment.'

'Giving you business advice,' he corrected. Warning bells sounded in his head. Her shop and her problems were nothing to do with him. He should keep well out of this. Hand over her notebook and leave.

Yet his feet remained firmly rooted to the spot.

'How does your father know your bank manager? I'd have thought that information about your loan would be confidential – unless your father was involved in helping you get set up.'

'Oh, Dad wasn't involved,' she said quickly. 'I used my savings as a deposit and arranged the loan myself. But he plays golf with the bank manager. Dad prides himself on having lots of . . . connections like that.' She sighed. 'I think the bank manager has lost faith in me and realised I don't have what it takes to do this. Turns out I'm no good with the accounts and the business side of things. I love sewing – and helping people sew – but that alone isn't enough to make my shop profitable.' Her gaze fleetingly met his before she admitted, 'I'm afraid that if the shop goes bankrupt I'll have to go back to London and a job I hated. Or, worse, back home to live with my parents.' She shuddered at the thought and strands of hair fell over her face as she looked at her feet, downcast.

Her openness surprised him, her air of vulnerability, too. He felt a curious and unfamiliar impulse to step forward rather than back off, as was his habit. 'If you expect to fail, you will undoubtedly fail,' he warned softly.

Her dimples flashed. 'Thanks. That's just what I needed to hear. Words of hope and optimism!' She crossed the shop back to the counter and tidied up the bundles of fabric which her father had disturbed. He followed and watched as she stacked them in the basket and fanned them out in a pretty display. Her fingers moved quickly and deftly.

'The reverse side of it is that if you believe it can work it most likely will.'

'I like that much better.' She smiled, though only fleetingly. 'But Dad's right – I can't do this. I was stupid to believe I could.'

He couldn't believe what he was hearing. He'd had her down as an eternal optimist.

Then again, he'd heard her parents speaking to her. They were so critical, they'd have sapped anyone's confidence. Even Pollyanna's.

'Why did you open this shop?' he asked.

'Because I love sewing.'

'Why? What do you love about it?'

'Is that a trick question?'

'Not at all. I can't see the appeal. I want to know.'

'Come with me,' she said, and led him into the back room. 'It's easier if I show you.'

On the large square table in the centre of the room there was a sewing machine and what looked like half-made curtains. Evie walked past and stopped beside a side table on which were laid out dozens of fabric hexagons. 'See the colours?' she said, scooping up all the crimson pieces and pointing to the remaining shades. 'See how the chocolate brown is the main anchor? Then the creams add contrast and warmth? And this beige and brown check bridges the gap between the light and the dark . . .'

He looked blankly from the fabric to her. She continued regardless and replaced the red hexagons: 'And finally the red adds a burst of colour which brings all the rest to life.' She stood back with a satisfied smile that lit her eyes.

'That's what you enjoy?' Her passion was obvious, but he didn't get it at all.

'Yes! Putting colours and patterns together. Each combination is unique. It's a bit like painting, I suppose. And then there's the sewing. Not so much making curtains, but the quilt-making. There's nothing more relaxing or satisfying than hand-stitching. But you have to try it to understand.'

'Show me.'

'Really?'

He nodded.

'Okay.' She grinned, as delighted as a child on Christmas morning, and picked up a couple of hexagons, then a needle and thread. 'Have you done this before?'

'Never.'

'You line them up back to back like this, and stitch. Tiny little stitches – look.' She leaned in closer to show him. The needle darted over and through the fabric – so fast he could barely see it. Her fingers were nimble and precise, and reflections of light bounced off her thimble. Within a few seconds she had stitched the two pieces together and unfolded them for him to see the reverse side. Her stitches were barely visible, a row of tiny neat lines. 'Here, you try it.'

He did it to humour her, but his effort looked ragged and clumsy. 'I never was much good at sutures,' he muttered.

'Try to keep the space between the stitches the same,' she encouraged.

He concentrated hard, but accidentally stabbed himself with the needle. He cursed. 'And you enjoy this?' he asked, sucking the blood from his finger.

Her laughter was like the tinkling of a bell. 'When you get the hang of it it's wonderful. And I'm not the only one to think so. At my workshops people often tell me how much they've enjoyed it – especially those with desk jobs. There's something about working with your hands and being creative that's incredibly satisfying.'

'I'll have to take your word for it.' He handed back the hexagons. 'So, you make curtains because you need the money, but you'd rather be making quilts?'

She nodded. 'And serving customers. I love helping people choose colours or chatting to them about their sewing projects.'

'Yes, I can imagine you'd be good at chatting,' he said drily.

Her cheeks bloomed with colour and she smiled. Her bashfulness was curiously endearing.

'If the shop is what you love most, why don't you focus on that?'

'I have – I do. But it's always so quiet and the few customers I have only come in for the odd reel of thread. She gave a sad little laugh. 'Tim – my ex – predicted that my shop wouldn't last six months. It's beginning to look like he was right.'

'You're a talented seamstress and you enjoy helping others. There's no reason why your shop shouldn't succeed. Have you asked yourself how you can attract more customers? How much advertising have you done? Have you really tried everything to make it succeed?'

'Well, not everything . . . I've been so busy making curtains, it's difficult to concentrate on the shop too.'

'Maybe think outside the box. Something tells me you'll be good at doing that.' His gaze dropped to her multi-coloured striped cuffs. 'You need to believe in yourself. Invest one hundred per cent in making your business succeed. Otherwise, with half-measures, things will continue as they are now.'

'Believe in myself?' she repeated.

He nodded.

A strange look crossed her features. Then she stilled, as if something had just occurred to her. 'What brought you here?'

He'd completely forgotten about the notebook. He

reached inside his coat. 'You left this at my place. I thought you might need it.'

'I've been looking everywhere for that! Thank you! But you shouldn't have gone out of your way. If you'd called, I would have picked it up.'

'I didn't have your number to hand, and it was just as easy to drop by. I was passing anyway.'

She picked up a business card from a pile beside the till and scribbled something on the back. 'Here's my mobile number – in case you need to get hold of me again.'

'Thanks, but I hope you're not going to make a habit of leaving things in my bedroom.'

'Of course not! That's not what I meant . . .'

He gave her a wry smile and held up the card. 'Any time I have a sewing emergency, I know who to call.'

She smiled, and her eyes glistened under the shop lights. 'Actually, while you're here would you like to choose any fabrics for the quilts I'm going to be making for you?'

He recoiled at the idea. 'No.'

'You're really not interested at all?'

'I'm sure you're perfectly capable.'

'What if you hate what I choose?'

'I won't.'

'What if you do?'

He shrugged. It didn't matter one jot to him. He'd only ordered them to help because she'd said she had cash-flow problems. And because he was still haunted with guilt about the night of the snowstorm?

Hastily, he brushed aside the thought.

'Okay. Well, in that case, I'll be careful to stay away

from anything overtly flowery and feminine. Stripes and checks, nothing fussy.'

'Please don't bore me with the detail.'

Her eyes widened, and she frowned. 'You're so rude – you know that, don't you?'

'Plain-speaking,' he corrected. 'And life would be more straightforward if others followed my lead.'

'I bet you don't speak to your customers like that.'

She was right. He didn't. But he wouldn't admit it. 'Your father was rude too, but you didn't stand up to him.' And, curiously, he wished she had. Something about the way she'd absorbed the criticisms levelled at her disturbed him. He much preferred the fireball in front of him now.

Evie ducked her gaze away. She snatched up a square of fabric from a pile behind the counter and her hands were ever so slightly unsteady as she folded it.

'My parents . . .' Her voice wavered. 'It's difficult for them.'

Difficult? He thought of the way her father had laid into her, belittling her, ridiculing her efforts. Jake felt an unfamiliar emotion stir inside him – what was it? Indignation? Anger on her behalf? Whatever it was, it came as a surprise because for the last two years he'd been incapable of feeling anything but grief. Perhaps he did still have a heart. 'To criticise and berate you in the way they did was totally unjustified. How can you let them—?'

'You don't know anything about my family!' she cut in. Fire flashed a fierce warning in her hazel eyes.

He held her gaze defiantly. Perhaps not, but he hadn't liked what he'd seen.

She picked up another square of fabric and folded it with quick, nervous movements, but even he could see that it wasn't straight. He looked at the card in his hand with the Button Hole's logo, and for the briefest moment thought about giving her his number too. Forget it, Hartwood. He didn't do friendships or get entangled in the affairs of people who worked for him.

'Right,' he said. 'I'd better go. Smoke will be cold waiting outside.'

Her head lifted. 'Smoke's here?'

Jake couldn't understand why her obvious pleasure at the news sent a dart of jealousy through him. 'Yes.' He glanced outside, and she followed his gaze.

She reached under the counter, then quickly crossed the shop and opened the door. He followed, only to find her feeding his dog treats and fussing over him. Out here the air was cold as ice, but she didn't seem to notice. Smoke, of course, was thrilled by the attention and barked with excitement. 'Someone's pleased to see you,' Jake remarked.

'The feeling's mutual,' she said, her dimples flashing, like sunlight breaking through cloud.

Smoke jumped up and she rubbed her cheek against his.

Jake rolled his eyes at the pair of them. 'Don't hold back on my account.'

She glanced over her shoulder. 'He's definitely the more approachable of the pair of you.'

He met her gaze, saw the challenge and the humour that danced in her eyes. How long had it been since anyone had teased him like this? 'That may be so, but I don't chase my own tail or have unmentionable personal habits.'

A giggle escaped her. 'I'm glad to hear it.'

He reached to untie Smoke's lead. 'Goodbye, Pollyanna,' he said.

'Bye,' she called after him, 'and thanks for returning my notebook!'

'It was nothing.' He hurried away into the cold.

Smoke tugged on his lead as they wove a path through the tiny lanes and cobbled streets. When they reached the edge of the village and crossed the stream, Jake unclipped the dog's lead and Smoke bounded up the hill and the shortcut they'd found to the Old Hall. As Jake followed, his boots crunched as they sank into the snow and his breath left little clouds in the air as the path grew steeper, yet he felt energised. He wondered what had caused the lightness in his step, the quickening in his blood. It was unfamiliar – but it was welcome. Any respite from the pain in his chest was a relief.

He pictured the wounded look in Evie's eyes as she'd faced her parents, the brave upward tilt of her chin. She was a curious combination of courage and vulnerability, and he was intrigued.

Not that he intended to get involved, he reminded himself sharply. She was supplying curtains for his house, that was all. There was no need for him to get embroiled in her life or difficulties.

Yet as he glanced back to the village in the valley below, the image of her standing behind her counter twisting her long plait around her fingers played on his mind. Evie Miller wasn't an easy person to forget.

Well, who'd have thought Mr Arctic had a human side after all? thought Evie, as she watched Jake and his dog disappear around the corner at the end of the street. It had been one surprise when he'd appeared in her shop, but it was quite another when he'd jumped to her defence and stood up to her parents. He'd seemed indignant on her behalf, yet he could still be inarguably brusque and sarcastic. She couldn't work him out. She shook her head and went back inside, shutting the door on the freezing air.

Oh, God. Now Jake knew all about her financial troubles and her private fears. Heat filled her cheeks and she rubbed the woollen sleeves of her dress.

If you expect to fail, you will undoubtedly fail. Jake's ominous words rang in her head as she sat down at her sewing machine to work on yet another pair of curtains for the Old Hall. The blue satin embroidered with metallic silver thread shimmered like frost in the sun.

Had she expected her shop to fail? Surely not. She smoothed the blue fabric, flattening out the creases before she began to sew.

And yet she hadn't dared to hope for success, had she? Because if she didn't hope, she couldn't be disappointed. And although she was an optimist in every other aspect of life, when it came to her own plans, her track record was consistent: one disappointment after another. Academically, she'd failed to live up to her parents' and teachers' expectations, then she'd failed in her career, and she had a failed relationship behind her too.

Listening to her dad, part of her had wondered what the point was in spending all these long hours sewing, when she was only just managing to keep her head above water. Rather than fighting her parents, wouldn't it be simpler to throw in the towel and accept that she'd failed yet again?

She reached the end of the hem and stopped.

You need to believe in yourself. Jake's words had resonated with her more than he could know. No one had said that to her or looked at her so intently – as if he believed in her – for a long time.

Zara used to. Evie remembered her big sister helping her up when she'd fallen off her horse and saying, '*Come on, Eves. Try again. You can do this, I know you can.*'

She looked around her colourful little shop, its neat shelves of fabric and display quilts hanging from the walls, and remembered that owning a shop like this had been her dream for so long before she'd finally plucked up the courage to do it. Sewing was her passion, it was what she loved more than anything in the world, and she really wanted her little shop to succeed. She wanted it more than anything. Perhaps Jake was right. Perhaps she needed to believe in it – and in herself.

She picked up her phone. 'Natasha? It's me. Are you busy tonight? Only I need your help with something . . .'

Chapter Six

'So, I need to come up with a plan to turn my shop around,' said Evie, opening her notepad, pen poised. 'I've come up with a few ideas – will you tell me what you think of them?'

Her friends nodded. They were gathered around the log fire in Natasha's living room. Her husband, Luc, was in the USA on a business trip, and their two-year-old daughter, Lottie, was asleep upstairs. On the coffee-table there were three cups of hot chocolate, and a plate of cakes Evie had bought from the bakery next to her shop: vanilla slices, sticky buns, and jam tarts.

'Of course,' said Suzie, helping herself to a vanilla slice.

'And maybe we can help you brainstorm some more,' said Natasha. 'But, first, why did you call us tonight, Evie? Did something happen? Has the bank been on your back again?'

She opened her mouth to tell her friends about Jake's visit to her shop – then changed her mind. For some reason, she didn't want to admit how much his words had affected her. Her friends would read too much into it. 'My parents came to see me. They think I should abandon the shop and go back to Tim. Give him a second chance.'

Suzie and Natasha looked horrified.

'After what he did?' asked Natasha, incredulous.

'I need the shop to become profitable so I can prove to them that I'm not a failure.'

'Of course you're not a failure.' Natasha picked up a jam tart. 'Your quilt-making workshops are really popular. Why don't you run more of those?'

'Yes, and I was thinking maybe I could invite other people to come and run classes too. They might be able to teach things that I can't, like crochet, or more unusual sewing projects.'

'Great idea. And how about running classes for smaller projects?' asked Suzie. 'Making a quilt is too daunting for a complete novice like me. Could you teach something more basic?'

Evie thought for a minute. 'How about pot grabbers? Or a mobile phone case?'

'Perfect. That's exactly the kind of thing.'

'And perhaps I could sell vouchers, too, in case people want to gift someone else a place on a course.'

Natasha nodded. 'If you incorporate those into your window display, I'm sure it'll inspire passers-by who are stuck for gift ideas. Christmas is only two weeks away.'

Suzie licked a dab of vanilla cream off her finger. 'What about starting up a knitting group? Something social rather than a class, where people meet to knit and chat over a cup of tea. It would get them through the door and let it be known that your back room is available for craft groups to hire.'

'A "Knit and Natter" session – my neighbour Dorothy

would love that. And I could buy in cakes from the bakery next door,' she said, nodding at the plate in front of them.

'That will definitely bring people in. These jam tarts are delicious,' said Natasha. 'Are you on any of those websites selling craft goods?'

'I've registered,' Evie admitted, 'but I haven't had time to push things. I'm going to put up photos of my quilts, and I'll advertise that I can make them in any design or colour to the customers' specifications.'

'Bespoke quilts,' said Suzie, approvingly. 'People will love that.'

'And there's the Christmas fair tomorrow,' said Natasha. 'Do you have a stall? I know it's a bit of a jumble sale, but everyone in the village goes along. It'll be a great chance to meet people, if nothing else.'

'Yes. I'm going to display curtains and quilts, and I've made some Christmas tree decorations and cards in the hope they'll draw people over to chat.'

Evie looked at her list. She'd covered two sheets of paper with scrawled notes. Plenty to get started with. 'Thank you both so much. I've been really worried about the shop, but now I feel more optimistic that I can turn things around. I have a plan, and the profit I've made on Jake Hartwood's curtains should buy me time to focus on making the shop more profitable.'

'I hope your parents get off your back. I can't believe they want you to go back to your ex,' said Suzie. 'From what you've told us, he was a controlling pig who totally crushed your confidence.'

'He did.' Only now did Evie realise how anxious she

had felt when they'd lived together: she'd been worrying constantly, trying not to make a mistake, do something clumsy or say the wrong thing. It was difficult to explain why she'd stayed with him for as long as she had, or how gradual, almost imperceptible, the changes in him and in her had been. At first she had been drawn to his confident wit. Also, their parents moved in the same circles, which had made it so easy for them to become a couple. But as he'd risen through the ranks in his work, he'd become tense and critical. He'd begun to compare her with his colleagues' partners, who all seemed to be top lawyers or other professionals, and he'd found her wanting. Perhaps he'd been frustrated because he was overlooked for promotion a couple of times. Whatever the reason, he'd begun to chip away at her self-esteem with judgements and mockery so subtle, at first, that she'd believed she was the problem.

Now she knew better.

'Since I came here, I can just be myself – and that's such a relief.'

'Of course you can be yourself,' said Natasha. 'You're perfect as you are and don't you forget it, Evie Miller!'

She laughed and, for some reason, thought of Jake saying *Goodbye, Pollyanna* with a twinkle in his eye. 'I don't think "perfect" is the right word – not for someone as clumsy as me.'

'Of course it is. You're one of the kindest and most positive people I've ever met, clumsy or not. I hate to think what your ex told you in the past. He really knocked your confidence, didn't he?'

'I don't think he intended to . . .' she began, then wondered why she was making excuses for Tim. 'He just wished I was more like the person he wanted me to be.'

The logs crackled gently in the fireplace.

'That's how my great-aunt made me feel when I was growing up,' Natasha said quietly. 'But it's a recipe for disaster – in any relationship. You can't change who you are. You can only be yourself, and if he couldn't accept that, he was wrong for you.'

Suzie nodded. 'If he really loved you, he would have appreciated all your good qualities rather than being so critical. Has he stopped calling, by the way?'

Evie glanced at her phone and realised it had been almost a week since he'd rung the shop. 'Yes, he has,' she said, brightened by the realisation.

'Good,' said Natasha. 'Fingers crossed he's got the message that you don't want anything to do with him.'

'Yes, fingers crossed,' said Evie, with a smile.

Although, her parents had admitted Tim had been in contact with them. The smile faded. She reached for the end of her ponytail and absently wound it around her fingers. She wondered how Tim would take the news that her parents had been unsuccessful in persuading her to reconsider. She had a horrible feeling he wouldn't take it well at all.

The following evening Evie locked her front door and walked the short distance to the Dog and Partridge. Her steps were light, and she was buzzing with adrenalin. The pub car park was almost full, which was usual for a Saturday night, and as she pushed open the doors, the place was crammed. The noise of chatter and laughter hit her, along with a rush of warm air. Evie paused, then spotted Suzie and Natasha sitting at a table nearby. Suzie waved and beckoned her over.

'We thought you might have sore feet after today, so we got you a glass of white wine to save you queuing at the bar.'

'Thanks,' Evie grinned, 'and you're right about my feet!' She unbuttoned her red coat and sat down heavily.

'So how was the Christmas fair?' asked Suzie. 'Your stall looked amazing. Those display quilts and curtains were so eye-catching. They were drawing lots of interest when I popped by.'

'Yes,' said Evie, pleased. Her stall really had stood out from the rest. All the others seemed to have been selling second-hand jigsaw puzzles and dog-eared books, and no one else had gone to as much trouble as she had. But, then, no one else had an ailing business or a bank's ultimatum hanging over their head. 'It couldn't have been better. I'd printed lots of leaflets advertising the new classes and workshops we talked about, and I sold all the Christmas tree decorations and greetings cards I had made. In fact, they were so popular I promised people I'd make more in time for the shop opening on Monday.'

She'd have a busy day tomorrow making them and finishing Jake's curtains.

'That's wonderful!' said Suzie, and raised her glass. 'To Evie and the Button Hole!' The three chinked glasses.

'I'm so glad for you,' said Natasha. 'You worked hard to prepare your stall.'

'I can make those felt decorations in my sleep now!' Evie giggled. 'But I enjoy it.'

'How difficult are they to put together?' asked Suzie. 'I could come round tomorrow and help you, if you like.'

'They're simple, really. And it would be lovely to have help. Thanks, Suzie.'

A gust of cold air slid past her feet and Evie glanced up. A solitary figure stood in the doorway. Her smile froze.

'If they're not too fiddly,' Suzie continued, 'perhaps I could make a simpler version with the children at school for them to give as gifts. They love craft activities like that . . .'

Evie didn't hear the rest. The blood pounded in her ears.

'Evie? What's wrong?' laughed Suzie. 'You look as if you've seen a ghost.'

She swallowed. Suzie and Natasha frowned and followed her gaze to the man standing in the entrance. He was scouring the busy pub, searching for someone. Evie ducked to the left, hoping he wouldn't spot her, but she was too late.

Seeing her, his expression instantly changed, and he pushed his way through the crowd towards her.

'Who's that?' asked Suzie.

'I have to go,' Evie said quickly, and darted to her feet. 'He can't – I can't – not here!'

But she was too late. He stopped in front of her. 'Evelyn.'

Cheeks flaming, she tried to get past him, but there were too many bodies blocking her path and he was too close. She saw her friends exchange a look of concern.

Realising there was no way out, Evie straightened her spine and glared at him. 'Go away, Tim. I don't want to talk to you. We have nothing to say.'

'Please, darling,' he said, with the easy smile she had once found so charming. Not any more. Now she knew he used it purely to serve his own ends. 'Just hear me out.'

The blood rushed to her head in a red mist. 'No! Nothing you say will make any difference.'

Around them, the chatter stopped, and the pub went quiet. Everyone turned to stare. Ice stole up Evie's spine, and Tim must have clocked her horror, because his expression changed to one of triumph: now he had a captive audience.

'Come back to me. I'll marry you. We were good together.'

Not here, not now. Her heart hammered angrily. Well, fine. If that was how the snake wanted to play it . . .

'Seriously? After I found you in bed with someone else?'

Gasps of surprise echoed around the room and she heard a ripple of whispers. Evie steeled herself, determined not to let him walk all over her. He'd done enough of that when they'd been together. Back then, his subtle but perpetual criticisms had ground down her self-esteem, but now she'd put some distance between them she saw how unjustified most of them had been.

Tim's eyes narrowed. There wasn't a trace of remorse in his expression, only irritation that she'd brought up the subject of his betrayal. 'I made a mistake. Just one.' He placed his hands on her shoulders, and instantly she stiffened. 'Don't be heartless. Let's move on. Put this behind us.'

She batted his hands away. 'The fact that you're talking in clichés suggests that you don't mean any of this. You never had feelings for me, Tim. I doubt if you'll ever have feelings for anyone other than yourself.'

'Not true. I loved you, Evelyn. I still do.'

'Really?' she said. 'And yet I was never slim enough or elegant enough. I never said the right things or laughed at the jokes your misogynistic friends found so funny.'

His eyes widened with surprise, and his mouth worked but no sound came out. The king of smooth talking seemed to be stunned into silence. And she knew why: she'd never stood up to him like this in the past. Her shoulders went back. Well, she was a different person now. Leaving him to move here was the best decision she'd ever made. His betrayal had broken her heart, but it had also been a blessing: the catalyst she'd needed to leave him and start a new life.

'You didn't love me before, and now I could never love you again.' He opened his mouth to speak but she held up her hand. 'And I won't change my mind, so please leave, Tim. Now.'

The landlord, Gary, stepped forward. 'You need me to show this gentleman the door, Evie?'

She threw him a quick smile, touched at this gesture

of support, before she turned back to Tim. 'Thanks. But I'm sure he can find it himself.'

Tim hesitated, glanced around the pub at all the angry faces watching him, then turned and left.

Evie sank back into her seat and Suzie wrapped an arm around her in a reassuring hug.

'You okay?' asked Natasha.

'I'm fine,' said Evie.

Though she wasn't sure how she'd ever live this down. Talk about airing your dirty laundry in public! Now everyone in Willowbrook would know her secret, and that was mortifying.

Jake was working in his study when his phone rang.

Louisa.

He sighed. Not again.

'Have you thought any more about my invitation?' asked his sister. When he didn't immediately respond, she prompted: 'For Christmas?'

'Louisa, I gave you my answer already,' he said impatiently, and tapped his pen against the desk. Evie Miller was fitting curtains in one of the bedrooms and the sound of her humming and singing to herself travelled down the stairs.

'But I asked you to reconsider, remember? Please, Jake. I can't bear to think of you spending Christmas alone.'

At the other end of the line he could hear his nephews shouting and laughing. 'Not even if it's my choice?'

'Not even.' She sighed. 'We're not that bad, are we? I

know the boys can be a bit boisterous, but you were once—'

'Louisa,' he cut in gently, 'it's not about you or the boys. Remember last year? I don't want to spoil things again.'

'I'm sure that won't happen. And even if you—'

'No!' He sighed and stared out of the window at the frosted valley and the church spire that protruded from the village. He'd been through this several times already, not just with Louisa but with his younger sister, Scarlett, too. He was getting tired of having to explain himself.

Aware that he wasn't alone in the house, he kept his voice down. 'I don't want to do Christmas at all, okay? I'm not in the mood for festivities.'

'We can keep it low key. Scarlett agrees.'

'That's not fair on the kids.'

'It won't be the same without you, Jake. Please.'

His head began to pound. What would it take for his sister to drop this? 'It's better for everyone that I stay away.'

'You can't be on your own. What will you do?'

Ignore Christmas. Pretend it wasn't happening. 'It really doesn't matter. I'll be fine.'

She took a deep breath. 'Listen, Jake, Scarlett and I both think—'

'Sorry, sis,' he interrupted. 'Got another call coming in. Got to go.'

'I don't believe you. You're just saying that to—'

He cut her off. The light went out on his phone and he stared at it, not liking himself or what he'd just done.

You're a coward, Hartwood. A better man would grit his teeth and go through the motions for his sisters' sake.

But he wasn't that man. He closed his eyes briefly.

Maria had loved Christmas. She came from a big Italian family and he'd often caught her looking longingly at his nephews and niece. He and Maria had hoped one day to have children of their own. At least four, she used to tease him. And she would have made a great mother. Patient, loving, and talented in so many ways. He used to picture her at the piano, a child on her knee, another beside her.

Jake hung his head. He gripped the desk as if it was a life-saving device. What was he doing, allowing his thoughts to unravel like this?

The noise upstairs grew louder and he scowled at the ceiling. What was she singing? He recognised the song from some musical or other.

His phone began to ring again. He sighed, thinking it was Louisa – then realised it was a potential supplier he'd been trying to get hold of for several days.

'François, hello,' he said. 'Did you receive my email?'

The winemaker launched into rapid French and Jake covered one ear to block out Evie's singing. 'Can you repeat that?'

A few minutes later, he hung up. Neither of them had been able to make himself understood. He rubbed his forehead, wishing the throbbing in his head would quieten down. The squeak of a stepladder being moved made him look up, and the high-pitched singing started up again. Exasperated, Jake pushed his chair back and stamped up the stairs.

Perched at the top of her stepladder, Evie paused to admire the breath-taking view of the diamond-encrusted hills and glittering rooftops of the village. She had been tempted to curl up in her cottage and hide for a month until everyone in Willowbrook had forgotten about the fiasco with Tim in the pub. Unfortunately, hiding was not a luxury she could afford right now. She had work to do, and top of the list was delivering another set of curtains to the Old Hall.

She turned back and got on with her task, humming as she worked (she'd been listening to *The Phantom of the Opera* on her way over and now she couldn't get the tune out of her head). Anyway, on the bright side, she had exciting plans for how to improve her business, and this morning she'd been out in the village asking local shopkeepers to display posters advertising her new classes. She had also updated her page on the craft website by uploading pictures of quilts she'd made, and tomorrow she would make a new window display with some eye-catching gift ideas. Hopefully, her efforts would kick-start some interest in her shop soon.

She finished hanging the curtains, then climbed down the stepladder and stepped back to admire her work. They hung beautifully. Made from a slate-blue satin with a scrolling pattern of silver embroidery, they gave the room a luxurious finish. She began to dress them, carefully gathering the fabric into neat, even pleats. What was it Jake had told her? *Believe in yourself*. She smiled and lifted her chin. Yes. The confrontation with Tim had been humiliating, but she wasn't going to let him hold her back any more. She was determined to put her all into making the shop succeed. Energised by the thought, she started to sing again. She was just getting to the Phantom's part when someone cleared their throat. She stopped and spun round.

Jake was standing in the doorway. And judging by the look on his face, he wasn't there to join in with the duet. 'Can you please keep the noise down? I'm trying to work.' His features were all dark shadows and hard angles.

'Oops – sorry! It's such a big house, I didn't think you'd be able to hear.' Hot colour rose in her cheeks.

'My office is directly below this room, and the noise is very distracting. Especially when I'm on the phone to a client in France.'

'Of course. Sorry.' She had to stop herself curtsying. What was it about the man that he seemed to have stepped out of a Victorian Gothic novel?

He gave her a curt nod, then disappeared again. As she listened to his footsteps on the stairs she wondered why, when he'd come to her shop, she had believed he had a human side. Brittle and bad-tempered was his default setting.

Reaching into her bag, she pulled out the tie-backs she'd made from buttons and beads threaded onto wire and attached them to the ornate hooks in the wall. She had tied back one curtain and almost finished the second when she accidentally knocked her box of curtain hooks off the windowsill. The tiny plastic hooks scattered across the wooden floor. She crouched to pick them up, but when she tried to get up again, her hair tugged and she gave a little squeal. It had caught in the tie-back.

She twisted her head to see and tried to loosen it, but she could hardly move her head. Working blind, Evie felt around with her fingers. It wasn't just a thin strand of hair but a thick chunk, and it was caught near the root. She twisted it one way, then the other, trying to work it loose.

Five minutes later, she was no closer to freeing herself – in fact, she might have tangled it more – and her heart fluttered with panic. She looked at her sewing bag. It was within reach, and inside it were her scissors, but she'd have to cut her hair at the root, and that would be very noticeable.

She ran through her options: Jake was downstairs in his study, but he was the last person she could ask, especially after his stern words earlier. She reached into her pocket for her phone and scrolled through the names until she found Natasha's.

'Nat?' she said quietly.

'Evie! Why are you whispering?'

'I'll explain later. Where are you?'

'At home. Lottie and I are making a Christmas cake. Why?'

'You've got to help me. I'm stuck . . .' She explained what had happened.

'Is Jake home?' asked Natasha.

'I can't ask him. He already thinks I'm ditzy and this will just confirm it. I'd rather cut my hair than ask him.'

'Don't cut your hair! Whatever you do, promise me you won't cut it, okay?'

Evie bit her lip. She couldn't very well stay here indefinitely, could she?

'Evie, you've got gorgeous hair. Promise me!'

'Okay, I promise.'

'Give me five minutes and I'll sort this.'

'Thanks, Nat. See you soon.'

She tucked her phone back into her pocket and tried to get as comfortable as she could, kneeling on the wooden floor. She opened her mouth to sing and cheer herself up, but the sound of Jake's phone ringing downstairs reminded her of why that wasn't a good idea. It wasn't the first time she'd found herself in a scrape like this. When she was small she'd once got her head stuck between the wooden bars of the banister at home while spying on a visiting aunt downstairs. In the end, a spindle of the eighteenth-century mahogany banister had had to be sawn out to free her. Her father had been furious. Evie shifted on her knees. If he could see her now, he'd say, *For Heaven's sake, Evelyn, not again! Why can't you be more careful?*

She was twenty-eight years old, and still asking herself the same question.

The sound of the door opening behind her made her start. 'How did you get here so quickly?' she asked, and twisted her head as far as she could – which wasn't much – to see Natasha.

'It's not that far really,' said a deep male voice.

She stilled, horrified that he'd found her like this. 'Jake?'

She heard footsteps on the wooden floor as he approached. 'Natasha called me.'

Evie closed her eyes. *Thanks, Natasha. Thank you very much.* What would he think of her now?

'I – I don't know how it happened. I bent down to pick something up, and now I just can't untangle it.'

He appeared at her side and bent to look. The smell of his aftershave wove through the air, stirring her senses.

'There are scissors here if you need them,' she said dolefully. Suddenly, cutting her hair and removing herself as fast as possible didn't seem like such a bad option. In fact, anything would be better than finding herself trapped in this embarrassing situation with Jake Hartwood.

'Natasha made me promise not to cut it,' he said. She could hear from his voice that he was concentrating, and she could feel his fingers working busily to free her.

'It might be unavoidable.'

'Tell me if it pulls,' he said quietly.

'It's not pulling.' His touch was gentle and he worked patiently. She pictured his long, delicate fingers, and her skin tightened with awareness.

'It could take a while.'

'I'm not going anywhere,' she said, with a weak laugh. Of all the people to find her in this humiliating situation, why did it have to be him?

She could hear the soft, regular sound of his breathing, and it felt strangely intimate. Her muscles tensed. Her skin glowed like a log burner. Perhaps Natasha had been right when she'd said he was hot.

But it only made this more excruciating.

'I hope your ex hasn't bothered you again since Saturday night.'

Evie's eyes widened with horror. A prickly sensation spread from her chest up her neck. 'You heard about that?' She twisted her head to try to see him.

'Don't move.'

'Sorry.'

'I didn't hear about it. I was there.' A short pause followed. 'I was sorting out a delivery of wine.'

Oh, God. First he'd met her parents, and now he'd witnessed her row with Tim. What must he think? 'Not all my relationships are dysfunctional, honest! Just those with my parents . . . and my ex.'

'I believe it's commonplace for there to be hostility with ex-boyfriends.'

'Ex-fiancé,' she corrected. Though why it mattered, she had no idea. The toad was out of her life for good. 'You're right. Still, it wasn't nice to have it aired in public like that. I wish he'd just accept it's over between us and stay away from me.'

'He's been harassing you?'

She nodded – then winced as the movement tugged at her hair. 'Only since his girlfriend dumped him, and it was just phone calls until now. Saturday was the first time he'd come here in person. Hopefully the last.' It worried her that he knew where she was. 'The thing I can't understand is, he doesn't seem to feel any remorse for what he did. If it was down to him, we'd still be having meetings with the vicar and going ahead with the wedding.' She gave a bitter laugh. 'God knows what kind of marriage it would have been. He hasn't grasped the concept of fidelity.'

'Some people regard marriage as a convenient arrangement rather than a lifelong commitment.'

'Yes . . . I don't know what I ever saw in him.' Evie forced a bright smile. 'Still, he did me a favour because now I know for certain that I'm better off without him. Without any man. And it's good timing, really, because I need to focus all my attention on the shop and getting it off the ground.'

'Pollyanna,' he said quietly, and she heard in his voice the faintest of smiles, 'do you look for the silver lining in every situation?'

'Absolutely. And it's true – I don't have time for a relationship, so it's good that he's vaccinated me against Man Fever.'

He sniggered and she blushed, realising she'd divulged an awful lot, considering he was a client.

The room fell silent, but it was a comfortable silence. Darkness had fallen outside, and she heard the distant call of a fox. Downstairs, Smoke barked in response.

'Thank you for your advice about my shop, by the way. I've drawn up some plans and I feel a lot more hopeful now.'

'Good.'

'Do you want to hear them?'

'Your plans? Not especially.'

No matter how much time she spent with this man, his blunt manner never failed to catch her out. 'Oh,' she said, unable to hide her disappointment. Why had she, even for a second, thought that he would be interested?

'Sewing is not my area of expertise,' he added, in a conciliatory tone.

'I suppose not.'

'But I'm glad I helped in some small way. It sounds as if you've been putting all your energies into curtains and not enough into making the shop successful.'

'Yes. I was. Silly of me, really . . .'

'Not silly. Perhaps a little short-sighted, but when money is tight, I'd imagine that's an easy mistake to make.'

He was right. She'd been so worried about paying her rent and bills that she'd pounced on any commissions for curtains that had come her way. Now, however, she was going to focus on her shop. Once she'd finished kitting out the Old Hall with soft furnishings, of course.

'There,' he said, a few moments later.

She felt her hair release and breathed a sigh of relief. 'Thank you so much.' She got up, rubbing her aching knees, then did her best to pat down her hair. 'I interrupted your work – again. I'm so sorry.'

'It was nothing,' he said mildly, but she knew that wasn't true. She remembered how sharply he'd asked her to stop singing.

She couldn't tell from his expression what he was thinking, but she was mortified that he'd found her trapped like that, and had witnessed her altercation with Tim in the pub. Now he knew all her embarrassing secrets: her financial difficulties, her tricky relationships with her parents and Tim, and her unbelievable clumsiness.

'I'll go. I – I'd nearly finished anyway.' Her cheeks flamed. Hurriedly, she began to collect up her belongings, but she dropped her phone, then her bag. He said nothing, but she felt his stern gaze on her as she dug in her pockets for her car keys. She pulled them out, but immediately dropped them too. They hit the wooden floor with a clatter.

Jake picked them up and handed them to her. 'You're not having a good day.'

'Thanks,' she muttered. Christ, he must think she was hopeless. Heat spread across her chest. 'I've always been clumsy – ever since I was a little girl.'

He absorbed this with the faintest nod. 'But it's worse when you're nervous or in a hurry, right?'

How did he know? 'Right.'

'And you're always in a hurry to leave this place. No wonder you forgot your notebook last time.'

She frowned, unsure what he was driving at. 'I'm sorry,' she said quickly. 'I'm pretty sure I've got everything this time. I won't bother you again.' She grabbed her ladder and went to leave.

'Wait!' he said.

She turned. There was a strange look in his eyes and his mouth was a flat line. An awkward silence filled the room as he stood there, hands in his pockets, looking fierce.

He must be fed up with her disturbing him, constantly interrupting his life. She had done her utmost to keep out of his way, yet no matter how much she tried, they seemed to keep bumping into each other. Evie braced herself for what he was about to say. He'd run out of patience: he was going to ask her to leave and not bother coming back. From now on, he'd get his curtains elsewhere.

Jake swallowed. He rarely cared what others thought of him, but seeing a woman so jittery around him made him feel deeply uncomfortable, and guilt speared him. He remembered what she'd said to her ex: *I was never slim enough or elegant enough. I never said the right things . . .* She'd had vivid spots of colour in her cheeks and a wounded expression. Jake had witnessed both her parents and her ex – unjustifiably, as far as he could see – belittling her. Making her feel inferior and jittery, with precisely the nervous look in her eye that she had now.

Yet only now did he realise that he'd done the same: that she fled from his house whenever he appeared, in such a hurry to escape his presence that she became a fumbling nervous wreck.

And that was his fault.

It had been playing on Jake's conscience, gradually building, even before Natasha had called. Now he couldn't ignore it any more: he'd been unforgivably rude the first time he'd met her, the night of the snowstorm.

'You don't need to leave. Finish your work.'

'I'll do it another time. I've disturbed you quite enough already – what with this and my singing . . .' She blushed, and her cheeks were the colour of peaches. Velvety dark peaches.

He pressed his lips together, not happy with himself.

'About the singing – I'm sorry. You caught me at a bad moment. My French is limited and the line was bad. The winemaker and I were finding it difficult to understand each other – even before you started singing.' He cleared his throat. 'I shouldn't have been so abrupt. It wasn't your fault.'

She frowned and narrowed her eyes warily. 'It – it's all right. I know you value your privacy and I respect that.'

'Well, you shouldn't.'

Her head whipped round. She blinked at him.

He asked softly, 'Would you really have cut off your hair rather than ask me for help? Am I so bad?'

Her eyes widened with horror. He noticed they were the colour of a deciduous forest, a fascinating blend of greens and chestnut brown.

'Natasha shouldn't have told you that.' She turned on her heel and hurried away.

He caught up with her, lifted the stepladder out of her hands and carried it down the stairs. 'Natasha has just given me a talking-to about remembering my manners. I realise you haven't seen me at my best – not today, but especially not that night of the snow.'

They reached the bottom of the stairs and stopped. She'd been in such a hurry to get away that now she was out of breath. She frowned at him but didn't reply. Smoke, waiting obediently at the bottom of the stairs, rubbed his head against her thigh.

'I – ah . . .' Jake raked a hand through his hair. 'I apologise, Evie.'

She stared at him, her mouth a perfect circle, her face framed by loose strands of hair. She was pretty, he realised suddenly. Or, rather, other men must find her pretty. Especially when she relaxed – as she did now, visibly.

'Apology accepted,' she said quietly, and smiled.

'And I owe you an explanation,' he added.

'What for?'

'That night we were snowed in. It wasn't typical – I mean, I wasn't . . . my usual self.' He dragged in air, feeling the hive of pain stir. Just talking about it was painful – which was why he never broached the subject. Normally, at least.

'You mean, you don't down a whole bottle of whisky every night?' she asked shyly. Her eyes gleamed with mischief, and her dimples flashed.

He wanted to smile, but he was also intent on explaining himself. He inhaled deeply. 'It was the anniversary of my wife's death,' he said, aware that this was no excuse for how hostile he had been towards her.

'The anniversary? I – I didn't know . . .'

'How could you? I deeply regret the way I behaved that night, the things I said and did.'

If he could have wound back the clock, he wouldn't have attacked the whisky with such abandon. He would have apologised the moment Smoke had knocked her off her ladder, and he would have behaved with concern, instead of lashing out at her for intruding on his private grief.

But, then, if he could wind back the clock, there were a lot of things in his life he would have done differently.

'I turned to alcohol hoping it would act as an anaesthetic. It didn't, of course.'

'I understand.' Her hazel eyes locked with his.

He cleared his throat. 'I was about to start supper.'

She followed his gaze to the open door of the kitchen. On the worktop a packet of rice, a solitary onion and a piece of fish were laid out ready. 'Of course – sorry – I won't keep you any longer,' she said, and turned to go.

'Would you like to stay?' he said quickly.

She stopped. Wide-eyed, she blinked at him.

'I know I don't have a track record for being the most welcoming host where you're concerned,' he said ruefully, 'but I'd like to make amends and show you that I'm not always such an antisocial beast.'

'Stay for supper?' Confusion but also excitement chased across her features.

His gaze narrowed. He didn't want her to get the wrong idea. This wasn't a romantic date he was proposing – just a meal. A simple meal, at that. Then again, he wasn't arrogant enough to believe she'd be in any way attracted to him, given the first impression he'd made on her.

'Salmon risotto – if you fancy it?'

Her eyes sparkled like the frost-covered pines outside. 'That sounds delicious!'

'I take it that's a yes, then?' His lips curved at her enthusiasm.

'The offer of a meal, plus the possibility of hearing Mr Arctic thaw a little? Only a fool would refuse! I'll just put these in the car.'

He picked up the stepladder and followed her outside.

Darkness had fallen and the air was freezing, yet an unfamiliar warmth touched his chest.

It was relief, he told himself – relief that he had the chance to explain and atone for his behaviour on the night of the snowstorm.

She locked her car. 'I'll give you a hand with the cooking. I could be your sous-chef!'

Had he done the right thing in inviting her to stay? She really was relentlessly cheerful.

Jake quickly peeled and diced the onion. Evie sat across the island watching him. She was perched on a bar stool drinking orange juice, and Smoke was settled in his bed, which now lived in the corner of the kitchen. In the short time he'd been living there, Jake had found that this was the room he used most, along with the study.

Evie pointed to the window. 'Look – it's snowing again!'

'Don't worry,' he said wryly. 'I have fully furnished guest rooms now. There's no danger of being stuck in the same room with me again.'

Her dimples showed as she smiled.

'Is this weather affecting your business?' he asked, stirring the onion and grateful to return to a neutral subject of conversation.

'It is, actually – people aren't willing to travel far in the snow. And the weathermen say it's set to stay cold until Christmas. It is beautiful, though, isn't it?' She turned to the window, a dreamy look in her eyes. 'Like a fairy-tale wonderland.'

'It's a damn nuisance. And all my customers are experiencing a drop in custom when usually this is the busiest time of year for restaurants. Even walking the dog is twice as hard as it should be.'

'You don't mean that. I bet you love the snow, don't you, Smoke?' The dog looked up sleepily from his bed in the corner of the room. She turned back to Jake, who tipped the rice into the pan and stirred a jug of hot stock. 'You look like a real pro. Do you cook every night?'

'Not every night, because I'm often away with work. But when I'm home I find it relaxing. How about you?'

'I cook in batches. I make a big pan of soup or stew, then eat it every night for a week.' She smiled and reached for her glass but knocked it over. The sudden noise made Smoke bark, and orange juice splashed everywhere.

Evie jumped to her feet. 'Oh, no – I'm so sorry!'

'It's no big deal,' he said, picking up the glass, and waving her hand away when she tried to help. 'Look. It's not even broken. No harm done.'

'I'll get a cloth.' She picked up a plastic bowl and came to stand beside him.

Their shoulders rubbed, their hands collided as they cleared up the spillage. He felt an unfamiliar dart of something – awkwardness? Yes, that must be it. After all, he wasn't used to having his personal space invaded.

'Why don't you watch the risotto for me?' he suggested, and nodded at the pan behind him. 'Just keep stirring and adding the stock a little at a time.'

'Okay,' she said sheepishly.

When he'd finished clearing up, he poured her another drink and took charge of the risotto again.

'I'm so sorry,' she repeated.

Something about her cowed expression reminded him of Smoke when he'd first found him. 'What for? We all knock things over from time to time.'

She shook her head. 'I'm clumsier than most.'

Jake remembered the red-faced temper her father had displayed in her shop and wondered if that had anything to do with her shamed expression. He stirred the contents of the pan again. 'It's not deliberate, though, is it?'

'Of course not.'

'Well, then,' he shrugged, 'no apology needed.'

Her shoulders dropped and she seemed relieved. He dipped a fork into the risotto and tasted it. 'This is ready,' he announced, and dished up.

'Delicious!' said Evie, after the first mouthful.

It was a simple dish, nothing special. But, then, everything with Pollyanna was worthy of excessive praise and beaming smiles.

'Lemon?' he asked, passing her a wedge.

'Thanks.'

'What? Why are you looking at me like that?'

'I can't work out what colour your eyes are. They look blue, yet the left one has a patch of brown in it.'

'Segmental heterochromia iridum.'

'Pardon?'

He repeated the name. 'It's hereditary. It can affect an eye completely or partially. In my case, it's partial.'

'I've never heard of it before.'

'Only one per cent of humans have it.'

'One per cent? How lucky are you?' She grinned.

He tipped his head to one side. 'I've never thought of it like that.'

'You should! You're special. One of a kind. But, then, we already knew that, Mr Arctic.' She winked, and he knew she was teasing him.

Curiously, he quite liked it when she took this irreverent tone and her eyes gleamed with mischief. It was refreshing.

'You said you're away a lot with work,' she said. 'Where do you travel to?'

'Mostly France. I focus particularly on importing French wine.'

He noted how she ate with genuine pleasure. He had no time for people who picked at their food. Sitting so close, he was aware of her perfume: a warm fruity scent that made him think of apples.

'Why French?'

'Personal preference. Plus, many people would agree that it's the best in the world.'

'Have you visited Luc's family? Nat told me their vineyard and château are beautiful.'

'Yes. He gave me a guided tour when I first set up my business.'

'What made you leave medicine and begin importing wine?'

He stopped chewing. Memories invaded his head, making it difficult to speak or think. Evie glanced at him.

'When Maria died,' he said tightly, 'I left my job. I wanted to start again. A new challenge.'

She nodded, but still looked puzzled. 'Was it difficult – to start again with a new career?'

'Yes. But I was happy to learn, and I didn't mind working long hours. In fact, I welcomed it.' Like alcohol, work was an anaesthetic – it kept his mind busy, too distracted to think or feel. Although it didn't take away the lead weight in his chest. And at the end of the day, when all the emails had been sent and the phone stopped ringing, the snarling monster of grief was still there, waiting for him.

She sent him a look of sympathy. 'I know what you mean. I don't mind working long hours because it's always been my dream to open a quilting shop and do what I love for a living.' She speared a piece of fish, and he noticed that for someone who said she was clumsy, she was also very graceful. Her slim fingers reached up and tucked a loose strand of hair behind her ear. 'I never get bored like I used to in my old job.'

Her cheerful expression faded. The change was so dramatic he was intrigued to know more. 'What did you do before?' he asked.

'I worked at a jeweller's in Knightsbridge. It was the dullest job in the world.'

Chapter Seven

Evie frowned, remembering the days when she'd had to drag herself out of bed each morning. She'd been lucky enough to live in a nice flat with green spaces and parks nearby, but life in the city had felt so . . . grey. All the tarmac and traffic and tall buildings closing in on her. She'd sometimes worried that if she stayed there any longer she'd turn to concrete, like her surroundings, or become another face in a suit sitting on the Underground, staring at her feet.

'You weren't bewitched by all the diamonds and gold?' Jake asked.

She shook her head in distaste. 'At the end of the day, they're just rocks. Yes, some are very beautiful, but they're not worth spending hundreds of thousands of pounds on.'

'I take it your customers were very wealthy?'

She wrinkled her nose. 'Disgustingly rich. Yet some of the men who bought the most expensive rings hardly looked at their fiancées. They weren't in love. You could tell from the way they talked to them – or didn't talk to them, in some cases. Even if Tim hadn't done what he did, working there was enough to put a girl off the whole engagement business.'

He raised an eyebrow. 'I thought most women dreamed of being given a ring.'

'Not me.' Evie thought of Tim's weighty diamond, which she'd been relieved to wrench off her finger and throw at him. 'I won't make the same mistake again.'

She had loved Tim once, but warning bells should have sounded when he'd delayed their wedding by two months, then six. Now she realised he'd hoped she would change and become the woman he wanted her to be, but she hadn't been slim or beautiful enough, and she'd had no successful career or achievements to her name. Even working in the jeweller's she'd consistently failed to hit her sales targets because she tried to meet customers' needs rather than persuading them to buy the biggest, most expensive diamond.

Jake casually dug his fork into the rice on his plate, but she saw him cast her a sidelong glance. 'You're going to let one bad experience dictate your future?'

'It's not just about Tim and what he did. It's also me. I . . . I'm not cut out for all that stuff. My sister was, but I'm not.'

'You have a sister?'

'Had.' She stabbed a piece of fish. 'She died.' She rushed on before he could offer his condolences. 'Zara had an amazing career, she was pretty, clever – the kind of girl every man dreams of settling down with. She and her fiancé were perfect for each other.'

Finally she ran out of steam, and her mouth clamped shut.

'When did she die?' Jake asked quietly.

'Five years ago.'

The job at the jewellery shop had been meant as a stop-gap, but after Zara died, she'd felt so lost that she didn't have the energy or the courage to look for something else.

'I'm sorry.'

She shrugged. 'Working in that jeweller's drove home to me that love can't be measured in silver or platinum. It's about how someone treats you, how they look at you, where they prioritise you in their life. And when someone truly loves you, the size or price of the ring doesn't matter at all because you know your relationship is going to last.'

She stopped to catch her breath, and blushed because she realised she was sounding a little passionate. Why? She had no idea. She took another mouthful of risotto and hoped Jake hadn't noticed.

'When I met Maria I was in the middle of exams,' he said, 'working all hours at the hospital. I had no time for a relationship. I wasn't looking for love – but the moment I saw her, I knew.'

Evie stared at him, astonished. She'd never heard him speak so openly – or without any hint of cynicism. 'At first sight you knew you loved her?'

'I knew she was the one, yes. My soulmate.' The look in his eyes was one of unquestionable and unconditional love.

How romantic, she thought. And how tragic that his wife's life had been so abruptly cut short. '*How* did you know?'

He reached for his glass and took a swig of water. His cashmere jumper clung to the solid lines of his shoulders and chest, and she saw muscles flex and tighten as he moved.

'Because I was blown away. In that moment when I met her, it was as if everything else shrank and was of no importance any more. We were at a party, and she was talking about music. She was so knowledgeable and passionate about it – I could have listened to her all night. She was intelligent. Talented. Beautiful.'

Evie thought of the photo beside his bed: his wife had indeed been beautiful. That she was also talented and intelligent came as no surprise. Zara had been the same, and her death had left a gaping hole in the lives of all those she'd left behind.

'Wow.' She stared at him. How romantic. And how unexpected coming from this abrupt, blunt-talking man.

What would it feel like to meet somebody and be swept off your feet like that? To feel such instant and overwhelming attraction? Her and Tim's story had been nowhere near as dramatic. They had known each other as children but hadn't seen each other for a few years when one day she bumped into him at a summer party. He took her number and hit her with a charm offensive. It had been exciting . . . but not passionate. They'd dated a few times, and it felt natural – inevitable – when, before long, they became a couple. After all, she'd known him all her life and his parents were like family.

Yet now she realised she'd hardly known him at all. Beneath his smooth-talking and seductive good looks had lurked a selfish snake. She hadn't seen it because she'd been too busy worrying that *she* was the problem.

'She was so perfect,' Jake went on, 'that I didn't think she would even notice me. When she did, I was bowled over. I bought a ring the next day and took it with me on our first date.'

Her jaw dropped. 'An engagement ring?'

He nodded. 'I didn't give it to her until later – I didn't want to scare her off – but I knew.' He sucked in air. 'I knew I'd never felt like that about anyone else . . .'

'I heard lots of engagement stories when I worked in the jeweller's, but I never heard of a man buying a ring before the first date.' She stared at him. It was difficult to marry up this romantic gesture with the bitter cynic she'd met here that night of the snowstorm. 'So, you believe in love at first sight, then?'

'I believe we all have a soulmate, yes.' His head dipped and she glimpsed the desolation in his eyes. His grief suddenly filled the kitchen, thickening the air. It was so palpable, she felt it too and her heart twisted with sympathy for him.

'It gets easier,' she said softly. 'You just need to give it time.'

She knew from first-hand experience how the passing of time eased the pain. Now, although she still missed her, she was able to think about Zara and smile.

'No,' he said definitively. His back straightened. 'My feelings will never change. I'll never love anyone the way I loved Maria. She was the love of my life and always will be.'

Distractedly, he reached into the collar of his sweater and pulled out a chain. Threaded onto it was a slim band of gold. His wedding ring, Evie guessed. Not platinum, not white gold, not even expensive gold by the look of it – just a simple plain ring that symbolised his commitment to a woman who was no longer here. She tried to swallow but found she had a lump in her throat.

'What happened?' Evie asked softly.

He pushed his empty plate away.

'Brain tumour.' His voice was rough with pain.

Evie had the urge to reach out and touch his arm, but something stopped her. He was her client, remember. And there was something untouchable about him. Despite his passionate words, his demeanour was like a shell around him, shutting everyone out. 'They couldn't operate? Remove it?'

Something flickered in his eyes and, for a second, he looked as if she'd hurt him. Then a curtain fell, and his expression frosted over. 'No. She died only a few weeks after they diagnosed it.'

'I'm sorry.' She knew how hard it was to lose someone unexpectedly, without any warning or time to prepare. For months after Zara's death Evie had found herself picking up her phone to call her sister – before she remembered Zara was gone.

He shrugged. The stony expression was back and she realised, with a jolt, that it wasn't disapproval, as she'd first thought when she met him. She'd compared him with Tim for being obnoxious and haughty, but now she saw that the deep lines that dug into his brow and the haunted look in his eyes were symptoms of his grief. Heartache for the love he'd lost.

He picked up their plates and carried them round to the sink. They clattered loudly as he stacked them in the dishwasher, and Smoke opened one eye at the sudden commotion. Evie followed Jake's lead and helped, passing him the pan and the chopping board, and wiping down the worktop. She watched him surreptitiously and noticed how his movements had become slow and weighted. He carried his grief like a heavy overcoat. It must be exhausting. It must be lonely.

'People tell me I should have moved on by now . . .' he said suddenly.

Evie stopped, cloth in hand. She watched as he raked a hand through his hair and his features twisted with anguish.

'. . . and I wish I could,' he finished wearily.

She put the cloth down, choosing her words carefully. 'It's not that easy. These things happen in their own time.'

His gaze lifted, met hers and held. And in his eyes she saw his pain and fear. 'What if it doesn't? What if it will always be like this?'

Back home in her cottage, Evie switched on the lights, lit the log fire, and settled down with a hot drink and her sewing, a new quilt made up of brightly coloured triangles that radiated out from the centre. The pattern was called Beacon of Hope. The sound of Dorothy's television next door was so loud it permeated the thick stone walls, but Evie didn't mind. As she spooned the marshmallows from her hot chocolate, she thought about Jake Hartwood. Her mind was haunted by his tragic story and the sorrow she'd seen in his eyes when he'd spoken about his wife.

'I hope that from now on you won't feel you have to run away next time you see me,' he'd said, as she left.

'I won't,' she'd promised, unsure why she felt a curious buzzing in her veins.

It must be the shock of having heard him divulge such intimate information, she'd told herself, yet that didn't explain why she hadn't been able to meet his gaze.

She picked up her sewing and switched on the television, but she wasn't paying much attention to the programme about polar bears. Instead, she looked around her, taking in the wicker heart strung from the back of the door and the patchwork wall-hanging she'd embroidered with sequins and beads so it sparkled in the firelight, and she counted her blessings that she could call this cosy cottage home. When she'd first moved in she'd held back with the decoration, knowing that Tim would have criticised her choices as tacky and twee, lacking in good taste. Then, little by little, she'd added a lamp here, a cushion there, a picture frame – until finally she'd decided that this was *her* home, and she could decorate it as she wanted. She could leave her sewing machine out and there was no one to complain about the clutter, nobody to criticise. It had taken her a little while, but now she was free of Tim's influence. She'd arrived in Willowbrook heartbroken and alone, but now she loved her independence.

And listening to Jake speak about his wife, she knew her feelings for Tim had never been that strong.

Yes, he'd hurt her, but she didn't miss him. She wasn't pining for him the way Jake was for Maria. In fact, she was certain she was better off without him.

The buzz of her phone interrupted her thoughts. Natasha's number flashed up and Evie answered straight away.

'Have you forgiven me?' Natasha asked.

Evie smiled. 'I thought you were coming to help me!'

'I know, but it would have taken me much longer to get there and he's really not that bad. I don't know why you two started off on the wrong foot.'

'I do,' Evie said quietly. 'At least, I do now – since he told me tonight. He explained that the first night I met him was the anniversary of his wife's death. He'd come up to the Old Hall to be alone. And then I turned up.'

'Ah.'

And suddenly it all made sense: how drunk he'd been, how hostile when he discovered he wasn't alone. It was difficult now to maintain her opinion of him as rude and antisocial, because she understood. On the anniversary of Zara's death she always kept herself to herself. It was difficult to be around people, difficult to explain the complex emotions that the day awoke.

'He invited me to stay for supper by way of apology,' she told Natasha.

'Did he?'

She could hear the smile in her friend's voice but chose to ignore it. 'And he talked about Maria.'

'His wife?'

'Yes.'

'Luc said he never mentions her. What did he say?'

I'll never stop loving Maria. She was the love of my life and always will be.

'Oh, Nat, it's heart-breaking how much he still loves her.' She thought of him alone in that big house, with only Smoke and his grief for company. He isolated himself and kept his distance from others, and he could be abrupt and rude. But now Evie knew why, she couldn't help but feel sympathy.

'Sounds like you two had a real heart-to-heart. You're not mad at me for calling him, then?'

'No, of course not. Turns out he's not the ogre I thought he was.'

'And he didn't have to cut your hair?'

Evie remembered how gentle his fingers had been as he'd worked to free her, and goose-bumps touched the back of her neck. 'No, he didn't.'

'Good. Well, I'm glad everything was all right in the end.'

'It was.' She felt privileged that he'd divulged so much to her about his loss and his feelings for his wife. And he'd made her promise she wouldn't avoid him in future. There was nothing to stop them being friends.

And if she brought a little sunshine into his life, it might make a small but important difference.

Jake tugged at the lead, but the dog refused to budge. 'Dammit, Smoke, what's the matter with you?'

It wasn't the snow that was bothering the dog because the roads and pavements around the village green had been cleared. Not that Smoke minded the snow when they walked in the hills, anyway.

'Come on, boy. You've had a good walk. Now we need to get home.' Jake gave him a reassuring pat, then pulled him gently by the collar, but Smoke gave him a withering look. 'Okay, we'll stop for a rest, then. Though I must say you could have chosen a quieter spot for it.'

The moment he relaxed his hold on the lead, Smoke set off towards the high street, pulling him along. It was all Jake could do to keep up with the stubborn animal. 'Smoke, you're going the wrong way,' he muttered. 'Where are you taking me? Ah, I see,' he said, as the Button Hole came into view and understanding dawned.

What was it about Evie Miller that his dog simply couldn't resist? She wasn't difficult to spot. Wearing a dotty red dress, she was a lantern of brightness in the stripped white window as she put up a new display. She flicked a side plait over her shoulder and reached up to steady an enormous Christmas bauble. It was only as he got closer that he realised the dots on her dress were buttons of all different colours and sizes sewn on to the red fabric. Smoke barked and bounded forwards, yanking Jake along, too. Evie looked up and waved.

Jake's mouth curved. He had to give it to her, there was something alluring about her quirky character, something intriguing. Her dimpled smile and upbeat nature were a breath of fresh air. Somehow she made the sky seem bigger, the sun more dazzling, the world more colourful. Her eyes seemed to smile right at him.

And when he'd seen her with her ex and her parents, it had stirred unfamiliar emotions in him. He'd gritted his teeth at the way they'd spoken to her, he'd been moved to step forward and intervene. Why?

He wasn't sure. His usual policy was to keep to himself. He certainly didn't make a habit of baring his soul the way he had over supper last night. But Evie had made it so easy. Maybe because she'd lost her sister and she understood. The clouds in her eyes had spoken volumes.

Still, it had been a mistake to open up as he had. The consequence was that sleep had eluded him, and he'd spent last night reliving the memories of when he'd first met Maria.

Breathless, he arrived outside the Button Hole where Smoke stopped at Evie's feet, panting and wagging his tail. Jake nodded a greeting, and while she fussed over his dog, he bit back the bitter blend of nostalgia and despair. *Oh, Maria. Will this ever get any easier?*

Evie had been changing her window display when she saw Smoke tugging Jake down the street towards her shop. She giggled because the Dalmatian was straining at the lead so hard that Jake was struggling to keep up. She went out to say hello. The air was icy despite the winter sun, and the sky was a flat sheet of cobalt blue.

'I must apologise for my dog,' said Jake, when they

reached her. 'He's decided he can't pass the end of this street without visiting your shop.'

A few days ago, she would have ducked out of sight to avoid Jake, but since last night she was no longer intimidated by him. In fact, she'd enjoyed his company. She liked his dry sense of humour and the way his eyes sparked when she teased him.

She laughed, glad that she'd remembered to refill the bowl of water by the door, and stroked the excited Dalmatian. 'That's wonderful! Hello, Smoke, and I'm really happy to see you too.' Straightening, she added, 'I wish I had more loyal customers like him.'

'Don't kid yourself that he's interested in sewing. He just wants your dog treats.'

She hesitated, then said, 'I was about to make a cup of tea. Why don't you come in?'

'Thank you, but I can't leave Smoke out in the cold too long.'

'Ah.' She had to give it to him: he might not be very sociable, but he really cared about that dog. 'It is cold, isn't it? Beautiful weather for walking, though. Bright and clear, with snow everywhere, and that lovely smell of winter . . .'

'Winter has a smell?' His raised brow and disparaging look would once have made her shrink, but not any more. Now she saw the gleam in his eye, the hint of humour in his expression. And it made her skin tingle.

'You know, cinnamon and mixed spice and log fires, the scent of pine trees, and oranges, and fruitcake baking.' He was looking at her blankly, but she was on a roll now. She hugged herself and couldn't help but smile as she went on, 'I love this time of year. It's all about soft wool sweaters and crackling log fires and . . .'

He held his hand up. 'Please stop. I'm worried you're going to break into song about the hills being alive with the sound of music.'

She laughed again. They stepped aside to let a couple pass who had just emerged from the bakery next door.

'I take it you like Christmas, then?' Jake asked drily.

'Winter,' she corrected him. 'I love winter.' Her smile faded. She didn't look forward to Christmas any more. Not since Zara had gone. Now it was a time when pain was felt more acutely, when empty chairs at the dining table highlighted those who were absent, and her parents' voices had a false edge as they tried to fake a cheerfulness they didn't feel.

'And the run-up to Christmas,' she said, choosing her words carefully, 'the anticipation. But . . .'

Smoke cocked his head, his dark eyes trained on her, as if he were listening intently too.

'But?' Jake prompted.

'I would quite happily miss out Christmas Day,' she said honestly, feeling dread at the prospect of going home to the pretence put on by her reduced family. 'You've met my parents. When I go home, I spend the whole time feeling I don't measure up and I've disappointed them with the choices I've made. Or not made.'

'Don't go home, then,' he said, with a shrug.

Surely even he, Mr Antisocial himself, could see how impossible that was. 'I have to. Family is family, and – and I'm all they've got.'

'You don't have to do anything. You're a grown woman.'

'We all have obligations and duties. I couldn't not go home unless I had a good reason.'

'Such as?'

'I don't know. This is all academic, anyway. Christmas is coming and there's no avoiding it. How about you? What are you doing for the holidays?'

'Nothing.'

She felt a pang at the idea of him alone in that enormous house. 'No family coming to visit?'

'No.' His mouth tightened and a muscle pulsed in his jaw.

Evie hated to think of anyone being alone at Christmas. Surely that would be even worse than spending it with her parents. 'Do you have any family?'

'Two sisters.'

'What about them?'

'They'll do their own thing. They know I don't do festivities.'

Ah. So, it was his choice to be alone. 'You don't do festivities? Why doesn't that surprise me?' She shook her head, teasing him. 'You're the Grinch himself.'

He didn't deign to answer that, but she was sure she saw a gleam of humour flash through his eyes before he said to his dog, 'Come on, Smoke. We'd better be heading back.'

Evie felt a tug of concern. She understood why he chose to isolate himself, but it couldn't be healthy to spend so much time alone with his grief, could it?

'Christmas is a difficult time when you've lost someone,'

she said quietly, 'but it doesn't mean you have to hide away on your own.'

His forehead pulled into a sharp frown. 'You sound just like my sister. What I choose to do is my own affair.'

His clipped words and fierce expression made her step back. He urged his dog on and left. Evie watched them go, wrapping her arms around herself to keep warm.

Just when things between them had started to improve, she'd said the wrong thing. Again.

Evie listened as her customer finished explaining what she had in mind for the small collection of fabric pieces laid out in front of her. She had chosen some beautiful patterned fabrics in a bold combination of emerald green and fuchsia.

'Do you think that's too ambitious to do by myself? I'm a beginner, really, but I do enjoy sewing and these fabrics will look perfect in my living room. The videos on YouTube make it look so simple, but maybe it's harder than I first thought.'

'It's not too difficult and I think you should definitely have a go, but since it's your first time, I suggest you make an envelope cushion cover. It's the simplest design because there are no zips or buttons involved. Here,' she reached behind the till for a folder she kept especially. 'This leaflet explains how to do it.'

'Oh! Thank you.' The lady beamed. But worry lines reappeared as she scanned it.

'I know the technical terms can seem a bit daunting,

but it's really straightforward, I promise. And if you're unsure about anything at all,' she reassured the lady, 'give me a ring or pop in any time.'

The worry lines vanished. 'Thanks. I'll have a go, then—'

The shrill ring of the telephone interrupted, and they both turned.

Evie stiffened. Even though Tim had left the pub with a flea in his ear, she still felt nervous every time the phone rang.

'I'll let you get on,' said the lady, and collected together all her pieces of fabric. 'Thanks for all your help. Bye!'

Evie picked up the phone. 'The Button Hole. How can I help you?'

'Hello, darling. I tried your mobile but it went straight to answerphone.'

'That's because I'm at work, Mum.'

Her mother ignored that and continued: 'I need to talk to you about Christmas.'

Evie's curiosity was piqued. She looked around to check the shop was empty before asking, 'Christmas? What about it?'

There was a whisper of hesitation before the reply came: 'We've been invited to Rupert and Angela's.'

Tim's parents. Evie frowned. 'When? I don't understand.'

She couldn't mean . . .

'On Christmas Day . . .'

Evie's head swam. She reached for a stool and sat down heavily. 'No!'

'And we'll stay the night, of course. That way we can have a few drinks and not have to worry about driving.'

'You're not going to accept, are you?'

'We're thinking about it. That's why I called – to see what you think.'

There must be something she hadn't understood. Her parents couldn't really expect her to go along with this, could they? 'Will Tim be there?'

'Of course. And with all that mistletoe around, you never know what might happen.'

'Mum, I can't go! You – you can't expect me to.'

'Oh, Evie, please. Think about it.'

She was, and the thought alone was making her break out in a cold sweat.

'They're our closest friends—'

'Tim did the dirty on me! Have you forgotten that?'

'This isn't just about you, Evie,' her mother went on. 'And – and it might be nice to do something different for Christmas.'

She heard the wistful edge in her mother's voice and Evie bit her lip. The undercurrent of pain and the unspoken message were clear. This time of year was so hard without Zara. Maybe it would be good for them to do something different . . .

Evie was torn. On the one hand, she wanted to help them get through the holidays in any way she could. If being with friends helped them escape the pain, Evie was willing to consider it. On the other, she couldn't spend Christmas with Tim. Anyone but him.

Was that selfish of her? Should she be trying harder to lay aside her own feelings for her parents' sake?

She looked up. One of the giant decorative cotton reels suspended from the ceiling spun lazily to the right, then to the left. She closed her eyes. What should she do?

'Evie! It's me! Evie – are you there?'

Jake banged on the door of her cottage, faintly aware that he was making enough noise to disturb the whole lane. His heart thumped against his ribcage just as hard as his fist was pounding the white-painted wood.

'Evie—' he began again, but the door swung open.

'Jake! What?'

'Smoke,' he cut in breathlessly. 'Is he here?'

'Smoke? No. Why?'

The words tumbled from his mouth: 'He ran away. I was walking him in the fields near the village when some kids let off fireworks. It spooked him. He just bolted! I thought – hoped – he might have come to you.'

He held up the redundant lead, and his fist was white with tension. What if Smoke got hit by a car? What if he spent the whole night out in these sub-zero temperatures? Jake couldn't bear to think of it. He stared down the lane into the darkness.

'Oh, no!' Evie pulled the belt of her dressing-gown tighter.

'He was gone in a flash. I ran after him, but it was so dark I lost him within seconds. I've been looking for him for ages, calling him. I've been back to the house, thinking he might have found his way home, but there's no sign of him anywhere. Nothing. I don't know where he is . . .' His voice broke and he raked a hand through his hair. He couldn't hide his despair. Or his fear for the dog. 'Smoke—'

He couldn't put it into words. Smoke meant everything to him. During the last few years they'd been through it all together. The darkest of times.

'Okay. Think. Where were you when he ran off?' asked Evie. 'Which direction did he run in?'

'We were by the stream. And he ran towards the village.'

'Right – let me grab my coat and a torch, and I'll help you look for him.'

'Thanks,' he said weakly. It wouldn't make any difference – he'd looked everywhere already – but it was good of her to offer and two pairs of eyes were better than one.

'Have you called Luc?' she asked, when she reappeared a moment later, wearing her red coat and an enormous scarf. As she pushed her feet into a pair of furry boots he realised she was wearing pyjamas.

'No – I – ah . . .' Evie was the first person he'd thought of, he realised.

'Why don't you call him now? Ask him to check the area near Poppy Cottage, and then perhaps he could go up to the Old Hall in case Smoke does find his way back. I'll call a few friends too.'

Jake nodded and pulled out his phone. While he spoke to Luc, Evie knocked at her neighbours' doors, and soon they were joined in the narrow lane by a small huddle of people.

'This is George,' Evie told him, as he hung up. Jake nodded at the man with the greying beard. 'George is a retired fireman.'

'I've looked for a few missing pets in my time,' George said proudly. 'Don't worry, Mr H. We'll conduct a thorough search of the village.'

'We will,' said the middle-aged lady beside him. 'Poor animal. Stupid kids messing about with fireworks. If I find out who it was, I'll give them a good talking-to!'

'Where did you last see the dog?'

Jake pointed. 'Just outside the village, over there.'

George followed his gaze. 'We'll fan out in groups to search the village itself and the nearby fields. Evie?' He turned to her. 'Stay with Mr Hartwood and we'll call you straight away if we find Smoke.'

She nodded and checked her phone was on full volume.

'Right, everybody,' George continued. He'd divided everyone into small groups and now he pointed at each in turn. 'You take that street, you head for the village green . . .'

'Come on,' Evie told Jake. 'Try not to worry – he's a really intelligent dog. He's probably just hiding somewhere and he'll come out when he's calmed down. We'll find him.'

Jake followed her red coat down the lane towards the village green. As they scoured the pavements and hedges for any sign of a cowering Dalmatian, doors were opening and more people emerging with torches and dog whistles.

Soon there were dozens of them, in couples and small groups, all searching and calling Smoke's name. And Jake felt the tight knot in his chest give a little. Warmth seeped through him: these people he'd never met had, without hesitation, come out to help with the search. To help him.

Chapter Eight

'I shouldn't have gone out so late with him,' said Jake, as they followed the road to the edge of the village and checked the stream carefully. 'I meant to take him out earlier, but a customer called, then I got tied up with paperwork . . .'

Evie pointed her torch at the bushes, checking carefully behind each one. 'There's no point blaming yourself. You were just unlucky those kids were setting off fireworks.'

He shone his torch across the water. At this time of year the stream was full, the water icy. Evie tried not to think about that. She tried not to think about poor Smoke, lost out there somewhere in the dark, scared and alone.

'I should have been quicker to clip his lead on, I should have . . .' He sighed and shook his head. The torch dropped to his side. 'If anything happens to him . . .'

Evie had never seen this side of Jake Hartwood before. Pale, tight-lipped and tense, yes, but never so openly fraught with worry. With emotion. How much had it cost him to ask for help when usually he kept his interactions with others to a bare minimum?

'Come on,' she said. 'Let's carry on along this road.'

As they climbed back up the bank, she could see torch

beams further down the lane, and heard people calling Smoke's name. Everyone shared the same concern: they were all pulling together to look for the Dalmatian. And with all these people searching the village, they were bound to find him eventually. In the meantime, she needed to help Jake stay calm.

'How long have you had Smoke?' she asked, deciding that distraction might help.

'Since he was a puppy.'

She shone her torch on the snow-covered shrubs and pots of flowers clustered around the front doors of the stone cottages. In the dim street lighting they took on ghostly shapes and their shadows stretched and waved. But Evie kept hoping she'd find the Dalmatian's distinctive black and white spots.

'You bought him?'

'No. I found him. Or, rather, he found me. He turned up on our doorstep one day. We thought he'd been run over because he was bruised and beaten, but in fact his behaviour suggested he'd been maltreated by his previous owner.'

We? Did he mean him and his wife?

'He was timid?'

Jake nodded. 'He cowered when we came near him. It was a while before he learned to trust us. Anyway, I took him to the vet, who treated him and advised me to take him to the rescue shelter once his injuries had healed.'

'Did you?'

They reached the end of the road and turned the corner. The lights became brighter as they walked back towards the village centre and here the street was clear of snow. Their footsteps were amplified by the sleepy silence.

'I took him, but when I got there, I changed my mind and couldn't leave him.' He clamped his mouth shut, unforthcoming as always.

Evie smiled, knowing that his words concealed a deep well of love for his dog. 'Why?'

'I don't know. Seeing the other dogs all caged up and so big, when he was just a small puppy and had been through so much . . .' He shrugged. 'Plus he was already showing signs of attachment.'

'Smoke adores you.'

'He's misguided. He's just grateful I don't hurt him like his previous owner.'

'Nonsense! Is he friendly with everyone?'

'Actually, he's mostly wary of strangers. You were the exception.'

'When did you find him?'

'Three years ago.'

Before his wife had died, Evie calculated. 'So he knew Maria?'

'Yes.'

She was glad Smoke had been there to help Jake through the difficult times after her death. He needed Smoke as much as the dog needed him.

'He was gentle with her even before her tumour was diagnosed. It was as if he knew what we didn't. And he was a huge help to me after she died. There were mornings when he coaxed me out of bed. If he hadn't been there, I don't know what I would have done . . .' He didn't finish the sentence, but he didn't need to: it was all there in his eyes.

'I'm sorry, Mr H,' said George, after they'd been searching for two hours. It was almost midnight. 'We've done all we can for tonight. I'll go out first thing tomorrow when it's light, but until then it's best we all get some sleep.'

Jake gave a tight nod, but Evie knew he wouldn't get a wink of sleep. She squeezed his arm. 'Smoke will be all right,' she told him. 'He's a clever dog. And, you never know, he may find his way back to the Old Hall.'

He didn't reply and his look of fear tugged at her heart. She watched as he drove away in his old car, and in her coat pockets she crossed her fingers tight.

'If the dog's run for the fields, we've no hope of finding him in the dark,' said George, as they trudged back to Love Lane.

'Jake didn't think he would do that. Smoke has a few chosen routes that he prefers, and he loves the village.' The Dalmatian was the opposite of his owner: friendly and uninhibited. At least, he was with her.

'We've conducted a thorough search of the village. If he was here, we'd have found him by now.'

Evie's heart sank as she pictured the dog alone in the snow-covered hills. 'But it's so cold. He'll struggle to keep warm in the snow.'

George patted her on the shoulder. 'Dogs aren't stupid.

They have excellent survival instincts. I've no doubt he'll find himself somewhere warm to curl up.'

'I really hope you're right, George.'

Back at the Old Hall, Jake put bowls of food and water outside by the front door, in the desperate hope the smell might carry and lure his dog home if he was nearby, then paced around the hall. He couldn't go to bed. If Smoke came home and Jake was upstairs, he wouldn't hear him. And he was too agitated to rest anyway.

He'd already searched the gardens earlier, but he searched them again, calling for Smoke, stopping and listening, hoping to hear a distant bark. But the night was silent, the snowy fields glowed white, and down in the valley the village was a cluster of faint gold lights. After doing five laps of the house and gardens, he ran a hand through his hair, and looked to the sky for inspiration. What more could he do?

Nothing. He had to wait. His head was beginning to spin with exhaustion, and his legs felt shaky. He went back inside.

Leaving the front door ajar in case Smoke came home, he made a makeshift bed for himself with sofa cushions and a duvet. He set up a heater nearby to ward off the chill, then lay down and stared at the sliver of sky through the open door.

It was cloudless, which meant the temperature would drop.

He closed his eyes briefly, and despair rolled in. *You've got to prepare yourself for the worst, Hartwood.*

He knew how cruel life could be. Just because you loved someone it didn't mean they'd be immune to harm, that they'd always be there with you. There were no guarantees. Needing and loving only made the wrench more violent when the worst happened.

The stars blurred and a fat tear slipped down his cheek. He tasted salt.

He owed Smoke his life. Without a doubt, he couldn't have got through the period after Maria's death without him. When everyone else, even family, had backed away from his flares of anger, frustration and silence, Smoke had stayed at his side, asking only for food and a bed. Undemanding. Faithful.

And look how badly Jake had let him down tonight. He rolled onto his side. Christ, he hadn't believed he was capable of feeling so much, but his chest squeezed as he pictured Smoke shivering in the dark.

This was the price you paid for letting anyone close.

He'd thought he'd lost everything when Maria died, but now he knew he'd been wrong.

Evie groaned as her alarm went off. She opened one eye to read the time. Why had she set it for so early? She'd had only a few hours' sleep after staying up so late searching for Smoke.

The workshop. That was why. She had a group of ten people coming to learn how to make a padded tablet cover, and there were still a few things she needed to prepare.

She got up and checked her phone. No message from Jake. Or anyone else. Her heart sank.

Resolving to phone Jake later, she grabbed a quick shower, pulled on a stripy sweater dress, and drove to the Button Hole. It was still dark, the village quiet. She parked her car and hurried towards the shop. As she turned the corner, she rooted in her bag for the keys. She was a short distance away from the shop when she noticed a shadow on the pavement by the door. She squinted in the dim light and increased her pace.

'Smoke? No, it can't be . . .' The shape was too small, too still.

The shape moved. Two eyes gleamed, and as she drew closer, the spotted coat was unmistakable. The dog barked and leaped to his feet.

'Smoke!' she cried, as he jumped up to greet her. 'Oh, my goodness! You found your way back. You clever, clever dog! I can't believe it!'

Smoke barked again and wagged his tail.

Evie reached into her pocket, not wasting any time before calling Jake. While she waited for it to ring, she petted Smoke. 'I know someone who's going to be so happy we found you.'

Evie had barely switched off her car engine before Jake pulled open the passenger door and Smoke bounded out to greet him, with a lot of excited tail-wagging.

'Am I glad to see you, buddy!' Jake exclaimed, clasping his excited dog.

Evie got out and smiled as the pair were reunited.

'I gave him some treats,' she said, 'but I think he's still hungry.'

'He must be starving. Come on, Smoke. Let's get you some food.'

Evie followed them inside, stepping over a rumpled duvet in the hall. Clearly Jake hadn't gone to bed last night.

In the kitchen, Smoke wolfed down his food and Jake crouched beside him. 'Where was he, then?' he asked.

'Outside my shop. Asleep. I don't know how long he'd been there.'

Jake rubbed the dog's back. 'I'll take him to the vet later and get him checked out.'

'I'm sure he'll be fine once he's warmed up.'

'I'm taking no chances. God knows what he's been through . . . Christ, I feel so bad!'

He straightened up. His skin was grey and pale from lack of sleep and Evie was reminded of the first night she'd met him. Only there was no smell of alcohol in the air this time. 'Jake, it's not your fault.'

His mouth was a tight flat line as he watched the dog. 'During the last two years there have been days when the only things that kept me going were work and Smoke. Work kept my mind busy, but Smoke . . .' He rubbed a hand over his unshaven face. 'He was just there.'

Evie watched as he bent to pat the dog.

'Weren't you? Yes. Good boy.' The dog nuzzled his hand, then went over to his basket and lay down. He looked up at them both as Jake went on, 'I think he understood what I was feeling – what I needed – better than anyone. My sisters would be on the phone and calling round, chattering away about inane stuff that was supposed to distract me, or asking intrusive questions that reopened everything – but Smoke, he just stayed close.'

Emotion roughened his voice and Evie swallowed. The look in his eyes as he gazed at his dog was one of pure love.

'When I was angry or falling apart, he was simply there. And when it became too much and I wanted to close my eyes . . .' he paused '. . . he would nudge me and whine. He had a sixth sense, I swear. So many times he persuaded me to take him out, and when I came back from our walks my head was clearer. I was in a better place. All down to Smoke.'

Evie blinked hard. 'Well, he's safe now,' she said.

Jake frowned. 'Maybe I should keep him on a lead in future.'

'Oh, Jake, I know he means the world to you but, really, that isn't necessary. The fireworks were a one-off, and I'm sure that when the kids who did it hear what happened they'll think twice about doing it again.'

'I suppose. And he's still getting used to this place. We've only been here a couple of weeks. It must still feel like unfamiliar territory for him.'

'Exactly.'

He cleared his throat. 'Thank you, Evie. I'm very grateful for your help. Everybody's help.'

'Oh, it's nothing. That's what it's like round here.

Everyone pulls together to help each other. It was fun, actually, seeing everyone with torches.'

'I can't believe how many people came out. I'd like to repay them. What can I do?'

'You don't need to repay them. Smoke is safe, and that's all that matters.'

They gazed at the dog curled up in his bed. Jake crossed the room and crouched to stroke him. 'He's exhausted,' he murmured. 'Go to sleep, boy. You're home and safe now.'

The dog's tail thumped on the floor and his eyes closed.

'I feel indebted.' Jake straightened up. 'People got out of bed to come and search for him. It was . . . incredible. Most of them don't even know me.'

She considered this. 'Well, if you really want to make a gesture of goodwill, there is something you could do . . .'

'Go on.'

'You won't like it, though.'

'What is it?'

'The Christmas ball. Here, at the Old Hall.'

'But Christmas is only ten days away!'

Her stomach lurched. Time was passing so fast. She wondered if her parents had reconsidered the invitation from Tim's parents. Goose-bumps prickled her arms. She hoped they'd see reason and decline.

'It is. But you have the venue already. How hard can it be to organise some music and a bit of food? You could even ask people to bring a dish, and I'm sure someone in the village would volunteer to do the music.'

'I don't know . . .'

'Where there's a will there's a way.' She smiled.

'Ever the optimist,' he said, but his eyes gleamed with amusement.

For some reason she couldn't fathom, his teasing words made her feel as if she was freewheeling downhill, and her heart beat double time. She flashed him a smile. 'You did ask what you could do to repay everyone . . .'

'I can't believe it!' said Natasha. 'He's going to host the ball?'

'That's what he said.' Evie was restocking her basket of felt tree decorations. They were selling like hot cakes, and so were the vouchers for her shop, which she'd tactically positioned next to them on the counter. Her till had never been busier, which was wonderful, but she needed to find a way to keep sales steady after Christmas, too.

'How did you persuade him?'

'I hardly needed to. He was so emotional when we found Smoke.' Natasha raised an eyebrow and Evie laughed. 'I know – Jake Hartwood and emotion don't often go together.'

Natasha rested an arm on the counter and looked out of the window. Today her nails were painted with Christmas puddings. 'Well, it's a wonderful thing. It doesn't leave us much time to get an outfit, though, does it?'

'I know.' Evie chewed her lip. 'I don't have a dress that's smart enough.' Neither did she have the money to buy one. Paying off her loan was her priority.

'I might have one you could borrow.'

Evie looked at her friend's petite figure and tiny waist.

She'd look ridiculous in one of Natasha's dainty tea dresses – if she didn't burst the seams first. 'That's a really kind offer, but I don't think your dresses would fit me.'

'Are you going to buy one, then?'

Evie shook her head. 'Who needs to buy a dress, when there's all this fabric to make my own?' She grinned, gesturing to the shelves around them. 'I'd better start now.'

Natasha was at the door when she stopped and looked back. 'By the way, are you still okay for dinner at our place next week? It'll be good to see you before we leave for France. Suzie can't make it because she's going home tomorrow for the holidays.'

'Of course. I'm really looking forward to it.' She was looking forward to dinner with her friends a lot more than she was Christmas with her parents. She just prayed they didn't accept the invitation from Tim's parents.

'Are you going to the ball, Dorothy?' Evie was putting the finishing touches to a quilt, hand-stitching the binding, and keeping her neighbour company for the evening. Dorothy hadn't dared leave her cottage since the first snowfall.

'What's that, dear?'

Evie repeated the question.

'Of course. George said he'd drive me. I wouldn't miss it for the world.' Dorothy's knitting needles clicked away, a rapid drumbeat. 'It's always a grand affair at the Old Hall, you know.'

'I'm not sure it will be this year, with so little time to prepare.'

Dorothy reached for her glass of sherry and drained it. 'Will you top me up, please, dear?'

Evie obliged. Dorothy always offered her a glass too, but she preferred to stick with hot chocolate.

'I met my husband, Charlie, at that ball,' said the old lady, with a glint in her eye. She finished a row and switched her needles round.

Evie adjusted the quilt on her lap, smoothing it out. 'You met for the first time?'

'Not the first time, exactly. We knew each other by name, but we'd never spoken properly. The ball gave us the opportunity to get to know each other better.' She winked.

'Dorothy!'

The clicking of needles resumed, faster than ever. 'Oh, there's been many romances have resulted from the Christmas ball, you know. Too many to count.'

'Have there? Do you think there'll be any this year?'

'Of course. There's the new owner, for a start.'

'Jake?'

Dorothy nodded. 'It would be nice to see him paired off. Such a big house for a man on his own . . .'

'That's not going to happen,' Evie said quietly, thinking of his vulnerability when he'd lost Smoke, his undisguised joy and relief when he was reunited with his beloved dog. Just to think of it made her heart turn over.

'What, dear? I didn't catch that.'

'I said, Jake's not interested in romance.'

Dorothy tutted. 'Even the most buttoned-up characters can get carried away by a bit of music and tinsel and Christmas magic.'

Evie shook her head. 'He hasn't got over losing his wife yet.'

'Well, maybe he needs a little push in the right direction. He's still young. And very dashing, don't you think?'

She blushed. 'Well . . . Ow!' She winced and a tiny drop of blood welled from her finger. She sucked it, and pushed the quilt to one side, afraid of staining it.

'He can't mourn her for ever. A bit of romance in his life might be just what the doctor ordered. If I was forty years younger . . .'

Evie giggled.

Dorothy put her knitting down. 'Tell you what, I do hope he'll get in a good supply of sherry.'

Evie stepped out of the taxi and paused, wide-eyed, to admire the sight in front of her. Christmas trees speckled with white lights lined the drive, and the Old Hall was illuminated with golden up-lighting. It looked stunning. Tasteful and majestic.

She smoothed the long, straight skirt of her dress, feeling a shiver of panic. Until this afternoon, she'd loved how the silver and blue satin caught the light and shimmered like a mermaid's tail – but now she felt self-conscious. She bit her lip, knowing Tim would have disapproved of the eye-catching fabric and the way it hugged her figure. He would have told her to change into something looser that would hide her hips and not draw so much attention to her chest.

She spotted Natasha at the front door and waved.

Well, it was too late to worry about her outfit now. Taking a deep breath, she drew her shoulders back and went in.

The entrance hall was strung with baubles and beads, and a band had set up beside the grand staircase. The musicians, dressed in denim and leather, and sporting grey ponytails, were playing well-known sixties hits that everyone could sing along to. But while his guests were either dancing or milling around, drinks in hand, Jake stood at the top of the stairs, a lonely figure surveying the party from behind the wooden banister.

Evie circulated, chatting with Luc, Natasha and little Lottie. Then, seeing Jake was still alone up there, she decided to join him. 'I've brought you an orange juice,' she told him.

'Thanks,' he said, and took the glass she offered.

She sipped her own drink. 'Like your bow-tie,' she said, nodding at the blue silk spotted with red dots. She'd never seen him wear anything but black, grey or navy. 'The colour suits you.'

Perhaps it was the lighting or the effect of being surrounded by glittery Christmas decorations, but tonight his cheeks had more colour, his eyes more life in them. She tapped her foot in time with the music, which was so loud she had to shout. 'How's Smoke? I hope he's wearing a bow-tie too.'

Jake shot her an amused glance. 'He's in the kitchen where it's quiet and there are plenty of treats. I gave the caterers instructions to tell me if he gets in their way.'

'I'll go and see him later. Say hello.'

'Say hello? Do I need to remind you that he can't speak?'

'Smoke likes me. He's always happy to say hello.' She was familiar now with Jake's dry sense of humour, but he'd be a lot easier to get on with if he were less reserved and as friendly as his dog.

She tugged at her skirt, wishing she'd opted for a looser design and worrying that the top was showing too much cleavage. 'It's very good of you to host this party. And at such short notice. How did you do it?'

'Heidi called in a few favours. It's astounding what people can do if you're willing to pay them enough,' he said wryly.

The band finished their song with a triumphant flourish and a short break followed. The sudden drop in volume was a relief.

'Why are you up here on your own and not enjoying the party?'

'I'm not a party person.'

She studied him for a moment, then said, 'I think you secretly like it.'

'Like what?'

'Being lord of the manor,' she teased. 'Looking on as the grateful but common villagers are having the time of their lives.'

'You're guilty of stereotyping me. I'm no lord of the manor.'

'Are you denying that you're aloof and you shun company?'

He held her gaze, but she couldn't tell if he was amused

or annoyed. He was so difficult to read, yet she knew that a current of intense emotion flowed beneath the surface. It had been more than evident the night Smoke had gone missing.

She elbowed him playfully in the ribs. 'Why don't you prove me wrong and come and dance?'

'I don't think so.'

'You don't fool me. Beneath that stern exterior there's a warm-hearted man who secretly wants to boogie the night away.'

'Boogie?' He wrinkled his nose. 'As if . . .'

The music started up again, this time with a faster tempo. People began to twist at the hips, and everyone, including the older generation, got up to join in on the dance-floor. Even old Dorothy picked up her walking stick and heaved herself to her feet.

'Ooh, I love this song!' said Evie, and began to jiggle on the spot.

He gestured towards the dance-floor. 'Don't let me stop you.'

'You won't dance?'

He shook his head.

Shrugging, she left him and made her way down the stairs. She found her neighbour, George, and twisted along beside him. Everybody was laughing and enjoying the music.

A little later she glanced up and saw the landing was empty. She scanned the room. Jake had come down, but not to dance: he was talking to the waiting staff and to his guests. Telling herself it was none of her business, she turned away. The band played another seventies classic, then a couple of Beatles songs, to which everyone sang along. The hall filled with people, and when Evie felt a tap on her shoulder, she ignored it because it was so crowded, arms being flung in all directions. It was only when George gave her a knowing look and pointed behind her that she turned.

There was Jake – and he was dancing with old Dorothy! Well, Dorothy wasn't exactly dancing, but shuffling around her walking stick.

'I couldn't leave him standing there on his own.' Dorothy winked, with a mischievous smile.

Evie grinned because Dorothy's idea of persuasion had most likely involved taking him by the hand and pulling him onto the dance-floor. And Evie was certain Jake would have been too polite to put up a fight. But he didn't seem unhappy. A little reserved, a fraction reticent, possibly, but not unhappy.

'That's enough for me!' said Dorothy, when the song finished, and the next one started. 'What I need now is a glass of sherry. You dance with Evie,' she told Jake, and gave him a gentle shove.

Evie and Jake grinned and watched as she shuffled away, one arm waving to the beat of the music.

'She's not as frail as I thought,' said Evie. 'She hadn't left the house since the first snowfall, but perhaps she has a touch of cabin fever from being cooped up inside by herself.'

'She told me she likes the music because it's loud enough for her to hear,' said Jake, and the corner of his mouth curved.

They got pushed a little closer by the crowd and Evie tried not to stare, but his black suit and slim-fitting white shirt were so flattering, and her eyes were level with his chest. The fabric pulled and stretched as he moved, and she was conscious of how solid his torso was, how lean. Her skin prickled, and not just because it was hot.

'So, you are dancing, after all. Who'd have thought?' she teased, trying to keep her tone light.

'Dorothy didn't leave me much option.'

'You looked like you were enjoying it.'

'You have me pigeon-holed as a stick-in-the-mud. I can't spoil my reputation by admitting I enjoyed myself.'

Her eyes lit. 'You pigeon-holed yourself, Mr Arctic!'

Jake caught her hand and whirled her around. 'Perhaps you were right,' he said, leaning in so she could hear him above the music. 'Maybe I did want to boogie after all.'

Evie spun and sang along. She was amazed at the transformation in him. He'd shaken off his stiff-backed demeanour, and his shoulders were relaxed. The music suddenly slowed, and he gave her his hand, placing the other on the small of her back, where his touch triggered explosions of awareness. It was magical, thrilling. But what delighted her more than anything was seeing him enjoy himself. Her chest tightened.

It felt like a small miracle.

Jake wandered through the dining room, surveying the food the caterers were serving. It had a casual, rustic feel: lamb hotpot with chunks of bread, cheese and nibbles, fruit and bite-size desserts. He didn't stop to eat, but wove his way through the room, pausing when people stopped him to chat.

'It's good to see you're keeping up the tradition of the Christmas ball, Mr Hartwood.'

'Great party, Mr Hartwood. When are you going to visit us in the pet shop? We've prepared a little gift for your dog in return for this evening.'

'That's very kind but there's really no need.'

'Ah, Mr Hartwood – do you know Lynn? She delivers the post around here.'

'Nice to meet you,' said Jake, shaking hands.

And he realised with surprise that he meant it. He'd been dreading tonight. The thought of opening his home to strangers had made him want to flee. But he knew that to do so would counteract the sentiment with which the invitation had been issued. He was determined to express his gratitude to the people of Willowbrook for helping him find Smoke so had gritted his teeth and prepared himself for the invasion. It was only a few hours, he'd told himself. Yet now the party was under way, he didn't feel the sense of intrusion he'd expected. Some of his guests were familiar, not just Luc and Natasha, who had left early because Lottie was tired, but Bob from the petrol station, and Jean who always served him in the village shop.

And, of course, Evie.

He picked his way back through the hall, where the band was still playing and people were dancing. When he'd spun Evie round, her eyes were sparkling and her cheeks crimson. She was so relentlessly cheerful, so stubbornly optimistic. His polar opposite. The corners of his mouth lifted – and then there she was, as if he'd conjured her with his thoughts, helping Dorothy to the front door where a taxi was waiting. Jake followed them out into the snow.

'Goodnight, Dot,' Evie called, and watched the taxi turn full circle and drive away into the night.

The blue and silver fabric of her dress shimmered in the moonlight. It looked vaguely familiar, though he wasn't sure why. And she had tied her hair back in an unusually neat, sleek ponytail. It drew attention to her elfin features, her tiny nose and beautiful eyes, and gave her a look of Audrey Hepburn.

'Another good deed done, Pollyanna?' He admired her thoughtfulness, her kindness. Dorothy and George had told him how generous she was with her time, always quick to help anyone who needed anything.

She whipped round in surprise. 'Oh, it hardly counts as a good deed! Anyway,' she went on, 'I was glad of some fresh air. It's getting a bit warm in there on the dance-floor.'

'And noisy,' he agreed, appreciating the peaceful stillness around them.

'Yes. We'll all be as deaf as Dorothy tomorrow.' She smiled.

His heart picked up in response. She always had this effect on him, he realised, like a shot of caffeine. 'Nice dress, by the way.'

She glanced at him as if to check he wasn't mocking her. 'Thanks. I was worried.'

'Why?'

'That it was the wrong shape, the wrong colour. Tim always told me I should wear black.'

'Black? Why?'

Spots of colour splashed her cheeks and she looked away, embarrassed. 'Because it makes you less visible . . . He said I wasn't slim enough to carry off bright colours.'

She spoke quietly, but he heard the edge of hurt in her voice. He stopped, irritated that the rat had said such a thing but more so that she was still affected by it. He swept his gaze over the floor-length dress, taking in her shapely hourglass curves. She was pretty, she was feminine, but what was most attractive about Evie Miller was her bright smile and long, thick hair that invited a man's touch.

'I can't believe you listened to that idiot. You look beautiful.'

Surprise flickered across her face. Then her dimples appeared as she flashed him a delighted grin. 'Thank you,' she whispered. Then cleared her throat. 'Do you recognise the fabric?'

He squinted at it. 'Should I?'

Her laughter was like bells ringing in the night. 'Of course you should! It was left over from a bedcover I made for you.' When he still didn't twig, she prompted, 'The guest bedroom two doors along from yours.'

'You're telling me I paid for your dress?'

'No!' He suppressed a smile at her affronted expression. 'I only charged you for the material I used! I over-ordered, so I used the remnants to make this. It worked out cheaper than buying a frock.'

She was resourceful and talented. He was impressed. But when she wrapped her arms around herself and shivered, he frowned. 'You're cold.'

Her teeth chattered. 'A little.'

'Here.' He removed his jacket.

'It's okay . . .' she began, but he'd already draped it around her shoulders. 'Thank you,' she said, and drew the lapels closer.

He glanced at the front door and the crowded hall. Inside, the drumbeat was loud enough to make the floor vibrate. Out here the white landscape was silent and still, watched over by an almost full moon in a cloud-studded sky.

'Fancy a stroll?' he suggested, and pointed to the path that circled the hall and led round to the landscaped gardens at the back of the house.

The moon reflected in her eyes as she looked at him, hesitating. 'Yes, that would be nice.'

They moved away, passing the busy dining room, with its silhouetted figures, bowls and plates poised in their hands.

'The food's delicious,' said Evie.

'Glad to hear it.'

'You haven't tried it yourself?'

'I wasn't hungry.'

Her foot slipped on a patch of ice and she grabbed his arm to steady herself.

'Are you okay?' he asked. The path had been scattered with salt, but it was getting to that time of night when any melted snow would turn to black ice in the sub-zero temperatures.

She nodded.

'Take my arm,' he said. 'I don't want you to fall and hurt your ankle again.'

She slipped her arm through his and he felt an unfamiliar stirring. It was just Evie, he told himself. The pretty, clumsy girl who'd had the courage to stand up to him and had an unusual affinity with his dog.

'You're not cold?' she asked, looking at his white shirt.

'No.' In fact he felt strangely alive, aware of his heartbeat, of the moon hovering in its own halo, and the way its glow picked out sparks of frost.

They skirted the dining room and rounded the corner of the house, heading towards the Italianate gardens. He led her down the steps and they slowed their pace to weave their way through the formal beds. The plants were all covered with snow, but the outlines of the square and circular beds neatly edged with box hedging were still visible.

'Something wrong, Pollyanna? It's not like you to be so quiet.'

She shook her head. 'I wish you wouldn't call me that.'

'What?'

'Pollyanna.'

'Why not? It's a compliment.'

'Is it? You always make it sound like I'm an irritation. I talk too much and I'm childish and silly for being an optimist.'

He stopped and faced her, realising he probably had said it rather derisively the first time he'd met her, but his opinion of her had changed since then. 'I don't think you're childish or silly,' he said. 'And being an optimist is a positive trait.' From her expression, that was the last thing she'd expected to hear. 'Although I must admit, you do talk more than is necessary,' he finished with a wink.

She laughed and punched his arm playfully. Instinct made him catch her hand, which took him by surprise as much as her. His gaze dropped to the slender fingers wrapped in his, and he rubbed his thumb over them, savouring the softness of her skin, remembering how quick and clever these hands had been when he'd watched her sew. She didn't try to pull away but looked at him questioningly.

He should release her, he thought distantly, yet something had taken hold of him. He looked down into her eyes, dark against the moonlit snow, as adrenalin rushed through his veins.

'Jake?'

Her words sliced through his thoughts and he released her hand. 'Sorry, I – I . . .' He didn't complete the sentence. He couldn't explain what had come over him.

He walked on, hastily changing the subject. 'So, has my party lived up to everyone's expectations?'

'Your party?' She was looking a little flustered. A moment later the knot in her brow cleared and her smile returned. 'Definitely. It's a huge success. You're going to be the most popular guy in Willowbrook.'

He laughed.

'Not that you care what others think of you,' she added. They walked a couple more steps in silence before she confessed: 'You know, I thought you were a beast the first time I met you.'

'You weren't far wrong.'

'Nonsense. Now I know you better, I see a lot of it is for show. Your bark is worse than your bite,' she added, with a mischievous grin.

'Really,' he said.

They stepped onto another path. It had also been gritted, but not so well, and they had to step carefully to avoid patches of ice. To their right the land sloped away and in daylight there were stunning views over the rolling countryside.

'Yes. You just say and do things to keep people at arm's length, but beneath it all you're a good guy with a soft spot for old ladies and vulnerable animals.'

'Stop trying to see the best in me, Pollyanna,' he said. 'Your first impression was more accurate than you think.' His voice took on a warning note. Since Maria's death, he hurt everyone who tried to get close to him. Like a snarling animal, he was best left alone.

Nevertheless, she persisted: 'You care deeply about Smoke, you put this party on tonight—'

He stopped her before she could go on. 'Granted, I have a soft spot for my four-legged friend, but that doesn't make me a good person.'

'It shows you have a heart,' she said quietly.

'That's where you're wrong.' His jaw clenched and he walked on past the long Victorian-style greenhouse. The brittle glass structure had been cleaned and emptied for the winter and now a thick layer of snow blanketed the roof, casting a dark and eerie shadow over the interior.

He'd lost his heart when he'd lost Maria and, contrary

to what people had predicted, it hadn't healed. Time hadn't changed a thing. Yet tonight something felt lifted, the pain eased a touch. Why? Was it the party atmosphere? Or Evie?

Guilt flashed through him. Of course not. Maria was always foremost in his thoughts.

An icy breeze swept up from the valley and touched his shoulders. He upped his pace a little and Evie's heels tapped on the stone path as she hurried to keep up. The fabric of her dress swished and whispered as she moved. They reached the end of the greenhouse and the gardener's tool shed, and passed the sprawling, ancient yew tree. A fat snowflake fell in front of him. Jake frowned as a couple more parachuted into his outstretched hand.

'It's snowing again!' squealed Evie.

'Damn. Well, it's time we went back inside anyway. Come on. This path leads back to the kitchen.' He pushed open the door in the wall and gestured for her to continue, but she had stopped.

Snow fluttered down around her, and she tipped her head back and held her hands up to the sky, laughing. 'Isn't it wonderful?' she said, blinking as flakes landed on her lashes.

'It's cold, and you'll be wet through before long.'

'I don't care. It's magical!'

She spun on her toes, a blur of glittering blue satin and whirling snow.

'There's been snow on the ground for two weeks now. Anyone would think this was the first time you'd seen it.'

'Oh, but fresh snow is always special,' she said, 'don't you think?'

He bit his tongue, not wanting to spoil her delight as she took his hands and pulled him around. Snowflakes showered down, like spring blossom, landing in her hair and on her face, and although the moon had been swallowed by cloud, her smile lit the night. His pulse beat a little quicker.

This, he thought fondly, was what marked her out from anyone he'd met before: her infectious smile, her awed appreciation of whatever life bestowed on her.

'Maybe the whole village will be snowed in with you tonight!' she teased.

He shook his head. 'I took precautions. I have a garage full of salt now and all the equipment needed to clear the drive. No one will be snowed in here.'

'Oh!' she gasped, eyes wide. 'I think I just got a snowflake down the back of my neck!'

He laughed and drew her into the shelter of the yew tree. 'Let me brush the snow off you before it melts,' he said, and swept the flakes off her shoulders and her hair.

'You've got some in your hair, too.' She reached up on tiptoes. 'And on your face.'

Her touch felt electric on his cheek. Her fingers smoothed his skin and he stilled. Time halted as they stood beneath the branches of the ancient tree. She drew her hand back, but he stopped her. He caught her fingertips and held them against his cheekbone, closing his eyes, inhaling the sweet apple scent of her.

When he opened his eyes, she was staring at him.

Something stirred inside him. She looked beautiful. She was fun and kind, and she brightened the lives of everyone around her. He was the opposite. And yet she had somehow wormed her way into his life and kept coming back, despite everything she knew about him.

He kept hold of her fingers with one hand, and slipped his arm around her waist, drawing her up against him. His body stiffened at the contact – foreign to him after the months and years he'd spent alone. She was all warmth and curves and softness against the wall of his chest. His heart pummelled his ribcage. She gazed up at him with those melting eyes, and he bent his head and brushed his lips against hers in a tentative, unspoken question.

The contact sent a flurry of sparks through him. His pulse drilled. He drew back, searching her face for a reply, but saw only raw desire. She was dishevelled, and he realised he must have done that in threading his fingers through her hair. Her lips were full and dark. He kissed her again. This time he didn't hold back, and it consumed him, it blew him away: the heat, the hunger, the urgent pleasure.

Chapter Nine

Evie felt as if she'd been whisked away to an enchanted world, there in the moonlit garden with its lattice of footpaths and ice-frosted plants. Away from the crowd, just the two of them. The band's music was muffled and it was intimately quiet. She heard only their snatched fevered breaths as Jake kissed her. Her heart thudded. Her body, pressed against his, hummed in a way it never had before. Need coiled deep within her, so strong she ached for more. Her fingers tunnelled into his hair, hungrily seeking—

The sound of the kitchen door creaking open pierced the night. The music suddenly became louder, there was barking – and seconds later Smoke came galloping round the corner, panting happily as he discovered them.

'Smoke!' cried Evie. 'What are you doing here?'

Jake's brow creased in a sharp frown.

'Hello, gorgeous,' she said, bending to pat the over-excited dog.

The distraction was welcome because her heart was pounding furiously as she tried to make sense of what had just happened. Jake's kiss had been so heated. So unexpected. Where had it come from? She didn't care.

He'd kissed her, and it had been magical. She laughed as Smoke nuzzled her face.

But when she straightened, the look on Jake's face wiped away her smile.

He cleared his throat. 'I think we should go back inside,' he said brusquely.

'Oh – okay.' A rush of cold air hit her as she watched him duck through the doorway in the wall and stride towards the house, his jaw set.

'Smoke!' he called sharply, although the dog ignored him and bounded around Evie, giddy with excitement. She tried to calm him with quiet words, but all the while she watched Jake's retreating figure. What had caused his sudden change in mood? What had she done?

Her stomach knotted as she reached the house. Jake was waiting like a sentry at the back door for the two of them to catch up.

'You're wet through,' said Evie, as she stepped past him. 'You must be freezing.'

'I'm fine,' he said tersely. 'I'll change my shirt.'

Confused and hurt, Evie nodded. A moment's silence hovered uncertainly between them before she slipped his jacket off and handed it back to him. 'Thanks for the loan of this.'

He nodded and pushed the back door closed, shutting out the snow, the navy sky and the icy air.

'Mr Hartwood?' The head caterer approached. 'What would you like us to do with the leftover food?'

Jake stepped into the bright kitchen to speak to him and Evie slipped away, cheeks burning. When Smoke tried to follow, she told him firmly to sit, then hardened her heart and closed the kitchen door on his pleading brown eyes.

It was only then that she realised how long she and Jake had been outside: the party was over and people were leaving in droves, climbing into the train of waiting cars and taxis that snaked up and around the drive. As she collected her coat, Evie heard mutterings of 'Hurry! It's snowing again . . .'

She stepped outside into the chilly night, scouring the crowd for a familiar face.

'Evie!' George leaned out of his car window and waved. 'We've got space for a little one if you want a lift home?'

'Yes, please!' She ran over to the car and slid into the back, forcing a brave smile for the couple, Anne and Roy, next to her.

'I wanted to thank Mr Hartwood but couldn't find him anywhere,' said Anne.

Evie said nothing but stared out of the window at the house, feeling hurt, feeling small. Clearly, he'd instantly regretted kissing her, and was that really a surprise to her, the girl who'd always been a disappointment?

The car in front finally moved off and George followed, turning full circle in the drive before heading down the hill towards the village.

Back in her cottage, she slipped off her shoes and rubbed her toes, which were sore and tinged blue with cold. Jake had looked annoyed, but *he* had kissed *her*. That was what didn't make sense, she thought, as she ran a hot bath and unzipped her dress. Her mind rewound frantically, searching for clues.

He'd told her Pollyanna was a compliment.

He'd told her he didn't have a heart.

He'd brushed the snow out of her hair with care, with tenderness. She'd done the same for him – and when he'd looked into her eyes he seemed to have shed his overcoat of grief, and she'd seen only desire. Uncomplicated, fiery desire – for her, Evie Miller.

She got into the steaming water and waited for the shivering to stop. Her dress lay crumpled on the floor and she tried not to look at it because all she saw was Jake's icy expression before he'd turned and marched away.

Her eyes stung and an old memory flashed up of when she'd accidentally dropped a bottle of Tim's favourite claret. It had smashed on the kitchen tiles and Tim had looked at her with exactly the same disgust as Jake tonight.

She closed her eyes, inhaling slowly and deeply, breathing in the citrus-scented bath oil. Resolve stole through her, silent but certain. Coming here to Willowbrook had been a fresh start for her. She was doing the job she loved and living her life the way she wanted to for the first time. She wouldn't allow anyone to make her feel small or inadequate or disappointing any more. Certainly not Jake Hartwood.

And he was her client. Yet another reason not to get

involved with him. Although her bank balance was healthy enough now to see her through to the New Year, she didn't want to lose a customer.

Anyway, Tim had taught her a lesson she wasn't planning to forget in a hurry. She didn't need a man in her life. Certainly not a complicated ice man, who was still grieving for his dead wife.

Jake opened one eye and looked at the clock.

He looked again. How late? He couldn't remember the last time he'd slept so long, or so soundly.

But the feeling of peace didn't last. He stilled as he remembered last night.

The ball.

Evie.

He tossed aside the duvet and strode across to the window. He swept the curtains open and his gaze homed in on the knot garden and the ancient yew tree under which they'd taken shelter from the snow.

What had he been thinking?

He hadn't been thinking. That was the problem. He'd been *feeling*.

Lust, hunger, need. Just the thought of Evie in that eye-catching figure-hugging dress and those big wide eyes smiling up at him was enough to reawaken the sensations in him, and they were so strong, so fresh, that panic ripped through him. He marched into the shower, slamming the door behind him. Water and soap streaked over him, but he couldn't wash away the guilt or the shame.

What did it say about him that he'd so easily forgotten Maria last night? What kind of man was he that he could use Evie like that? Leading her on, kissing her as if it meant something – when he knew full well it didn't. Disgusted with himself, he snatched up a towel and dried himself with quick, angry strokes. Had he really laid aside all thoughts of his wife for a few moments of physical pleasure? How could he trample her memory like that, undermining the promises they'd made and the love they'd shared? It was the ultimate betrayal, when he had loved her – still loved her – so deeply.

He pulled on a black sweater and looked at his watch. He had to speak to Evie and set the record straight.

Jake knocked on the door, then stepped back. The cobbled lane was quiet. Some of the upstairs windows still had their curtains drawn, but Evie's were open, and a reassuring spiral of smoke was weaving its way up from her chimney.

'We won't stay long,' he promised Smoke, and patted the dog, who peered at him with questioning eyes.

The cottage door opened.

'Jake! What are you doing here?'

'I – ah – can I have a quick word?'

'Yes, of course. Come in.' Her hair spilled freely around her shoulders, the honey-coloured threads catching the morning light as she stepped back to let him enter. 'Smoke can come in too.'

The dog licked her hand enthusiastically as she greeted

him and followed her to a small kitchen area where she put a bowl of water out for him.

Jake eyed the stove. 'Your pan's boiling over.'

'Pan? Oh!' Evie snatched it away just in time. 'Hold on, I'd better switch everything off or I'll burn the place down.'

Jake nodded politely. His stomach growled fiercely when she pulled a tray of bacon out from under the grill. It smelt delicious and he suddenly regretted not having eaten breakfast before leaving the house.

'Tomato soup and bacon sandwiches,' she said. 'Do you want some? I've made plenty.'

On the counter there were three bread rolls and she quickly filled them. Jake's mouth watered. He dug his hands deeper into his coat pockets and shook his head. 'No, thanks. I'm afraid I can't stay.'

Her shoulders dropped. 'Oh. In that case, I'll keep them warm for later.' She hurriedly piled them onto a tray, chattering as she did so. 'They're not all for me, by the way. I always make extra for George and Dorothy. They both love a bacon sandwich, but you know what it's like when you live alone – it doesn't seem worth the trouble . . .'

He listened to her cheerful patter and guilt twisted inside him as he prepared himself for what he had to say. But what alternative did he have? To lead her on would be even more wrong.

'Ow!' She snatched her hand back from the open oven and sucked her finger.

'What happened?' asked Jake.

She blinked rapidly. 'I caught my finger on the shelf. Burned it.'

He crossed the small space in a couple of strides. Her finger glistened an angry shade of red. 'Run it under the cold tap. Here.' He flicked open the tap and took her hand, carefully angling her finger down so the water flowed over it.

A few seconds had passed before he became aware of how close they were standing, the touch of her hand in his, and the way she was looking up at him from beneath her lashes. Warily. A pulse flickered at the base of her throat and he thought of their kiss last night. Of how her lips had looked so dark and full in the shadowy light and how his head had spun with intoxicating need. His muscles tightened. He remembered how it had felt to press her body against his, how soft and warm she'd been despite the cold night air. He remembered clearly the sensations he'd experienced as he'd brushed his lips against her petal-soft skin and she'd sighed with pleasure—

Abruptly, he stepped back. 'Keep it there – like that,' he ordered, motioning to her finger.

She ducked her gaze away and gave a tiny nod. He closed the oven door, then moved away. The sound of running water filled the small cottage as they stood in awkward silence.

'You said you wanted a word?' Evie said quietly. She barely looked at him but kept her gaze on her injured hand.

'Yes. About last night. I – ah –' he cleared his throat '– I kissed you and I – I . . .'

Smoke finished lapping water and settled himself near her feet.

'And?' she said, darting Jake a hooded glance.

He swallowed. 'I shouldn't have done it. I'm sorry. You see, I, ah . . .' He felt as if he was about to hit her with a sledgehammer, and in that moment he hated himself for what he'd done – and what he was about to do.

'Let's not make a big deal of it,' Evie jumped in quickly.

He looked up in surprise, quickly followed by relief.

'It was just a kiss at the end of a great party. No big deal.'

He didn't know what to say.

'I really enjoyed it,' she went on, adding hastily, 'the party, I mean.'

'You did?'

'Yes.' She shot him a halogen smile, bright enough to light up the entire village. It suddenly occurred to him that perhaps she kissed men all the time. She was young, pretty and single – why not?

'And that kiss – it was a rebound thing.'

Jake was struggling to find words. This wasn't how he'd expected her to react at all. 'Okay . . . Well, that's fine, then.' He breathed a sigh of relief.

Yet he felt a plunging sensation too. Disappointment?

His fingers reached for the chain around his neck. Of course he wasn't disappointed. Evie was an acquaintance, nothing more, and what had happened last night had been a momentary aberration on his part, a glitch. Primitive urges taking over.

She nodded, and for the briefest of moments he thought

he saw a splinter of hurt flicker in her eyes. But then she smiled again. 'So, can we agree to pretend it never happened?

'It never happened,' he confirmed.

Evie closed the door behind him, then sank down into the sofa. Oh, God, could that have been more humiliating? His visit had caught her so much by surprise that she'd initially hoped—

Fool that she was. With hindsight it had been obvious why he'd come.

She buried her face in her hands as she thought of how his eyes had been clouded with shadows and how pale he'd looked, dressed all in black like a mourner.

What had she thought – that he'd kissed her because he felt something? She knew he was still grieving for his wife – he'd told her how much he missed her. *She was the love of my life and always will be . . .*

His wife had been intelligent, sophisticated and accomplished. Evie could never compete with a woman like that. She couldn't even hope to come close. She was just Evie Miller, klutz extraordinaire.

That kiss had been a mistake. He'd probably had one glass of wine too many. Usually mistakes were her speciality, but it seemed even Jake Hartwood was capable of them. She lifted her chin and made herself breathe deeply.

Pretend it never happened, she'd said. It couldn't be that hard. They simply had to go back to how things had been before. She could do that. She really could.

Her phone lit up and her parents' number filled the screen. Her mind still working nineteen to the dozen, she answered distractedly.

'Evie,' said her mum. 'I'm calling about Christmas. We've decided to accept Rupert and Angela's invitation.'

Her palms began to sweat and she had to grip the phone tighter to prevent it slipping out of her hand. Her heart thumped. No. This couldn't be. Just when she'd thought today couldn't get any worse.

Chapter Ten

'Nat, I can't.' A long strand of hair had escaped from her messy bun and Evie wound it around her finger. She'd popped into the flower shop to deliver a Christmas card when Natasha had broken the news to her that Jake was also invited to dinner with her and Luc on Wednesday.

'Please, Evie. Lottie's really looking forward to it, and we'd like to see you before we go away.' Natasha put down the bouquet she'd been making and wiped her hands. She unfastened her apron, revealing a fifties-style tartan dress as colourful as the buckets of bright flowers that surrounded her.

'It's kind of you,' said Evie, 'but I can't – not if Jake's there. Things are . . . awkward between us now. Perhaps we could do gifts another time, just you and me.'

Natasha's blonde head tilted as she considered everything Evie had told her about the ball and the kiss and his visit the previous day. 'Are you sure you don't have feelings for him?'

'No!' Evie said quickly. She felt a flicker of hesitation as she remembered the heat of his kiss. Did she?

No. Definitely not. She enjoyed his company, she

sympathised over his loss and desperately wanted to see him smile again, but she didn't have feelings for him.

'He's still in love with his wife, Nat. I doubt he'll ever love anyone else.'

'Of course he will. He just needs time to get over his grief.'

'No . . . No one else will ever measure up in his eyes.'

A motorbike roared past and they glanced out of the window. Across the road the Button Hole was still in darkness. It was nearly nine o'clock and time to open for the day; Evie didn't have long.

'You know,' Natasha said carefully, 'living in a place as small as Willowbrook you're bound to run into him again. Especially since you're both good friends of ours. There's no avoiding him. Isn't it better to get it out of the way sooner rather than later?'

Evie bit her lip. Natasha had a point.

'It's just dinner, Evie. Please come.'

Her friend's imploring look tugged at her. Natasha was right: there would be no avoiding him completely. And wouldn't it be better to get that next awkward meeting over and done with? Plus, she could tell her friend would be disappointed if she pulled out now. Natasha had been such a good friend to her since she'd moved to Willowbrook. When Evie had arrived in the village knowing nobody, Natasha hadn't lost any time in coming over to introduce herself and invite her out for drinks with Suzie and to meet her family, Luc and Lottie. Evie didn't want to risk damaging that friendship for the sake of Jake Hartwood and a kiss.

She sighed. 'You're right. If I avoid him it will look as if I care. What time should I come over?'

Evie lifted her hand to knock at the door of Poppy Cottage, then hesitated. She looked down at the bouquet in her hand. She could still leave – it wasn't too late. She could run away and text Natasha to say she wasn't feeling well . . .

She glanced behind her at Jake's classic car parked by the verge.

No. Running away would be a coward's way out. She drew her shoulders back and knocked hard and loud.

Natasha opened the door and greeted her with open arms. Evie hugged her and gave her the flowers.

'What's this?' asked Natasha. 'A bouquet of fabric flowers?'

'Well, I couldn't very well buy a bunch from you to give back to you, so I made these instead,' Evie explained. She had used vintage fabrics which reminded her of the tea dresses Natasha liked to wear, and she'd glued the roses onto twigs and fixed them in a wooden display box. The overall effect was modern and unique.

'They're amazing! I love them.' Then Natasha whispered, 'If it's any consolation, he looks dreadful. Really pale and drawn.'

'Only because he regrets what happened,' said Evie.

'Teevie!' Lottie came galloping into the hall.

'Hey, Princess!' Evie crouched to say hello to the little girl who was all ready for bed in yellow striped pyjamas.

Natasha smiled down at her daughter. 'It's Auntie Evie – can you say that, Lottie?'

Lottie nodded and repeated solemnly, 'Teevie.'

Evie and Natasha laughed and went through to the lounge. The cottage looked gorgeous, decorated for Christmas with fairy lights strung across the ceiling, suspended from the wooden beams, and Evie could smell the pine scent of a real tree in the corner.

Luc rose to greet her with kisses – she always forgot that the French kissed on both cheeks – and as he did so, Jake stood up too.

'Evie!' he said. 'I didn't know you were coming tonight.'

Evie glanced nervously at Natasha, who looked with surprise at her husband. 'Luc, didn't you mention Evie was coming?'

'I can't remember.' He shrugged in that characteristic French way. 'My mistake if I didn't. But I'm sure you're as happy to see Evie as we are, aren't you, Jake?'

'Yes – of course,' said Jake. A little too quickly. He bent to kiss her lightly on one cheek, but she couldn't bring herself to meet his eye.

'Have you finished making all Jake's curtains?' asked Luc, glancing at Lottie, who was riffling through a box of toys, searching for something.

'Not yet. There are still a few rooms left, but I did the important ones in time for Christmas.'

Jake was watching her with an unreadable expression. She glanced away quickly and kept her attention on Lottie, who toddled across to him with a book.

'Thank you, Lottie.' He opened it with exaggerated pleasure, which made the little girl beam. He patted the seat beside him and Lottie climbed up. She popped her thumb into her mouth and settled down.

Watching him with the toddler, Evie had the strange sensation of a seam unravelling. She ignored it. So he was good with small children. Why should she care? They'd clearly established that he wasn't interested, and she was concentrating on building up her business. Nothing else.

'Why doesn't Uncle Jake read you that book upstairs, Lottie?' suggested Natasha. 'It's bedtime for sleepy girls.'

Lottie seemed happy with that arrangement and Evie watched, fascinated, as Jake lifted her easily into his arms and carried her away. It was difficult to reconcile the man before her with the haughty figure she'd met on the night of the snowstorm.

Luc vanished into the kitchen, and Natasha went through to the orangery, where she began to lay out plates and cutlery. 'Here, let me help with that,' said Evie.

They could hear Jake's deep voice over the baby monitor. Lottie was babbling away and he was coaxing her into her cot. She quietened down and he read her the story, not in a monotone, but with child-friendly inflections that made Evie and Natasha giggle. The low rumble of his voice was soothing.

'He's good with Lottie, isn't he?' said Evie, as she smoothed a linen napkin.

'Don't sound so surprised,' said Luc, coming in with a bottle of wine in each hand.

'I am surprised,' said Evie. 'He's not the most sociable of men usually.'

When he'd kissed her he'd taken her by surprise, too. She thought of the passion that had unexpectedly darkened his eyes as he'd drawn her to him and their lips had met . . .

She cut off that train of thought. Forget it happened, she told herself, but the heat coiled from her centre regardless.

'He is good with Lottie,' Natasha agreed. 'She adores him.'

A short while later the monitor went quiet, and they heard Jake's footsteps on the stairs. 'I left the book with her,' he told Luc and Natasha. 'She wanted to look at the pictures.'

'Yes, she reads to her teddies,' smiled Luc, as he popped the cork on the red wine.

'Well, she tries to,' said Natasha. 'She makes the sounds but they're not necessarily real words. Sit down. Dinner's all ready.'

Evie tried not to feel offended when Jake sat diagonally opposite her, putting as much distance as possible between them. Natasha served them with a tomato puff-pastry tart, glazed and golden from the oven. Evie's mouth watered and she was glad she'd chosen to wear her red dress. Made from a soft cotton jersey, Tim had hated it, but she loved the colour and the fact that it stretched so she could eat as much as she wanted without worrying about buttons popping.

'Evie?' asked Luc, the wine bottle poised. She nodded and he filled her glass. 'Jake?'

Jake shook his head.

'You're driving?' asked Natasha.

'I am, but I'm not drinking at the moment.'

Evie looked up. 'Not at all?'

'I haven't touched a drop since the night I first met you.'

The snowstorm.

Luc and Natasha looked from him to her and back again. Jake's gaze held hers, as if he was silently communicating a message, and Evie puzzled over what it could be. Had he resolved not to drink again because he was ashamed of his behaviour that night? But at the ball – that kiss – she'd assumed it had been a drunken blunder. If he'd been sober, what did that mean?

'I suppose you taste so much wine with your work, perhaps it loses its appeal?' suggested Natasha, as they all began to eat.

'I just decided it was a sensible thing to do,' he said dismissively. He turned to Evie and changed the subject. 'Lottie adores that pink quilt you made for her. She wouldn't lie down until I'd fetched it for her.'

'The princess quilt?' said Natasha. 'We can't go anywhere without it.'

Evie smiled. 'I'm glad she likes it. I could make a smaller one if you like – one that's more portable.'

'Please,' said Luc. 'We live in fear of losing the damn thing. She'd never sleep again without it.'

Evie nodded. 'I've got some scraps of fabric left. A doll-sized quilt will be a good project to take to my parents' house over Christmas.' She sliced another piece of tart. The pastry was buttery and delicious.

'I'm so looking forward to spending Christmas in Provence,' said Natasha.

'All my family will be there this year,' said Luc, with a smile. 'Lottie will be so excited to see all her cousins.'

Evie knew he was close to his family. He and Natasha liked to visit as often as possible. She wished she could feel the same eagerness about going home, but her heart was heavy at the prospect. Even more so than usual this year.

'Have you got guests coming for the holidays, Jake?' asked Natasha.

'No.'

Evie wondered if the others noticed how his mouth tightened, if they recognised it as a sign of his bitten-back grief and the strain he felt at times like Christmas.

'What are your plans, then?' Natasha had painted her nails sparkly red with white-bearded Santas. They glittered in the candlelight as she reached for her glass.

'I don't have any.'

'It's only five days away. Haven't you left it a bit late?'

'No.'

Evie glanced at him, remembering the conversation they'd had on this subject outside her shop. His plate was empty and he sat straight-backed.

'You're not going to visit your sisters?' asked Luc, reaching across the table to refill their wine glasses.

Jake shook his head. 'I hate Christmas.'

'You don't mean that.' Natasha smiled.

'I do.'

Her smile faded and a moment's silence punctuated

the conversation. Natasha and Luc glanced at each other, puzzled, but Evie understood.

She understood perfectly. 'It's a difficult time of year for anyone who's lost a loved one,' she said quietly. 'Everyone has high expectations of a perfect family gathering, but emotions run high, and people are forced together who don't normally spend time with each other. I dread it too,' she finished, darting Jake a weak smile.

'You do?' asked Luc. He sipped his wine.

She nodded, picturing her parents' faces. Her relationship with them had never been easy, but at Christmas they went into overdrive with a particularly artificial act of jolliness, which set her nerves on edge.

It hadn't been like that when she was a girl. She had fond memories of childhood Christmases. But everything had changed, and now she was torn between feeling her parents depended on her, their only surviving child, and knowing her presence wasn't enough to make them happy. Christmas was the most acute reminder that, no matter what she did, she could never fill Zara's shoes. They always looked as relieved as she felt when the holidays were over and she left.

'Usually my plan of damage limitation involves arriving as late as possible on Christmas Eve and leaving first thing Boxing Day, but this year is going to be different . . .' She took a sip of wine, but it didn't chase away the leaden feeling in the pit of her stomach. 'We're going to Tim's parents.'

'No!' said Natasha, wide-eyed.

'His parents are good friends with mine. They're like family, really.'

'But won't that be incredibly awkward for you?'

'Yes. Big-time.' This Christmas was going to be the worst ordeal for her.

'And can't they see that?'

She shook her head, smoothing out her napkin and remembering her conversation with her mother. *'Why don't you go without me, Mum?'*

'You know we can't leave you on your own at Christmas.'

'I'd rather that than spend it with him.'

'Oh, Evie, darling. Please try to be more mature about this.'

More mature? Her fingers squeezed the linen napkin because, no matter what she did, they always saw her as the difficult one. Tim had cheated on her! And hindsight was beginning to reveal what she hadn't seen at the time: how he'd emotionally abused her, persistently undermining her self-esteem. There was nothing unreasonable about not wanting to spend Christmas with him.

'Tim can do no wrong in their eyes. They still think I should get back with him.'

Natasha touched her arm in sympathy. 'Oh, Evie, what are you going to do?'

'I don't know.' She pinched the stem of her wine glass. 'I really don't know.'

'Could you invite your parents to your place instead?' asked Luc.

'I suggested that, but they've really got their hearts set on going to Tim's parents. I think they're hoping that being with friends and doing something out of the ordinary will shake off the memories and make the day more bearable.' She sympathised. She wished she could wave a magic wand and make the holidays easier for them. Less painful. 'Like I said, Christmas is difficult.'

She caught Jake's eye as she said this, but rather than looking sympathetic, he glowered.

Natasha got up and began to collect the plates. 'I'll get the main course. Prepare to be impressed! Luc has made a delicious stew. *Boeuf bourguignon.*'

'You should tell your parents you're not going,' said Jake, when Luc and Natasha had left the room and he was alone with Evie.

'What?'

'To spend Christmas with your ex. You should point-blank refuse.'

She shook her head. 'I can't. I don't have a legitimate reason to miss it.'

'I'd say you do. And if they can't see that, they're fools.'

'They're not the ogres you think they are. They wouldn't want me to spend Christmas by myself.'

'Yet they're leaving you no option but to spend the holiday with your ex who cheated on you and continues to harass you?'

'You don't understand . . .'

He understood better than she gave him credit for. She was too kind-hearted. She spent too much time considering how difficult Christmas was for her parents, while they clearly didn't consider her feelings at all. 'You should stand up to them. Stand up for yourself.'

He would stand up for her. He'd fight her corner. He didn't care what others thought of him.

But her affairs were none of his business.

'I have considered crying off sick at the last minute,' she admitted, after a moment, 'pretending I have flu or something.'

'And spending Christmas where?'

'At home. Alone.'

He could see from her expression that she wasn't looking forward to it. Unlike him, she was friendly, she was sociable, and she would hate to spend the holiday alone.

Let it go, Hartwood. He'd spent the last few days cursing himself for the thoughtless loss of control that had pushed him to kiss her. He'd be wise to learn from his mistakes and keep his distance.

Silence settled in the room, like an unwanted guest, and Jake couldn't think of anything more to say. He pressed a finger to his forehead. Another fitful night had left him tired. Again. He wasn't sure why life felt as if it was grinding to a halt this week, each day slow and dull and grey, when it had been like that for the last couple of years.

Since he'd arrived in Willowbrook, though, things had changed a little. He'd grown used to being stopped to chat as he walked through the village. He and Smoke had begun to look forward to their stops at the Button Hole and Evie's visits to the Old Hall with deliveries of soft furnishings followed by cheerful conversations over a cup of tea.

Perhaps that was what had been missing the last few days – her bubbly presence and bright-eyed optimism. The realisation dawned on him that he'd grown to regard her as a friend. He glanced at her, trying to ignore the buzz she provoked in him. Had he felt this before or was it the consequence of that kiss? Or was it simply that she looked pretty tonight, her eyes smoky with make-up, her luscious thick hair draped over one shoulder? She was lost in thought and unusually quiet as she fiddled with the end of her long plait.

He cleared his throat, racking his brain for a neutral topic, some small-talk to fill the silence. But it wasn't easy: he wasn't practised in small-talk. 'Has the – er – snow hampered your Christmas shopping?' was the best he could come up with.

'Not at all.' Her face brightened. 'I've made all my gifts this year.'

He tried to dampen his awareness of how well that dress moulded her curvaceous figure and how the colour accentuated the rose of her cheeks and the hazel of her eyes. She looked even more beautiful than she had on the night of the ball, and the urge to reach out and brush the loose strands of hair away from her face was difficult to suppress.

'Let me guess – patchwork quilts?' He didn't know how she had time. She'd produced so many curtains and bedcovers for his home alone, as well as running her shop.

Her cheeks dimpled as she smiled. 'No – but you're not far wrong. I've made Dad a case for his tablet, and for Mum I knitted a handbag.'

'You knitted a handbag?'

Her chin lifted. 'What's wrong with that?'

'It's all kinds of wrong. It sounds terrible.'

'I made one for myself, too,' she said, reaching down by her feet. 'See?'

She held up a bag, grey-brown in colour, with a cabled pattern and leather handles. 'It's fully lined,' she said, opening it up, 'with small pockets inside for her keys, lipstick and so on.'

He had to confess, it looked nothing like the picture he'd had in his head of stretched and saggy knitted squares. In fact, it looked completely professional and the kind of thing his sisters would pay a lot of money for.

'Still don't like it?' she asked, her eyes dancing with challenge.

'Actually,' he cleared his throat, 'it's – very nice.'

She arched a brow and put the bag down. 'Thank you. Now, tell me, was that painful?'

Her dimples flashed, her eyes gleamed, and he felt a curious skip in his chest. 'Was what painful?'

'Paying me a compliment.' Her smile lit up the room. 'I know it's difficult for you to do.'

Her teasing words triggered a warm sensation in the pit of his stomach, and he was relieved that he hadn't destroyed their friendship after all.

Luc and Natasha returned with a big pot of stew and a bowl of green beans.

'Will you be taking a break from work over Christmas, Jake?' Natasha asked, as they tucked in.

'Probably not.' Though what would he do when his phone went quiet and his customers were all busy with their families?

He found his gaze kept drifting back to Evie. The flickering light of candles around the room caught the gold threads in her hair and made them shimmer. He'd never noticed before how smooth her skin was, how easily it coloured when she dropped something or when she made everyone laugh with her upbeat humour.

'Seconds, anyone?' asked Luc, taking the lid off the stew.

Evie's forehead creased. 'I'm tempted, but I shouldn't . . .' She bit her lip, and absently touched her stomach.

Jake frowned. 'Why shouldn't you?'

Her cheeks filled with colour. 'Because I only need to look at a plate of food and my hips get wider.'

'Nonsense!' he said, more fiercely than he'd intended. He knew her ex was responsible for her hang-ups about her figure. How could the other man not have appreciated her fresh-faced beauty, her bright-eyed optimism, her sweet-natured charm? She was generous with her compliments and her ready smile – she had an uplifting effect on all those around her.

'You have a lovely figure,' said Natasha. 'But Jake brought dessert, so perhaps you want to keep some room for that.'

'Yes, I will,' said Evie.

Jake got up and began to collect the plates. When

Natasha moved to do the same, he held up his hand. 'Sit down,' he told her. 'You two have worked hard to make us that delicious meal. Now let me do the rest.'

'Thanks, Jake.' She smiled.

Evie helped too, and they carried everything through into the small kitchen. As he rinsed the plates and she stacked them in the dishwasher, he caught a drift of her scent – apples and cinnamon – and his body tightened, remembering how it had felt outside in the cold night to press her against him, to brush his lips against the softness of her skin, to hear her sigh with pleasure.

Irritated with himself, he tried to wipe it from his mind. Pretend it never happened, they had agreed. Most likely, Evie had already forgotten about it. So why couldn't he?

'I'll take these through,' she said, scooping up a pile of plates and dessertspoons and hurrying away with them.

Jake nodded and opened the fridge. He followed her into the orangery and put the dessert in the middle of the table. 'Lemon cheesecake,' he said.

Evie's eyes widened. 'You made that yourself?'

'I did. Is that so hard to believe?'

'You're a dark horse, Mr Arctic. A dab hand with young children *and* you bake desserts!'

'I like cooking. I find it relaxing.' Natasha handed him a knife and a cake slice, and he cut the cheesecake.

'What did you call him?' Natasha asked Evie.

Evie's dimples flashed. 'Mr Arctic. He's a bit of an ice man on first acquaintance.'

Luc laughed. Natasha looked at Jake. 'I like it,' she said. 'Mr Arctic . . .'

'He calls me Pollyanna,' said Evie, 'so it's only fair he should have a nickname too.'

Natasha looked at her friend. 'Pollyanna? That's perfect!'

'I think so. Evie's eternally optimistic,' Jake said, 'even when there's nothing to be optimistic about.'

'There's always something to be optimistic about!' Sparks of indignation lit her hazel eyes.

'Is there?' He slid a piece of cheesecake onto a plate and handed it to Natasha.

'Yes! It's just in some situations you have to look hard for it.'

He shook his head at her naivety and handed her the next plate.

'The trouble with you, Mr Arctic,' she said, with a mischievous glint in her eye and a nod to the dessert in the centre of the table, 'is you're as sour as the lemons in this cheesecake.'

He couldn't help smiling at that. Why did Evie's teasing send ripples of pleasure shooting through him? Was it because she was one of the few people around who spoke to him with such irreverence? Or because he was beginning to understand how many demons she had overcome to find that cheeky confidence?

Natasha laughed, and he realised she was watching them both, fascinated. 'Yes, you both have quite opposite personalities, don't you?' she observed thoughtfully.

Evie's dimples winked and she threw him another look of amusement before tucking in to her dessert. The candlelight made her lashes look incredibly long and dark, and her cheeks glowed. He tried to concentrate on eating his own cheesecake, but his muscles wouldn't relax.

Ignore it. Give it time, and it would inevitably wear thin. Lust always did. His fingers slid down the collar of his sweater searching for the chain around his neck.

The metal ring had a sobering effect.

'I'd better head off,' said Jake. 'Let Smoke out into the garden before I call it a night.'

'Yes, I'll be off too,' said Evie, hugging Natasha. She'd had such a lovely evening. 'Thank you for dinner, and I hope you all have a wonderful time in France.'

'Thanks,' said Natasha, and she and Luc shared a look so loving that Evie's heart skipped a beat.

There had been a time when she would have wished for what they had: that special closeness, the elusive once-in-a-lifetime love that young girls dreamed of and so many stories had been written about. But Tim had disillusioned her of all that. She was twenty-eight, and she had a business to rescue. Making the Button Hole succeed was the only thing that mattered to her. It was her dream.

Still, she couldn't help feeling a faint pinprick of envy.

'Oh, and Jake,' said Luc, stepping forward as if a thought had suddenly occurred. 'Our villa is empty over Christmas if you want to get away from it all.'

Jake tilted his head as he considered this. 'That's an idea, actually. There's a couple of winemakers I've been meaning to visit. Are you sure?'

'Absolutely. In fact, you'd be doing us a favour. There

have been a few burglaries lately and I'm worried about the place being empty during the holidays. Here,' Luc reached behind the door, then handed Jake a bunch of keys, 'take these. You know where everything is.'

'Thanks. I'll think about it and let you know what I decide.'

The door of Poppy Cottage creaked shut behind them, and Evie pushed open the garden gate.

'Want a lift?' asked Jake.

'Thanks, but I'll walk,' she said. 'It's not far, and you can't drive down Love Lane anyway.'

'I'll walk with you, then. See you get home safely.'

'How chivalrous of you.' She smiled, appreciating the gesture, although it would be easier to avoid him. Being alone with him made her skin tingle and her blood rush. She had to constantly remind herself that her awareness of him wasn't reciprocated. That his heart belonged to someone else.

But as they fell into step, she relaxed again. Despite the hiccup of that kiss, she enjoyed being around him. She found him fun – in a dour kind of way. He was reserved, a little uptight, very pessimistic and grumpy too, but she understood him. She got why he was so down on life – who wouldn't be after what he'd been through? – and she felt . . . What did she feel exactly? An affinity with him.

Plus, she enjoyed their teasing. When he called her Pollyanna it set off sparks inside her, and she loved teasing him back. Perhaps by doing so she was even helping him in a small way. It wasn't much, but if she could make him smile even once, wouldn't that be better than if he hadn't smiled at all?

'I didn't know Luc had a place of his own in France,' she said. 'I thought they always stayed at his family's château.'

'He bought the villa a long time ago and renovated it. But now that he's healed the rift with his father, he prefers to stay at his parents' place. They have plenty of room.'

She thought of how Luc had given him the keys. 'Have you been to the villa before?'

'Several times. I use it for business trips. It's in the country – handy for visiting my suppliers and their vineyards. And it's peaceful, too. Secluded. My kind of place,' he added.

She smiled, but felt a pang at the thought of him alone on a business trip when everyone else would be with their families, celebrating. They approached his old Bentley and the crescent moon's reflection in the windscreen made her look up.

'Isn't it a beautiful night?' she said softly. The moon shone so brightly, lighting the linen-like drifts of cloud that slid silently and serenely beneath it.

'It's cold enough to get frostbite.' He pushed his hands deeper into the pockets of his coat.

'I'd have thought you'd like the cold, Mr Arctic.' His lips were tight, but she saw the amused glint in his eye. 'How does your car fare in this weather?'

They crossed the road. 'Fine. The salt on the roads doesn't do her bodywork any good, but she starts without any problem.'

'Your car's a she?'

'Definitely.' His eyes creased and Evie felt a coil of heat unfurl from her centre. It was impossible to ignore, no matter how hard she tried.

She giggled. 'How long have you had it – I mean, her?'

'She's been roadworthy for five years now, but I bought her a few years before and it took a good while to have her restored.'

'She wasn't in good condition?'

'Terrible. Eaten up with rust and needed a lot of replacement parts – but we found them all eventually.'

'Couldn't you use new ones?'

He threw her a look of mock outrage. 'That wouldn't be authentic! No, I hunted all over the world for the original parts. But my patience paid off. Now she goes like a dream. I can't imagine being without her.'

She remembered he'd said almost the same thing about Smoke the night the dog had gone missing. And, now she thought about it, wasn't there a parallel between having lovingly restored his old car and having nursed the injured, frightened puppy back to health? Jake Hartwood was a man who didn't commit easily, she could tell, but when he did it was irrevocable.

Like his undying love for his wife, she thought, feeling the bite of envy. She bowed her head and kept her gaze on the cobblestones underfoot. Beneath that abrasive exterior there was a strongly beating heart.

'Did you know she has a heated rear window?' he said.

'Er – no.'

'Quite astounding for a car built in 1952. It's a privilege

to drive such a rare piece of history.' His eyes lit when he was talking about the car, and he looked so animated, the silent battle to overcome his grief momentarily gone. It made her wish she could erase it completely.

She grinned. 'Well, it takes one to know one.'

'Are you saying I'm old?' His eyes glistened in the golden glow of the streetlamps. 'I'm only thirty-five!'

'Practically antique.'

He shook his head, but she saw his lip curl and she was relieved they could still laugh together, that they'd managed to leave behind any awkwardness.

They arrived at her cottage and stopped. She glanced at the wreath on her door and the mistletoe berries that shone white, like the moon. 'Well, here we are.' Evie shrugged, suddenly feeling self-conscious. Her cheeks felt warm and she knew that wasn't just from the walk. She hoped the street lighting was too dim for him to see.

'Goodnight, Evie.'

Why did he have to have such a deep, sexy voice? In the quiet of the night it vibrated right through her and made her wish for things she couldn't have.

'I'm glad we can still be friends,' she said.

'Yes, so am I.' He chuckled softly. 'Good job, too. You keep turning up wherever I go.'

'That's village life for you,' she said, trying to sound cheerful. Trying not to look at his lips.

Everything was still in the cobbled lane. He stood just a couple of feet away from her, within touching distance, and she longed to run her fingers along the chiselled line of his jaw, to reach up on tiptoe and press her mouth to his again.

Pretend it never happened, she had said. But her body hummed, remembering. Longing for a repeat. That kiss had woken something in her, something she'd never felt before, and she cursed it. He'd pushed her away already. Being attracted to Jake Hartwood could never lead to anything. She had to ignore it. Get over it.

'Goodnight, Mr A,' she said, and forced herself to turn away, to unlock her door and shut it quickly without looking at him.

Jake clicked open a spreadsheet. He was throwing himself into his work, although with just four days left before Christmas the phone had gone quiet and his inbox was almost empty. All his clients' cellars were well stocked. Their hotels and restaurants would be snowed under with reservations right through until New Year. January was a quiet month, so he didn't expect business to pick up until February. But the thought of all those empty days stretching ahead of him made him tense.

He picked up a pencil and tapped it absently against the desk. His gaze wandered to the window and he watched a distant plane's vapour trail dissolve in the sky. He was still considering the possibility of a trip to France and waiting to hear whether a couple of winemakers would be around to meet him. In the meantime, he had to keep busy, keep his mind occupied, so he was getting his finances in order, and making sure he was up to date with all his paperwork. It was dull, but he forced himself to concentrate on the columns of figures.

I'm rubbish at doing accounts, Evie had said, last time she was here. *I always came bottom in maths at school.* Yet he'd watched her calculate in a flash how much fabric was needed for the study window.

He rubbed his face. He had to stop thinking about Evie Miller.

The sound of a car engine made him sit up, and Smoke barked. Jake hushed him. 'It'll be the cleaner. Sit down. Good boy.'

But the doorbell rang. He frowned. The cleaner had her own key, so it wasn't her. He thought about ignoring it, but his phone simultaneously lit up with a message.

Answer the door. I know you're in.

Jake stilled. Louisa was here?

Damn. There was no escaping his big sister.

Chapter Eleven

'Jake!' Louisa threw her arms around him in a vigorous hug.

Affection for her rolled through him. As kids they'd been close, and they'd chosen similar career paths. All through his time at medical school she'd been a constant source of advice and encouragement. It was only recently that cracks had developed in their relationship, and he regretted that, he really did. But he was powerless to change the way things were, or the way he felt.

She drew back and looked him over. Her dark bob was as glossy and tidy as ever, but he noticed faint lines around her eyes that hadn't been there last time he'd seen her. When had he last seen her?

'Jakey, you're so thin.' She frowned. 'Are you eating?'

He rolled his eyes. 'Yes.'

'Taking regular exercise?'

'What are you now – my mother?' As soon as he'd said it, he cursed himself because, growing up, she had been exactly like a mother to him.

After their own mother had died, they'd been raised in the care of nannies and housekeepers – which had been fine. It had been a pragmatic arrangement, and the women their father had employed to look after him and his sisters had done what was required of them. But none had provided the affection of a mother. They'd been professional and detached. Perhaps that was why Louisa, the eldest, had instinctively taken on a more maternal role with Jake and his younger sister Scarlett.

'Smoke keeps me fit and active.' He glanced behind him at his dog, but Smoke was hanging back, a little uncertain. He patted his head to reassure him but was surprised. He'd thought the Dalmatian had got over his fear of strangers: he'd bonded instantly with Evie.

'Hello, Smoke,' said Louisa, holding out her hand to the dog. 'Remember me? You probably don't. Jake's made himself quite unreachable these last few months.' She threw her brother a weak smile.

'Not intentionally,' he said, and regret twisted through him. He knew she'd found it difficult to understand his withdrawal these last couple of years. She was hurt by his self-imposed solitude but he was coping in the only way he could.

'I know.' She hugged him again. 'But it's not good to hide away, stewing, keeping it all locked in. It might do you good to talk about it.'

'Is that why you're here? I hope not.'

'That's not why I'm here,' she said, and gave him a sharp look, which clearly communicated that she wasn't at all intimidated by his clipped words. 'I brought you gifts – we received yours, by the way, thanks – and I was curious to see your new place. See how you are. To keep in touch. I waited a couple of weeks for you to invite me, but since you didn't . . .' She shrugged, as if he'd left her no choice.

'You thought you'd invite yourself?' he finished mildly, a ghost of a smile playing on his lips.

She pushed her hands into the pockets of her navy padded gilet. 'John's got a couple of days' annual leave. He's taking care of the kids and doing the last-minute shopping – so I'm free to spend some quality time with you!'

'Quality time? Right.' He tried not to panic at the prospect of spending two full days with Louisa. She was his sister, after all.

'You've got a spare room I can sleep in, haven't you?'

'One or two,' he said.

'Good. It'll be great to catch up properly,' Louisa went on. She peered over his shoulder to see the wide staircase, now stripped bare of all the decorations from the ball last weekend. 'I can't wait to see this place, and for you to show me round Willowbrook. I drove through the village on the way here and it's gorgeous! I've never seen so many cute cottages.'

She picked up a small overnight bag and Jake tried to quell his panic. He had a feeling there was another reason why she'd come here. She was going to pressure him over spending Christmas with her and her family, wasn't she?

'So, what *are* you going to do for Christmas, then?'

Jake gritted his teeth. It hadn't taken her long. A ten-minute tour of the house, and no sooner had they come down to the kitchen for a coffee than she'd launched into her offensive. 'Louisa, we've been through this a hundred times!'

'And you still haven't answered the question. I can't bear the thought of you being here in this enormous house alone.'

He dropped a sugar cube into his coffee and stirred it more violently than was necessary. 'I'm not alone. I have Smoke.'

'A dog doesn't count! Not at Christmas!' She took a deep breath, as if she was struggling to contain her frustration.

She wasn't the only one.

'Jake, why don't you want to come to us?' she asked more quietly. 'Tell me. Please. I won't be offended, I promise. I just need to understand why you'd rather be alone than with family.'

'Louisa, it's nothing to do with you or your family – or Scarlett's, for that matter. It's me. I'm not ready to face . . .' he grappled for the words '. . . all the emotion that Christmas entails.'

His sister studied him closely, concern in her blue eyes. He downed his coffee and carried the cup to the sink in a vain attempt to escape her scrutiny, but she followed him with her gaze.

'Jake,' she said gently, 'it's been two *years*. When will you be ready?'

He gripped the cup and closed his eyes. Why did everyone have such an obsession with how much time had passed? The gap Maria had left in his life would always feel vast to him. The pain ran so deep it could never heal. But how did he even begin to explain this to those who had never experienced it?

'There isn't a cut-off date,' he said. 'There isn't a day, a time, when you suddenly wake up and think, That's it! I'm better now. You of all people should know that. Would you tell a patient that they should have finished grieving now?'

She held his gaze a moment longer, then sighed. 'You're right. I'm sorry. I'm just . . .'

'Concerned,' he finished for her. 'I know.'

Louisa opened her mouth to speak, then closed it again. The sympathy in her eyes made him turn away. He didn't want her pity, or to be forced into spending time with family. He'd only spoil their Christmas.

'That reminds me,' she said, eyes brightening suddenly. 'Did you know there's a vacancy for a GP in the next village?'

He rinsed his cup and put it into the dishwasher. 'So?'

'So you could apply.' She sipped her coffee but watched him over the rim of her cup.

'Why would I do that?' He reached for a tea towel and dried his hands.

'Because you're a good doctor. Your skills and training are going to waste.'

Her words probed the place he didn't like to think about. 'They're not.'

'Can you honestly tell me you get as much job satisfaction from organising shipments of wine as you did from helping sick patients?'

'You're interfering again, Louisa.' His voice struck a warning note.

'I'm not! Okay, I am. But only because I care about you, Jakey.'

Louisa had been mothering him since he could remember, but couldn't she see? He was thirty-five now, not three.

'Actually, talking of wine shipments, there's the possibility I might be in France for Christmas.'

'The possibility?'

'Yes.'

She eyed him suspiciously. Then her features lit with hope. 'Who with?'

'No one. A work trip.'

Her shoulders sank. 'Is that supposed to make me feel better? You're not only going to spend Christmas alone, but in a foreign country too.'

Damn. He'd hoped it would get her off his back, but that had backfired. Still, Louisa had helped him make up his mind: he would book his flight. Because if he stayed here, she'd only hound him right up until Christmas Day.

Smoke trotted over to him and dropped a tatty, discoloured tennis ball at his feet. It was a not-so-subtle hint that he wanted to go out.

'Excellent suggestion, you clever dog,' Jake murmured, and rubbed him behind the ears. He turned to his sister. 'Why don't we take Smoke for a walk and I'll show you the village? We could get lunch while we're out.'

Louisa's face brightened, though he could tell from her

forced smile that her worry wasn't appeased. 'A walk would be lovely.'

'There's only the pub and the bakery café that do food, but they're both rather good. I was surprised. This is the bakery here,' said Jake, as they stopped outside it. He glanced at the Button Hole next door and had to grip the lead tightly because Smoke was straining to continue to Evie's.

Louisa peered inside. The window display was brimming with savoury bakes and pastries, and inside were a dozen or so small square tables. 'Let's stop here, then.'

He held the door open for her and they placed their orders for soup and toasted sandwiches.

'So, there's no American coffee chain here?' asked Louisa, when they were seated.

'Willowbrook isn't that kind of village. It's very English, very quaint, and . . .'

'And what?' she prompted.

He bit his lip. A few weeks ago he would have said 'stuck in the last century', and he wouldn't have meant it as a compliment – but now? Now he'd come to know a lot of the locals by name and, of course, there had been the search for Smoke when he'd gone missing. He was still astounded at the generosity and kindness others had shown him.

'. . . and there's a real community feel,' he finished.

Louisa arched an eyebrow, looking sceptical. 'How do you know?'

'Know what?'

'That there's a community feel. Somehow, little brother, I can't picture you joining the local book club or volunteering to deliver meals for the elderly.'

'It's a small place and people are friendly.'

'Jake, tell me the truth – have you met anyone here in the village?'

'Yes, I have,' he said indignantly.

'I don't believe you. You won't even pick up the phone to call your own sisters – and I know because I checked that you don't call Scarlett either – never mind speak to strangers.'

'I've met lots of people.'

'Name some,' she goaded, pressing the same buttons she'd used when they'd been children. 'Go on.'

He was riled. 'Luc and Natasha, for starters . . .'

'Luc doesn't count – you knew him already.'

'Well, there's the cleaner, the gardener—'

'They're paid staff! I'm talking about friends! Have you made any friends, Jake?'

The door of the café opened and Evie walked in. She was wearing another colourful outfit. It looked as if she'd cut out fabric flowers and stitched them onto a blue denim dress, and around her neck was a red scarf that matched her boots. Her hair was tied on top of her head in a messy knot, and her lips were the colour of raspberries. She was a picture of brightness as she joined the short queue, and when she spotted him, she raised her hand and slanted him a shy smile. He noticed she glanced curiously at Louisa, though he and his sister were so alike that he was sure she'd have no problem deducing who she was.

'Evie!' he said, and beckoned her over.

She hesitated – probably unnerved by his uncharacteristically friendly behaviour – then came over. 'Jake, hi. What can I do for you?'

He stood up to make the introductions. 'I'd like you to meet my sister, Louisa.'

They shook hands. It was a little formal and perhaps he was more enthusiastic than necessary because Evie shot him a quizzical look. He couldn't reveal how grateful he was that she'd spared him from his sister's inquisition. He was off the hook – for now, at least.

'Evie owns the fabric shop next door,' he explained. 'She also made the curtains for my new house.'

'And a few bedcovers, too. Although, being a man,' Evie leaned in conspiratorially, 'I'm not sure he's even noticed them.'

Louisa smiled. 'Well, I noticed them. They're beautiful. Did you make the blue and silver one in my guest room?'

Jake recalled the dress she'd worn to the ball and his cheeks burned, which didn't escape his sister's notice. She glanced from him to Evie in puzzlement.

'Yes. That's one of mine.'

'You must give me your number,' said Louisa. 'I'd love something like that for my bedroom at home.'

Evie looked delighted and pulled a card out of her purse. 'Of course. Here you are.' She glanced at her watch. 'I'd better go – can't leave the shop closed too long. I only popped in for a sandwich.'

'Oh, that's a shame. We didn't get chance to chat

properly. Why don't we meet for a drink tonight after work?' Louisa suggested, with a wide smile.

Uncertain, Evie turned to Jake, who was staring at his sister. 'Am I invited to this?' he asked.

Louisa laughed. 'Yes, of course.' She turned back to Evie. 'My brother leads a quiet life. He won't arrange an evening out for my benefit, so I'm doing it myself. It would be really nice to get to know you better.'

'What she means is she's checking on me,' he muttered.

'Checking on you?' asked Evie.

'She doesn't believe I have enough interaction with other human beings.'

'She'd be right, then, wouldn't she?' Evie grinned. 'You're not exactly a party animal.'

'I knew it!' said Louisa. 'He spends too much time alone, doesn't he?'

Evie nodded. 'Alone with Smoke, but I've told him a dog –'

'– doesn't count,' they finished together. Then laughed.

He looked from one to the other: his sister with her conventional beige trousers, well-ironed shirt and expensive handbag, and Evie with her wild hair and cheerfully embellished dress. He was seriously regretting having introduced them.

'That's not fair.' Jake shook his head. 'The two of you are ganging up on me.' Trust Evie to make such a swift connection with someone she'd only met five minutes ago.

'I close the shop at five. Want to meet in the pub then?' she asked his sister.

'Perfect. See you there.'

'Do I get any say in this?' asked Jake.

'No!' they told him simultaneously.

Evie shook the snow off her leather boots outside the Dog and Partridge, then pushed open the heavy oak door and went in. She spotted Jake sitting by the fire, brooding over a glass of orange juice.

'You're looking more Arctic than ever. Where's Louisa?' she asked, sitting down opposite him.

'She left her purse in the car – she's just coming now.'

Evie peered out of the window and saw Louisa, purse in hand, locking up his Bentley. 'I like your sister. She seems fun.' She looked just like him with the same dark hair and blue eyes, but instead of wearing a permanent scowl she had a ready smile.

Evie wondered if he'd told Louisa about their kiss. She hoped not. On reflection, she couldn't imagine him divulging such a thing. Especially something he'd instantly regretted.

'She likes you too. Apparently, your company is preferable to mine,' he said, with his usual wry humour.

'Is she older or younger than you?'

'Can't you tell by how bossy she is? Two years older.'

'Are you close?'

His gaze slid away from hers. 'We were.'

Evie waited for him to explain. When he didn't, she asked, 'You're not any more?'

He took a swig of his drink and she watched his Adam's

apple rise and fall. He hadn't shaved and his face was dark with stubble. It was disturbingly sexy, although he looked pale in the navy sweater he was wearing.

He stared out of the window before answering. 'Louisa thinks there's something wrong with me. She believes I should be over Maria's death by now and move on.'

Evie sympathised. Experience had taught her that grief was complicated and intensely personal. Even after five years her parents hadn't come to terms with Zara's death, and she wasn't sure they ever would.

'She also has the irritating habit of calling me all the time and checking I'm all right. I've told her I want to be left alone, but she won't listen. She's insufferable.'

Evie smiled at his dry humour. 'You mean she cares about you.'

He didn't smile back. Instead he added, 'And she won't accept that I don't want to spend Christmas with her and the family this year. It's . . . causing friction between us.'

'Ah.'

The pub door swung open and Louisa headed towards their table.

Evie got herself a glass of wine and they settled down for a chat. It was strange, but conversation with Jake's sister came so easily that it was as if they'd known each other for years. In the space of five minutes Evie learned that Louisa worked as a GP, lived in London with her husband, two dogs, and three boys aged between six and twelve, who enjoyed sports more than academia, if their latest school reports were anything to go by.

'My school reports were bad, too,' said Evie. 'They

always began with the words, *Unlike her sister . . .*' She began to tick off on her fingers. '*Evie does not pay attention, is not able to solve even a basic equation, is disappointingly slow to grasp even the basic principles of physics, blah-blah-blah.*'

'Ouch,' said Louisa. 'Your sister was a good student, then?'

'She was top of the class in every subject. She won prizes, she was a prefect, then head girl. I was always in detention for forgetting my homework, or in the nurse's office because I'd hurt myself. The teachers used to sigh and say *I can't believe you two are sisters . . .*'

'Tough act to follow,' said Louisa. 'Did that drive a wedge between you?'

'Not at all,' said Evie. She added quietly, 'She died a few years ago.'

Louisa's eyes widened. 'I'm sorry.'

'It didn't drive a wedge. I adored her.'

She sipped her wine and tried to ignore the lump in her throat. Talking about Zara was hard, but at the same time they were precious memories. And she refused to let her sister be forgotten by *not* speaking about her.

'Even though everyone compared you both?'

Evie nodded. 'We had such fun together, running around having adventures in the countryside, horse-riding, having midnight feasts. We were best friends . . .' She finished her drink and gazed thoughtfully into the bottom of the empty glass. 'I miss her a lot.'

The pub door opened and the noise level jumped as a group of men came in, talking and laughing loudly.

Jake pushed his chair back. 'I'll get more drinks. Same again?'

Evie looked up in surprise. Their glasses were still half full. He didn't wait for a reply, though. In a few strides he had crossed the pub and was standing at the bar.

'Did I say something wrong?' asked Evie.

'Who knows?' Louisa sighed. 'My brother doesn't like to share what he's thinking or feeling. He prefers to run away. Or bury his head in the sand.' Her dry words and the set of her mouth were so much like Jake's it was uncanny. She had the same clear blue eyes too, though without the fleck of brown that marked out his so distinctively.

'You mean he doesn't like to talk about grief?' Evie watched him hand a note to the barman. 'I shouldn't have said I miss Zara. It was insensitive of me.'

'Actually, I meant emotion. Any emotion makes him feel uncomfortable. And it wasn't insensitive of you to talk about your sister. Like I say, Jake is the one with the issue here.'

Louisa's reassuring words brought Evie a rush of relief. Perhaps she worried too much about saying the wrong thing. Tim's perpetual criticism of her had left its mark.

'Jake didn't mention you were coming to visit.'

'It was a last-minute thing. I decided to surprise him because I knew that if he had any warning he would have made sure he wasn't in.'

Evie smiled. That did indeed sound like the kind of thing Jake would do. However, she could see how hurtful it must be for Louisa. His sister clearly adored him.

Jake returned with more drinks and put them down on the table. 'I'm just going to check on Smoke,' he said.

'Where is he?' asked Evie.

'In the back room with the landlord's Chihuahua. I'd better make sure he's not been deafened by its yapping.'

He vanished.

There was no denying how much Jake doted on that dog, and Evie was about to make a joke about that, but before she could, Louisa turned to her. 'So tell me,' she said, with a wink, 'are you two an item?'

'No! Definitely not!' Evie thought of that mortifying morning after the ball and her cheeks fired up. Her heart rattled as furiously as her sewing machine with the pedal flat down. 'I don't want a relationship – neither of us does . . .'

If she was honest, she still found Jake attractive. But he'd made it clear as day that it was unreciprocated.

'We're friends, that's all. I know he still has feelings for Maria and always will. He told me.'

Louisa's mouth pinched. 'It would be good for him to move on.' She paused a moment, then said urgently, 'Evie, I'm worried about my brother.'

'Worried? Why?'

'He's become a recluse. Did you know he's planning to spend Christmas alone in France?'

Evie sent her a look of sympathy. 'I knew he was thinking about it.'

'It breaks my heart to see him like this. He's changed so much these last couple of years. He used to be the life and soul of the party, you know.'

'The life and soul? Jake?' She simply couldn't imagine it.

Louisa nodded, smiling at the memory. 'He had a wicked sense of humour. He used to make us laugh, cracking jokes all the time, and he was the one who instantly made everyone feel at ease.' Her smile faded. 'He's changed so much since Maria died. Now, well, you've seen him. You know what he's like.'

Evie couldn't even picture him smiling, never mind cracking jokes. Although, now she thought about it, he did have a dry sense of humour. Was that the remnant of a man who had once been the life and soul? 'His bark is worse than his bite,' she said, though she wasn't sure why she felt pushed to defend him. Perhaps because she'd also lived through a period when grief had made it impossible to laugh or smile.

'I'm glad you think so. Some people find him intimidating and aloof. Still, to shun his family at Christmas is taking aloofness to another level.'

Evie could see how hard it must be for Louisa, but she also sympathised with Jake. She shared his dread of Christmas – although her family was very different from his. 'Don't be upset about that,' she said carefully. 'He just needs time . . .'

'But how much time? It's been two years already!'

'I know it's hard when he's your brother and you care about him, but he might be thinking it's better this way. He's not the type to put on an outwardly cheerful face, is he? Perhaps he's worried he'll spoil your Christmas by being miserable.'

Louisa nodded and blinked hard.

Across the room someone put money into the jukebox and Evie recognised the opening chords of an old Christmas hit. It took her straight back to her childhood and opened the floodgates to memories. She tried to block them out. Unfortunately, there was no avoiding those songs at this time of year.

'He must have loved Maria very much,' she said, and wondered what kind of person Maria had been. It sounded as if she'd been an exceptional woman: talented, intelligent, beautiful.

Louisa agreed. 'He did. They were made for each other.'

For some reason, Evie felt a sharp twist in her chest, so unexpectedly painful she had to take a deep breath and wait for it to ease. She frowned and told herself she wasn't jealous. Anyway, she'd resolved to forget any kind of emotional involvement with Jake Hartwood. Yet that hadn't happened, had it? Even when she was alone in her shop, she often found her thoughts wandering his way, wondering what he was doing, picturing him with that haunted look in his eyes, and wishing there was something she could do to help.

She shivered. She couldn't help feeling concerned. It was only the same as when she checked on Dorothy next door. The pub door opened again, and a flurry of snow blew in, reminding her of how dark Jake's eyes had looked in the moonlit snow, how his fingers had curled around hers as he'd held her hand against his cheek . . .

Her heart skipped. Okay, maybe what she felt was a little more than concern.

'Perhaps he wants to be alone so he can be free of the

memories and begin new traditions,' she said, wishing she could do the same.

Next year, she thought, when her business was more established and she'd furnished her spare room, she would invite her parents to her cottage for Christmas.

'Begin new traditions on his own?' asked Louisa. 'Unlikely. I'm worried he's just going to sit and mope.'

Evie remembered the night she'd first met him, how he'd locked himself away in the Old Hall with a bottle of whisky. She suspected Louisa might be right.

'And in France he won't even have Smoke to keep him company.'

'I wish I could help,' Evie said.

'So do I. I'd feel heaps better knowing he wasn't alone.' Louisa laughed. 'If only you could go with him to France. But I'm sure you have your own plans.'

There was a long pause. Evie reached for a loose strand of hair and, deep in thought, wound it around her finger. 'I do,' she said eventually, 'but I'm not looking forward to them . . .'

Christmas was just three days away, and although her parents assumed she was going to Tim's, she still hadn't come up with a solution to her dilemma. What should she do? Acquiesce to her parents' wishes and face Tim? Or cry off sick and spend Christmas alone? Her stomach churned at the thought of being holed up in her cottage by herself. Nothing could be lonelier.

Then again, Tim would be insufferable. For thirty-six hours there'd be no getting away from him, and he'd see it as a challenge. He'd launch the ultimate charm offensive against her and her parents. And with his parents added into the mix, it would be her versus the five of them all breathing down her neck to get back with him. She felt sick at the thought.

'Actually, I'd love to have an excuse *not* to go home for Christmas,' said Evie.

'Really?'

She smiled, and Louisa's face lit up.

'What's going on?' Jake's deep voice made them turn. 'You both look like the cat that got the cream.'

Jake sat down. His gaze flickered from Louisa to Evie and back again.

Louisa grinned. 'I've found the perfect solution for you, little brother.'

'I didn't realise I was a problem that needed solving.'

'You know I'm worried about you being alone at Christmas.'

He rolled his eyes. 'Not this again,' he muttered, picking up his drink.

'Well, Evie would be happy to go with you to France!'

He stilled, glass in hand.

'It's perfect, isn't it?' Louisa went on excitedly. 'You two get on so well, Evie doesn't want to go home . . .'

The silence stretched and both women smiled at him expectantly.

France?

His plans to hide away alone?

Evie?

Jake thumped his glass down. 'Why can't you just respect my wishes, Louisa? Respect my feelings, for that matter! I told you I *want* to be alone.'

Heads turned. Louisa blinked.

Evie reached for her handbag. 'I – I'd better go.'

'No.' He put his hand out. 'Stay. This isn't your fault. It's between me and my interfering sister.'

'Your sister who cares about you,' Louisa bit out quietly. Her eyes gleamed, reflecting the light from the fire, and an arrow of guilt hit him between the ribs.

He made himself take a deep breath. 'You're right. I'm sorry . . . But despite your good intentions, Louisa, you can't barge in and reorganise other people's lives for them. It's not fair. Especially taking advantage of kind-hearted folk, like Evie.'

He didn't need to have been there to imagine how the conversation had gone: his sister would have lost no time in railroading Evie into complying with her plan. And Evie, always eager to help, would immediately have agreed.

'Er, actually,' said Evie, 'I thought it was a great idea.'

'You did?' He remembered their conversation at Luc's and her look of undisguised dread when she'd spoken about spending Christmas with her ex.

She nodded so eagerly that a strand of hair fell loose. She tucked it behind her ear. 'I don't want to spend Christmas by myself.'

'That's what you're planning to do?'

'I can't face seeing Tim.' She looked away.

Ah.

Perhaps Louisa's idea wasn't such a bad one, after all.

Now he felt guilty for reacting so angrily. Evie would leap to the conclusion that he didn't want to spend the holiday with her. Which wasn't true. He enjoyed her company, valued her friendship. But friendship was all it was. All it could be. His mind returned to that kiss. *Pretend it never happened* had been easy to say, but would it be as simple to follow if they were alone together for a week?

He stopped himself. Evie was desperate to escape her family. He wasn't going to stop her coming to France because he lacked self-control. There would be no repeat of that kiss. He had this under control. He did.

'As far as I can see,' said Louisa, 'you're good friends and you both have reasons why you want to get away.'

Evie put her hand on Louisa's arm. 'Louisa, stop. Jake doesn't want me there. He wants to be alone and I get that. I'd drive him mad.'

'Not true. Though I can't guarantee that I wouldn't drive you mad.' He tried to picture the two of them alone in Luc's villa, and found his pulse picked up at the prospect.

'That's okay. I know what you're like – cranky, antisocial, rude . . .'

Her teasing smile set off a ripple of heat. He did his best to ignore it. 'What about your shop? Could you leave it for a week? And so close to Christmas?'

'There's more snow forecast tomorrow so I don't expect to have many customers until the new year.'

He nodded. 'You understand, don't you, that I don't want the rigmarole of meals and gifts and rituals? I want to pretend Christmas isn't happening.'

'I know,' she said softly, and their eyes connected. 'I understand.'

Another thought occurred to him. 'How will your parents take it?'

'Oh, they'll be fine. Going away with a friend is a legitimate excuse for missing Christmas. They'll probably read too much into it and start planning my wedd—' She stopped suddenly, and two red spots coloured her cheeks. 'Of course, we both know it wouldn't mean anything. We're just friends.'

'You can wipe that smirk off your face,' he told his sister. 'We *are* just friends.'

'Of course you are,' said Louisa, though amusement danced in her eyes.

Evie bit her lip. 'But I've just had a thought – how much would it cost? Things have picked up at the Button Hole, but I can't afford to blow all my profits on a holiday.'

'Luc isn't charging me any rent for the villa and, technically, it's a business trip so I'll pay any utility bills. And the flights are really cheap. I had a look this afternoon.'

'So what do you say?' Louisa asked Evie.

Jake realised, to his surprise, that he wanted her to come. And after being so uncouth earlier, he felt he should make amends. 'If you agree to come with me, Evie, my sister will be reassured that I'm not alone, and she might finally get off my back.'

Louisa confirmed this with an eager nod.

Evie beamed. 'You have a deal then, Mr A,' she said, and reached across the table to shake his hand. 'Let's escape Christmas together.'

Chapter Twelve

'What did your parents say?' asked Jake. 'I don't want to be the cause of tension between you.'

Evie laughed. 'Tension? There's nothing but tension between me and my parents. I don't think there'll ever be anything else.' She put the rotary cutter down and shuffled the squares of fabric she'd cut into a neat stack. 'They were fine about it. Relieved, in fact. Apparently this means they can spend Christmas with Tim's parents without worrying about me "sulking".'

She blinked hard. In their eyes Tim would always be perfect husband material and she was a fool for turning him down. What would it take for them to listen to her? To side with her just once?

But all that stuff was exactly what she was hoping to get away from. She loved the idea of escaping Christmas, with all the tension, emotion and memories it brought. A week away in the winter sun with Jake. Her skin tightened. It would be perfect. No complications, no demands. Just friendship and good company. She couldn't wait.

'Who will look after Smoke while you're away?' she asked, picking up the bolt of fabric and crossing the shop to put it back on the shelf.

'Heidi always has him. He loves it there. Actually, I'd better go – I said I'd drop him this afternoon.'

'I can't believe we're leaving tomorrow!' Evie had to stop herself bouncing on the spot. 'I'm so excited! I love a bit of last-minute spontaneity.'

Jake's lip twitched. 'You did check your passport is still valid, didn't you?'

She sighed. 'You just love being a kill-joy, don't you? Yes, it's valid.'

'Good. Well, I'll pick you up tomorrow – early.' He glanced out of the window. 'Provided this snow doesn't get any deeper and hamper our journey.'

'I'm sure it won't.'

He went to leave, then stopped. 'Thanks, by the way.'

'What for?'

His blue eyes fixed on her. 'For agreeing to come.'

'I'm seeing this trip as a Get Out of Jail Free card. It's got me off the hook.'

'Well, I appreciate it. My sister went home much happier.'

She tilted her head. 'You're lucky – she cares about you.'

'I know.' He weighed the car keys in his hand. 'I know.'

They arrived in Nice the next morning. With only two days left until Christmas, the airport was bustling, but a gentleman in a smart suit was waiting serenely to greet them. In his hand a set of keys jingled as he led them to the other side of the car park.

Evie's eyes widened as they stopped beside a small open-topped car parked away from the rest. It was cherry red and vintage. 'Is that the car you've hired?'

Jake nodded. 'A 1960s Alfa Romeo Giulia Spider,' he said reverently.

She knew he loved classic cars, but it hadn't occurred to her that he'd hire one abroad.

'You want to look at her first?' asked the gentleman in accented English.

Evie stood back as Jake walked around the car, pausing to examine the paintwork and inspect the tyres. Sunlight bounced off the silver bumper and headlights. The car was beautiful in its simplicity, but she hoped the boot would be big enough for all their luggage. She hadn't travelled light. She'd filled half a case with a quilt she was working on.

When Jake straightened up, his blue eyes gleamed like jewels in the sun and she felt a little wobbly to see his usual scowl replaced with such delight.

Once he'd signed the papers and they were alone, he asked, 'So what do you think?'

Evie looked at the dashboard, with its retro dials and the comically simple gearstick by her knees. 'It's quirky, but wouldn't a modern car be more reliable?'

'Probably,' he conceded, 'but it wouldn't be beautiful or steeped in history.' He smoothed his hands over the slim steering wheel. 'This is a design classic, perfect for the area. If you could go back in time you'd see dozens of these driving around the French Riviera. Ready to go?'

'Aren't you going to put the roof up? It's not that warm.'

'I can, if you want, but I like to feel the wind on my face. It's more . . . authentic.'

'I see. Well, if we're going to be authentic . . .' Evie slipped on her sunglasses and grinned. 'I feel like Brigitte Bardot.'

She couldn't believe how sunny it was, the air fresh with the scent of pine. This was so glamorous and exciting, a world away from what she'd thought she'd be doing today. Her parents were probably packing to go to Rupert and Angela's tomorrow. She could picture exactly what would happen when they arrived: there would be sherry before dinner, then a long-drawn-out meal in Rupert and Angela's splendid dining room. And Tim.

She inhaled deeply, so glad that Jake had thought of coming here.

He started the engine. 'Right. Let's go, then.'

'Not far now,' said Jake. 'The turning is somewhere on the left. Ah – there it is!'

They turned off the road at two slightly shabby-looking iron gates, then wound up a snaking drive through forest. The villa finally came into view.

'Luc said it was a wreck when he bought it,' said Jake. 'He completely rebuilt the frontage.'

It was luxurious but not extravagant, a simple architectural design with Italianate touches, such as tall, arched windows and a voluptuous balustrade along the front.

Evie's eyes widened. 'He did a great job. It's beautiful.'

They parked in the shade of an umbrella pine and

she raced up the stone steps to check out the huge terrace.

'Wow! Look at that view!' she said, gripping the balustrade. 'I can't believe we can see the sea!'

Her excitement sparked a little thrill of pleasure in him. 'We're very high up here on the hillside.' Though they were a good way inland.

He strolled around the side of the villa and looked out at the olive trees, pines and shrubs that stretched away into the forest behind. He hoped he'd done the right thing coming here, and that the memories didn't follow, snapping at his heels as they so often did. He just wanted respite from it all. This trip had been spur-of-the-moment, but now it was reality he wondered. Had he thought it through properly? Had Evie? Would she really be happy hiding away from the world – with him?

He heard light footsteps approaching and she appeared around the corner. Her apple scent invaded his senses as she joined him, and he tensed. Throughout the journey here he'd been troubled by the way he responded to her, the flickering of desire. Would being here with her bring its own complications?

'There's a village about ten minutes' walk away with a bakery, a restaurant and a bar,' he said, as she joined him. 'Other than that, this place is pretty secluded so we're guaranteed complete privacy.'

'Is that your only goal in life?' she teased. 'To avoid human interaction?'

'We've come here to get away from it all. Not to spend time with strangers.'

'Well, it's perfect. I love it!' She spun on her heel, closing her eyes and savouring the sun's heat on her face.

He watched her with amusement and felt a tightening in his stomach. The sound of leaves rustling carried on the breeze like music.

They were friends, nothing more. Granted, that kiss had left him with a residual awareness of her, but he had enough self-restraint to deal with that. She wouldn't notice a thing. They would simply be two friends escaping their families and enjoying a break in the South of France. What could be more straightforward?

'Want to choose your bedroom?' he asked.

'I get first pick? Yes, definitely!'

He lifted their cases out of the car and she followed him into the enormous house. Upstairs there were several bedrooms, and she went wide-eyed from one to the next.

'They're all so gorgeous and elegant – it's impossible to choose!' She lifted a finger to her chin as she weighed up her decision. 'I'll have that one,' she said in the end, 'because it has the most beautiful bedcover.'

'Does it?' He looked again at the faded red and ivory patterned fabric. Granted, it did have a faintly regal air, or perhaps that was simply down to the size of the enormous bed.

'Yes! That's a Toile de Jouy. It's gorgeous!'

Evie crossed the large, airy room and flung open the French windows, which gave onto a small private balcony. 'Look at that view! I'll be able to see the sea from my bed when I wake up!'

The corner of his lip curved. 'Calm down, Pollyanna,'

he said. 'I'm worried this trip is provoking too much excitement in you. You're like that orphan girl when she goes home with the millionaire.'

She grinned and took the cue to launch into her favourite song from *Annie*.

Jake rolled his eyes. 'I'll be next door,' he said, and disappeared with his case.

'How about we drive to the next town and visit the market?' Jake suggested, when they'd unpacked. 'If we're quick, we'll catch the tail end of it and we can stock up on food. I've booked the restaurant for this evening but tomorrow is Christmas Eve and everywhere will be shut around here.'

'Sounds good.'

They drove for twenty minutes and parked in the street, like everyone else. Their car attracted curious looks and animated discussion among the men sitting outside the *tabac* opposite, but Jake didn't stop to chat. Instead, he led her directly to the market.

It was a riot of colour and vibrant noise. The stallholders all shouted to each other and chatted happily to their customers, who were filling baskets with fruit and vegetables, meat and fish. Evie was so busy taking it all in that she tripped on somebody's trolley. Jake caught her. 'You okay?' he asked.

'Fine,' she said, blushing furiously as she straightened her sunglasses. Forget Brigitte Bardot – she was very much still clumsy Evie Miller.

'What do you think?' he asked, steering her out of the way of an oncoming pushchair.

'It beats queuing in the supermarket back home! It's wonderful. And there's so much here, too!' Not just food, but also fresh flowers, straw bags, leather goods, jewellery, clothes – the list was never-ending and there was a surprise around every corner. 'Look – there's some Provençal fabric! I've heard about it but never seen it in real life.'

She stopped to examine the huge rolls of vibrant cotton material. They were so unusual, and the colours so intense: deep red, rich ochre, and a blue as inky as the Mediterranean sky. She smoothed her fingers over the napkins and tablecloths that had been sewn from them. These fabrics would be perfect for quilting, and they'd add a truly unique touch her customers would love.

But she'd only just got her finances under control: she couldn't justify spending heaps of money on a whim. Reluctantly, she pulled her hand away.

'How about we buy a chicken to roast?' suggested Jake, when they strolled past the meat stall.

'Great idea,' said Evie. Anyone listening to them could be forgiven for thinking they were a married couple. The thought sent a little vibration buzzing through her, but she brushed it aside.

'I know a recipe for a vegetable bake that would go nicely with it,' said Jake, as they left the stall. 'They call it a *tian* around here. It's very simple to make.'

Evie nodded and made a few suggestions of her own for easy meals they could put together over the next few days. Glancing at the Christmas tree in the village square, she wondered if Jake would buy something special to eat on Christmas Day, but he didn't mention it so she kept quiet. The whole point of coming here was to get away from the festivities. There was no pressure whatsoever to cook a special meal or decorate a tree or follow any of the other seasonal customs, and that was liberating.

When they'd finished at the market, Jake gave her a quick tour of the town before they stopped for a snack in one of the cafés that lined the main road. 'So where are we going tonight?' asked Evie.

'It's called Le Rouge Gorge. It's a tiny place but the food is remarkable. The chef is a French *grandmère* who loves cooking. The story is that when her four children grew up and left home, she hated cooking only for herself, so she opened a restaurant.'

'Sounds fantastic.'

'It is.' He glanced at her jeans and rainbow-striped sweater. 'Did you bring something smart? The locals tend to dress up for it.'

'Ready?'

Evie pulled at the neckline of her dress, glancing nervously at her reflection in the mirror. 'Yes,' she said hesitantly.

Natasha had warned her that the temperature dropped quite low in the evening, so she'd brought a cream knitted dress, which she'd made and embellished with red and orange beads. She loved the long chunky sleeves and the A-line shape, which nipped in at the waist, but was it too revealing?

'Stop fussing,' said Jake, who was waiting by the door, car keys in his hand. 'You look lovely.'

Her head jerked up, eyes wide.

'Why the astonished look?'

'I – I don't know. I thought – is it a bit tight? I must have put on weight . . .'

'Forget what your ex told you! None of it was true. You're a beautiful woman, Evie Miller, and you look great in that dress. Feminine, shapely . . .' He swept his gaze over her and seemed to struggle to find the words. 'You look beautiful,' he said finally.

'Thanks.' Her cheeks seared with heat. 'If you didn't look so angry, I'd think you were paying me a compliment.'

'I'm angry that that idiot ex of yours is still influencing you, eating away at your confidence. You have a figure other women would envy, and those colours suit you.'

'Thank you,' she said quietly.

Beautiful, feminine, shapely. Wow. She felt herself grow a little taller at this vote of confidence. And he was right. She shouldn't care about Tim's opinion.

'You look good yourself.' She smiled, with a nod to Jake's smart but sombre jacket and trousers. Although she wished he would sometimes wear something other than black, navy and grey.

They arrived at the restaurant, which looked tiny and unassuming from the outside, but as the waiter led them to their table Evie realised the interior was bigger than it appeared, with lots of alcoves and rooms that led to others. She sat down opposite Jake and tried to concentrate on reading the menu, but his words had unsettled her. He was making her feel things she shouldn't. Making her tingle inside, her blood quicken, sending heat coiling through her body.

But she mustn't let it go to her head. The compliment may have meant a lot to her, but for him it had been an inconsequential remark.

They ordered, and Evie tucked in to her starter of homemade terrine and crispy thin toast. The food was delicious, and she loved the rustic decorations of pottery, woven straw and wicker that hung from the exposed beams. The restaurant had a timeless charm with a great atmosphere.

'Do you like the food?' asked Jake, and sipped his water.

'I love it.' She beamed. 'You?'

He'd chosen fish for his starter. 'Very good,' he said.

She glanced around at the other diners. Mostly family groups, they were all engaged in loud and lively discussions. Jake, however, was quiet and concentrating on his food, his expression grave. Evie smiled. She found it endearing that he looked so serious so much of the time. Only when she teased him did his eyes crease a little and a glimmer of humour dance in their ocean-blue depths. She wondered what he was thinking about. She had a suspicion that she knew, and his enigmatic silence made her curious. She burned to know more about the woman who should have been here with him now.

She cleared her throat and tried to sound as casual as possible. 'Did you come here with Maria?'

He looked up. 'No.' His brow pulled into a sharp frown, and she felt a flicker of fear that perhaps she had crossed a line into forbidden territory. 'Why would you think that?'

'You seem to know the area well, that's all – where to shop, where to eat . . .'

His expression relaxed a little. 'I've spent a lot of time here since I set up my company.'

'I see.' She laid her knife and fork down across her empty plate and waited, thinking he might divulge a bit more, but he remained silent.

He might have told Evie she looked beautiful tonight, but his wife had been stunning. She pictured the other woman sitting here opposite him in a slim-fitting dress, with her smooth dark hair sliding down her back. Evie glanced down at her side plait, suddenly regretting not having spent more time on her own hair. It was messily casual and, as always, strands had worked themselves loose all over the place.

'Did you travel much before that?' she asked.

He finished eating and sat back. 'Mostly to Italy. Maria had Italian heritage and she loved it there.'

'Italian heritage?' Well, that explained her dark-haired beauty and sophistication.

He nodded. 'Her grandfather was Italian. I never met him, but she had visited often as a child and, of course, she spoke Italian fluently.'

'Of course,' murmured Evie, feeling herself shrink with each crumb of information he revealed about her.

Jake looked away, his jaw set. She should stop asking questions, but she couldn't stop herself. It was stronger than her, the need to know more about the woman who had captured his heart.

'Are you still in touch with her family?'

'No,' he said tersely. 'It was easier for me to cut all ties. Since we didn't have children . . .'

He didn't finish the sentence. His chin lifted, and he looked haughty, unapproachable. But she knew this was simply the armour of a wounded man.

She let the subject drop, and as the waiter cleared their plates, she thought of how Louisa was counting on her to watch out for him. They hadn't come here to dwell on the past or reopen old wounds. She was determined to erase his frown, and what she wanted more than anything was to see him smile. From now on, she resolved, she would quash her curiosity and be careful to avoid any mention of Maria.

'What would you like to do tomorrow?' he asked.

Evie considered this. 'I'd love to visit the area. Maybe we could go for a drive.'

'A drive?'

'You have a beautiful car. Why not make the most of it? With the sun on your face and the wind in your hair, it's exhilarating! Don't you think?'

His lips curved. 'Yes. Yes, I do.'

When they got back to the villa, Evie lit the log fire while Jake made hot drinks.

'Considering how accident-prone you are, you're a dab hand with matches and a wood fire,' he said, as he handed her a wide, bowl-shaped cup.

'I have one at home. There's nothing cosier, don't you think?' She'd left just one light on, so the flames cast an orange and gold glow over the whole room. It was cosy and warm, and she curled up on the sofa, cradling her hot chocolate.

'You've never had to call on George next door to put out the flames?'

'Never!' she said indignantly.

'I don't believe you.'

She threw a cushion at him. 'I haven't!'

There was a pause. 'Although I did once have to use the fire extinguisher . . .'

'Knew it.' His eyes creased, and she felt a pool of heat in her centre.

This was what she loved about Jake Hartwood. The flashes of humour, of teasing warmth. She didn't want to see him buttoned-up and bleak-eyed any more.

Her hands were itching to be kept busy, so she opened her sewing bag. She was making a lap quilt for her first online customer.

'This is supposed to be a holiday, remember? Don't you want to use the time to relax rather than working on your patchwork?' asked Jake.

She smiled. 'It's not patchwork, it's a wholecloth. The quilt top is made from a single piece of fabric, see?' Her stitches would form the pattern in the plain cream sateen fabric. 'And it's really relaxing. I've always done it, since I was nine or ten.' There was nothing more soothing than having a warm quilt on her lap and the rhythmic motion of pulling the needle through, a few stitches at a time.

'Nine or ten? That's young. Who taught you?' Jake sipped his coffee.

'A teacher at school. Miss Shaw. She showed us how

to stitch hexagon pieces together to make a pincushion and I was hooked straight away. I used to spend my evenings sewing while all the other girls were reading.'

'You went to boarding school?'

She nodded. 'All my family did. Eventually Miss Shaw taught me how to make other things, which was a relief because there are only so many pincushions a girl can use.'

She could feel Jake watching as she threaded her needle and began to stitch again.

'Did you do a course? Do you have qualifications?'

'I did one in my own time when I worked in London . . .' she gave him a mischievous smile '. . . in secret. I told Tim I was going to Zumba classes.' She pushed the tiny needle up and down through the layers of fabric and wadding, careful to keep her stitches small and even.

'Why didn't you tell him the truth?'

'Because he would have disapproved. He thought my sewing was a silly hobby. He told me my quilts were old-fashioned, that I had the same interests as an eighty-year-old granny. I used to sew in secret and hide it all away before he came home. Luckily he often worked late.'

Jake's eyes became shards of flint. 'What did you ever see in him?'

She laughed. 'I often ask myself the same question. He wasn't like that in the beginning. He changed over time – or maybe he revealed his true colours. Anyway, my parents thought sewing was old-fashioned too. I know it's an unusual hobby, these days.'

'I'd say that in your case it's more than just a hobby – it's a passion, a rare skill.'

His words reminded her of the first time someone had said that to her. 'When I did my City and Guilds someone asked me why I wasn't making a living from it and that got me thinking of opening a shop. It became my dream.'

'But let me guess, you didn't find the courage to realise that dream until your life hit rock bottom?'

'How did you know?' She looked up, horrified that he could read her so accurately. After she'd left Tim and London, she'd been jobless and alone. Yet this was when the seed of the idea had begun to take root. Without her ex's undermining criticism, she'd begun to dream. And she'd realised she was free to do as she wished. She had money her gran had left her and, with a loan to supplement it, she had the means to buy stock and open a shop.

'Educated guess. Your optimism is exemplary, Pollyanna, but your nearest and dearest have seriously eroded your self-esteem.'

'You're wrong. It's just hard to follow the high standard that my sister set. I'll never be as clever or as successful as Zara was. And I never choose the conventional route . . . the path my parents would like me to follow.'

'You're a different person, Evie. Your parents should value you for who you are, instead of always comparing you to your sister. Do they appreciate how talented you are?'

She bit her lip, not wanting to admit the truth. They had never looked at her needlework with anything but a fleeting, derisory glance. They would have preferred her to come home with brilliant academic results, a high-status job title and a fat salary to match. The only time they'd looked at her with pride had been when they'd seen the glittering engagement ring Tim had put on her finger. They hadn't noticed how uncertain she'd felt, even then, that she'd done the right thing.

'My point exactly,' said Jake, and put his cup down.

She shook her head. 'You never knew Zara,' she said quietly. 'If you had, you'd understand. She was so much cleverer, taller, prettier, more interesting than me. She was . . . perfect.'

His sharp gaze was pinned on her, studying her, scrutinising. 'No one is perfect. Can't you see, Evie, how we're all different? The world is populated by individuals. Some of them are businessmen or -women, others are nurses, sailors, teachers, racing drivers . . . The list goes on.'

'But they're all successful,' she said, with a rueful smile. 'They don't have a huge loan and a shop which is losing money.' She looked down at the sewing in her lap.

'My point is we all have different skills. We're all good at different things, but you don't seem to value your own talents as much as you should.'

Her cheeks flushed again, just as they had earlier when he'd told her she looked beautiful. 'Two compliments in one evening. Anyone would think you were thawing, Mr Arctic.' She tried to make light of his praise but she was glowing inside.

And perhaps he had a point. Perhaps it was time she stopped measuring herself against her parents' idea of success and accepted that she was different from Zara.

They sat up chatting until the early hours. Eventually, tiredness overcame her and Evie yawned.

'How about we go to bed?' he said, and his velvety voice reached across the dimly lit room to her.

Evie felt the tiniest shiver at his suggestive words. However, he didn't seem to notice and carried their empty cups through to the kitchen.

He had meant it innocently, Evie berated herself, as she folded her sewing away and followed him upstairs. She had to stop the sparks of lust she felt whenever he was around. They were just friends.

Outside her room he paused. 'Night, Pollyanna,' he said softly.

Evie smiled. 'Goodnight, Mr Arctic.'

He hesitated for a flicker of a moment, then bent his head and dropped a brief kiss on her cheek. Her skin tingled at the contact and she remembered the closeness they'd shared, the intimacy, when he'd kissed her.

Then he walked away, closed his door, and her stomach sank.

Why was she disappointed? She pulled shut the door of her own room. Wasn't the memory of how he'd instantly regretted that kiss still vivid enough? She bit her lip as she undressed and slipped into bed. Whatever physical attraction she felt for him, she had to ignore it because he didn't share it at all.

Chapter Thirteen

The car raced round the bends in the hillside, clinging beautifully to the road, the speed and the wind making the blood in his veins pump faster. The classic car handled every bit as well as Jake had hoped, and beside him Evie giggled with delight as they headed home to the villa. He hadn't felt this lightness in his chest, this buzz, for months. Years, even.

Perhaps it was because he'd slept so soundly last night, or because they'd spent a relaxed afternoon exploring an ancient hilltop village in the winter sun. Or perhaps it was down to Evie – her enthusiasm and sunny disposition were infectious.

'I can't believe how beautiful this place is!' she said. 'Or how quiet the roads have been!'

'It's Christmas Eve,' he reminded her. 'The celebrations here begin tonight.'

Families would be coming together, preparing gifts and food for this evening's festivities. But he and Evie weren't constrained by any of that. They were free to do as they pleased, to go wherever they wanted whenever they liked. And that was what was so liberating about this trip.

When they got back to the villa, Evie brought her laptop

down to the kitchen to check her emails. 'Sorry to be a bore,' she said, throwing him a sheepish look, 'but I've had lots of enquiries from the online craft site I joined. It's really time-consuming to answer questions and give quotes, but I feel I ought to reply promptly or customers might go elsewhere.'

'Absolutely. And it's not a problem.' He got out his tablet and skimmed through the news.

But Evie's gasp made him look up, and she squealed with delight.

'What is it?' he asked.

Her dimples winked and her eyes shone. 'Look!' She angled the laptop so he could see the screen. 'Each of those there is a commission for a quilt!'

He counted seven. 'You sound surprised.'

'I *am* surprised. I didn't think so many would translate into sales! They must like my work!'

'Of course they do.'

'And they're willing to pay a lot of money for them to be bespoke.'

He nodded. 'People value custom-made quality items. Why wouldn't they pay a lot for your work?'

'I've only sold one quilt in my shop. I thought people didn't like them,' she admitted.

He pressed his lips flat because he had witnessed her father telling her just that. Couldn't she see how distorted her parents' view of the world was, and how unfair their criticisms of her were? Was he the only one to appreciate her bright optimism? Her generosity? Her determination and dedication?

'But this is so exciting!' She grinned.

'Will you be able to keep up with the demand?'

She nodded. 'I've already found an assistant to help me in the shop, and when she starts, I'll be able to dedicate as much time as I like to making quilts. This is a dream come true!'

His lips curved and he got up. 'Shall I make dinner?'

'Yes, I'm starving,' she said, and snapped her laptop shut. 'I'll help you. We can make it together.'

They worked side by side. Evie sliced the tomatoes, courgettes and aubergine for the *tian*, and he put the chicken in to roast and prepared an onion soup. As she worked, she hummed and sang.

'What's that song you're singing?'

She looked surprised that he didn't know. '"Somewhere". From *West Side Story*.'

'What is it with you and musicals? Is that all you ever sing?'

'Mostly, yes,' she said, lifting her chin. 'I love them.'

Her defiant tone amused him. He stirred the onions, careful to keep the heat low so they'd retain their sweetness.

'I suppose you don't like them, Mr A?' Her dimples flashed as she threw him a taunting smile.

'Actually, I did – I do.' He didn't tell her that he hadn't listened to music for two years because it seemed to bypass his brain and trigger visceral reactions in him. Uncontrollable emotions, which he preferred to avoid.

Yet Evie's cheerful singing didn't bother him. In fact, he

found it quite charming – even when she didn't quite hit the high notes.

She stared at him. 'Really? Which is your favourite?'

'*Les Misérables*.' He smiled wryly and pushed the glistening slices of onion around the pan.

'How apt.'

He lifted a brow. 'What's that supposed to mean?'

'Nothing.' She giggled, and gave him a kittenish look that made his blood heat.

She innocently ran her tongue over her lips and fire shot through him. He had to make himself exhale. He tried to resist, but it sucked him under, this pull, this need to get close to her. He left the pan and stalked towards her. She giggled and danced away from him, but he caught her by the waist. She shrieked and squirmed to get away, but he held her fast.

'What were you implying about me?'

'Nothing,' she repeated. Then squealed as he tickled her waist.

His pulse rocketed as she laughed and twisted and tried to tickle him back, though not with much success.

'Okay, okay!' she cried, laughing.

He released her and she brushed the hair back from her eyes and smoothed down her crumpled top. They were both breathless. His pulse spiked and he watched her, enchanted by the blush in her cheeks and her dimpled smile. He couldn't tear his gaze away. She was so good-natured, she radiated fun and *joie de vivre*, and this was her special brand of beauty.

She looked up and her eyes widened as his gaze connected with hers. For a heartbeat – or an eternity, he couldn't tell – their eyes remained locked.

Until a nasty hissing sound made them turn.

'The onions!' she said. 'They're burning.'

He cursed, rushed back to the pan and swiped it off the heat. An acrid smell rose into the air, and he tipped the charred remains into the bin.

'Sorry,' he told her. 'Soup's off the menu, after all.'

Her smile was ever so slightly bashful, her cheeks spotted red, like the tomatoes she had gone back to slicing. 'Never mind. We've already got a feast with all this, haven't we?'

He turned away, perplexed by what had just happened. His fingers reached for the ring on the chain around his neck. This, he thought, was exactly what he'd felt the night of the ball: the lick of desire, the uncontrollable urge to pull her close. It hadn't faded. If anything, it was growing stronger the more time they spent together, making his muscles coil tight whenever she was near. And interwoven with this attraction was the sharp sting of guilt. He didn't want to betray Maria's memory, yet his body had other ideas. His awareness of Evie stubbornly refused to fade. When she was in the same room, he found himself watching her, enthralled by her infectious laughter, intrigued by her fragile self-confidence, thrilled by her mischievous smile. When he'd kissed her outside her bedroom door last night, it had taken all his self-control to walk away.

Evie Miller had got under his skin.

He took a deep breath. So, what was he going to do about it?

Jake sat up in bed, shocked at how late it was. He'd slept ten hours straight through. It was unheard of. For years his nights had been broken, haunted by memories and by his own personal demons.

He got up and pushed open the shutters. Christmas Day. The sky was smudged grey, and he could see swollen clouds billowing in off the sea. Never mind. He wondered if Evie was up yet, and the prospect of her breezy smile lightened his step as he padded down the stairs.

'Whoa!' he cried, shielding his eyes as he entered the kitchen.

Evie was sitting at the table with her laptop open. She looked from him to her outfit and her brow creased. 'Is it too bright?' she asked.

Her dress was vibrant pink, as bright as a highlighter pen, and over it she wore a jungle green cardigan with a scarf around her neck, which featured – he peeped through the slits in his fingers to see – pink and green parrots.

He couldn't prevent himself from smiling. 'It'll be all right,' he said, 'once I find my sunglasses.'

She stuck her tongue out at him, and he flicked the coffee machine on.

'How long have you been up?' he asked.

'Hours! Unlike you, lazybones. I've got tons of work

done.' She beamed and sat back in her chair, looking very pleased with herself. Her hair was in two loose pigtails, playful and girlish. Sexy, too, if he was honest.

'Oh, yeah?'

'Yes. I worked out a few quotes and did some quilting.' She glanced towards the lounge where she'd left the quilt laid out across an armchair, her pincushion and threads scattered across the coffee-table. 'I'm making really good progress on that wholecloth.'

He sat down with a plate of bread and jam, then took a hungry bite. 'How about we go to the beach today?'

'For a swim?' She tugged her cardigan tighter. 'Won't it be too cold?'

He laughed. 'If you're feeling brave I won't stop you, but I was thinking of a walk. With any luck it'll be quiet.'

He drove to one of the smaller coves on the coast, which, at the height of summer, would be heaving with noisy tourists. Today, however, the crescent of sand was empty, and the only sounds were of water lapping against the shore and the wind shaking the tops of the pines. He got out of the car and looked up at the sky. It was less threatening now, but still dreary. He patted the roof of the convertible, wondering how waterproof it was.

'Look away,' said Evie, as she unzipped her long boots and reached under her skirt.

He did as he was told but asked warily, 'What are you doing?'

'Okay, you can look now.'

She was bare-legged in the sandy car park and tucked her discarded tights into one of her boots. 'We have to walk barefoot.'

'Why? Do I need to remind you that it's winter?'

'Because there's nothing like the feel of sand beneath your toes.'

He frowned and looked down at his comfortable and warm canvas shoes.

'Come on,' she goaded. 'You know you want to.'

The memory flashed up of how delighted she'd looked when he'd joined in with the dancing at the ball and, with a shrug, he bent and untied his laces.

They walked side by side in companionable silence. And it turned out Evie was right about going barefoot. There was something sensual about feeling the rough grains beneath his soles, the yielding of the sand as his feet sank into it, the lick of cold as the waves tickled his toes. He had the sensation of something long since dormant slowly wakening.

'How far away is Luc's vineyard?' she said. 'Should we arrange to meet up?'

'They live a couple of hours west, towards Aix. And Luc promised not to disturb me so I feel I ought to return the favour. He values time with his family and I don't want to encroach on that.'

'Fair enough. He and Natasha are so happy together,' she said, with a dreamy smile. 'They really have the fairy-tale romance.'

He steered her around a large stone before she could trip on it. 'There's no such thing as a fairy tale.'

She hesitated a moment, before saying quietly, 'You had it with Maria.'

The crunch of pain was inevitable. He saw the hospital room where she'd withered away, and a vice clamped itself around his chest. 'And look how that ended,' he said bitterly.

Evie's mouth snapped shut, and she fixed her gaze on the rocks ahead. She looked like a child who'd just been told Santa didn't exist.

The only sound now was the whisper of waves and the ringing of regret in his ears. Well done, Hartwood, for that nice bit of cynicism. Perfect for bringing the mood down.

There had been a time when he hadn't given a jot what others thought of him or his outlook, yet as they reached the end of the beach and turned back, he found himself wishing he could swallow his words – because he didn't want to be the one who had wiped the smile from Evie's face.

But, then, he hadn't counted on how fast she was able to spring back, as chirpy and buoyant as ever.

She peered up at him with a cheeky gleam in her eye. 'See that tree over there?'

He followed where she pointed and nodded. But it was a ploy to distract him.

She gave him one hard shove and he landed in the water on his backside. 'What the—?'

'Last one there has to cook supper tonight!' She raced off, laughing.

He chuckled. 'Just you wait, Evie Miller! Just you wait until I catch up with you!'

'It's been like having our own private beach,' said Evie, as they headed back slowly towards the car. 'I can't believe how lucky we are.'

He looked up at the ash-grey blanket of cloud. 'The weather could be better.'

'It's dry and warm.' She hugged herself and threw him a lopsided smile, 'Well, warmish. You're not too cold, are you?'

'I suspect I have hypothermia, thanks to your prank.' His trousers were wet through, but fortunately he'd brought a towel, which would protect the car seat.

She giggled. 'I'm so glad we did this. I can't tell you how much I was dreading the holidays. It's wonderful to be here, and to be free. This is the best Christmas.'

She was right. This was what he'd wanted, wasn't it? To forget Christmas, forget the past and numb the pain? And it was working. He was enjoying himself, enjoying Evie's company. The tension had seeped from his body and his shoulders felt relaxed. It was working better than expected, and he felt a prickle of guilt. Did the easing of the pain mean he was betraying Maria in yet another way?

Evie tipped her head back, enjoying the fresh breeze on her face. He smiled. She was colourful through and through, in her smile, her optimism, her brightness. She opened her eyes and saw him watching her.

'What?' she asked.

'Nothing.' He grinned. Then muttered, 'Pollyanna.'

'Wait a minute!' She peered at his face more closely, then reached for his chin and turned his head towards her.

'What are you doing?' He did his best to ignore the tingling where her fingers touched his skin.

'No – don't stop!' she cried.

'Don't stop what?'

She let go of his chin and placed her hands on her hips, grinning. 'That's the first time I've seen you smile properly, so it reaches your eyes,' she said quietly. 'It suits you, Mr A. You're almost good-looking.'

He loved the mischievous glint in her eyes and his mouth curved again. 'Almost? Damned with faint praise.'

Her gaze dipped to his lips, but this time something changed. It turned smoky. Time slowed. He swallowed, fighting back the rush of heat, the tightening of his muscles.

Then an icy wave washed over their feet, dispelling the heat.

'Okay, you're extremely good-looking when you smile,' she said. 'You should do it more often.'

They'd had such a good day, and Evie couldn't believe how relaxed Jake was. The shadows had gone from beneath his eyes, the lines of tension in his brow had smoothed, and his skin was taking on a faint bronze tint. Perhaps this was what he'd needed all along, she ruminated, as she towel-dried her hair: time off work, at the beach, then a swim in the heated pool with a lot of splashing about and laughter back at the villa.

She gave her hair a quick blast with the hairdryer and went downstairs. 'Time for an apéritif,' she said, as she poured them drinks and tried to open a bag of peanuts. It didn't open, so she tugged harder.

'Don't!' Jake stuck his arm out and leaped to his feet to stop her, but he was too late.

The peanuts exploded all over the place.

'Oops.'

'You're supposed to tear the bag open,' he sighed, 'not detonate it.'

She watched him warily as he crouched to pick up the peanuts. But he didn't seem angry. On the contrary, he was shaking his head and smiling, and relief rushed through her. She fetched a brush. They'd have to throw away the peanuts, and that reminded her of the burned onions Jake had tipped into the bin yesterday. She was still confused about what she'd seen in his eyes. His gaze had been intense. Hungry. It had pinned her to the spot and made her heart defy gravity.

Then he'd turned away and she'd wondered if she'd dreamed it.

More likely, she was reading too much into it, seeing what she wanted to see. He'd just been horsing around, having fun. That was all.

When they'd tidied the kitchen, they carried their drinks through into the lounge and sat by the window with its view over the hills and treetops to the Mediterranean beyond. Evie sipped her pastis. She had developed a taste for the anise-flavoured drink, which Natasha had recommended she try.

Jake put down his orange juice and reached beside his chair. He handed her a parcel wrapped in deep blue tissue paper and gold ribbon. 'Happy Christmas,' he said quietly.

Evie blinked. It was soft in her hands. 'What is it?'

'Open it and see.'

She pulled the ribbon loose and the tissue paper rustled as she unfolded it. Inside was a neat bundle of fabric, striped with neat patterns and in shades of paprika, turmeric and cobalt blue. Provençal fabrics.

'Oh, wow! They're gorgeous, thank you! They're just like the ones I saw at the market the other day.'

He nodded. 'They're the very same. I went back while you were in the supermarket.'

'You told me you'd left your car keys behind!'

'I did.' His eyes glittered, like water in sunlight. He handed her a small business card. 'Here's the supplier's name, too – in case you want to order more for your shop.'

She stared at him, blown away by how thoughtful his gift was.

But she didn't have anything for him. 'I, er – I thought we weren't doing Christmas.'

'We're not. I just saw you looking at these at the market and thought you'd like them. It's no big deal.'

But to her it was a big deal. Evie swallowed and got up. 'I just need to finish yours. I'll be back in a little while.'

She galloped up the stairs. In her room, she shut the

door, leaned against it, and took a deep breath. Think, Evie, think!

She yanked open her sewing bag and rummaged through, pulling out scissors and cotton reels and all the odd scraps of fabric from past projects. Thank goodness she wasn't a tidy person, she thought, as she held up one brightly coloured scrap after another. There was even a length of blue satin in here which would do very nicely. She laid them out, played with the order, then threaded her needle purposefully. Without her sewing machine, this was going to have to be the most fast and furious job she'd ever done.

A while later, there was a loud knock at the door.

'Don't come in!' she cried.

'You've been gone nearly an hour. What are you doing?' His deep voice was muffled, but it still sent her blood rushing through her veins. Or perhaps it was adrenalin.

'Just putting the finishing touches to your gift.' She snipped a couple of threads, held her work up to the light, and smiled.

'Evie, I know you didn't get me a gift.'

She folded it and slipped it into a paper bag bearing the Button Hole's logo. 'How do you know?' she asked, through the closed door.

'By your look of horror when I gave you yours.'

She threw open the door. 'Well, Mr Know-it-all, that's where you're wrong.' She handed him the bag, then stood on tiptoe to kiss his cheek. 'Happy Christmas!'

He opened it and unfolded it in his hands. 'A patchwork scarf?'

She beamed. 'Do you like it?'

'It's – er – very unusual . . .' his forehead creased, as he searched for the right words '. . . and – er – colourful.'

It stood out against his navy sweater and black jeans like a flashing neon sign in a dark alley. Her smile faded. 'You don't like it. It's too bright, isn't it? Too different.' It wasn't his style at all. What had she been thinking?

'Not at all,' he said gravely. Earnestly. He looked her directly in the eye. 'Actually, I love it. It's like you.'

'What do you mean?'

'Unique. I've never met a woman like you before.'

Her heart sank. 'Yes, well . . . people have been telling me that all my life.'

'Why the frown? It was a compliment.'

She looked up in surprise and the warmth in his eyes made her tingle.

'You're creative and resourceful, you don't follow the crowd, you think outside the box. I admire that.' The satin stripes shimmered as he ran the scarf through his fingers.

Her chest swelled and she glowed with pride. Being around Jake Hartwood was turning out to be a real confidence-booster. She loved the way he paid her compliments in that matter-of-fact tone, she loved the way he made her feel ten foot tall. *Unique.* He didn't seem to mind that she was clumsy. In fact, it seemed to amuse him. He didn't share Tim's view that she was overweight, and although they'd spent the last three days together, he seemed to enjoy her company rather than regarding her as an irritation.

They'd had a lot of fun together, she thought, recalling

how they'd splashed around in the pool earlier. With him she didn't feel like she was a disappointment or an embarrassment. Her pulse fluttered. She could be herself and it was okay.

Jake held up the scarf. 'I mean, how many women could have improvised a gift like that? With anyone else, I might, at a push, have received a box of chocolates.'

'Damn!' She slapped her thigh and grinned. 'I didn't think of that.'

Chapter Fourteen

'Hey, nice jacket!' said Evie, when Jake appeared. He was wearing the scarf she'd given him, too, she noticed, with a little flip of delight.

She stepped forward to run her palm over the pale mint jacket. It was soft to the touch, quality linen, and it looked fantastic with those cream chinos. It brought out his blue eyes. 'That colour really suits you,' she said admiringly. Though she suspected any colour would suit him. His usual choices of black, grey and navy were so draining.

'Thanks,' he said.

'So what's with the new look?'

'It's not new. I just hadn't worn this jacket for a while.' He swiftly changed the subject. 'You ready to go?'

'Wait a minute . . .' She riffled in her bag and pulled out her sunglasses. 'I am now!'

An hour later they arrived at the Château Blanc vineyard. The owner, François Laurent, came out to greet them. He looked very French, Evie thought, with dark hair and black-coffee eyes that gleamed when he smiled at her and made her blush. He was extremely good-looking, and she couldn't say she minded when he vigorously shook her hand and told her she was glamorous.

She noticed Jake glance from François to her and back again, frowning.

François gave them a guided tour of the property and the fields behind the château, proudly showing them his vines, although at this time of year they weren't much to look at. Evie could imagine they must look impressive in summer when they were in leaf, the long rows climbing all the way up the hill and stretching into the distance.

Finally, François led them back to the wine cellar, where he opened several bottles for Jake and Evie to sample. Jake seemed more relaxed now they'd got down to business, and he confidently took his time, tilting his glass this way and that to examine the wine, inhaling its aroma, then finally rolling it around on his tongue and spitting into a pewter bowl.

Evie giggled, but the two men ignored her and conferred in ultra-serious voices. She tasted the wine, too, but couldn't bring herself to spit.

'You'll get tipsy,' warned Jake.

'On a mouthful? I don't think so. Besides, it's too delicious to spit out.'

He shrugged and went back to discussing the ageing process with François. Evie began to get a little bored, so when they weren't looking she helped herself to another taste – or two. After the ninth bottle, however, she began to feel a little light-headed.

'This one has a good nose,' said Jake.

He looked so serious that she had to giggle.

'What?' he asked.

'Wine doesn't have a nose!'

The two men looked at each other. But while Jake was clearly unimpressed, François smiled. 'Do you work with Mistère 'Artwood?' he asked.

'Oh, no.' She laughed. 'I know nothing about wine – except how to enjoy it, *bien sûr! Ils sont tous délicieux,*' she added, raising her glass in a mock toast. In truth, the wines had begun to taste the same after the sixth bottle.

François' eyes creased. 'Ah. You speak French?'

'*Oui!*' Evie dug in her mind for a phrase or two. She had once been almost fluent, but that was a long time ago. '*J'ai passé un an à Paris quand j'ai quitté l'école.*'

François raised his arms in delight. '*Elle parle couramment – c'est formidable!*'

'What did you say?' asked Jake. He frowned.

'Just making small-talk.' She was secretly pleased that her French wasn't so rusty after all.

'Why didn't you tell me your girlfriend speaks French?' François asked, with the irritating smile that never seemed to leave his face.

Jake gritted his teeth. 'She's not my girlfriend. And I didn't know—'

But François wasn't listening. He'd launched into another tirade of French directed at Evie, who listened carefully then replied.

Over the last few days he'd heard Evie say a few phrases – asking for a baguette or a glass of wine, that kind of thing – but he'd assumed that was the extent of her vocabulary. Jake didn't speak French, which wasn't a huge problem most of the time since many suppliers spoke enough English to make business possible, but right now it meant he was excluded from whatever the two of them were discussing.

He spat the last of the wine, and picked up the bottle, playing for time as he superficially studied the label. Really, he was keeping an eye on François. He didn't understand what he was saying, but the guy's body language was clear enough as he took Evie by the shoulder and led her through the cellar, pointing to the barrels, leaning close to speak to her, smiling, laughing. Her skirt swished around her knees, and her black tights and flat shoes showed off her legs. And she smiled and laughed with François too. In fact, she looked up at him with rather adoring eyes.

Jake's fingers curled around the stem of his glass. She was tipsy. That was the only reason she was so taken with the man. He might be good-looking, but anyone could see he had an eye for the ladies. He probably thought that if he charmed her, they'd buy a lorryload of his wine. Jake's jaw clenched.

Without warning, François hurried away, waving one hand in the air and saying, 'I come back!' and Jake and Evie found themselves alone in the cellar.

Evie glanced at him, then again, and her smile slipped. 'What's wrong?'

'Nothing. Why?'

'You look angry.'

'Why would I be angry?' He nodded at the door through which François had disappeared. 'Where's he gone, anyway?'

'He said he was going to fetch something.'

'To fetch what?'

'I don't know. He speaks so fast it's hard to follow.'

Jake's eyes narrowed. 'Bet he wants to show you his magnum,' he muttered.

'His what?'

François reappeared holding a huge bottle of red wine. '*Un magnum!*' he announced triumphantly, and presented it to Evie. '*Pour vous, Mademoiselle!*'

'For me?' Evie's eyes widened. Her dimples appeared. 'Oh, but I couldn't! It's enormous!'

Jake rolled his eyes. 'Please. Don't encourage him.'

'What's wrong with you?' asked Evie, as they got into the car.

Jake yanked it into reverse. 'What do you mean?'

François stood by the entrance to his cellars, watching them leave. Evie waved politely, which made Jake scowl all the more as he thrust the car into gear and drove away.

'You've gone all sulky and mean-looking. Even more mean-looking than normal,' she added.

The car made a brief rattling noise, as if it, too, was irritable.

'Thanks,' he said sarcastically.

'It's true! And I have a right to know why.' She sighed. 'Tell me – what have I done?'

He glanced sideways at her, noticing the stiff upward tilt of her chin, as if she were bracing herself. It reminded him of that time in her shop when he'd witnessed her parents laying into her. 'You haven't done anything,' he said finally.

'Then why are you so cross?'

'Because watching François come on to you like a hormonal teenager is not my idea of fun.'

Her cheeks flushed with indignation. 'He didn't come on to me like a—'

'He did. He fancied you.'

'Fancied me?' She laughed. Then hiccuped. 'Oops, that wasn't me – it was the wine!'

'He was like an octopus, putting his arm around you, taking your hand, telling you you're beautiful . . .'

'I'm not complaining. It's quite nice to have the occasional admirer.'

'Even one who's so blatant about it?'

Her cheeks flushed. 'He's French! They're famous for being more forthright than Englishmen. It's a cultural thing.'

'It's a libido thing,' he corrected. 'But he should learn to control his forthrightness if he wants to do business with me.'

'You mean you're not going to buy his wine because he flirted with me?'

'I didn't say that.'

'You implied it.' She laughed, but at the same time reached for her ponytail and wound it rapidly round her finger.

Would he really be so petty as to pass by a business opportunity because the guy had annoyed him? And why had it irritated him so much to see François flirt with her? She was perfectly entitled to flirt with whomever she wanted.

Jake's fingers gripped the steering wheel, his knuckles white.

The car engine made another rattling noise, louder this time.

'What's that?' asked Evie.

He glanced at the bonnet. 'I don't know.'

There was a slight pause before the rattling began again.

'Why are you slowing down?' asked Evie.

'I'm not.' His foot was pressed down flat on the accelerator, but still the car slowed. 'We're losing power.'

He glanced at the hill ahead and muttered a curse. The car coasted to a stop. Jake put the hazard lights on. There was only the dusty road, fields of vineyards and pine forest for as far as he could see.

He tried to restart the engine. Nothing. 'Great,' he muttered. 'That's just what we need – to break down in the middle of nowhere.'

She looked at him cautiously. 'You do have breakdown cover, don't you?'

'I do.'

'Well, isn't there a number you can call?'

He hunted around for the paperwork, but his pockets were empty. 'Damn! I must have left it in my other jacket!'

'Maybe there's something here.' She opened the glovebox but it was empty. 'Have you got the number for the rental company? They'll be able to help.'

Colour streaked his cheekbones. 'All the paperwork is back at the villa,' he confessed.

'Ah.'

He cursed again. 'I'm sorry, Evie. Hiring a classic car was self-indulgent of me.' It had been a selfish whim.

'It's not your fault. And we're not in a rush to get somewhere. Look on the bright side – what a beautiful place to break down! It beats the M4 any day.'

'I'll walk to the nearest place and ask for a car mechanic's number. You can wait here, if you like.'

'Why? I'll come with you.'

He glanced at her shoes. They were flat and delicate, the kind of things ballerinas wore. They didn't look sturdy enough to walk any distance. 'It could be miles to the nearest town.'

'I'll be fine. I like walking. Besides, the sun's shining and it's a lovely day.'

He shook his head. 'Fine. Come on, Pollyanna. Let's head this way,' he said, pointing to the road ahead. 'If my geography's correct, there should be a village soon.'

They walked in silence. He was still ruminating on why François' flirting had enraged him so much. The conclusions he drew were unsettling. Perhaps he should be relieved that the car had broken down: it had cut short a conversation he wasn't ready for.

'This is a much better way to enjoy the scenery, don't you think?' asked Evie, after they'd walked a mile or so.

'Personally, I'd rather enjoy it from the comfort of a moving vehicle.'

'But then it all flashes past so fast you can't appreciate it properly. Listen – can you hear those doves calling?

And that woodpecker? You wouldn't have heard those over the noise of the car engine.'

'True. But I would have felt cooler.' He wiped his forehead. The temperature was supposed to be around eighteen degrees, but it felt much hotter walking in full sun.

Evie smiled. 'You can't complain about the sunshine when that's exactly why we came here – to get away from a cold English Christmas.'

He shrugged. 'I suppose. At least here there isn't a carol singer or a snowman in sight.'

'For now, anyway.' She grinned.

He threw her a flicker of a smile in return.

They crested the hill and rooftops came into view, gradually revealing a huddle of houses ahead.

'Aha,' he said. 'Not far to go now.' Which was a relief because it was getting late in the afternoon and the sun would be going down before they knew it.

When they reached the village, he tried to explain in English that they'd broken down, but the lady at the petrol station didn't understand so Evie stepped forward and translated. Immediately, the lady's face broke into a smile and understanding dawned. She replied in rapid French, picking up the telephone and making a call.

A stream of more French followed, then Evie turned to him. 'A mechanic's on his way,' she translated. 'He's going to tow the car back to his garage. If we leave the keys here, he'll collect it.'

The lady was speaking on the phone again.

'We can go with him,' said Jake. 'In the tow-truck.'

'No need,' smiled Evie. 'She said there's a really nice hotel up the road where we can stay the night. The car probably won't be ready before tomorrow lunchtime at the earliest.'

Jake opened his mouth to speak, but the lady was beckoning them to follow her to the back of the building where a car was parked. She spoke in rapid French again as she opened the door for them. From the driver's seat, the lady added something else. Evie laughed, then translated for his benefit: 'She said no one wants to be stranded without a bed for the night – especially at Christmas.'

Evie stared as they drew up outside a breathtakingly beautiful old château. 'Is this the hotel?' she checked.

The lady from the petrol station assured her it was. They thanked her for the lift and got out of the car. She drove away, and Evie and Jake blinked, wide-eyed, at the spiky turrets and multi-coloured roof tiles that glinted in the sun and made her think of storybook dragons.

Inside, their footsteps echoed in the big entrance hall and, through a stone archway, Evie could see what looked like a reception desk.

'*Ah, vous voilà!*'

They both turned as a woman in her fifties hurried down the stairs, exclaiming, '*Bonjour!*'

She shook their hands, introduced herself as Christine, and told them she'd given them the best room in the place; it had views over the fields and hills behind.

'Just one room?' asked Evie, forgetting to speak French.

'Oh, no, we need two, please. We're not – we're not, em . . .' Her cheeks heated and she glanced at Jake.

Thankfully, Christine nodded. '*J'ai compris. Vous voulez deux chambres. Pas de problème.*'

Christine showed them the dining room and explained that, strictly speaking, the hotel was closed for the holiday. She could cook them a meal tonight, but it would have to be something simple like *steak-frites*. Was that all right?

'Perfect,' said Evie.

Christine led them to the sitting room with a television and shelves lined with old books. 'And after dinner,' she explained, 'feel free to use this room to relax. There's a fire so you won't be cold,' she said, pointing to the pile of logs ready to be lit.

'That's wonderful,' said Evie. 'Thanks.'

'Now I need to take payment for your rooms,' she said.

'Oh – yes.' Evie got out her purse and followed Christine back towards the reception desk. A place as nice as this would be expensive, she was certain, but since Jake had refused to accept any money for the car hire or other costs, this was the least she could do.

'What are you doing?' asked Jake. Their footsteps echoed in the corridor.

'Paying.'

'Put your purse away.'

'Why? I want to pay. You've been so generous.'

'I won't hear of it,' he growled. 'This is all my fault – I chose to hire that car. I will pay.'

She took in his fierce expression and backed down. 'Fine. Have it your way.'

Christine showed them upstairs. The exposed stonework and wooden beams were a reminder of the château's age and history, but they blended beautifully with the cream modern décor and a luxurious bathroom boasting all the mod-cons. Evie had no change of clothes, but Christine had supplied them with all the toiletries they needed and it was nice to have a shower and wash the dust out of her hair before dinner. She left it loose to dry and put her tights and skirt back on, and her peach-coloured sweater.

When it was time for dinner, Jake knocked on her door. He had tucked her scarf into his shirt, like a cravat, and the effect was both quaint and smart.

'Your hair looks nice,' he said, as they made their way down to the dining room. Their footsteps echoed on the empty staircase.

'It's a bit knotted,' she said, running her fingers through it. 'I don't have a hairbrush with me.'

'It suits you like that.'

She glanced at him and noticed a strange look in his eyes that she couldn't decipher. Perhaps she should leave it loose more often. She always tied it back because it got in the way when she was sewing.

The dining room was at the base of one of the large turrets, so it was circular and had been furnished with small tables, all of which were bare except one, where a white tablecloth, cutlery and napkins had been laid out ready for them.

Christine brought them a bottle of wine. 'This is complimentary,' she explained. 'It's a good one – made locally.'

Jake examined the bottle and tasted it, then nodded his approval. Christine filled their glasses.

When she'd gone, Evie asked him, 'You're drinking?'

'Just a glass. It would be rude not to when she's offered it to us as a gift.'

As she took a sip, Evie twisted the bottle to look at the label. 'Château Blanc? Wait a minute – isn't that François' vineyard?'

Jake nodded, tight-lipped.

She laughed at the withering glare he cast the bottle. 'I don't know why he upset you so much.'

'I told you why.'

'You didn't like him flirting with me when he should have been doing business with you.' She sighed. 'But it's not as if there's anything going on between you and me.'

Jake looked at her. 'Isn't there?' he asked quietly.

His words made her still. She put her glass down. His blue-eyed gaze held hers in what felt like a look of challenge. Evie frowned.

Isn't there? She thought of how her heart did a small flip each time he walked into the room, of how she lay awake at night thinking about him in the next room. How her skin tingled in response to his deep voice. She could deny that there was anything between them, but the truth was, she did feel something. Did he feel it too?

'What are you saying?' she asked.

'What we both know. That there's . . . a connection between us. And it isn't going away, despite our best efforts to ignore it.'

His expression was earnest. Intent. And he was watching her closely for her response.

She shook her head, remembering the painfully awkward conversation in her cottage the morning after the ball. The memory of his rejection was still vivid and still hurt. 'Jake, if you're talking about when we kissed, you regretted it straight away.'

'It took me by surprise, that's all. And – and I was worried you might think it meant more than it did.'

She stared at him. She'd been so sure that he'd regretted it.

But, then, she'd been quick to brush it off too, pretending it hadn't meant anything.

'The truth is, Evie, I didn't enjoy watching François flirt with you because . . .' he fiddled with the stem of his wine glass, then looked up and his gaze locked with hers '. . . because I was jealous.'

She blinked. So the attraction wasn't one-sided, after all.

Christine arrived with their food, cutting short the conversation, and Evie had to admit the interruption was welcome. She was stunned by his admission. She'd been so sure he didn't want anything from her but friendship. Christine laid down their plates of food and wished them *bon appétit*, then left.

In silence, they picked up their cutlery and began to eat.

There's a . . . connection between us. And it isn't going away . . . Her mind kept returning to his words, mulling them over. They made her temperature rise. Heat rippled through her, making her muscles tighten in discreet places. She stole secret glances at him, remembering how he'd spoken about his wife. How he'd said he'd always love her, and his feelings would never change. And Evie understood. Her heart was still fragile, and she wasn't ready to open it again either.

But she missed being intimate with a man.

Jake put his knife and fork down and reached for his wine. Her gaze drifted to his long fingers as they delicately held the stem of the glass.

She longed for the warm touch of hands on her skin, for the closeness of bodies nestled together in the night, and limbs intertwined in sleep. She ached for relief from the pent-up need she felt whenever he was near. It had only intensified since they'd arrived in France.

He sipped his wine and she watched surreptitiously, her eyes drawn to his lips. She ducked her gaze away, but the image of them burned in her mind. When he'd kissed her in the snow it had felt magical. His touch had been gentle yet sure. Her body, pressed against his, had felt molten. Her muscles tightened just thinking about it. Her throat dried.

She took a swig of wine. Perhaps Jakc was the perfect man for her just now. With him there could be no emotional complications because his heart was off limits too. She could trust him. She wanted him.

'Not like you to be so quiet, Pollyanna.'

She looked up and his blue eyes were fixed on her. Had he read her thoughts? Her cheeks reddened. She hoped not. 'I was just thinking that things don't always turn out how we plan,' she said quietly.

'You can say that again.'

She heard the faint bitterness in his voice and thought of his wife's sudden illness, of the plans they must have had, which had died with her. He was so full of pain and anger. Perhaps Evie could help him heal.

'I have to say, things might have turned out very differently today if it hadn't been for your interpreting skills. You got us out of a sticky situation, and I'm very grateful. When did you learn to speak French so fluently?'

'Oh, I've forgotten most of it now,' she replied, 'but I spent a year in Paris after I left school.'

His brow lifted. 'Didn't you want to use your French in your work?'

She shook her head. 'To be honest, I only went to France to get away from my parents. They were very disappointed that I'd flunked my exams and hadn't got into university.'

'Well, you're clearly gifted in languages.'

'Only for speaking. I was never any good at all the written stuff – grammar, translations, essay writing.'

He threw her a long, hard look. 'I wish you wouldn't do that.'

She took in the rigid line of his jaw. 'Do what?'

'Put yourself down. Focus constantly on what you can't do, rather than what you're good at.'

She opened her mouth to answer but found she didn't know what to say.

'It's strange,' he went on, 'because in other people and in everything around you, you always focus on the positives. Yet you berate yourself, you belittle your talents. Why are you so hard on yourself, Evie?'

'I – I don't know. Because I'm not like other people. I'm clumsy, I never follow the conventional route. I'm different.'

'But don't you see that different is good? Unconventional is unique?'

'My parents wouldn't agree. They wish I would—'

'Forget about your parents for one moment,' he cut in, with an impatient wave of his hand. 'Listen to me. You should be proud of your talents. You're a skilled seamstress, you speak French fluently, you're a kind and generous person. And good company.'

'Good company?' She was overwhelmed. Coming from Mr Arctic himself, that was the biggest compliment. 'That's not what you said the first time I met you. When we were snowed in.'

'Yes, well . . .' His eyes held hers. 'I behaved like an idiot that night. I was wrapped up in self-pity. Now . . .' He sucked in breath.

'Now?' she prompted quietly.

'Now I know you, Evie Miller, I realise I have a lot to thank you for.'

He knew her? He wanted to thank her? Tonight was turning out to be a night of revelations, and it felt . . . magical.

'A lot to thank me for? What do you mean? I should be thanking you. You're the one who brought me here.' She looked around at the beautiful château in the stunning Provence countryside.

He nodded. 'You came into my life like a bright light, altering my perspective, challenging me, standing up to me. I admire you for that.'

They had come a long way since that first night snowed in at the Old Hall. 'You admire me for arguing with you?'

'I've had to rethink the way I see the world, and that's in no small part due to you.'

Her heart flipped over. Did that mean she'd made him happy? She hoped so. 'It hasn't all been one way,' she said. Her voice was surprisingly low and a little frayed around the edges. 'You've become a good friend too.'

He was fiercely supportive, always shining a spotlight on her achievements and encouraging her to believe in herself. Despite his brittle outer shell, he had a nurturing personality. She'd seen it in the way he cared for Smoke, too.

Which led her back to a question which had been niggling ever since their first meeting when he'd examined her ankle with gentle, capable hands. 'Why did you give up practising medicine?' she asked.

He stilled. She felt a flash of panic at the sudden ice in his eyes, at the hard set of his chin, and her heart sank. She'd done it again, said something wrong.

'I was ready for a change,' he said dismissively.

But he would be a great doctor, she was sure of it. Knowledgeable. Calm. Committed.

'That doesn't answer the question. Being a doctor must have been far more rewarding than the job you're doing now.'

He didn't look at her, but stared into the depths of his glass.

'Be honest with me, Jake. Do you enjoy importing wine?'

'It's not about enjoyment. It's about earning a living

and keeping busy.' His mouth snapped shut, signalling that that was the end of the conversation.

Footsteps approached and the hotel owner came in. Evie leaned back in her seat and smiled politely as Christine cleared their plates.

'Was everything all right with your meal?' Christine asked.

'It was perfect,' said Jake. 'Thank you for letting us stay. It's very kind.'

Evie sat back, wondering why he was so evasive. She knew there were things in his past which were difficult to talk about, but surely his job wasn't one of them? She remembered what Louisa had said about how he used to be the life and soul of the party – before he'd changed. His wife's death had transformed him into a man with dark secrets, a man who stoically kept his pain and feelings close to his heart, and Evie wondered, would anyone ever be allowed to get close to him again?

Christine led them through to the lounge and made it clear that she was leaving them in privacy now and would be back in the morning to prepare breakfast. They thanked her and she closed the door behind her. The fire was burning, but the clear skies meant that the temperature outside had dropped dramatically when the sun had set, and now Evie hugged her arms around herself, wishing she had more than just a light sweater with her.

'Want to watch television?' asked Jake, as they sat down on the sofa in front of the fire.

Evie wrinkled her nose. 'My French isn't that good.' She pulled a strand of hair forward and absently began to plait it. Her fingers itched to sew but, of course, she had nothing with her, not even a needle and thread.

'What will you do, then, without your sewing?' The corner of his mouth lifted in a teasing smile.

'You read my mind.' She shivered. 'A warm quilt would have been nice to wrap around me.' She leaned forward and held her hands out as if to catch the heat from the fire.

'You're cold?'

'A little.'

Jake took his jacket off and draped it around her shoulders. Then he crossed the room to pour cognac from the tray Christine had left for them. Evie followed him with her gaze and pulled the jacket close. The mint-coloured linen was warm from his body and carried the scent of his aftershave. It made her feel a little light-headed.

'Here.' He handed her a wide-bottomed glass, just like those her dad used for his post-dinner drink at home. 'This will warm you.'

'On top of all the wine I had? I'll be drunk,' she said, curling her fingers around it and throwing him a mischievous smile. 'I might do something I regret.'

Or something daring, she thought, holding her breath and watching from beneath her lashes as he sat down beside her. She felt that spark again – the simmering bite of desire that was becoming so familiar.

She had a choice: she could carry on ignoring it or she could be honest with him. She didn't want the complications of a relationship, and he didn't either. He'd made that clear.

A new and unexpected surge of courage flowed through her and she knew it was thanks to him. Each day she had grown in confidence. Tonight, she knew what she wanted.

She just hoped he wanted it too.

He sat down. 'Pollyanna regret something? Doesn't she always look on the bright side? I'd have thought this would be your cue to tell me how breaking down was actually a blessing because it led us to this gem of a hotel, a delicious meal, and an unexpectedly pleasant evening.'

She laughed. 'It has been a lovely evening. And an adventure. Sometimes Fate leads us down unexpected paths . . . and they can be more interesting than the ones we would have chosen.'

He threw her an indulgent smile.

She took a sip of the cognac and her eyes widened with shock. It burned her throat and made her cough. 'Wow!' she spluttered. 'That's strong!'

His eyes creased as he laughed and warmth unfurled from her centre, heating her blood. She put the glass down. She wanted to keep a clear head tonight.

'Warmer now?' he asked.

'Much.'

She leaned back, letting the pillowy sofa absorb her weight. He took another slow slug of his cognac and gazed thoughtfully at the fire. Silence settled around them.

Evie took a deep breath, mustering all her courage. 'So . . . where do we go from here?'

He looked at her. She held his gaze.

'I take it you're not talking geographically?'

'No,' she said softly. 'You said you feel it too – this attraction. If ignoring it doesn't work, what next?'

'You ask that as if I hold all the answers.' His glass chinked as he put it down on the glass table beside him. 'I don't. And even if I did, I could only speak for myself.'

She swallowed. 'We agree we don't want a relationship, but it doesn't have to be complicated. It could just be . . .' her cheeks flamed '. . . what it is.'

As long as they were clear this was just physical, no one would get hurt.

Jake's chest rose and fell with each breath. Was it her imagination or did it pick up pace?

'And what's that?' he asked softly.

She swallowed. 'Fun. No strings.'

His silence was unbearable. Oh, God, why had she said anything? She'd probably misunderstood what he'd said earlier.

Suddenly, her fledgling confidence deserted her. She'd been mad to make such a suggestion, setting herself up for certain humiliation. Now his opinion of her would sink so low there'd be no redeeming herself. Mortified, she looked at her knees and steeled herself for his rejection.

Chapter Fifteen

Jake had to admit it was the last thing he'd expected. Yet a no-strings fling made sense. For both of them.

The jealousy he'd felt at François' vineyard today had taken him by surprise, but it didn't mean he was ready to embark on a full-blown relationship. He almost reached for the chain around his neck but stopped himself. He wasn't ready at all, but his attraction to Evie was becoming difficult to ignore. As long as this remained purely physical, it wasn't a betrayal of his wife's memory, was it?

'It doesn't matter,' she said, moving to get up. Her face was flushed, her skin the colour of the fruity young Syrah they'd drunk with dinner. 'I shouldn't have said anything. This was a mistake.'

He put his hand on her arm to stop her. She looked beautiful with her hair loose around her shoulders, luxuriant and gleaming in the gold light of the fire. 'Don't run away,' he said, his voice rough.

She shot him a nervous glance.

He licked his lips, conscious of what was at stake. Their friendship meant a lot to him. He'd almost lost it once already after the ball. He didn't want to risk losing it again. 'Evie, I want this. I want it more than anything, but you need to know it can never be love. If that's what you're looking for, you should walk away now.'

Those big hazel eyes stared up at him. 'I understand. You don't want a relationship, and neither do I, remember?'

'But you might—'

'No,' she cut in firmly, and he was glad to see her confidence had returned. Her dimples winked at him. 'This would be just fun. No complications. A no-strings fling is exactly what I need after Tim. And when we get back to Willowbrook we'll go back to normal life. Agreed?'

His heart hammered against his ribcage. He brushed the loose strands back from her face, and the desire to kiss her almost overtook him. However, he held back. It felt imperative that they got this straight, that there was no misunderstanding. 'What do you mean by normal life?'

'Being friends. Hanging out together.'

'There'll be no going back from this. We won't be just friends any more.'

'Then we carry on having . . .' the fire in her cheeks was impossibly endearing '. . . fun. The point is, we don't let it spoil our friendship. I love seeing Smoke. I don't want to have to stop because we've fallen out.' She looked up at him from beneath her lashes with pure mischief and it made his heart pole-vault.

This was Evie through and through: teasing, cheeky, joyful. The demon of self-doubt well and truly banished.

His lip curled. 'So, you admit you like my dog more than me? I knew it.'

Her smile lit her eyes. But they both became serious as he dipped his head and kissed her gently. Tentatively.

The brush of their lips was electric. Desire crashed through him, but he reined it in and searched her face. If she showed the faintest sign of hesitation he would stop immediately.

She didn't. The hunger in her eyes made his muscles tighten. His pulse thrummed in his ears. She reached up and drew his head down again. This time she took the lead and kissed him, and for some reason it thrilled him. Their breathing became ragged, and their hands began to seek each other urgently, feverishly.

He glanced up at the door, fairly certain their host wasn't going to return, but not willing to take any chances. 'Why don't we go upstairs?' he murmured.

At the top of the stone staircase he pushed open his door simply because it was the closest. He shut it and drew her to him. Her body felt achingly soft against his. She slipped off his scarf, and he groaned as she unbuttoned his shirt slowly, darting him shy looks, running her tongue across her lips in a way that made the blood speed through his veins. With any other woman he would have assumed she was being deliberately provocative – but this was Evie. Sweet, trusting, clumsy Evie, who only did genuine.

Finally, she unfastened the last button and he pulled his shirt off impatiently, closing his eyes as she spread her fingers across his chest, her fingertips brushing his nipples, her palms smoothing over the dips and ripples of his torso.

He drew breath and ran his hands through her long hair, trying to keep things slow, resisting the urge to undress her and pull her over him so those honey locks would spill down onto him. But then her fingers moved to his buckle and fumbled, and his self-control snapped.

He took over. The belt came undone, his trousers were discarded, and he was naked. Charmed by the colour that touched her cheeks, he kissed her again and made equally quick work of removing her clothes too. Her sharp intakes of breath as he kissed her throat and her neck only made his pulse race faster, and soon they both lay on the large bed, their bodies touching, heating, rubbing beneath the crisp white sheets.

'Jake, I want you,' she whispered.

His blood pounded. 'Evie—' His voice cracked. He had to call on all his self-restraint. 'It – it's been a long time. I might be . . . out of practice.'

Her eyes widened. What had she thought? That because he was a man, sex was something he did regularly, and with anyone?

'Of course,' she said, and kissed him. 'We've got all night.'

But neither of them slowed down. It was hot, urgent, hungry. With Maria it had always been reverent. Slow. They had—

He pushed his wife out of his mind to concentrate on Evie. This might be no-strings but that didn't mean he couldn't give her his full focus. That was what she deserved at the very least. He ran his hands over the indent of her waist, savouring her pillowy softness, breathing in her sweet scent. And as he did so, the ghost of his wife's memory gradually receded.

Evie moved over him and her hair spilled down, brushing his face, his shoulders, his chest. And it felt even silkier and sexier than he'd imagined. Her lashes fanned out across her cheeks as she closed her eyes, lips parted, and sucked in air.

Jake watched her, determined not to let go but to keep tight control for her benefit and her pleasure. But as her hips moved beneath his hands, the energy between them rose and brimmed and became so overpowering that he closed his eyes in surrender. He held her as she collapsed against his chest and their hearts hammered.

He felt lighter and more alive than he had in a long time. He stroked her hair, murmured quiet words in her ear and wondered why had he waited so long for this. It might not be love, it might be nothing like what he and Maria had shared, but it was pleasure of the most potent kind.

And for a moment there it had helped him forget.

Evie watched Jake sleep. The frown had gone from his brow, his chest rose and fell slowly, unhurried, and she was glad that in sleep, at least, he had found peace.

She smiled, like a very contented cat, and watched as the rising sun lit the distant hills and the mousy light of dawn was replaced with a coral glow. Closing the shutters had been the last thing on their minds last night. They'd been— It had—

She struggled to put into coherent thought the bliss, the exquisite sensations, the revelation that it had been for her. Frankly, she'd never known sex like that.

With Tim she'd never felt a wildfire of desire as she had last night, or the sense of giving herself up to an unstoppable force. And he'd never taken his time getting to know her as Jake had, his fingers tracing the outline of her hips, her thighs, smiling when she moaned, making her sigh and gasp and explode with pleasure over and over again. She'd never felt as if she'd given so much of herself, either. It made her feel . . . vulnerable.

Fear fluttered in her belly.

Just fun, she had confidently proposed. A no-strings fling. It sounded so simple. But today her head was spinning and her heart was doing somersaults just remembering it all. Could she really separate her emotions from what had happened last night?

A cockerel's call pierced the morning silence, but Jake slept on undisturbed.

Of course she could. Especially knowing that Jake's heart was with Maria. And this was nothing like her relationship with Tim.

It was better, a devilish voice whispered.

Her pulse quickened in panic. No, not better. Different. Jake had always been honest with her about his feelings. *This can never be love*, he'd warned.

And yet last night when he'd held Evie and looked at her with those kingfisher-blue eyes, there had been intensity in them. All grief and pain had been completely erased, and in that moment it had been tempting to believe he felt something for her.

But he didn't. And she didn't, either. She was just a little dazed and dazzled by the sex. That was all.

She'd suggested this fling, and she would keep to the terms they'd agreed: no emotional involvement, no complications. She would enjoy this time with Jake, but make sure her heart remained carefully tucked away and safe.

The cockerel crowed again, and this time Jake stirred, squinting against the morning light that streamed in through the window.

Confused, he looked around the unfamiliar room and Evie tensed, watching his reaction as the fog of sleep slowly lifted and he remembered where he was and what had happened. His gaze settled on her and she saw the moment when realisation dawned. His lips curved in a slow, lazy smile.

'Morning,' he said, in that deep voice of his, and reached for her.

'*Bonjour*,' she whispered, as she dipped her head.

She kissed him long and hard, and their bodies sought one another once again and became entwined. As he rolled her onto her back Evie closed her eyes, smiling with pleasure but also with relief that there were no regrets and last night hadn't been a dream.

By the time they were up and dressed, it was almost noon. Christine advised that their car was ready and arranged for a taxi to drive them to the garage.

The workshop was quiet, presumably because it was the holidays. Spotting the red convertible, Jake strode across the deserted garage in search of a member of staff and Evie followed.

'The floor's just been mopped,' muttered Jake, 'so there must be someone around.'

Evie slipped and landed hard on her bum. She gasped, then winced. Oh, great. She'd arrived here walking on air after a night of the best sex a girl had ever known, and now she found herself on the floor with a very sore bruise. As she rubbed the base of her back, she steeled herself for Jake's reaction. Tim would have rolled his eyes and marched away.

Jake turned and rushed back, his features narrowed with concern. 'Are you hurt?' he asked.

'I'm fine,' she said, trying to be brave. In truth, it did hurt.

'Can you get up? Here, let me help you.'

'I'm okay,' she said, but it was nice to feel his arm around her waist, supporting her.

A door opened and a man in overalls appeared. He was wiping his hands on an oil-stained rag when he saw what had happened and hurried over.

She opened her mouth to make a joke about how clumsy she was, but before she had a chance Jake told him, 'You should have put a sign up to say the floor was wet!'

The mechanic apologised profusely, and Evie's mouth snapped shut.

She wasn't used to having someone stand up for her. She could happily get used to it.

'So, what do you want to do now?' asked Jake, as they drove away. 'Go home? Or do some sightseeing?'

Her hair streamed behind her and shards of sunlight

flashed off the car's metal trimmings as they sped along the deserted country roads. Truth be told, she was tired and sleep-deprived, but she didn't want to miss out on a day of their holiday when they had only a few left.

'Why don't we go back to the villa,' she said, 'and get a change of clothes? Then maybe we could go for a drive? Explore the countryside.'

'Yesterday's experience hasn't put you off using the car?'

'Not at all. Like you said, it was a blessing in disguise.' Evie closed her eyes, savouring the rush of wind on her face and the gentle heat of the winter sun. A night of passionate sex in a beautiful hotel – it couldn't have turned out better, really.

'I'm glad you feel that way,' he said, under his breath. 'Maria would never have set foot in a classic car, especially one that had broken down.'

Evie's eyes snapped open. He was thinking about Maria? Of course he was. She would never be far from his thoughts. She tried to force down the emotions that rose up inside her.

'Oh, yeah?' she said, relieved at how casual she sounded. 'What about the Bentley?'

He kept his eyes on the road, concentrating as he slowed for a bend. 'She refused to go near it.'

Instinct told her it would be wise to drop this subject. Talking about Maria only made her feel jealous, small and inferior. She was willing to bet that Maria had never slipped and landed with her feet in the air and her knickers on show to the world. But now he'd revealed this tiny morsel of information about his wife, Evie couldn't help herself. She was desperate to know more.

'Why didn't she like old cars?' she asked.

'She liked life's luxuries. Air-conditioning and heating in a car were basic essentials, she said, and she didn't want to feel every bump in the road.'

Evie didn't know what to say. Her high spirits suddenly dissipated, leaving her deflated. Although last night had been a revelation for her, earth-shattering, clearly the same couldn't be said for Jake. His thoughts were still with the woman he loved. It was a reminder that what she and Jake shared was only superficial. Just fun.

And she was fine with that. She really was.

The light beside his bed cast intricate shadows across the ceiling. Jake gazed up at them, savouring the warmth of Evie's body tucked against his chest, and the faint rhythm of her heart beating in time to his. Absently he ran his fingers through her hair. His phone buzzed and lit up with a message. Jake reached to take a look, then put it back.

Evie's eyelashes brushed against his chest. 'What is it?' she asked sleepily.

They'd had a lazy, laid-back afternoon wandering through a medieval walled village, soaking up the atmosphere and historic beauty of the centuries-old houses, then sitting in a café and watching the world go by. Watching each other, feeling the rocket of heat as their eyes met and held. It had simmered beneath the surface all day, the electric charge that last night had finally been released and allowed to flourish.

Then they'd driven home to the villa. He smiled wryly. Tonight was the first evening Evie hadn't done any sewing. Instead, they'd gone to bed early. To his bed.

The sound of a night bird calling pierced the stillness and Evie shifted, the velvet of her thigh rubbing against his, making his body stir again, causing his muscles to tighten. He kissed the top of her head, inhaling her apple scent. It was a relief to have this thing out in the open. To be able to kiss her when he felt the urge, to draw her against him and let lust lead them down its alluring path.

'Just Louisa.'

'Shouldn't you reply?'

'I will in the morning.' It was eleven o'clock. His sister wouldn't expect an immediate answer.

'Nothing important, then?'

'No. She's checking on me. Mothering me, as usual,' he said fondly.

'She cares about you.'

'I know. She's been doing it since I was three. I'm used to it now.'

'Since you were three?'

He nodded. Louisa had always been more than just a big sister to him. 'When my mother died.'

Evie sat up and rested her head on her hand to look at him. 'That must have been hard for you.'

For some reason her sympathy made him want to pull back. 'Not really. I don't remember her. She died shortly after Scarlett was born. There were complications . . .'

'It must have been hard for your father, then, being left to raise three children alone.'

'He hired nannies. And our housekeeper was around to help, too. He left it to them, really.' His father had never seemed like a man who was struggling. He'd always worked long hours, and when he was at home, he'd been a remote figure, preoccupied, never getting involved in the children's daily routine.

'He didn't remarry?'

'No.'

'I wonder why.'

He'd never asked, and his father had never told him. 'We never talked about it. Or about anything . . . emotional. We didn't have that kind of relationship.'

Evie traced circles on his chest with the tips of her fingers while she absorbed this. 'You don't have any regrets about missing Christmas with your sisters?'

'None.'

'It will get easier.' She lay back and twisted her head to look at him. Her dimples appeared. 'I used to adore Christmas before Zara died. I had a CD of Christmas songs and I used to play it from September until February – or until everyone else lost patience and they hid it from me.'

'I can imagine that would be mildly irritating.' But he smiled indulgently at the thought, because it wasn't difficult to imagine. She was so overly enthusiastic about the things she loved. About life. He pictured her, head thrown back with delight and hands in the air as snow had fallen all around them. And in his car, beaming as the wind rushed at her face. Maria would never have enjoyed those things. He had forgotten how stubborn she used to be.

'I used to cut out paper snowflakes and hang them around my bed, and I would make personalised cards for all my friends and family . . .' She sighed wistfully. 'I miss Zara.'

Hearing her voice so ragged with sadness made his chest tighten. He kept his gaze fixed on the ceiling while she continued.

'Sometimes I miss her so much it feels . . . physical. A bone-deep pain, you know? I think of her every time I hear a song we used to dance to, or smell her perfume, and I feel . . .' she faltered, then wrapped her hand in a fist and touched her heart '. . . I feel it here.'

He swallowed.

'We were different in so many ways, yet she understood me better than anyone.' He heard her take a breath before she added quietly, 'Sometimes I think it would have been easier for my parents if I'd been the one who died, rather than her.'

His eyes narrowed and he turned onto his side to face her. 'I don't believe that for a second,' he said sharply.

'I see it in their eyes.'

Perhaps that was how her parents made her feel. He'd seen what they were like. But no parent should make their child feel so. Especially not their only surviving child.

'Why don't you stand up to them?' he asked, his voice gruff with anger.

'What do you mean?'

'That time when I saw them in your shop, your father

was completely out of order. You should tell him to cut the criticism or sling his hook.'

She looked horrified. The streaks in her hair glinted in the gold light as she shook her head. 'I can't say that!'

'Why not?' She was too good, too kind for this world. He wanted to protect her from those who would take advantage of her openness and were so quick to destroy her self-confidence.

'Because they – they're still grieving.' He glimpsed her pained expression before she dipped her gaze. 'They've never got over Zara's death. You know how hard it is. They can't accept that she's gone.' She hesitated, then admitted, 'They took all her belongings from her flat and turned her old bedroom at home into a shrine. The wardrobe is full of her clothes and shoes. They won't throw anything away. It's been more than five years now, but they can't let go.'

She glanced at him as if this was her guilty secret, and it was indeed extreme. But it didn't justify their behaviour towards her. Her parents had had years to come to terms with their grief. It was no excuse for belittling Evie.

Then again, he knew better than anyone that the passage of time didn't necessarily lessen the grief. *It's been two years now. Don't you think it's time you moved on?* His sister's words rang in his head. Was he guilty of the same thing as Evie's parents? Allowing his grief to hurt those who were closest to him? He thought of Louisa's pleas for him to spend Christmas with his family. He'd avoided doing so, but he'd hurt them in the process. His skin prickled uncomfortably.

Perhaps, once he returned to England, he should visit both his sisters. Perhaps it was time he made more effort and stopped shutting them out of his life. His nephews and nieces were growing up fast, and he didn't want to miss out on their childhood completely.

'Why do you care so much about what my parents do?' Evie asked, running her hand over his stubbled chin.

He caught it and kissed it. 'What do you mean?'

'You get so angry, telling me I should stand up to them. Why does it matter to you?'

A long pause followed. He didn't know how to answer. He was completely thrown by the question. Why did it matter? 'Because you're a friend,' he managed eventually. 'A good friend. And I don't like to see anyone trampled on by others.'

'You care about the underdog, don't you, Jake?' she observed quietly.

'The underdog?' Was that how she saw herself? As someone he'd taken under his wing, the way he'd done with Smoke as a puppy? A hot rush of indignation flowed through him, and he battled to contain it as he looked down at the beautiful woman beside him, her hair spilling over her pillow, her eyes smoky in the low light of the bedroom. 'No,' he corrected her brusquely. 'I care about you, Evie Miller.'

Her eyes widened, then shone like stars. He saw them light with hope and immediately regretted his choice of words. No strings, they'd said. No complications. His pulse hammered in his ears with sudden panic. He cared, but his heart still belonged to Maria. It was mothballed and safely tucked away, out of reach, and that was exactly where it would stay.

Evie was fun, she was talented, she lit up the room with her sunny smile. But she wasn't Maria.

Chapter Sixteen

'Evie, put the knife down.' His heart was in his mouth as the blade glinted in the kitchen light. 'Please. Put it down.'

Evie whirled round. Spotting him in the doorway, she stopped, and blushed. Abba's "Dancing Queen" continued to blast out at full volume, and something delicious-smelling was baking in the oven.

Jake stepped forward. He took the knife out of her hand and laid it down on the worktop beside the tomatoes and cucumber she'd been slicing for a salad before she'd been distracted by the music. Now the element of danger had been removed he could smile. 'Caught you,' he said.

'I was only dancing!'

'Knowing how clumsy you are, dancing with a knife in your hand is not a good idea.'

She laughed and resumed the whirling and jiggling she'd been doing when he came in. 'Come on, admit it,' she said, 'this song makes you want to dance too.'

'I don't dance.'

'You did at the ball. I saw you.'

'Only to please Dorothy. That was exceptional.'

'Suit yourself.' She spun on the spot, smiling, her head tipped back, her arms in the air.

He couldn't help but smile. Her joy was infectious. The beat of the music made his pulse pick up. She swivelled her hips and his gaze lingered just a little too long on her shapely figure and the indent of her waist. He tried to clear his mind, but lust tore through him, like adrenalin.

If you can't beat them, join them, he told himself. He seized her hand and waltzed her round in a circle, but the kitchen table and chairs got in the way so he waltzed her out onto the terrace. She tipped her head back, laughing, and the stars were reflected in her eyes as they spun faster. And Jake found himself singing the words with her, not just to that song but the next one too. They laughed and danced, and energy surged through his body, fed by her uninhibited delight and his answering joy. When the song finished and a slower one started, they were both breathless and flushed. Spots of colour splashed her cheeks, almost as scarlet as his new sweater. He grinned and pulled her to him for the slow dance, not wanting the moment to end or the spell to be broken.

'You see? You do dance,' she said, then let her head rest against his chest.

'Shush. Don't tell anyone.'

'Why not? It was fun. Or is that the problem? Mr Arctic can't be seen to have fun?'

He smiled, loving how she teased him. 'It was fun,' he agreed. 'You, Pollyanna, are fun.'

He felt happy, he realised, for the first time in months – years. His heart thudded as if in confirmation.

'Ha! You wouldn't say that if I'd trodden on your foot. And, believe me, it happens a lot when I'm dancing.'

'I believe you.' He grinned.

When had they stopped dancing? When had their gazes locked so all he could see were her long lashes and gleaming eyes looking up at him? Hungrily. Seductively.

'Yet you're still here?' She gave a soft laugh. 'You're brave.'

She felt warm in the cool night air. 'Not brave. Privileged. Thank you,' he said, his voice low. 'Thank you, Evie, for making me feel so alive. I'd forgotten what it was like.'

He was sleeping more soundly than he had done in months. He was looking forward to each new day, waking up beside her. Previously, he had lived a grey existence, but she had quite literally brought colour into his life.

'Oh, Jake . . .' Her voice broke, but it didn't matter because he dipped his head and stole the words from her lips with a lingering kiss, loaded with the need to avoid confronting his emotions or thoughts, and just feel.

Because being with Evie felt so right, so good. And he wasn't ready to think about anything beyond that.

When they'd eaten – a little later than planned, since they'd been side-tracked in the kitchen – they settled themselves in the lounge for a quiet evening in front of the fire.

'I wonder what Smoke is doing,' said Evie.

'You don't need to worry about him. He loves staying at Heidi's. She spoils him rotten.'

Jake watched her, head bent as she sewed. Her long

plait had fallen forwards over her left shoulder. As usual it was untidy, and strands had come loose. He remembered how neatly tied back she had worn her hair for the ball. It had looked sleek and elegant, it had looked beautiful – but she hadn't looked like Evie.

The real Evie was sitting here sewing, eyes sparkling as she chattered and laughed, wincing as she accidentally stabbed her finger with the needle, then sucking it and fiddling with the end of her plait while she waited for the bleeding to stop.

'I miss him,' she said.

He rolled his eyes. 'What is it with you and my dog? You haven't known him that long – or intimately.'

She giggled. 'I know. But sometimes you feel an instant connection.'

'With a Dalmatian?'

'With anyone or any animal! Don't pretend you don't know what I'm talking about.' She laid the quilt aside and came and curled up next to him on the sofa.

He wrapped his arm around her, feeling a surge of protectiveness.

'He's just adorable,' Evie went on, 'so friendly and affectionate. And he worships you. I hate to think of him missing you while you're away. Pining for you.'

'He's not pining, I assure you.'

'How do you know?'

'Tell you what, why don't we Skype Heidi now?'

'Yes!'

They called, and sure enough Smoke was fine. They could see him with a Golden Retriever in the background, playing with Heidi's son, who was rolling an old tennis ball around the kitchen for them to fetch. Evie smiled, reassured.

'Better?' asked Jake, when he'd hung up.

'Much,' she said.

Jake was thoughtful for a moment, then asked, 'What do you say we stay here a few days longer than planned? Into the new year, maybe?'

'The new year?' She counted on her fingers. 'Three extra days?'

He nodded. 'Smoke's happy, your shop is closed anyway, I don't have anything to rush home for, and this is . . . good. I'm enjoying spending time with you, Evie.' His voice was low, and heat simmered in him as he waited for her answer.

'So am I,' she said, looking up at him from beneath her lashes, her gaze darting to his lips, making his muscles tense, making him want to kiss her. 'Yes. Let's stay.'

Jake was smiling to himself as he listened to Evie singing in the shower. It was a song from *The Lion King*, and he chuckled to himself because she wasn't just singing the melody, but all the musical accompaniments too. The sound of running water stopped, and he pictured her stepping out and rubbing herself dry. Perhaps he should go up there and help her—

A loud crash slammed through that line of thought.

He frowned at the silence that followed. No *oops!*, no singing or humming. Nothing.

'Evie?'

No response.

Jake ran up, taking the stairs two at a time. He flung open the bathroom door, which, thankfully, she hadn't locked.

She was on the floor, out cold. A towel lay crumpled beside her. Evie was wearing a bathrobe, but her feet were bare and there was a puddle of water on the tiles. He glanced at the hard, square edge of the marble washbasin. She must have slipped and banged her head.

Horror slid through him, a sliver of ice. 'Evie!' he shouted. 'Evie!'

Nothing. He felt for a pulse.

It was strong – thank God. Her eyes fluttered open. She looked up at him. 'What happened?' she murmured.

Relief washed through him. 'You banged your head. You must have slipped getting out of the shower.'

'I'm fine,' she said, but stared past him, as if she couldn't see him. Her pupils were tiny.

Something was wrong. Panic gripped him.

'Help me get up,' she said.

'No. Stay right there. Don't move.'

He reached for his phone, but his hand shook so badly he dropped it. With a crack like a gunshot it hit the stone tiles.

This was why he'd given up medicine. He didn't trust himself any more: he couldn't be relied upon when it mattered. The phone's screen was shattered in the corner but it still worked. He called the emergency service and did his best to explain the problem. Fortunately, the operator spoke enough English to understand and told him an ambulance was on its way.

It couldn't come soon enough. Her eyes had closed.

'Evie, wake up!' He took her hand. 'Please, Evie.'

He couldn't do this again. He couldn't watch the worst happen, knowing he should have prevented it. Not a second time, not Evie. Memories flashed up in his mind, making it difficult to concentrate and sending his blood pressure rocketing. He heard the siren and jumped to his feet. He ran down to find the paramedics and explained what had happened, the symptoms she'd shown when she'd briefly woken. Then they took over.

He followed them into the ambulance, where he held her hand and kept up a string of meaningless words during the bumpy ride to hospital, hoping the sound of his voice might stir her back to life. When they arrived, the doctors took over and he was asked to wait while Evie was wheeled into a room for treatment. Only then did he sit down, head in his hands, drained and shaking, knowing there was nothing more he could do.

Minutes ticked into hours, and Jake stared at the poster on the wall opposite him, reading words that he didn't understand. This was a strange hospital in a foreign country, but he'd been here before. The smell of disinfectant, the endless waiting, the uncertainty and fear and growing inevitability of what was to come were identical. It all rushed back to the surface: the ferocious emotion and self-loathing – and the knowledge that he could and should have prevented it . . .

Finally, the door opened, and a nurse appeared. 'Evie's

come round now,' she said, 'but she's very tired and needs to rest.'

She led him to the window where he saw Evie asleep, looking peaceful, her long hair fanned across the pillow.

'Why don't you go home and get some sleep yourself?' suggested the nurse.

Jake blinked and looked at his watch. It was evening, already?

'We'll take care of her. Go home and rest. Come back in the morning.'

He did as he was told. But next morning he was back well before visiting hours. As soon as they opened the doors, he ran in and planted himself beside Evie's bed. There, he waited silently for her to wake, and eventually his patience was rewarded.

She opened her eyes slowly and blinked. 'Jake.'

Relief pummelled through him. And a barrage of other emotions, too, that hit him square in the chest. Unable to speak, he took her hand instead.

'You're wearing my scarf.' She smiled.

'Yes – well, it was cold this morning.' He glanced down at the patchwork fabric nestled so comfortably against his skin. The temperature had plummeted last night. He'd felt icy lying in bed staring at the empty space beside him, gritting his teeth as all the memories and guilt of two years ago had returned to torment him.

'You look as if you've seen a ghost. Are you okay?'

He gave a dry laugh. A ghost. How appropriate.

Chapter Seventeen

'Never mind me. You're the one who's been sick,' said Jake. 'How are you feeling?'

Evie remembered the nurse had spoken to her during the night and explained that she had concussion and must stay in for observation, but today she felt fine. Perhaps a little groggy, but fine. 'I'd be better if you weren't crushing the bones in my hand.' She smiled.

He snatched his hand away with a muttered apology.

'I feel completely fine,' she assured him. 'Just a bump on the side of my head – and that only hurts if I touch it.'

Jake, on the other hand, was pale as chalk, and she noticed the dark smudges beneath his eyes. 'Jake, is something wrong?'

He shook his head. 'You scared me, that's all.'

He picked up the keys for the Alfa Romeo and they rattled as he rotated them through his fingers.

'The nurse said you saved my life by calling an ambulance straight away. She said you knew exactly what to do. I don't know why you gave up being a doctor – you're brilliant!'

The keys became still, and his fingers were clenched so tightly around them that his knuckles showed white.

'Jake, what's the matter?' She sat up. 'Is it the hospital? Is it bringing back memories? Is it—'

'I was to blame for Maria's death!' The words exploded from him, rough and rasping.

'You?' She almost laughed, thinking he was joking in that dry, deadpan way of his.

But his expression was deadly serious, and her smile vanished.

'I missed the signs,' he said flatly. 'I didn't realise their gravity. I knew she was getting headaches, but I didn't put two and two together.' He hung his head. 'I failed her.'

Evie stared at him.

'My own wife, and I didn't even realise she was ill,' he went on. 'What kind of a doctor does that make me?'

Self-loathing was etched into his face.

But everyone made mistakes – she knew that better than anyone. She was the queen of mistakes, be it the wrong job choice, catastrophic relationships, or driving her car into a ditch.

'You're only human, Jake,' she said quietly. 'And hindsight is a wonderful thing, but perhaps her symptoms weren't so obvious at the time. I mean, everyone gets headaches . . .'

He shook his head, dismissing this. He'd retreated into himself. She recognised the distant look in his eyes, and it reminded her of the night they'd met during the snowstorm. Only now she understood what he was feeling, and her heart went out to him. 'You're being too hard on yourself. Maybe you were too close.'

'How could I not see?'

'Perhaps hers was a rare case where the symptoms weren't obvious. Perhaps she played down her symptoms because she didn't want to worry you.'

He glanced at her and she could tell by the way his brows lifted that he hadn't thought of this. She went on: 'Did her GP make the diagnosis?'

'Not at first.'

'And do you blame him for missing it?'

He blinked. 'What?'

'Do you blame the hospital for not being able to cure her?'

'Of course not. I—'

'Then why so hard on yourself, Jake? Doctors are only human. And you wouldn't judge another doctor so harshly. Why are you any different?'

'Because she was my wife! I lived with her. I loved her. I knew her better than anyone . . .'

Evie felt a needle of jealousy at the words *I loved her,* and it caught her off guard. She squeezed it out of her mind, telling herself she wasn't being rational.

'I should have seen the signs, but I didn't. By the time anyone knew it was a brain tumour, it was too late. I might have saved her life.' He jabbed a finger at his chest. Then the fight seemed to desert him and his arm dropped to his side. 'But I let her down.'

He stared at his feet, consumed by memories and guilt, and under the harsh strip lights of that hospital room he looked so wretched that Evie wanted to reach out to him. Suddenly it all made sense. His pain, his grief had always seemed intense. Now she realised they had been underpinned by guilt. It had been eating away at him all this time. And it explained why he'd given up his job as a doctor and had a sudden change of career.

What could she do to make him see that beating himself up like this didn't help? It only made him feel worse.

She sat up and touched his shoulder. He looked at her through haunted eyes. 'If Maria had been knocked down by a car, would you hold the driver responsible for her death?' she asked quietly, thinking of her sister.

He frowned. 'I don't know. It would depend on the circumstances, I suppose. If he'd been speeding or driving recklessly or over the limit, then, yes, I might. Why?'

'The man who hit Zara was none of those things. Just a father of three on his way to work, driving along a busy London street at rush-hour. She was crossing the road, and he didn't see her until it was too late.'

Jake blinked but didn't say anything.

'He had to have counselling after the accident. My parents didn't blame him, and the inquest ruled it was an accident, but he found it difficult to live with what had happened.' She took his hand. 'Jake, there isn't always someone to blame or a reason. Bad things happen, and we don't understand why they've happened, but they do. And sometimes we can't prevent them. It's not always easy, but if we can accept events without holding anyone responsible, sometimes that's better for all involved.'

Her throat was tight as she finished. 'I'm glad that Zara died instantly. I'm glad she didn't suffer.'

Jake saw the emotion well up and make her eyes shimmer. He covered her hand with both of his, and she smiled bravely. How typical of Evie, he thought, to see the positives in the bleakest of situations.

And perhaps she was right. Perhaps it wasn't anyone's fault that Maria had died. Perhaps if he *had* spotted the signs, her suffering would have been prolonged. There was certainly no guarantee that an early diagnosis would have saved her.

Something loosened inside him – something he'd been wrestling with for so long – and his shoulders dropped a little.

Evie lay back against the pillows and a solitary tear slipped down her cheek. She was brave: she talked openly about the sister she'd lost, but she felt the same grief that he'd been battling these last two years. She understood how it felt to lose someone irreplaceable. He sat on the edge of the hospital bed and held her against his chest, careful not to touch her head where it was sore, and wondered who was comforting whom right now. Her hands clutched him tight, and they became locked in each other's warmth.

'You speak wise words, Pollyanna,' he told her, when she pulled back.

'I know. Hold on to that thought.' She grinned.

'Were you always an optimist, or did Zara's death make you that way?'

'Always.' Her sunny smile lit her eyes. 'You know, you shouldn't blame yourself. It won't change anything. It won't bring her back. And wouldn't she want you to be happy rather than mourning her indefinitely?'

He felt an unexpected shift inside. It was like a kaleidoscope adjusting to reveal a new picture, a new perspective. What would Maria have wanted? He realised he'd never asked himself that question.

'Yes,' he said slowly. Then certainty filled him. 'Yes.'

'So, let it go, Jake. Stop blaming yourself.'

He'd been punishing himself for his mistake, but Evie was right: it hadn't changed anything. He was only human. He needed to accept that. The guilt and the blame would never bring his wife back. And his life would move on. It already had – moving to Willowbrook, meeting Evie. But rather than fighting this and staying stuck in the past, he saw now that it was all right to embrace the changes. And that realisation brought with it the sensation of a huge weight being lifted.

He shook his head and gave a dry laugh. 'My sister's been telling me for months that I need to move on. Maybe I should have listened instead of shutting myself off.'

Evie looked at him with understanding. 'These things happen in their own time,' she said, her voice tinged with sadness. 'They're not always within our control.'

'I'm fine,' said Evie, as Jake fussed around her, fetching her sewing, making her drinks, asking if she was warm enough and insisting that she didn't leave the sofa. 'Really

I am. If I wasn't, the doctors wouldn't have discharged me, would they?'

He threw her a stern look, but she saw through his flinty expression to the concern that underpinned it, and if she was honest it was quite nice to be cared for with fleecy blankets and Jake's grave solicitude. 'I want to wrap you up in cotton wool and make sure you never get hurt again,' he said, and she could tell he was only half joking. His aquamarine roll-neck sweater made the blue of his eyes even more intense.

'That's impossible. I'm always bumping my head and slipping, although this was—' She stopped and listened. 'Is that my phone ringing?'

It must be upstairs beside her bed, and she moved to get up, but he stopped her. 'Stay there. I'll get it.'

He returned a couple of minutes later. 'It was your parents. I rang them to let them know what had happened and I've been keeping them up to date with your progress. They said they'd call tonight to see how you are. I spoke to Natasha and Luc, too. They're back in Willowbrook now, but they send their love.'

She took the phone. 'Thanks. I'd better call Mum back.'

A little while later she ended the call. Jake was watching her. She didn't need to say anything for him to ask, 'What's wrong?'

'They want to come and see me when I get back.'

'They're worried about you?'

She nodded. 'I told them I'm fine and I said I'd go and visit them instead.'

That way she could go when she was ready to face

them. She felt guilty because she dreaded seeing them so much. But no one else had the power to make her feel as worthless and wanting. Reflecting on the conversation, she noticed they hadn't said much about their time at Tim's parents. No doubt they were saving it for when she was better, and then would undoubtedly follow all the usual adulatory praise of Tim.

'Want me to come with you?' asked Jake.

Her spirits lifted at the thought. 'Why would you do that?'

Her parents would leap to conclusions. They'd assume that, having just been away together, she and Jake were in a relationship. A real one. Then again, if they thought that perhaps they'd get off her back about Tim.

'To give you moral support.'

She smiled, touched by this. No one else understood her well enough to appreciate how much that meant to her, but Jake had proved he was the most dependable of friends.

It was funny because Tim had put a ring on her finger, yet he hadn't respected her: he'd hurt her. With Jake, on the other hand, their agreement was strictly no commitment, yet he made her feel like the most special woman in the world. She'd told him things she'd never told anyone else and he listened to her, he believed in her. It was difficult to imagine somebody respecting her more, caring more, and she knew he'd never intentionally hurt her.

Perhaps she had been rash to rule out all possibility of finding love and her own happy ending. Perhaps one day she would meet a man who would accept her as she was and love and cherish her.

Believe in yourself. Hope woke inside her and spread its wings. She pictured herself in a long sweeping dress with Lottie as a flower girl and a man gazing down at her with the adoring look of a groom who had eyes only for one woman.

But that was where the film in her mind abruptly ended.

Because she could only picture one man in that role. And Jake had been clear from the start that love was something he could never give.

'Thanks,' she said, and her voice was a little husky with emotion. 'I'd really appreciate that.'

Jake went into the kitchen to make hot drinks, but he was preoccupied, thinking about their conversation in the hospital earlier. He wasn't used to opening up, but Evie had helped him to realise that his guilt was futile, and perhaps misplaced. And, as he'd grasped that, a deep sense of peace swept through him. He knew he owed her for helping him let go of the guilt. He could move forward now, unchained.

And yet his mind lingered in the hospital waiting room, haunted by the fear, sick with worry for Evie.

He carried the drinks into the lounge, and they snuggled up in front of the fire. They talked, they touched. He smoothed her hair back from her face, she slid her hand beneath his sweater and his muscles flexed beneath her touch. Her lips found his, and they began to rediscover each other after the last twenty-four hours apart.

'This isn't a good idea,' he whispered, pulling back. 'You need to take it easy.'

Her smile was wicked. 'I am taking it easy. I want this.'

Desire tunnelled through him, tightening its grip on him. He felt the fire light, and the blood raced in his veins. She peeled away his sweater, his T-shirt. She ran her palms over his chest, waist, hips, making him shudder with anticipation. And when need had coiled itself so tight it became unbearable, their bodies finally connected and he looked into her eyes. Evie blinked back at him, her smile veiled with passion, and he made love to her until she closed her eyes and gasped with pleasure. He wasn't far behind, but as he watched her hurtle towards her climax, emotions welled up in him, powerful. Terrifying. Evie came undone in his arms, and shortly after his body exploded.

It should have been perfect. But as Evie whispered his name, a hook caught in his chest. The piercing sensation was both exquisite and terrible, and he shrank back from it.

Confused, he tried to make sense of what he felt: the rushing sensation, the dizzying feeling that his world was spinning on its axis, the finger of ice that scratched his spine.

He opened his mouth to say her name but no words came out. Instead, fear gripped him. He didn't want this – he didn't want to feel emotions as strong and vivid and acute as this, in neon colour and full surround-sound. Not again.

Memories rushed to the surface. The desperate

emptiness after Maria had gone. What if Fate punished him a second time? What if something happened to Evie? When she'd banged her head, it had been a taste of what might be. The fear for her life . . . It had been too much. He couldn't go through that again.

He waited until she was heavy in his arms, then he slowly levered himself away. He made sure the fleece blanket was tucked around her, and he left the room. Outside on the terrace, the darkness was waiting for him.

Familiar. Cold. Inevitable.

Chapter Eighteen

The first time she woke and found herself alone, Evie frowned, then went back to sleep. The second time, however, she sensed something was wrong, sat up and looked around.

The fire had burned itself out, and Jake had gone. She got up to go and look for him. The blanket wrapped around her, she noticed the French windows were ajar and spotted him outside on the terrace.

He was leaning against the balustrade, staring into the darkness, lost in thought. She shivered as the chilly night air swished about her bare legs. It was late, the early hours of the morning, she guessed. How long had he been out here?

'Jake?' she whispered from the doorway.

His head turned a fraction. His face was hidden in shadow.

'What is it?' she asked, as she joined him.

'You'll get cold. Go back inside.'

The gardens and forest around them were a black hole of whispers and rustling. She pulled the blanket tighter. 'Jake, what's wrong?'

'Nothing.'

'Something's worrying you.'

'I'm fine.'

'You don't look fine.'

Although the space between them was only a few inches, it felt vast. Her mind worked fast, rewinding, trying to work out what had happened. Something must have triggered this, but she couldn't work out what.

She mustered the courage to ask, 'Is it Maria?'

He didn't answer.

She wanted to help, but she couldn't reach him when he withdrew like this. It reminded her of the first time they'd met when his eyes had been bloodshot and he'd reeked of whisky and loneliness. She knew he missed Maria, but it hurt when he shut her out.

Evie thought they'd created something during the last few days, a new bond. All those tender moments alone together, all their whispered conversations and heartfelt lovemaking.

The tiles felt rough and cold beneath her feet as she stepped closer, trying to read his expression in the shadows. But all she could see was the rigid set of his shoulders and the hard line of his jaw.

'Jake, you're scaring me,' she said softly.

'I'm fine. Go back to bed.'

She hugged the fleece blanket closer. 'I can't leave you like this.'

'I'm fine. I don't need cheering up, Pollyanna.'

She stiffened as if he'd slapped her and stepped back. His words stung.

'I'm sorry,' he said quickly. 'I didn't mean that.'

She heard him sigh, she heard his disgust at himself.

'I warned you,' he said, shaking his head. 'I told you I'm not a good man.'

'Speak to me,' she said. 'You owe me that, at least.'

But he only closed his eyes. She bit her lip, battling frustration and hurt. She couldn't reach him. He'd retreated into himself and it made her feel invisible. Insignificant. And insignificant was exactly how she'd felt with Tim.

Whereas Jake had become very significant to her.

Her heart gave a dull thud. This wasn't just a fun fling any more, she realised, with a shiver. She turned and looked back at the villa, the warm glow of light in the lounge, the sofa where they'd made love just hours ago. Something had infiltrated her heart, a closeness she had never known before. Jake had knitted himself into her very being and become as much a part of her now as she was herself.

She dipped her head in despair. She'd gone and fallen in love with him.

When? She'd promised herself she wouldn't get attached. She'd been so confident she wouldn't get involved, wouldn't get hurt, couldn't get hurt. Yet here she was, feeling wounded, feeling raw at the sight of his rigid silhouette, silent and untouchable.

How had it happened? Was it their love-making, which had been so different from what she'd known before? Or the long days they'd spent together in quiet intimacy? All their whispered conversations at night when she'd opened herself to him?

They'd arrived here as friends, but in the space of a few days Jake had grown to know her better than . . . anyone, which shocked her. Yet even Natasha and Suzie hadn't witnessed just how difficult her relationship with her parents was, or how much Tim had eroded her self-esteem. She'd fallen in love with the man who'd told her – who'd always been honest with her – that he could never love again because his heart belonged to someone else. How was she going to fix this?

She couldn't. There was only one way this could end, and she knew it would be painful.

'Jake, I won't let you push me away,' she said, steeling herself. She had assured his sister she wouldn't let him mope, after all.

But it seemed that his grief had followed them there, after all. And hurt bubbled up inside her, making her fists ball with frustration that yet again she wasn't enough. 'I know you miss her, but it doesn't help, you know. It doesn't help to hide away in the dark wallowing in self-pity. You could – you could choose to be happy with what you have, rather than what you don't have!'

But even as she spoke the words, she knew she wasn't enough to make him happy.

She was beautiful when she was angry.

The velvet light from the house made her face glow, a star in the dark night. She looked beautiful and she looked strong, wilful, confident. And he was glad that she wasn't afraid to speak her mind and to tell him—

To tell him what he already knew. That things were just fine as they were. He'd been overthinking, overfeeling.

'I'm sorry, Evie. The last few days have been incredible. I've really enjoyed our time together. With you I –' his voice cracked '– I could almost forget everything else. For a while, anyway.'

He'd learned to live and laugh again. When they'd made love, he'd forgotten everything but the moment, her heart beating against his, the sound of his name on her lips. And it was life-affirming, exhilarating.

But no strings, no emotional involvement was what they'd agreed, and those were the terms he would stick to. Tomorrow they'd return home and he wouldn't miss her.

'Almost forget? But not completely?' The fleece blanket slipped a little, exposing her bare shoulder. Her skin was puckered with goose-bumps.

'Never completely.'

He pretended he hadn't seen Evie's look of hurt before she swiftly turned away, hugging the blanket tighter. He ignored the needles of fear that pricked the back of his neck. He refused to analyse why his heart thudded furiously in his chest and memories of her unconscious on the bathroom floor flashed through his head. She had recovered now, and everything was fine.

'I'm sorry I shut you out, but there are parts of me that . . . that will never be the same.'

'I understand,' she said.

But he could tell from the rough edge to her voice that he hadn't said what she'd hoped to hear. His spine stiffened.

His gaze met hers in a silent warning. 'It's been a great trip. Thank you.'

He'd made no promises. He enjoyed her company, but he didn't love her. When they went home to England normal life would resume and he'd be back to his routine, walking Smoke, working, travelling. She'd be just down the road in her shop or dropping in at the Old Hall to fit curtains and fuss over Smoke with that dimpled smile and mischievous glint in her eye.

But she didn't heed the warning. Instead, she took a deep breath, as if she were about to say something difficult. 'Jake . . .' she began.

He looked up just in time to catch the flutter of fear in her eyes before she asked quietly, 'What will happen when we go home tomorrow? To us?'

His skin prickled. 'What will happen? We'll go back to how it was before. That's what we agreed.'

Silence.

'But can we? Now?'

He tensed. Of course they could.

'It's what we agreed,' he repeated.

'I can't do that, Jake,' she said, and her words sounded raw. She looked down at her toes, which were curled under, rubbing against the terracotta tiles. 'I'd rather not see you at all.'

He swallowed hard. 'I see.'

Silence stretched. In the distance a night bird shrieked. He cast her another sidelong glance. She was biting her lip. She looked stricken.

What will happen to us? She'd rather not see him at all?

He had a feeling he knew where this was leading, and an ominous sense of dread settled over him, like a dead weight.

'Why?' he asked. 'Or is that a question I'm going to regret asking?'

'I know we said this would be no strings, that it was fun and nothing more.' She took a long slow breath in and her chin lifted. 'But you see – the thing is . . . I love you.'

He didn't move. His body was rigid with tension. *It can never be love*, he had warned her.

'But we said – I didn't . . .' He cleared his throat. 'You said you weren't interested in a relationship.'

Her eyes shimmered in the semi-darkness. 'I know. But we can't always control how we feel. I didn't ask to feel this way, Jake.' Her voice was small. 'But coming here – the last few days – things have changed between us. I thought you felt it, too. But even if you don't, I can't help it. I can't undo it.'

Jake blew out a long slow breath.

Dammit, Hartwood. What have you done?

Chapter Nineteen

She spoke the words, then quickly closed her mouth, and it was as if she'd just offered up her heart on a tray.

I love you. Such a terrifyingly revealing confession. Yet those words couldn't even begin to convey the swell in her chest, the loaded weight that had grown so fast and by such stealth during the last few weeks and days until now it filled her heart.

Evie made herself breathe. The cold, damp air crawled up her legs, making her shiver. Still Jake said nothing. His silence was torture.

Her heart sank. It was only what she'd expected. She'd heard the warning note in his words: *It's been a great trip. Thank you.*

Goodbye. So long. Farewell.

But she had felt compelled to tell him the truth, so she'd mustered all her courage in the hope that maybe, just maybe, he—

Sometimes being an optimist really sucked.

And now she steeled herself because, mortifying as this conversation was, it wasn't over yet. She could have left it there. She could have turned and fled, like she'd fled when she'd found Tim in bed with another woman, and she could have hidden away for the last few hours here in France, red-faced with shame and humiliation.

But if she did, she'd hate herself for being a coward.

She might not be perfect, but she was honest, and Jake needed to know how she felt. Because these feelings she had for him weren't going away. Before she'd come to France, she had believed she was done with love and romance, that engagements and wedding bells and happy-ever-afters weren't for her. But it wasn't just her confidence that had grown this week: her dreams had too.

'I thought – after Tim – that I didn't want another relationship, but now I know that he didn't so much break my heart as hurt my pride. Tim and I weren't meant for each other. It was never a lasting love.'

He blew out a long, slow breath, and her eyes must have adjusted to the darkness because now she could make out his features enough to tell he was horrified.

Yet there had been times this week when she'd been so sure he felt something for her too. When he'd laughed and danced, when she'd glanced up from her sewing to find him watching her, when he'd made love to her and looked into her eyes and whispered her name as if it were a prayer.

'Tim never loved me. He made me feel small and inadequate and stupid, but I see now that that doesn't mean I am those things. And – and I believe there is someone out there who will accept me as I am . . .' She gripped the balustrade. The rough stone dug into her fingers. '. . . and love me.'

She paused but couldn't bring herself to look at Jake. Instead, she kept her gaze on the emptiness ahead where the olive trees sighed, invisible in the night. 'And I know now that I *do* want my own happy ending.' She lifted her left hand and looked at the bare finger that had once worn Tim's engagement ring. 'I deserve to be loved for myself. I hope to find the one who has eyes only for me.' She took a deep breath and forced herself to meet Jake's gaze. 'I don't want to live in the shadow of another woman.'

He was silent. Her heart drummed as she allowed the silence to unfurl, giving him time to respond.

But he didn't. So she turned and went to leave, her shoulders, her feet, heavy with the pain of rejection.

'I never promised love.'

His rough-edged words stopped her.

'I was honest with you from the start, Evie.'

She looked at him. Contrition was etched into his features. 'I know,' she said. 'I know.'

A deep frown cut through his brow. 'And you're right. You do deserve those things. You are . . .'

Her breath caught as she waited for him to finish.

'You're very special, Evie.'

Her heart sank. She tried to smile but couldn't find her voice to speak.

Chapter Twenty

Jake heaved himself out of the car and trudged round to the back. Smoke bounded out, displaying a lot more energy than Jake felt after their overnight trip to see a client in London.

'All right, all right,' he muttered, as the dog turned in circles, impatiently waiting for him to open the front door.

If he was honest, it had been a wasted trip. He could have dealt with the supply issues by phone and email, but he had kidded himself that it was good customer relations to pay his client a visit. In truth, he was trying to keep himself busy. Trying to distract himself and prevent his mind from wandering, replaying moments and conversations from his holiday with Evie.

He closed the front door with a heavy thud and looked around. Everything was exactly as it had always been, yet his footsteps seemed to echo louder around the empty hall and the house felt uncomfortably quiet. He made his way to his study and slung his jacket over the back of his chair. His gaze instinctively drifted to the window and the rooftops of Willowbrook village. He surveyed the church steeple and the cluster of tall trees beside it, and he pictured the village centre. He'd passed the Button

Hole two days ago because Smoke had tugged him that way. He'd waved at Evie and hurried on, offering Smoke a treat in the hope that the dog wouldn't be disappointed that they hadn't stopped and spoken to her. Smoke had refused the treat and looked back at her shop with confusion – and longing.

Jake wondered what Evie was doing. He hoped she wasn't hurting too much.

He sighed and sat down at the desk. Guilt was eating away at him, but what else could he have done? She had been brave to admit she had feelings for him, and he'd had no option but to repeat what she already knew: that he could never offer her more than friendship. He'd always been honest with her.

Still, he was sorry it had cost them both so dearly. Their friendship had meant a lot to him. He missed her vibrant presence and her sunny outlook. He missed inhaling her apple scent as he woke up next to her and feeling her thick soft hair against his cheek.

He pulled out his phone and typed a text message to her. How was she? When was she going to visit her parents?

Then he sat back. She might not answer. He didn't really expect her to. Yet his thoughts kept leading back to her.

Out of concern, that was all. Concern for a friend.

He fingered the scarf she'd given him and examined the strips of brightly patterned fabrics, the crazy combination of stripes and squares and flowers that butted against each other, singing and shouting in a bizarrely compatible explosion of colour. He looked at the tiny neat hand-sewn stitches that bound it all together and pictured her, head bent in concentration, as she had sewn it. For him.

He only wore it because it reminded him of their trip to France. It had been the perfect holiday – until she'd spoilt it by saying those three words. He let the fabric drop and pushed his hands into his pockets.

She deserved better than him. She deserved a man whose heart wasn't blackened and damaged and twisted. She deserved the fairy tale she dreamed of, and he was sure she'd find her rainbow's end.

This was the best thing for everyone.

The next day his mood hadn't improved. In fact, he was even relieved of the distraction when his sister called to say she was in the area and could she pop in for a quick cup of tea? She wouldn't stay long, she assured him. She had to get back for the kids.

'Wow!' she said, when he opened the door. Wide-eyed, she looked him up and down. 'What a transformation!'

'What do you mean? Have I had a haircut and no one told me?'

She hugged him, then stepped back, but couldn't stop smiling. 'You look like a new man. There's colour in your cheeks, the frown lines have gone, and you're not wearing black!'

He glanced down at his red sweatshirt and blue jeans.

'Clearly that trip did you the world of good!'

'Yes,' he said, picturing the intense Mediterranean

colours, the warm sunlight, and Evie's dimpled smile and gleaming eyes as she'd teased him. Regret plucked at him, but he brushed it aside. 'It was a much-needed break.'

Louisa followed him inside, but he was conscious as he led her into the kitchen that she was watching him curiously, as if trying to decipher a complex puzzle.

'Coffee?' he asked, filling the kettle.

'Yes, please.' She sat on a bar stool and looked around. 'So . . . where's Evie?'

'Evie?' His fingers gripped the cups he'd just reached for and he was glad he had his back to her so his sister couldn't see his expression. 'I don't know.'

'You don't know?' She sounded disappointed.

'Why would I?'

'I thought you two were – you know . . .'

'What?' It came out sharper than he'd intended. The fridge door slammed, and he put the milk down with a clumsy thud.

'. . . an item,' his sister finished calmly, unaffected by his bad temper.

We can't always control how we feel. Evie's words echoed in his mind.

'We're just friends. I told you that before.'

She laughed. 'You really expect me to believe that?'

'Yes,' he said, through gritted teeth, 'because it's the truth.'

Her smile faded. She looked at him a moment longer. 'Whatever.'

Thankfully, she let it go, and over coffee recounted to him how she and her family had spent New Year's Eve.

'Right, I'd better go,' she said, a little later. 'If I'm quick, I might just miss rush-hour traffic.'

Jake accompanied her to her car. As they reached it, he cleared his throat. 'I – ah – I thought I might come and visit this weekend – if you're around, that is.'

Her head whipped round. 'Yes, we're around,' she said, beaming. 'That would be lovely!'

'Or perhaps you'd all prefer to come here? You could bring Harry and the boys, and I could invite Scarlett and her little ones too. We could have a belated turkey dinner together.'

Louisa was clearly delighted. 'That sounds wonderful! The boys will love this place,' she said, gesturing at the gardens and fields that surrounded them. 'There's so much for them to explore, so much space to run around!'

He was pleased that, for once, he'd made his sister smile. 'I'll arrange it, then.'

She planted a light kiss on his cheek. 'I'm so glad you're feeling better, Jakey.'

He heard the relief in her voice and felt a pinch of guilt for the worry he'd caused her these last couple of years.

'But do me a favour, will you?' She weighed her car keys in her hand.

'What's that?'

'Patch things up with Evie. Because she's good for you.'

'What is she – a medicinal tonic?'

'I like her,' said Louisa. 'She's open and honest. A ray of sunshine. She's exactly what you need.'

'Is she?' he said drily.

'Yes. And you miss her, don't you?'

He wanted to say no but his mouth refused to cooperate. He looked at his shoes, because he couldn't meet his sister's eye.

Louisa tilted her head a little. 'What happened between you two? Did you sleep with her?'

He stiffened. 'That's really none of your business.'

'I'll take that as a yes. Then what?' Her eyes narrowed. 'Wait. Let me guess – you ended it?'

He pressed his lips flat. It was pointless resisting his sister's interrogation. She could read him better than anyone.

'You bastard!' She glared at him.

'It wasn't like that!' he said quickly. 'We had agreed no strings . . .'

Louisa rolled her eyes. She made as if to leave, then stopped. 'Tell me something, Jake. How do you feel now? Do you ever think about her?'

His heart thudded. *All the time.* 'Yes,' he said quietly.

'You miss her?'

Terribly. 'A little.'

Memories assaulted him: Evie with the wind in her hair, head tipped back, grinning; the two of them whirling around the kitchen and out onto the terrace; falling asleep together, their limbs entangled, her hair splayed over his chest. Her laughter rang in his ears; her whispered words in the quiet of the night haunted him. His chest constricted.

Louisa placed a hand on her hip. 'So?'

'So what?'

'What are you going to do about it?'

He frowned. 'Do about what?'

She jabbed a finger at his chest. 'You love her. You're just too scared to face up to it.'

'I don't love her.'

He didn't. He never had. He pictured her lying prone on the bathroom floor, the white lights of the hospital room.

This can never be love. If that's what you want, you should walk away now.

Alone was familiar. It was safe. He tried to quash the hollow ache in his gut.

'And I'm not – never was – in the market for another relationship.'

Louisa stared at him, stone-faced. 'You're planning never to have another relationship, ever? You're going to lead a life of celibacy, are you?'

Anger simmered inside him. His jaw clenched. 'What would *you* do, after what happened to me?'

Her expression softened and she said quietly, 'Oh, Jake. You lost your wife and it was painful, it was unfair, it was tragic, and you were incredibly unlucky. But you're over the worst now. You will get through this and you are getting through this. And, be honest, Evie's played a big part in helping you get to this point, hasn't she?'

His chin went up and he bristled at the truth in her words but couldn't bring himself to reply. The blackness of the last couple of years rushed at him head-on, like a charging bull. He couldn't go through that again. If anything happened to her . . . He couldn't risk opening his heart to those levels of pain a second time.

And yet his sister's words resonated. Evie *had* helped him. She *was* good for him. She had brought out the man in him and helped banish the beast he had been when she'd first met him.

She had changed him.

'You're more positive, you're walking tall and even smiling – occasionally – again.' Louisa's eyes were warm with sympathy as she paused to draw breath. 'Whatever happened with Evie, you need to sort it out, Jake. You're hurting. I'm guessing she's hurting too, and there's an obvious solution to all this – but first you need to take your head out of the sand and admit to yourself how you feel.'

'I don't –' he began '– I never—'

But Louisa was striding away.

He watched as his sister got into her car, waved and drove off. He stayed there, long after her car had vanished from view. Smoke whined and tugged at his sleeve, asking none too subtly to be taken for a walk.

'Okay, Smoke. In a minute.'

He ran a finger under the collar of his sweater. It felt tight, his skin clammy. He unfastened the chain around his neck and cradled it in his palm. The slim gold band was duller than he remembered. It felt light in his hand.

The sensation of ice cracking and breaking loose made him frown. Overhead, pillowy thick clouds flowed past, driven by the wintry breeze, scattering like jigsaw pieces.

He would always love Maria, but he knew then that he was ready to let go.

Evie hurried to finish serving a customer, then turned to the next lady waiting in line. The Button Hole was so busy she'd taken on a new assistant, Liberty, to help in the shop, and all her new courses were fully booked, with waiting lists for some. The bank was happy. So was Evie. At least, she would be if she weren't so preoccupied.

'I'll have a metre of each of these four fabrics, please,' said her customer.

Evie unrolled the first and picked up her rotary cutter.

'Would you like me to do that while you go on your lunchbreak?' asked her assistant. 'You haven't stopped all morning.'

'Oh, thank you, but I'm all right,' said Evie, and sliced through the turquoise batik. It was totally out of character for her, but she'd lost her appetite recently. 'You go, Liberty. I can manage here.'

Liberty disappeared into the back room.

'Liberty, like the fabric?' asked the customer.

Evie smiled. 'Yes, but ironically she hates flowery material. Her quilts are all bold, bright colours and really modern designs.'

Her customer smiled, then returned her attention to the fabrics she was buying. 'I've never made a quilt before, but I've always wanted to, and my daughter bought me a voucher for your shop for Christmas. Now I'm retired I have the chance to try my hand at it.'

'It's the perfect time of year to start sewing,' said Evie. 'When the weather's cold and you can't get out as much as you'd like, nothing beats sitting in front of the fire with a cosy quilt on your lap, stitching.'

And yet for the last week she had lost her enthusiasm for sewing. She dreaded going home to Love Lane. The evenings felt long and lonely. She forced away the negative thoughts and tried to focus on her customer. 'These look really pretty. What are you making?' she asked, as she folded the pile of fabrics and slipped them into a bag.

'It's a throw for my sofa.'

Evie's mind drifted away as the lady described the pattern she was planning to use. Outside, a tall figure passed the shop, catching her eye – but her hopes sank when she saw it wasn't Jake.

She'd seen him passing with Smoke. She was hurt that he hadn't stopped, but she hadn't really expected any different. She pictured him, alone in his big house on the hill. He'd sent her a short text but she knew he was just being polite and it hadn't really said anything. He'd cordially enquired when she was seeing her parents, she'd answered, then heard nothing more since. He had clearly moved on, putting her out of his mind.

If only Evie could do the same. But her thoughts were stuck, like a knot of thread jammed in a needle. She wondered if he'd been glad to be reunited with Smoke, if he regretted their holiday. Did he think she was a fool? She'd suggested the fling, after all. She *was* a fool for not sticking to the rules they'd agreed.

Stop it, she told herself. Thinking about him was

pointless. He had chosen to live alone, and she understood he still had feelings for his wife. His loyalty was one of the things she loved about him. She felt a sharp pain, as if her heart had been torn and left frayed at the edges. To tell the truth, she was deeply envious of his loyalty to Maria. She longed to be loved like that.

And one day she would be, she told herself. She just hadn't met him yet.

Two weeks ago she hadn't dared to hope for such a thing, and she had Jake to thank for rebuilding her confidence in the way he had, for helping her to see that not all men were like Tim, and that somewhere there was a man who would love and accept her as she was. She smiled, but it was a thin, watery smile.

Evie warily eyed her reflection in the hall mirror. The scarlet wool of her coat made her look pale, and she traced a finger over the faint smudges beneath her eyes. Her heart was heavy, not helped by the prospect of visiting her parents today.

She pulled herself up tall. Feeling sorry for herself wasn't going to change anything. Look on the bright side: at least she could report to her dad that the Button Hole was beginning to turn a profit. A few weeks ago, nothing had mattered more to her. So why now did it feel like an empty victory? A short spell in France had been enough to turn her world upside down. She was reaching for her scarf when a loud knock at the door made her jump.

The door creaked as she opened it and she blinked as

she took in the tall figure in a long coat who stood there, his Dalmatian at his side.

'Jake!' she said, then made herself clamp down on the delight she felt at seeing him, and the hope that he might have had a change of heart. She pulled the scarf tight around her neck and looked about for her car keys. Where had she left them? 'Actually, this isn't a good time. I was just going to—'

'Visit your parents,' he finished for her. His smile was both conciliatory and wary. He watched her cautiously, as if he was unsure what reception he would get.

She blinked at him. 'How do you know?'

'You told me. Can I come with you? I offered to give you moral support.'

True. Although he had made that offer before her bumbled confession of love. But he was a man of his word, she thought, with a ripple of admiration. He was still offering to keep his promise, despite all that had happened between them. She weighed up his offer. Would it make the visit harder to have with her the man who had recently broken her heart?

No, she decided, remembering how he'd stood up to her father. Any kind of moral support was welcome. 'Well . . . I suppose so,' she said, trying hard to sound casual and not too eager.

Smoke gave a small bark and she rubbed his ears. 'Hello, gorgeous.' She looked up at Jake. 'Is Smoke coming too?'

'If that's all right with you? We can take my car.'

'It's fine. Mum and Dad have a big garden he can run around in.'

As he drove, she made one or two attempts at conversation. 'How's work?' she asked.

'Fine.'

She wondered if he'd struck a deal with François, but she didn't like to ask. It was too painful to be reminded of the night they'd spent at the château. That was when everything had changed. When she'd foolishly suggested they take their friendship to another level, and she'd believed she could handle the emotional consequences of doing that.

How naive she'd been.

'Bet you're glad the snow's melted.'

'Actually,' he said, 'I realise now that it was quite pretty.'

Evie stared at him. What had happened to Mr Arctic, who saw only the negatives in everything?

He smiled enigmatically and returned his attention to the road ahead.

'Have you been away much with work?'

'A little. Things are slow at this time of year.'

She couldn't think of anything else to say or ask, so she let silence settle. The gently undulating hills unfurled around them, the bare fields making a patchwork of muddy browns and grubby greens.

'I've got an interview for a new job,' he said suddenly.

Evie's head whipped round sharply. Her heart thudded. He was leaving?

She did her best to sound indifferent. 'Oh, yes? What kind of job?' God, she should have anticipated this. He was moving away to spare them the awkwardness of bumping into each other all the time. She felt deflated. Her eyes burned and she blinked hard.

'Working as a GP.'

'You're going to be a doctor again?'

He smiled. 'I miss it. You were right – it was much more rewarding than importing wine.'

'Jake, that's wonderful!' Her hands balled into tiny fists, she was so excited for him. He'd make an excellent doctor. 'I really hope you get the job.'

'If I do, you'll be seeing a lot more of me. It's in the next village.'

'The next village?'

He nodded. 'I won't need to travel any more.'

She wasn't sure how to respond. She wasn't sure how she felt about seeing more of him. It could be tricky. But she was glad he was finally settling down. Perhaps this meant he'd made peace with his loss. Perhaps he felt able to move on now. She hoped so. Her own feelings aside, she wished only the best for him. Just because things hadn't worked out between them didn't stop her hoping he'd find happiness someday, somehow.

'So how was your Christmas?' Evie asked her parents politely.

She put her cup of tea on the table beside her, worried that she might spill it over her mother's expensive white rug or, even worse, drop it and chip the vintage Royal Doulton china. Beside her, Jake sat back in his chair. His unexpected presence had caused her parents to raise eyebrows, but Evie had introduced him as a friend. Hopefully, having him there would put them off discussing her love life – or lack of it.

'Good,' said her dad.

'It was all right. Okay,' her mum agreed.

They glanced at each other, instantly sparking Evie's curiosity. What were they not saying?

Through the French windows she could see Smoke sniffing around the walled garden, chasing a robin, exploring.

'How was Tim?' she asked.

Her mother peered at her feet. Her father clasped his hands together. 'He – ah . . . It was a good job you weren't there, actually.'

Why did her father look so uncomfortable? Her curiosity was definitely piqued now. 'Oh. Why?'

Her parents exchanged another look.

Then her dad blurted, 'He turned up with another woman in tow! Would you believe it? We were quite shocked.'

'Were you?' Evie did her best to suppress a smile and glanced at Jake. A warm, smug feeling of *I told you so* spread through her.

'Yes. So were his parents. They knew nothing about it until he rolled up at the door with her. He said it was a recent thing but . . .'

When he didn't go on, Evie prompted, 'But?'

'Well, it seemed to me they knew each other very well.' He cleared his throat. 'Anna, her name is.'

'Oh, yes. She's the woman he cheated on me with,' said

Evie, pleased that the memory didn't sting any more. 'Are they back together, then?'

'Very much so, apparently. I'd say he's moved on from his engagement to you, anyway. That ship has sailed.'

'Yes.' It had sailed six months ago, she wanted to say, but bit her tongue.

'So,' said her dad, looking at Jake, 'you two. Is there something you want to tell us?'

Hot colour rushed to her cheeks. 'Oh, no!' Evie said quickly. 'No, I told you – we're just friends.'

Her dad nodded and reached into his inside pocket. 'In that case, you'll be interested to read this.'

He handed her a folded sheet of paper. A chill slid through Evie as she unfolded it. They wouldn't – would they? Not with Jake here, surely.

'I had a flick through my contacts and found a few names for you.'

'Names?'

'Of young men with good connections. From suitable families, you know.'

Evie put the sheet down and met her father's gaze square on. 'No. I don't know.'

'Oh, Evie, don't be facetious. We're trying to help you make a good match. Find a man who will support you when your silly shop fails.'

Jake sat up taller. He didn't say anything, but she sensed the tension in him, and a muscle flickered in his jaw.

Evie took a deep breath. 'Actually, my shop is doing really well. Things have turned around in the last few weeks. I've worked hard to—'

'It's no good putting it off, Evelyn,' her father cut in. 'You need to think about your future.'

'I have thought about my future, and it doesn't involve marrying someone my parents have picked out for me,' she said, through gritted teeth.

She reached for the end of her ponytail and darted a sidelong glance at Jake. Although she had changed her views on marriage now, she hoped that one day she might meet a man who loved her as Jake had loved his wife, with the same unfailing loyalty and devotion.

Her father's cheeks reddened. Anger pulsed from him. 'Well, then, you need to rethink your career, girl. Playing around with bits of fabric isn't going to keep a roof over your head. You had the best education money could buy, but it's been wasted!'

Was that really what they thought? She flinched. Her fingers had wound her hair so tight that it tugged at her scalp. She released it. 'I – I—'

'Take the list, darling, and at least have a look at it,' her mother said.

Her cheeks burned. What must Jake be thinking? She should never have agreed to let him come here with her. 'I don't need a list, Mum. This isn't the eighteenth century.'

'We're trying to help you but you're just being difficult!' said her father.

Evie stiffened. Why did conversations with her parents always descend into an argument? No matter what she did or said, it was never right, never good enough. Would they always look at her like this, with exasperation and fury?

Jake sat forward and opened his mouth to speak, but she held up her hand. This was a battle she had to fight herself. 'I'm not being difficult,' she said quickly. 'You're always telling me I'm not good enough, but please listen to me: I don't want the same things as you. Society connections don't interest me. Neither does the type of career you have in mind. Having a big salary and working in the City – that isn't what I want.'

She half expected her father to interrupt but for once he didn't. Perhaps he and her mother were caught off guard by her sudden show of assertiveness.

She tried to keep her voice as steady as possible. 'I love sewing,' she said. 'My business is starting to become successful, and I'm – I'm happy! Really happy running my shop and living in a place where people accept me for who I am. If that isn't good enough for you, then – then hard luck!'

Her father shook his head, and sighed. 'Why is it always like this with you? Your sister was never so difficult. She never argued with us or defied us like this—'

'Stop!' said Evie. Her parents stared at her, shocked. 'Stop comparing me to Zara. You refuse to talk about her most of the time, you've made her a taboo subject, yet you compare me to her and always find me wanting. Well, that's enough. It's not what she would have wanted, and it's not – not helpful.' She paused to catch her breath. Then added more quietly, 'I am not Zara, and I never will be. I'm me. Evie. And – and I'd really like you to accept me as I am.'

She felt an unexpected rush of relief to have finally

given voice to what she'd been feeling for so long. Silence bounced around the room. Even Jake looked startled.

Then his lips curved into a proud smile. He turned to address her parents. 'Evie's right,' he said softly.

'I beg your pardon?' said her father.

'In your eyes Evie's sister is perfect, isn't she?' Jake went on. His tone wasn't confrontational, but sympathetic. 'She's so perfect, she's almost . . . unreal.'

Evie stared at him. Where was he going with this?

Her parents' faces became flushed. It was clear they were upset, but Jake continued, 'But you know something? She wasn't really perfect. She was human too. She had flaws and failings just like the rest of us.'

'How dare you talk about our daughter like this? You never even knew her—'

'How dare I? Because I've done it myself.'

A look of deep sorrow made his eyes glaze with pain. And this cut through Evie.

He said gently, 'I'm as guilty as you are of putting a loved one on a pedestal.'

Her parents' eyes widened, and they glanced at each other, unsure how to react to this. Their anger seemed to have been punctured by this huge admission.

'I loved my wife more than life itself. I loved her long after she'd gone. No one could measure up to her – my memory of her. But now I see how distorted that memory was. How inaccurate. Idealised. And it's only now I've realised this that I can finally let go of her. Believe that I might one day love again. Love someone else.'

He turned to Evie. 'Maria wasn't as cheerful and extrovert as you. She didn't have your talent for sewing, for making beautiful things out of scraps of fabric, for finding the good in everything life threw at her or the people around her. She didn't have your work ethic, or your determination to succeed and your generosity with everyone you meet.'

A stunned silence swept through the room.

He told her parents quietly, 'So, instead of dwelling on what you've lost, why not open your eyes and appreciate what you have?'

Outside, Smoke barked. Then Evie heard the patter of paws on gravel, and his face appeared at the window. But no one else noticed. Her parents were looking uncertainly at each other.

Finally, her father spoke. 'We do accept her as she is,' he said weakly, and without conviction.

Evie frowned. 'All you do is criticise me.'

'Have you ever supported her?' asked Jake.

'We paid for the best schools, we arranged a job for her. We tried to introduce her to a young man with good prospects.'

'But did you ever give her emotional support?' They stared at each other. 'Did you ever support her in what *she* wants to do, in establishing her business? Have you noticed how hard she works, how much time and effort she's invested in trying to make her shop successful? Have you noticed how talented she is? Sewing is her passion, yet you've never shown any interest in it. In fact, from what I can see, you belittle it.'

His barrage of questions was met with an awkward silence.

Her father cleared his throat. Her mother shifted uncomfortably in her seat.

'I think we should go,' Evie said quietly. 'I'll get Smoke.'

No one responded, so she stood up.

Jake and Evie drove back in silence. She didn't like to leave relations with her parents so hostile, but until everyone had calmed down and had time to digest what had been said, she decided it was the best form of damage limitation.

She glanced at Jake. His brow was furrowed in concentration as he steered smoothly into a roundabout.

It's only now that I've realised this that I can finally let go of her. Believe that I might one day love again.

His admission had been so unexpected that she was still trying to absorb it, but it could only be a good thing that he'd finally come to terms with his grief. She imagined it wouldn't be long before he met someone. Evie tried to picture him with another woman, but it hurt too much so she bundled that thought away hurriedly.

'Thank you,' she said, finally breaking the silence.

'What for?'

'Saying what you did.' Standing up for her.

'I just said what I think.' He shot her a worried look. 'I hope I haven't destroyed your relationship with them.'

'I'll talk to them. To be honest, it felt good to bring those things out into the open.'

'Well, I hope they'll think about it.'

She paused. 'I'm glad you feel you can move on. I'm sure it's what Maria would have wanted for you.'

He didn't respond. His expression remained unreadable. They pulled off the main road and towards Willowbrook village.

'I – ah – I hope your interview goes well,' she said.

'Interview? Oh. Yes. Thanks.'

She reached for her ponytail and wound it around her fingers, wishing things weren't so strained between them. Jake looked preoccupied. He clearly had other things on his mind.

'Will you let me know if you get the job?'

He nodded. A deep frown sliced through his brow.

'Dr Hartwood.' She smiled. 'It has a nice ring to it.'

'Where should I drop you? At home?'

Her smile instantly vanished. He couldn't wait to be rid of her. She swallowed back the hurt of rejection. 'Actually, I need to collect some fabric from the shop.'

He parked outside the Button Hole.

'Right,' said Evie.

'Right.'

'Thanks for the lift. And – and everything.' She reached for the door, desperate to escape the stifling atmosphere, yet not wanting to leave him.

'We'll come with you,' he said, getting out. He opened the back door. 'Come on, Smoke.'

She was surprised. She thought the dog had already run around a lot in her parents' garden, but what did she know?

'I hear your classes are all booked up for the term,' said Jake, as she opened the shop. He bent to clip Smoke's lead on.

'Who told you?'

'Natasha.'

'Yes, they are. And I've been inundated with commissions for quilts too. They're so much more fun to make than curtains. More profitable too.'

It was everything she'd hoped for. But now her heart longed for something else, something more. She missed Jake.

'I'm glad,' he said, and his eyes creased as he smiled.

She felt a rush of warmth. 'Thanks.'

A car drove past.

She cleared her throat. 'The fabric's in the back room. I'll just get it.'

Jake waited outside while she ducked in to get what she needed. He could hear her humming to herself, a sad lament – from the musical *Oliver!*? He wasn't sure. It was slightly out of tune, but he found it impossibly endearing and smiled to himself.

She emerged clutching a bag of fabric, and while she locked the shop door he tried to muster the courage to say what he hadn't been able to say in front of her parents.

'That's everything,' she said. 'Are you—?'

'I love you, Evie.'

'What?' She blinked up at him.

He smiled. 'I love you, Evie.'

Her mouth fell open. The bell of the shop door could still be heard jingling faintly inside, and Smoke gave two happy barks.

'I love how you brighten my life and everyone else's. I love how passionate you are about sewing and this village and your life. I love how generous you are with your time and advice and helping others. I love how determined you are to see the positive in everything and everyone. I love how you're clumsy and creative and brave enough to stand up to me and tell me when I'm being an arse. You've taught me to live again and to laugh . . . and to love again.'

He stopped and held his breath, praying it wasn't too late, hoping against hope that she could forgive him for having pushed her away and hurt her and been blind to what his heart had felt all along but his head had refused to accept.

He realised now that Evie could never replace Maria, but she didn't need to. She was her own woman. Different. Unique. His Pollyanna.

'Oh, Jake . . .' she whispered, and her eyes shone.

'I love you, Evie.' He was surprised how easy thc words were to say. How natural they felt. Overdue, even.

She smiled. Smoke barked again.

'He's agreeing,' said Jake.

'Is he?'

'Yes. He loves you too. We both love you and miss you and –' his voice broke '– and need you.' He smiled ruefully. 'My life has no colour without you in it, Evie Miller.'

She frowned. 'But you love Maria,' she said softly. 'You said you'd always love her.'

'I was wrong. I was scared to love again. I still am, truth be told. Hanging on to the grief and guilt seemed less terrifying than taking another chance on love. But you've helped me live again, Evie. You fell into my life and changed everything! Changed me.' She had brought light where previously he'd seen only darkness, laughter where there had been silence, and warmth, energy, hope. 'I need you.'

She beamed. 'I'm here. I'm not going anywhere.'

'I'm going to do everything I can to make you happy and keep you close – if you'll let me, that is?'

Relief rushed through him as she stood on tiptoe, threw her arms around him and kissed him fiercely.

Across the street passers-by stopped and pointed and murmured to each other. Above their heads, a window opened and Marjorie from the bakery next door peered down at them, then grinned.

Jake shook his head. There really was no privacy in this village. But for once he didn't mind. He bent his head and kissed Evie one more time for good measure.

The small crowd clapped and wolf-whistled.

'Oh Jake,' Evie smiled, 'I love you too.'

Epilogue

Evie perched on the edge of the sofa, wishing she could relax. Smoke was curled up at her feet and Jake sat beside her. He reached for her hand and gave it a reassuring squeeze. She smiled her thanks.

'This is a nice place you have here, Jake,' said her father.

They'd invited her parents to the Old Hall rather than Evie's cottage simply because there was more room. The smell of something roasting in the oven drifted through from the kitchen, and next door in the dining room the table was laid, ready for the meal.

'I love the furniture,' said her mother, running a finger over the arm of her chair. The fabric was a modern print, but Evie had used it to re-cover a collection of mismatched antique chairs and sofas. With lots of rugs and cushions the effect was elegant and in keeping with the house's history, but warm and inviting at the same time.

Jake nodded. 'Evie chose the décor for this room. She has good taste, wouldn't you agree?'

Evie blushed and her parents murmured assent.

Her father looked at her. 'You made the curtains too?'

'Actually, we had them made. I'm too busy now with quilt commissions and classes in the shop.'

He nodded. A short silence followed.

'Did you know Jake has a new job?' she said. 'He's working as a GP in the local doctor's surgery.'

'Oh, yes? Are you enjoying it?'

Jake's eyes creased as he smiled. 'Very much. I had forgotten how rewarding it is. Plus I'm not travelling now, which means I'm around a lot more.'

He and Evie shared a look. They treasured their quiet evenings together.

Jake got up. 'I'll just go and check on the food.'

He closed the door behind him, and Evie braced herself. She and her parents had spoken on the phone, but this was the first time they'd met face to face since that terrible confrontation at their house.

Her father cleared his throat. 'I'm sorry we made you feel as if we loved Zara more. Her death hit us badly. But we shouldn't have been so hard on you.'

His quiet remorse was so out of character and so unexpected it took Evie by surprise. 'I know. It was a shock for all of us. I miss her too.'

'But we still have you, and we don't want to lose you,' her father went on.

Emotion welled inside her, sudden and fierce, and Evie jumped up to throw her arms around him. It felt unfamiliar and strange, but good. And she was relieved. She'd been so worried that she might have gone a step too far with her outburst last time they'd met. In fact, she seemed to have brought into the open what, previously, they hadn't been able to talk about.

She hugged her mother, too.

'We're going to clear out her room. Redecorate. Start afresh.'

'Really?'

Her mother nodded. 'It's time. We have to let go.'

Evie swallowed the lump in her throat. 'Would you like me to make a quilt out of Zara's dresses and shirts? Something to remember her by. I could make one for you and one for me.'

Her mother looked surprised, then thrilled. 'That would be lovely. Thank you.'

The door swung open and Jake appeared with a tray of glasses and a large green bottle. He took in the scene in front of him and grinned. 'Champagne, anyone?'

'Absolutely,' said her father. They filled the flutes and drank a toast. 'To new beginnings. We wish you both all the best – in your jobs, and in your relationship.'

Evie and Jake's eyes locked as they chinked glasses. 'To new beginnings.'

Acknowledgements

Thanks to Megan Carroll, my agent, for all you've done to get me here today. A publishing deal is the golden prize that others see, but I know how much more you've done behind the scenes, negotiating on my behalf, and generally being in my corner.

Thanks also to my editor, Kimberley Atkins and her assistant, Madeleine Woodfield, for taking a chance on me, being so professional and a delight to work with.

My grateful thanks to Peter Moss for his enthusiastic advice on Jake's Bentley (1952 R-Type, in case anyone was wondering). After speaking to you, Peter, I almost wanted to buy one myself – maybe one day.

Thanks also to Louise Barrett, who patiently answered my many questions on curtain fitting.

Huge thanks to my good friend Jacqui Cooper, who is always there and who understands. I couldn't do this without you, Jacq.

Thanks to Ian, who patiently listens to me moan about the latest plot hole I've got myself into, and always surprises me with his really good suggestions.

Special thanks to Marian Keall for reading my book and checking the sewing. And finally, thank you to

Bowdon Quilters for welcoming me into your group and advising me on numerous sewing questions, most especially the patchwork scarf Evie made (which would have been a tie if you hadn't warned me about the difficulty of making one! Phew). You're the most talented, knowledgeable and nurturing group of ladies I've met, and here's to many more evenings of companionable stitching. xxx

Read on for an extract from Luc and Natasha's story in *A Forget-Me-Not Summer*

Coming March 2020

Prologue

London, three years ago

'Is there anyone we can call for you?'

Natasha blinked. The nurse smiled kindly. Her eyes were the rich blue of hyacinths, filled with concern and pity.

'Your husband maybe?' The nurse looked at the ring on her left hand.

'I left him a message. He's abroad.'

'A family member?'

She shook her head.

'You're going to need a D and C. Dilation and curettage. It's a minor operation, but necessary. Do you understand, Natasha?'

She nodded. The baby was gone. Her heart folded up on itself and she squeezed her eyes shut against the pain.

Afterwards, she lay staring at the white ceiling. The fluorescent lights tinged everything violet. Losing the baby still felt too enormous, too violent to think about so she turned her mind to Luc instead. She had to come up with a plan. What would happen when he came? Would he even come at all? His work was so important, after all, she thought bitterly. She knew she ranked very low down in his life and he'd only married her for the baby. She held her left hand up and the platinum ring was a silver blur that swam and swayed. She blinked hard. When he'd proposed she'd hoped it would be the start of something new, that he'd put his freedom-loving days behind him, and they'd work to become a family. She'd hoped they'd both share the same goal, and the baby would bring them together. She'd hoped so hard.

The nurse came back. 'Did you have a name for the baby?' she asked gently.

Natasha nodded. She hadn't discussed it with Luc – they were barely talking – but it was certain in her mind. 'Hope. Her name was Hope.'

Now Hope had died there was nothing left, no reason for her to stay. The pain was crushing, intense.

The sound of quick heavy footsteps in the corridor made them both look up. There were raised voices, then Luc appeared, breathless. She was surprised.

'I came as fast as I could,' he said.

Her heartbeat picked up at the sight of him. His dark hair, his treacle-dark eyes. She wondered if she'd ever stop loving him. *He doesn't love you, though.*

He stayed with her as she drifted off, welcoming the anaesthetic of sleep. He was still there when she woke up and the nurses told her she could be discharged. He took her back to his penthouse, and she didn't have the energy to argue.

Back at his flat, he looked worried, he couldn't do enough for her. It was as if he was speaking to her through a funnel, his words were muffled and distant. 'Are you hungry?' he asked, 'What can I get you?'

She shook her head. Too little, too late, she thought. This wasn't the man he'd been the last few weeks. Since she'd told him about the baby resentment had filled this big flat, pressing against the glass walls.

He left the room, she heard the front door shut, and a memory came back of when she'd left her great aunt's house at sixteen. She'd made a promise to herself then that she'd never allow herself to be in that situation again: unwanted, resented. A plan was assembling in her mind.

It didn't take long to pack her clothes, toothbrush, and the tiny framed photograph of her parents. She was waiting by the door, ready to leave when he came back from the shops.

'What are you doing?' He stared at her.

He had a pint of milk in his hand. She looked at that. 'I'm going home.'

She thanked her lucky stars that she'd kept the lease for her bedsit these last two months. Perhaps a part of her had always known it would end this way.

'But you've only just come out of hospital. You can't go.'

'I am.'

'Why?'

She blinked. Her head was fuzzy, the room tilted left, then right. She put her hand out and touched the wall to steady herself. He doesn't love you, she reminded herself silently.

'You're not strong enough—' he began.

'Because it's over. The pregnancy was a mistake. We only married because of the baby, and now…' She couldn't stay where she wasn't wanted. Self-preservation kicked in and she lifted her head, she looked him in the eye. 'Now we can both get on with our lives.'

He didn't argue. He didn't say anything at all. His silence sliced through her, killing any doubts she'd still carried.

The intercom buzzed. Her taxi had arrived. She bent to pick up her case. Tears welled, salty and hot. She wished she wasn't so weak, she wished she didn't love him so much, so fiercely and completely.

'I'll take that,' he said nodding at her suitcase.

Their hands collided. He snatched the case away from her and she mumbled something about divorce papers, then left.

He didn't try to stop her. Far from it. He saw her to the taxi, he lifted her luggage into the boot, then stood back, hands in his pocket, his mouth a flat line, and watched as the taxi drove away.

He didn't love her, he never had. And that was why she had to go.

Chapter One

Present day

Natasha was slicing the thorns off a marshmallow-pink rose when he came in. The door chimed and she glanced up, ready to smile, then froze. The flower in her hand was forgotten and she stared, because there, in her shop, was Luc.

Her heart thumped hard. The shop flooded with cold air, as if it were the middle of winter, not this bright June afternoon. His tall figure and broad shoulders filled the door and his dark eyes fixed on her, but gave nothing away. She swallowed, feeling a sharp twist in her chest, and glanced at the back room. But of course Debbie had already gone home, so she was alone.

'Natasha,' he said, stepping forward and closing the door. 'Good to see you.'

The sound of his voice was as unsettling as an earthquake. Deep. Sure of himself.

'Luc,' she said. She couldn't disguise her shock. It had been – how long? – three years since she'd last seen him. 'Why are you here?'

He didn't answer immediately but glanced around her tiny shop, taking in his surroundings. She followed his gaze from the sunflowers to the gerberas, and for a moment she hoped this might be an accident. That, by some bizarre coincidence, he'd arrived in this tiny village and had walked in here to buy a bouquet. But then he turned back to look at her and his eyes, the colour of molten chocolate, fixed on her with such a fierce look of determination that she knew it was no accident. Her fingers gripped the rose a little tighter.

'You could at least pretend to look pleased to see me,' he said.

He was right, she thought. She might feel like she'd just been plunged back in time to a dark place of violent emotions, but she didn't want him to know how much he was affecting her. Not when, in the past, he'd been so cool with her.

Pretend, she told herself; act as if you're totally indifferent to him.

'I'm just – just surprised, that's all. I wasn't expecting you. You should have called.' As she spoke, she noticed that he'd changed. The details were subtle; small lines around his eyes, a few greys at his temples. He was still good-looking though, she noted grudgingly. And he looked effortlessly stylish, even in a simple cream jumper and jeans. She suddenly felt self-conscious. No doubt he would disapprove of her new, quirky style; he'd think her outfit was eccentric and too bright, not sophisticated like him. She fought the urge to hide her fingernails, painted pale blue with tiny daisies, telling herself it didn't matter what he thought. She might have tried to please him in the past, but those days were over.

'There wasn't time,' he said and looked at the flower in her hand, but there was an uncharacteristically distant look in his eyes. 'It was quicker to come straight here.'

Natasha frowned. Really? How much time would it have taken to call her from the train or the car or however he'd arrived?

'Don't tell me, you urgently need a bunch of flowers?'

He shook his head and the corner of his mouth tilted, almost a smile and impossibly sexy. She was certain that no woman could look at him and not feel a little weak in the legs.

'No. Not flowers. I need you.'

She put the rose down What did he mean, he needed her?

And why did her mind instantly fill with heated images? Memories of him and her. Naked.

She shook her head, feeling dizzy, struggling to think straight. 'Me? What on earth would you need me for?'

'I need your help.'

As he held her gaze steadily, she realised he was being serious and a spike of emotion shot through her, something between fear and anger. 'Luc, I'm your ex-wife. We're not usually top of the list for being keen to help.'

'I wouldn't ask if it wasn't necessary. Besides, I have faith in you to help, ex-wife or not.'

Did he now? She eyed him suspiciously: was he saying she was a pushover? But then she noticed he looked pale, and now she wondered if the lines around his eyes were signs of ageing or of something else – strain possibly, tiredness? Though she tried to prevent it, she felt a tug of concern. 'What's wrong, Luc? What's happened?'

A look flashed through his eyes: preoccupied, pained.

'You're not on the run from the police, are you?' she joked, but it was feeble, and she wished she hadn't said anything. She was just nervous, rattled by his unexpected appearance here, by the desperation etched into his handsome features.

'Is there somewhere we could talk?' he asked.

She glanced at the clock. 'I suppose I could close a little early ...' Then she threw him a stern warning look. 'But whatever you've got to say, you'll have to say it here.'

'OK.' He was so quick to accept that she knew something was seriously wrong and anxiety needled her more strongly than ever. He might be her ex-husband but that didn't prevent her from feeling sympathy for him. It just made her incredibly wary.

She locked the shop door, flipped the sign to 'closed', and dropped the roses she'd been trimming into a bucket of water. Then she returned to stand behind the counter. She felt safer with a bit of space between them. It seemed incredible that after three years apart he still had the power to make her feel so on edge.

'So what's the problem?' she asked, trying to sound detached and efficient, though her hands were unsteady as she swept up the thorns and leaves and cuttings scattered across the counter.

'My father is ill,' he said. 'Very ill, in fact.'

She stopped tidying and looked up. 'Oh Luc, I'm sorry.'

She'd never met his parents, not even when they were married, but her heart went out to him.

'He collapsed, it's his heart, and the next few weeks – days – are critical.'

She nodded cautiously, unclear how this had anything to do with her or how she could help.

Luc ran his tongue across his lips. 'I've just been to visit. All the family are there …' He swallowed again, then met her gaze. Steadily. 'But he was asking for you.'

'Me?' She laughed, a nervous and high-pitched sound. 'Why me? I've never even met him before.'

A flush of colour filled her cheeks and she turned to deposit the cuttings in a bin behind the counter, then briskly dusted off her hands.

'Exactly.' He picked up a half-clipped leaf she'd missed and absently rolled it between his fingers. 'He was unhappy when he learned that we got married without inviting anyone. Now he's asking that we spend some time with him. In France.'

'We? I don't understand.'

'You and me,' he said.

She frowned, and her tone was sharp. 'There is no "you and me" anymore. Anyway, why on earth would he want me to—?'

'Because he believes we're still married.'

There was a long pause. In the street outside a car rumbled past. Natasha blinked, not sure she'd heard properly, but the words settled around her like a handful of rose petals fluttering to the ground. *He believes we're still married.*

After three years? Why? She'd assumed his family didn't know about her: Luc certainly hadn't told them about his marriage at the time. He'd behaved as if he were ashamed of it. Of her.

Confusion made her head spin, and she felt a sharp point of irritation too. Let's face it, what did any of this have to do with her?

'Why on earth would he believe that, Luc?'

He ducked his head and looked away. When he'd appeared in her shop she'd thought Luc didn't look quite himself, but this was something new: the man who was never anything but one hundred per cent certain of himself now looked sheepish.

He said quietly; 'I haven't told him about the divorce.'

There was a long pause. 'Haven't told him?' she repeated incredulously.

He shook his head.

Luc wasn't a man to hide from the truth. He was bold and strong, with a core of steel. A core she'd once been sure was impossible to penetrate. 'Why not?'

His shoulders went back, his chin went up, and when he looked at her now there was a hardness in his brown eyes which warned her this was not safe territory. 'It's complicated. This isn't the time to go into it.'

Fine. Two could play at that game, she thought, raising emotional barriers of her own. Because she desperately needed them. She hung up her apron and ran her palms over the skirt of her dress, smoothing out the rosebud patterned cotton. She adjusted the small red scarf around her neck and touched her hair band: everything was in place, yet she felt ruffled. Irrational though it might be, seeing him made her feel vulnerable, like she had been when they were married, made her feel scared that the pain of that dark time in her life might return. But of course it wouldn't; she had to remember that.

'Well it sounds like it's time to have an honest conversation with your father,' she said briskly, then turned and lifted her jacket off the hook behind the door, hoping he'd get the hint and leave, vanish back out of her life as suddenly as he'd appeared.

'Natasha—' he said, but she just walked right past him, keys jangling in her hand, and held the door open for him.

She shook her head. 'No way. I'm not getting involved in this.'

Reluctantly, he moved past her and stopped in the street outside. With his skin the colour of caramel and his glossy dark hair, he looked as conspicuous in this English country village as an exotic flower.

'I wouldn't ask you if I had any alternative.'

'I'm sure you wouldn't. There's a reason why we got divorced.' She locked the door.

'It's just two weeks—'

'No!' she said. Then, more calmly; 'I don't owe you anything, Luc.'

'I know you don't. That's why I'm asking – appealing to you.'

She could see the desperation, the worry in his eyes, and guilt stabbed at her because he'd come here clearly counting on her help. Then her friend drove past them and waved. It was Suzie, on her way home from the village primary school, and seeing her was a reminder of all Natasha held dear. She'd built a life for herself here and she was happy. As she waved back, she contrasted that with the dark turmoil she'd lived through when she was married to Luc, and her instinct for self-preservation kicked in.

'No,' she said firmly, and began to walk quickly, taking a left off the High Street because it would be quieter on the back roads. She'd seen Suzie's eyes widen with curiosity at the sight of Luc, and Natasha didn't want anyone else to see her with him. 'It would be a lie. I won't do it.'

'My father is seriously ill and this is his wish – what am I supposed to tell him?'

'How about you tell him the truth?'

It wasn't far to her flat, just a couple of hundred yards, but today it seemed like miles. Her sandals tapped quickly along the pavement, but her pace didn't seem to bother him and it irritated her that he kept up effortlessly with his long strides.

'That our marriage lasted three months and we applied for a divorce as soon as was legally possible?' His tone was biting. Vicious. 'The truth would kill him. He's hanging on to life by a thread.'

She tried to ignore the guilt which she knew he'd intended her to feel. 'Then stall. Play for time. Tell him … I'm travelling.'

'How do you think I've explained your absence until now?' He sighed and raked the hair back from his eyes. 'We don't know how long he has left. He wants to meet you.'

She stopped beside a red letterbox and planted her hands on her hips. 'Why?'

'He wants to know who I married. He wants to see for himself that I am happy.'

She snorted. 'Well that's asking the impossible! Even if I came with you to France, we couldn't pretend to be a happily married couple if we tried.'

'We could.' His tone was resolute, his expression determined.

And a shiver touched her spine because Luc was renowned for his determination. What he wanted, he always got. Like a bulldozer, once on course, he was difficult to block.

Turning, she set off again. How did he manage to make her feel so churned up? For heaven's sake, shouldn't their divorce have made her immune to him?

He blew out a long breath. 'Listen, if there's something you want – anything – I will pay for it. In return for your time.'

She flinched and glared at him. 'You always thought money was what motivated me, didn't you? Well you were wrong, Luc. Then and now. I have everything I need already.'

She thought of her shop and the friends she'd made here in the village. She was part of this community now; she belonged. There was only one thing which might possibly make things even more perfect, but she wasn't about to tell her ex, whom she hadn't seen for three years, about that. It was nothing to do with him, her private dream. Her fingers automatically reached inside her pocket, checking for her phone as she thought of the call she was expecting.

'Then you're lucky,' he said flatly.

They reached her flat and she stopped. 'Yes, I am. Or maybe I don't want for much. Not the things money can buy, anyway.'

She marched up the steps to her door on the first floor, thinking she was settled now, but it hadn't always been like this. After their brief marriage, it had taken her months to get her life back on track. He had no right to come barging into her life, demanding favours of her. She owed him nothing. Nothing at all.

She opened the door and turned to face him one last time. 'I'm not doing it, Luc.'

'Natasha –'

Shaking her head, she waved away his protest. 'I'm very sorry about your father – and for what you're going through right now, but I can't help you.'

She went in and was tempted to say goodbye then push the door firmly shut on him and the tornado of emotions which was spinning through her – but he reached his arm out, holding the door open.

'Wait,' he said. 'Aren't you going to invite me in?'

She couldn't believe he'd even ask. And the thought of his tall figure filling her tiny flat, of being alone with him in such a private place made her skin tingle. It went against the grain to be so rude, but to let him in would be too … intimate. She shook her head. 'No.'

'I've come all this way – and we haven't seen each other in a long time. Let me buy you dinner, at least.'

'So we can catch up?' she asked dryly. 'Reminisce on old times?'

'So we can catch up, yes.'

She realised how bitter she sounded and regretted her words. She shouldn't be so affected by him; after all, she had long since got over him, hadn't she? She looked at her watch. He *had* driven a long way to get here, and it would be rude to send him packing without so much as offering him a cup of tea.

'We could go to the pub,' she said. 'The Dog and Partridge is just down the road. They do good food.' She'd hoped they wouldn't be seen, but perhaps being surrounded by other people would calm her jittery nerves and the tingling in her blood which had started the moment he'd walked into the shop.

He nodded. 'Sounds good.'

'But don't think this is another chance to persuade me,' she warned as they set off again, 'because I won't change my mind.'

'I just want to eat and spend a little time with you,' he said quietly.

Thankfully the Dog and Partridge was busy and, maybe it was silly, but she was reassured to see friendly faces all around. Gary the landlord greeted her and, when he cast Luc a curious look, Natasha introduced him. 'This is Luc. He's –' she hesitated, '– an old friend.'

'Friend?' Luc shot her a fierce look. 'We were married.'

Her cheeks burned as Gary, wide-eyed, turned to her and said; 'I didn't know you'd been married before. You dark horse.'

'Yes, well. We all make mistakes,' she said, darting Luc a sideways glance. But his expression remained grim. This wasn't the time to make jokes, she told herself; not when he was clearly worried sick about his father.

They got their drinks and ordered food, and Luc produced his wallet. He handed Gary a couple of notes, but Natasha shook her head.

'I'm perfectly capable of buying my own drink,' she said, pulling out her purse.

Her ears still stung as she remembered how, just after their wedding, he'd told her, *I suppose you'll want your own credit card now you're my wife*. From the moment they'd been married he'd behaved as if she were some kind of parasite, out to leach him of his wealth.

'No,' said Luc. 'This was my idea.'

'Tell you what. We'll each buy our own.'

His nose wrinkled in disgust. 'And have to split the bill in half? I don't think so.'

Her chin went up. 'Then I'll leave now. I pay my own way, Luc. I don't want anything from you.'

His phone rang and he scrabbled to answer it. 'Excuse me,' he said, his accent suddenly pronounced. 'This might be important.'

He walked away, his phone to his ear, and Natasha handed a note to Gary, who was still a little wide-eyed from watching them.

'He really presses your buttons, doesn't he? I've never seen you like this before, Natasha.'

She blushed. Luc didn't bring out the best in her. But then, how many ex-husbands did? 'He's only here because he wants my help,' she said. Then added quietly, 'But he's not going to get it.'

She carried their drinks over to a small table beside the window and sat down, then checked her own phone. There were no missed calls, but she was expecting a call so she left it out on the table because the pub was noisy, and she couldn't be sure she'd hear if it rang. A few moments later, Luc joined her.

'Everything all right?' she asked, taking a sip of her lemonade.

He nodded. 'That was my sister. She's at the hospital – there's been no change.'

He lifted the pint of beer to his lips and his throat worked as he swallowed. His coffee-brown eyes were clouded as he gazed out of the window, his mind evidently elsewhere.

Bookends

When one book ends, another begins...

Bookends is a vibrant new reading community to help you ensure you're never without a good book.

You'll find exclusive previews of the brilliant new books from your favourite authors as well as exciting debuts and past classics. Read our blog, check out our recommendations for your reading group, enter great competitions and much more!

Visit our website to see which great books we're recommending this month.

Join the Bookends community:

www.welcometobookends.co.uk

 @Team Bookends  @WelcomeToBookends